The Raincrow

By Darrell Gasaway

To my wife Judy,
who saw me through the dark side,

To Cory and Carol,
without whose help the Raincrow may never have happened,

and to the two most amazing young ladies in my life,
Reagan and Madison.

One

IT STARTED WITH PEACHES
APRIL 24, 1966

It started with peaches.

Life had become a continuous string of jungles with miserable heat that seemed to scorch my heart, as an endless supply of insects, delighted by my presence, swirled about me. Like everyone else in the company, black soil had worked its way into everything I owned, including my body, with crud caked beneath my nails and in my hair and scalp.

We were entering the third day of Operation Birmingham, the Republic of Vietnam on the Cambodian border.

Captain Alvin Novak, commanding officer of Charlie Company, most often referred to by his radio call sign Charlie-Six, called for a halt in a small area of the jungle where the canopy thinned slightly, allowing fluorescent-like light to pass through from above.

I dropped my pack and followed it to the ground, landing in a twisted heap. I stared at white concentric rings in the armpits of my blouse, the residue of salt from my body, and inhaled the stench from my shirt. The only relief came from the perfumed letter in my fatigue blouse, which I would savor. My hands were covered with filth from the soil, dirt as black as I imagined the Devil's soul to be. I looked up to see Darnell, my reconnaissance sergeant, sitting on his upside down helmet, his arm held out to me offering a small, green C-ration can and one of his trademark grins. "The best food in the world comes in little green cans, remember?" As I began to reach for it, B.J. Tucker, the captain's radio operator, walked to where I had just lain down against my pack.

"Lieutenant Pearce," he said, "Captain Novak has called a meeting of the lieutenants—he asked me to let you know—in five minutes."

I glanced at him and let out a long sigh. "Duty calls, I suppose." I raised myself slowly, sending shock waves through every bone in my body, and followed Tucker back to where the Captain was studying his map. He looked up, nodded to me, and said, "Lieutenant Pearce," and then resumed his study of the map before him.

I dropped my helmet to the ground with a metallic thud, dome side down, and sat on it. I opened one of my canteens and drank from the tepid iodine-treated water, then poured a small amount into my hand, and rubbed it over my face and into my hair.

I stared upward into the jungle canopy above with shafts of sunlight filtering through the foliage, wiped my neck with my black scarf, and rotated my head on my shoulders. I raised my chin and looked up to see Lieutenant Rose, the commander of the company's 1st Platoon, ambling toward where I sat, his wire-rimmed glasses pushed back onto a mop of dirty blond hair. He was reading a crumpled *Time Magazine* as he walked, eating what looked to be a piece of C-ration pound cake. With the blond hair and freckles, at the age of twenty-three, he looked considerably like Howdy Doody in a filthy uniform.

"Ah, if it isn't Lieutenant Craig Pearce, woman slayer!" he said as he approached, pushing his words through the remainder of the pound cake. "And how goes your day?"

"Why, thanks for asking. You are a wonder, Professor," I replied, "and my day is going fine. Just another day in paradise."

He lowered himself down beside me, shoving his helmet beneath his butt as he did. He placed his map on the ground and brushed the crumbs from his hands onto his filthy fatigue pants.

We turned to see Lieutenant Michael "Mike" Allegretti rise and stretch in the area of 3rd Platoon, his platoon fifty feet away, and begin his walk toward us. His details became clear as he approached. At six-six, he was a giant, a stout troll with exaggerated features. Although friendly, his face was a constant frown centered about the bridge of his large nose, and a black buzz-haircut covered the swarthy Italian skin on his head. He wore a crumpled, filthy jungle fatigue shirt, which had recently had something spilled down the front. All of this made him look somewhat like a distant thunder cloud moving our way. He nodded to each of us and squatted down, continuing the circle that was forming, leaving one more spot for Lieutenant Wilson.

We would wait for Lieutenant Terrance "Bama" Wilson, of Birmingham's Cherry Hills Heights Wilsons, who always seemed to be the last to arrive. And the wait would be worth it since he always brought his unique brand of humor with him. Sure enough, several minutes later he appeared out of a copse of hardwood trees, holding his helmet between his elbow and his side. Like the rest of us, sweat glistened on his exposed skin.

"We're so pleased that you could make it," Charlie-Six said to Lieutenant Wilson with a smile, as he removed his black-rimmed glasses and began smearing his lenses with a hopelessly fouled handkerchief. After almost a minute, he held the pair up to the sky and frowned at the result of his cleaning efforts. He took a moment to untwist the black cord that connected the earpieces and looped it over his head.

"Why, thank you, Captain. I'm always pleased to be in your company, no pun intended." Then turning to the rest of us, he sneered, saying, "What a rotten smelling lot the rest of you are. Grandmother would faint if she knew I was in the company of such trash." Allegretti allowed a wry smile as he picked up a twig and threw it, hitting Bama in the crotch. "You arrogant hillbilly prick," he said softly.

Charlie-Six continued, "We're two hours from where we'll spend the night—a short distance from the Cam Bach—that's the river that forms the border of Cambodia in this area."

Bama interrupted, "Why can't these people use simple names for their rivers like we do in Alabama, like Chattanooga or Choctawhatchee?"

"As you know," Charlie-Six continued, ignoring him, "we have been pushing the Viet Cong hard, and Battalion says that they are seeing results of our efforts. Army intelligence estimates that they are more exhausted than we are. They're trying to get across the river with tons of equipment and supplies into Cambodia, obviously more than they can carry, before we catch them. We have hit them in their mother lode over the past week, and they are trying to save as much materiel as they can." He turned his map case toward us and traced a thin black line with the handle of a plastic C-ration spoon. "We will join with Alpha and Bravo companies tonight to form a blocking wall, with B Company on the right and A behind us in reserve. This will deny the VC access to the major trail to the river, and they will have to start carrying supplies farther north instead of crossing the river here."

He looked up long enough to scan our faces, pausing to swat at some insect. "Stress to the men that this is a powder keg, and everyone has to be alert. I know it will be a tough bitch." He dropped his map case on the ground, looked down, and began to rub his temples. "After this meeting, we will move out roughly parallel to the trail on your map. Bama, you'll take the lead." He twisted and pointed with his plastic spoon to a dirt trail ten meters to the east, then turned back.

"A stellar command decision, Captain," Bama said, interrupting. "I'm sure we will all feel more comfortable with the 2nd Platoon leading the way. I know that *I* certainly will." He smiled broadly, pulling dimples deeply into each cheek.

"Allegretti, you'll follow Bama, and then you, Lieutenant Rose, will bring up the rear of the column."

He raised his head and looked at me. "Lieutenant Pearce, we'll continue to be supported by Alpha Battery." Alpha Battery—the communication call sign "Destroyer"—was a 105 howitzer battery located approximately six miles to the east, providing artillery support to us and other infantry companies within its range. "Stay close to me," he said. "I want to burn a lot of artillery rounds as we move through the shitty jungle we'll be going through."

"Like the Fourth of July all over again," Bama said, looking at me and smiling. "Light the little bastards up."

"Our final destination for the day is at—" He called off the map coordinates of a spot in the jungle to the northwest and waited until we had all found the evening camp location on the map. "Anyone have any questions?" Charlie-Six asked as he quietly scanned our faces, holding each man's gaze for several seconds. "OK, we move out—" he said, staring at his watch, "—in thirty minutes."

I stood stiffly and walked back to where my pack and the two men of my artillery section were. At five feet, ten inches tall, Darcy Darnell, my reconnaissance sergeant, was a husky, broad-shouldered specialist fourth class. We were about the same height, but at 200 pounds, he had me by at least thirty pounds—of solid muscle. He had big farmer's hands and wore EEE width boots that resembled those worn by Elmer Fudd, with arms that looked like Popeye's.

As I approached and dropped once more by my pack, he held out his hand, with the same army green can between his forefinger and thumb.

I took it and read the words stenciled across the top, as if examining a bottle of fine wine. "Peaches, sliced, packed in syrup. You devil, you. You certainly know how to please a man."

"Whoa!" Panther, the radio operator for my section, shouted, sitting on the ground to my left. "You two are starting to scare me. You're starting to sound like an old married couple. Just eat the damn peaches. No commentary, please," he said, smiling, as he turned to respond to a radio call. We watched as he did. "Nothing," he said after several seconds. "B.J. Tucker just put a new battery in his radio and was checking it out."

Just over six feet, six inches tall, Mathias "Panther" Raille had been created in the image of heroes from Greek mythology...an athlete. He was handsome with a flashy smile, deep brown eyes, and an ebony body, sculpted of solid muscle. He was my radio operator who kept us in contact with our support artillery battery, some six miles away.

I pulled the John Wayne can opener on my dog tag chain from beneath my T-shirt and removed the lid on the can, careful not to spill a single drop. I sipped some of the thick, sweet syrup, and then, with filthy blackened fingers, I stuck my thumb and forefinger into the juice, lifted one of the golden slivers, cocked my head back, and lowered it into my mouth. I repeated the process with another. With the third, I stopped and stared at the last joint of my forefinger and thumb. They were no longer filthy.

I spread my map on the ground between us, and we began to study it. Our current position was easy to spot, a small lime green patch on the map representing a clearing in a sea of sparse, dark green jungle. I paused to wipe a smudge of peach juice from the map with the side of my hand.

"After this meeting, we will move out, skirting this clearing to avoid the stream, to this road." I traced a dotted line that ran across the map with my finger and retrieved the last peach sliver, turned my face upward, and dropped it into my mouth. "Charlie-Six estimates two hours to our night camp. Destroyer will continue to provide artillery support." I ran my finger along the inside wall of the can and stuck it in my mouth. "It looks like we'll need—"

The sudden noise sounded like a firecracker—a shot. Every head in the command section twenty feet away turned to stare in the direction of the sound, like a group of startled meerkats.

Panther sat up quickly and spoke into the radio handset: "Destroyer Two-Three, this is Destroyer Niner-Three. Communication check, over." "Destroyer Niner-Three" was my call sign. Panther was doing his job, making sure we had good communications with the artillery battery.

"Destroyer Niner-Three, this is Destroyer Two-Three. I read you loud and clear," replied the voice of the battery radio operator. With that, Panther nodded to me and said, "We're okay."

"It's probably one of those friggin' greenhorns," I suggested, hoping that the sound had come from one of the "new" guys in Bama's platoon.

In seconds, three more shots rang out from the far side of the clearing that Bama's platoon was approaching. Charlie-Six was on the radio. He stared at me, then rose and placed his helmet on his head. Accompanied by his two radio operators, we all started to run in the direction of the firing. I could hear Panther behind me, already calling in the artillery support as he ran at my side. "Destroyer Two-Three, this is Destroyer Niner-Three. Fire Mission, over."

"Destroyer Niner-Three, this is Destroyer Two-Three. Send your mission," came the voice from the artillery battery.

"Wait one," Panther replied. I immediately pictured the artillery battery to our east where the men were scurrying about frantically and crawling over the howitzers to remove canvas as they prepared to support us by firing on locations that we wanted destroyed.

We joined Charlie-Six, all of us bent at the waist, hunched forward, loping toward the clearing we had just been discussing. We ran with the seventy pounds of equipment attached to each of us—our packs, rifles, helmets—and then dropped behind a low berm. We sounded like a truckload of scrap metal being dumped on a concrete floor as we fell beside Charlie-Six and his operators. In seconds, our packs were off and lying in front of us. The firing was coming from the edge of a small clearing covered with high grass and framed on the other side by gigantic trees. The continuous firing was coming from a large caliber machine gun, most likely 50-caliber, coughing steadily.

The sound of the rifles firing was now heavy, as all three of Charlie Companies platoons were engaged, firing into the wood line as they sought ways to reach the enemy.

It had begun.

Panther handed me the radio handset. "Destroyer Two-Three, this is Destroyer Niner-Three. Fire mission, over."

"Roger, Niner-Three. Send your mission." It was the voice of "Flash" Gordon, supporting us from the artillery battery we had discussed in the briefing earlier. His voice was calm and comforting like warm honey. It was like having a big brother joining you in a fight. I visualized the shaved sidewalls and the flaming red patch of hair atop his head.

I realized that I was squeezing the empty peach can. Darnell had already marked the location from where the firing was coming, the spot where I wanted the rounds to be delivered, and relayed the necessary information.

Flash read the information back to me, and I confirmed it. "Destroyer Niner-Three, roger. Wait," I said. I imagined the frantic activity at the battery as the howitzers were aimed toward the target in front of us. I imagined the soldiers of the battery, ammo-humpers carrying 105 caliber artillery rounds to the guns, adjusting the number of ammo bags for the mission, and sighting their 105 howitzers, all practiced and performed in controlled chaos.

In less than two minutes since the first shot, Flash was back on the radio. "Destroyer Niner-Three, on the way. Observe two rounds." Two thirty-pound projectiles were hurtling toward the intended target, a spot on my map where my finger now pointed. These were adjustment rounds.

Darnell was beside me, double checking everything I said. He had drawn the attention of B.J. Tucker, Charlie's radio operator, and was moving his flattened hand front to back over his head, a sign that artillery shells were on the way to the spot from where the enemy firing was coming. Tucker turned and shouted something to Charlie-Six. Charlie-Six turned to me and gave me a thumbs up signal.

Flash's voice came over the radio. "Splash," he said, a signal that the rounds were on their way to hit where I had requested. Splash meant they would hit in ten seconds. "Ten seconds!" Darnell yelled to those around us as he dropped down. The first two rounds of concussive explosions hit, sending a shock wave through the jungle, drowning out everything else. Gigantic trees vacillated as jagged chunks of hot steel careened through their branches. Flash and I now had a common point from which to adjust future rounds, just beyond where the Viet Cong were firing. I estimated the distance from where they had hit and where I had pinpointed the machine gunner. "Destroyer Two-Three, this is Destroyer Niner-Three. Drop three hundred, left one hundred." I had asked for two groups of six rounds, each to hit the spot from where the rifle firing was coming, at the new location.

"Roger, Niner-Three. Wait." I breathed deeply at the sound of the voice on the other end, still calm and deliberate, like a commercial pilot announcing the weather and flight time.

For the first time, I realized that we had soldiers down in the clearing in front of us, some apparently dead. At least two were moving less than twenty feet away. "Son of a bitch!" I yelled as I realized that one of them was the butcher, the company medic, screaming. He had most likely run into the clearing to help a wounded soldier and was shot. I could see at least three more wounded now. The enemy wouldn't kill them immediately. They would be allowed to live in order to draw more soldiers into the target area so that they, too, could be killed. The din of constant fire grew to incredible heights as Charlie Company soldiers fired back, sounding like a burning firecracker stand.

My artillery rounds hit. I made adjustments, hoping that the next rounds would hit the target. I glanced back to see Darnell on his elbows, his face twisted in agony as he cursed and stared at the Butcher, who continued to scream and writhe ten meters away. The sound of the enemy 50-caliber machine gun firing from the spot at the edge of the jungle foliage punctuated the air with its distinct bark. *Caulk-caulk-caulk.* The men of the company returned fire immediately as dozens of M16 rifles from Bama's platoon answered, firing into the thick, green jungle wall fifty meters away, as branches and leaves fell.

"Destroyer Niner-Three, this is Destroyer Two-Three. On the way, over." The next set of "two" rounds was on the way, to impact in front of us and just beyond where the firing was coming. Once they hit, I would make further adjustments, bringing more rounds toward the enemy line until shrapnel was "going up the enemy machine gunner's ass."

"Destroyer Two-Three, roger. Wait." It was my way of telling Flash that I would adjust and get back to him.

Darnell yelled at Swizzledick, Charlie-Six's radio operator, who turned to him. Darnell pumped his fist into the air, a sign that the rounds were on the way. I watched as Swizzledick, three yards away, turned to Charlie-Six, who was talking on the radio, and yelled at him. Charlie-Six looked up and then turned to me, nodding vigorously.

My stomach burned and sent caustic acid up my throat.

"Splash, wait," came Flash's creamy, baritone voice. It was his signal telling me that two rounds would hit in ten seconds—a warning to get down. "Splash!" Darnell yelled as loudly as he could to signal everyone to get down.

The artillery rounds hit in earth-shaking, terrifying explosions. Charlie-Six was animated in his conversation, waving his arms. I knew he was talking to Bama, who was directly in contact with the Viet Cong unit, to confirm that the last two rounds had hit where we wanted them. He turned his head toward me and nodded vigorously, pumping his free arm up and down. That was my signal.

"Destroyer Two-Three, this is Destroyer Niner-Three. Fire for effect." The two rounds had hit where we needed them. "Fire for effect" was my command to Flash, letting him know we had hit the "sweet spot" and it was time to lower the gates and let the hounds of hell loose. Instead of sending two rounds, this time eighteen would be heading toward the Viet Cong foxhole.

I looked at Charlie-Six, who was staring at the far side of the clearing, his mouth hanging open and his face covered in sweat. He turned briefly toward me, and I nodded. With all else going on in my mind, I realized that the right lens of his glasses was missing.

I stared at the small meadow in front of me as I waited, flinching at the constant explosions and the sound of shrapnel and bullets whizzing overhead. Earlier in the day, there had probably been birds in the trees basking in serenity. Now, I counted at least ten men down in the clearing; most were still, the rest were barely moving. Darnell was on my right side, Panther was on the left, and both flat behind the berm to the point where they could barely see over it. Darnell was staring at Butcher's every move with the intensity of a cat stalking a sparrow.

"Twenty seconds," came Flash's soothing voice, like a late night radio announcer.

"Twenty seconds," I thought to myself. I had made calls like this before, and yet I was terrified in anticipation of what was only seconds away.

Eighteen of my rounds—over five hundred pounds of steel and explosives—would hit just beyond the other side of the clearing where the Viet Cong 50-caliber machine guns continued firing at us.

Butcher screamed once more, a scream that seemed to carry fear, hatred, and pain, as bile rose once more in my throat.

"Splash," came the mellow voice over the radio. "Observe eighteen rounds on the way. God be with you."

Butcher screamed once more, and I caught movement from my left eye as I keyed the radio handset to respond to Flash. It was Darnell rising to charge over the berm in the direction of his wounded friend, like a bull, into the clearing, his boots pushing dirt away from him with each step.

"What the—damn you, Darnell—get your damned ass back here," I screamed as I grabbed his pant leg and was jerked forward, partially over the berm, his boot kicking my chin as my radio hand receiver was jerked from my hands. I rose to follow him. Suddenly I felt something strong and large— Panther, I realized—jerking me back behind the berm, landing spread-eagled on top of me as he did. *Caulk-caulk-caulk.* The Viet Cong machine gun continued to bark from the tree line.

In seconds, my rounds would begin to fall.

Two

SAIGON AND TAN SON NHUT
FEBRUARY 2, 1966

I was standing in the shade of a shed at Tan Son Nhut Air Base near Saigon, as sweat seemed to run down the length of my body. I realized that with each stop in my trip, the heat and conditions had gotten worse. Suddenly my thoughts of home and my future were disrupted as a Huey helicopter roared into view over the hanger where I was standing. It hovered there like a giant dragonfly, and then it sat down on the tarmac on a large yellow X painted inside an even larger red circle. It had barely touched down when a specialist fifth class, a soldier, jumped from inside and approached me. He wore nylon coveralls with wires sewn along the arms and legs and a helmet the size and shape of a basketball, with a visor in front. Buffeted by the downblast from the rotors, he trotted to where I was standing, my duffel bag at my feet. He raised the visor on his helmet. "Lieutenant Pearce?" he yelled, as he read from a scrap of paper, to be heard as he glanced down at the name tape above my right pocket, and nodded.

"I am," I shouted, barely heard above the roar.

"Well then, your chariot awaits you," he yelled into my ear. He grabbed my duffle bag and returned to the chopper, throwing it unceremoniously behind the pilot's seat of the aircraft. The pilot turned and looked at me over his shoulder, nodded his head, and gave me a thumbs up sign. The rotor blades picked up speed and began slapping the moist air, making a popping sound. The chopper tentatively rocked, then lifted, and we were on the way, the rotors clapping heavily against the stale and pungent morning air.

The seat was made of nylon wrapped around an aluminum frame and bolted to the back wall of the cabin. There were no seat belts or side doors on the craft. I grabbed the seat frame and prepared for the ride.

The chopper wobbled slightly as it lifted, tilted forward, and rushed upward on its rise. My amazement continued as we passed over stacks of green supplies and materiel being loaded onto or unloaded from green trucks by airmen in green fatigues, as well as operating green equipment to fill or empty green C-130 military aircrafts. Higher still, the views below changed into a crowded city—Saigon, I assumed—filtered through white wisps of clouds and smoke, as I marveled at the mass of humanity below.

Within seconds I was looking down on a kaleidoscope: visions of crowded streets, a man wearing a conical hat while carrying a pig under each arm, and antique black French Citroens honking as they vied for traffic lanes. Masses of people milled past crowded shops with corrugated roofs, and patchwork gardens seemed to be stuffed into every square foot of unused soil, as the din from the street yielded totally to the staccato chopping of the blades above me. Scents ranging from offal to sweet, rancid to aromatic, and chemical to petroleum floated through the open doors of the aircraft. The traffic was like a huge circus act with black cars, brightly painted motor scooters loaded with boxes, bicycles with cages of chickens stacked eight feet high, and oxen pulling massive carts laden with cargo...all almost touching each other as they passed.

We quickly rose above multi-level buildings to reveal patched asphalt roofs with twisted clotheslines stretched from wall to wall, filled with drying clothing, as smoke and steam rose from various pipes. At one point, I saw a group of dogs of various sizes inside a fenced area atop a multistory building. At our altitude, poorly planned roads and insistent drivers looked like Tonka toy-sized vehicles and caused traffic jams as we began to move to the east, leaving the expansive geometric views of Tan Son Nhut Air Base below and back to the south and west.

I watched the chopper crew, looking like huge insects behind the mirrored visors of their bubble-shaped helmets, working levers above their seats immediately in front of me as they punched buttons, twisted knobs, and spoke into radios. Within fifteen minutes, the chopper banked northeast over what I recognized as rice paddies being worked by what appeared as miniature men and tiny water buffalos. They plowed sheets of shining silver water, stitched together by narrow berms like one of my mother's handcrafted quilts. Occasional plantations of trees, what I assumed to be rubber trees, stood aligned in rows and columns like ancient French Legionnaires silently awaiting orders.

The noise of the chopper prevented conversation with the crew—a major, a warrant officer, and the specialist fifth class. I simply stared, wishing that I could just fly around up here for the next year. As we finally began to pass over jungles, a combination of the breeze passing through the cabin and the sweat of my clothes seemed to decrease as the temperature dropped considerably. I had never seen anything, with the possible exception of Johnny Weissmuller's Tarzan movies, that I could compare to the spectacle of the jungles that passed beneath us, their trees appearing like giant broccoli plants. As I stared, I wondered if this was where the Viet Cong hid.

My thoughts were drawn to southeastern New Mexico, where I was raised, on predominantly flat, open desert plains and farms, sparsely covered with scrub bushes, yuccas, and stunted mesquite trees less than five feet high. Flat country with views in any direction are either panoramas in shades of gray, tan, and dull green or the rich deep green of farms, all under a bowl-shaped sky of almost always azure blue. What rivers I had grown up with in Southern New Mexico were stingy trickles in comparison to those below me now.

Lush, green landscapes were laced by wandering rivers like giant anacondas trying to free themselves from the jungles. We flew over a convoy of fuel tanker trucks headed north along a dirt road, protected by a military police escort. There were occasional flashes of huts in tiny clearings, and at one point a flock of birds moved as specks against the eastern sky.

Finally, we began our descent toward a group of white buildings in the distance. As we approached, the buildings grew in size and details, the rust on the tin roofs and the specks on bicycles along the dirt roads becoming more and more visible. The scene changed to hundreds of brownish-tinted green Army tents, neatly arranged in ranks and files, with trucks and jeeps of the same color parked around them. They were intermixed with howitzers of all sizes, surrounded by walls of sand bags, like giant doughnuts. And finally, at several hundred feet, the UH1 helicopter reared back and slowed, the crew more animated in preparation for landing, as it made its final descent onto a crude air strip.

Three

PHUOC VINH AIRFIELD
FEBRUARY 2, 1966

I removed my army green baseball cap, adorned with the small
rectangular brass bar centered above the bill, and wiped the dust from my face
with my sleeve. "Welcome to your new home, country boy," I said softly.
"Play it right, and someday you might get to climb back on that chopper and
ride out the same way you came in. Just 360 more days," I thought, "or
whatever part of that time that you manage to get away with." I picked up the
duffel bag with everything I owned in it and carried it to the edge of the
airfield.

The airstrip was sterile looking, made of cream-colored compacted
caliche, or laterite, and about the size of three football fields. The only
building in sight, which appeared to be for storage, joined the dirt road at its
southwest corner. It was roughly ten by twelve feet with a roof that sloped
from front to back and was covered with tar paper. Judging from the lettering
on the boards that had been used to build the walls, it had been built from

salvaged wooden ammunition packing crates used for shipping artillery shells, probably scrounged from the gun batteries in the area. The roof, most likely built with the same crates, was covered with a tarpaulin. The only thing that seemed substantial about the structure was that it had a huge padlock.

Next to the dirt road entrance, which appeared to be the *only* entrance to the field, stood a sign stenciled on a four-by-eight sheet of plywood, painted white with red lettering and supported by two four-by-four posts that read "Phuoc Vinh Air Field." In the center was a replica of the "Big Red One" patch, an army green symbol shaped like an upside down baseball home plate with a large "1" emblazoned in red in the center, the words "1st Infantry Division" arched above. Four crudely lettered additional signs had been haphazardly attached. One read "San Francisco - 8,000 miles. There are currently no out-going flights scheduled." Another read "New York - 8,900 miles," and the bottom one simply read "Visit Adler, Oklahoma. I don't know how far away it is." The largest and crudest of the four read "Welcome to Phuoc Vinh, Vietnam - proof that not all cesspools are below ground."

Going both east and west from the opening were fences made of concerto wire, with a ten-feet opening to allow access to the airfield. Beyond that was what had apparently once been a jungle, cut to the ground to take away cover for snipers. It left short stumps, limbs, and what looked like stubs of sugar cane stalks or bamboo, giving the appearance of a hurricane aftermath. The only sign of life was a noisy group of Vietnamese civilians inside the perimeter seventy-five yards away, dressed in what looked like black satin clothing and thong sandals. They were building walls of sandbags around the fuel dump: four large, black rubber bladders that contained what I assumed to be JP-4 jet fuel lay on the ground like beached whales. I turned at the sound of yelling to see one of the Vietnamese workers, the boss, I thought, as he shouted and gestured wildly, pointing at the top row of filled bags. He then pulled two of them down, with his free hand screaming as he flailed his other arm. Then they all began shouting simultaneously as one of the others picked the two bags up and placed them back where they had been.

Well beyond the entrance to the field, I could see the tops of olive drab Army tents. I recognized the sound of 105 howitzers firing, obviously in support of some operation miles to the west.

On each horizon, towering white clouds stood like interested spectators. Shielding my eyes with my hand, I looked up at a magnificent blue sky and then turned to my watch, a green plastic Army issue with nylon straps. It was only 1000 hours. Sweat had already trickled down the inside of my fatigue shirt, forming familiar dark spots of sweat beneath my armpits, as the queasy activity in my stomach that I had felt for the past week continued.

Just a week ago I had been in Hobbs, New Mexico, saying goodbye to my friends and family. My brother had driven me to El Paso, Texas, for my first flight ever on a commercial plane, bound for Oakland, California. The flight that would eventually get me to Saigon left Oakland at 2030, a Boeing 707 under contract to the Department of Defense and filled only with soldiers in khaki uniforms, all on their way to Vietnam. Within 30 minutes, the view through the fishbowl window to my right was of total darkness. It seemed to be *interminable* darkness for seventeen hours to Tachikawa Air Base, Japan, with only a forty-five minute fuel stop somewhere around Anchorage. The first hint of light, some seventeen hours from when we left California, came as a thin, peach-colored line across the ocean. Five hours later, I was in Camp Alpha to begin my military in-processing at Tan Son Nhut Air Base in Saigon, Vietnam.

I turned at the sound and sight of a jeep approaching over a rise, dragging a cloud of dust as it came from the direction of the guns that had been firing earlier. In less than a minute, the jeep bounced along and turned through the space in the wire barrier, coming to a stop ten feet away. The driver stepped out and approached, saluting as he did. "Lieutenant Pearce?"

"That's me," I said, returning the salute.

"Specialist Darnell," he said. "I'm your section reconnaissance sergeant." He had been smiling an infectious smile constantly since the quarter-ton vehicle stopped. "Welcome. I took the liberty of booking you at the Phuoc Vinh Hilton. I hope that's okay," he said, as his smile grew even larger, crowding his eyes almost shut.

I had just flown in over Phuoc Vinh. There was no Hilton.

I smiled back as I said, "If that's all you've got, I'm sure it's fine."

He picked up my duffel effortlessly and threw it into the back seat of the vehicle. We climbed in and sat there.

"You have two stops to make as I understand it," he said as he continued to grin. "I can take you to The Plantation first, where you will be living, and you can drop your gear at the officers' tent there, or we can go directly to the battery. What's your pleasure?"

"What do you suggest?" I asked.

"Well, I would suggest that you turn around and go back home," he said, smiling with a grin that I thought might be broad enough to hurt him.

"Agreed. But since I'm here, let's see some sights."

"OK. Then I suggest we go to the battery first, I suppose. Captain Turner is anxious to meet you."

"The battery?" I asked.

"Our artillery battery. Alpha Battery," Darnell said. "The one we are attached to."

I nodded. "Let's try that first."

"And Captain Turner is the battery commander, I assume?" I had seen his name on some of my paperwork.

"You assume correctly," he answered, as he accelerated through the gate and away.

As he drove, Specialist Darnell seemed adept at hitting every pothole in the dusty road, causing me to recall my rodeo days.

My section would consist of me, Darnell, and a radio operator. My job, like most second lieutenants whose father was not a Congressman, would be a "forward observer." I would be attached to an infantry company to provide artillery support.

"And that would be Battery A, 1st Battalion, 5th Field Artillery," I said, recalling that from my orders.

"Right you are," he said. "That's 'Hamilton's Own.'"

"OK, I'll bite. What is 'Hamilton's Own'?" I asked, as he surprised me, turning so sharply that I almost fell from the jeep as he avoided a hole in the dirt road.

"Actually, it refers to Battery D, one of the most, if not *the* most, famous battery in the artillery, I suppose. It is the oldest continually operated artillery battery in the Army. It was formed and commanded by Alexander Hamilton in the Revolution. Been around ever since. The weapons have changed in that time, however," Darnell said with another infectious grin.

One more curve, one more rise, and we pulled up in front of a squad tent with a sign that read "Alpha Battery, 1st Battalion, 2nd Brigade, 5th Artillery." As we pulled in, men were wiping down the six howitzers, obviously the ones I had heard firing earlier.

Specialist Darnell came to a stop, and I waited as the dust that had been following us passed. Standing there beside a tent was Captain Carlton Turner.

Four

"Welcome to paradise," Turner called, as I stepped from the vehicle. "It's a bit chilly this morning, but it will warm up," he said with a deep chuckle.

I saluted and made an attempt to dust myself off as I stepped out, only to realize that the combination of dust and perspiration had coated my face with a light layer of mud.

"Sounds good to me," I returned.

We sat in the shade of his tent on folding stools as he told the story of the 1st Infantry leaving the states and its arrival in Nam. Finally, he said, "Let's look around."

It was to be an interesting morning of shaking hands and hearing names, most of which I wouldn't remember. We stopped by the mess tent and got two cups of iced tea. "This is the battery, obviously," he said, waving his arm in the direction of six 105 howitzers. Each was ringed by a wall of sandbags stacked three feet high and two feet wide to form a large doughnut, tamped with entrenching tools to the point that they looked like a mason had built them. In each ring, an opening had been left for access. The area inside the doughnut had been raked and packed until perfectly flat and swept, giving the appearance of a cement floor. Soldiers looked up from their chores as we passed, eyeing us with interest.

There were six 105 millimeter cannons mounted on two wheels that seemed to silently wait for the next forward observer, one of my counterparts, to call with a fire mission. Each one was attended by at least one soldier, diligently rubbing or repairing some piece or part of a howitzer.

I stepped inside and was met by the crew Chief.

"Sergeant Parker," the man said, rubbing his hand with a rag and then extending it to me. "Craig Pearce," I returned.

"Pleased to meet you, sir," he said. We talked. It seemed to be a good idea to become acquainted since these would be some of the men firing artillery rounds close to my position when I called for their support. I walked to one of the howitzers and stopped. Stencil letters, painted white and three inches high, read "Angry Anna" on the gun barrel.

"'Angry Anna'—that's the name?" I asked quizzically as I turned to the sergeant in charge of the piece.

"That's right. The section chief for this gun *was* married to a broad named Anna. After he left to come here, she started getting letters from two women whom he had apparently been seeing on the side before he left for here. The story, as I heard it, was that Anna sent him a letter with only one line: 'Sweetheart, please don't get killed over there. I want to do that myself when you get home.' The soldiers that work for him on this gun thought it was so funny that they voted unanimously for that name to go here." He slapped the barrel as he finished speaking...and laughed.

I stopped to shake hands and make small talk with the crews as we made our way to the two guns in the center of the battery. I moved to the two centerpieces, read the names on the howitzer, and turned to Captain Turner. "What's the story behind these two?" I asked.

He smiled. "When we first got here, we fired three rounds into a friendly village. Well," he continued sheepishly, "at least it had been friendly until *that* happened. Some of the data given to us by the battalion fire direction center caused us to fire on the edge of the village, hitting an outdoor privy. Fortunately, no one was in it. A big-assed inquiry followed and showed it had not been our fault. We had been given bad location data." He rubbed his sleeve over the painted name on the howitzer that we stood by. The first one had the word "Accused" stenciled on the barrel. The other bore the name "Acquitted."

Captain Turner and I went inside the mess tent long enough to get a refill of tea and then went to the fire direction center tent, the "brains" of an artillery battery, where we were met by another second lieutenant.

"This is Lieutenant Jack Gordon," Captain Turner said, holding his hand out toward a lieutenant with a reddish-blonde hank of hair on top of his head and shaved sidewalls. "Better known as 'Flash' Gordon." He was wearing fatigue trousers, an olive drab T-shirt, and red shower shoes. "Flash, this is Craig Pearce. He has been assigned to C-company to replace Lieutenant Swenson."

I flinched at the use of the word "replace," as it occurred to me that *I* was replacing a dead man. The word had been used as casually as if describing the process of *replacing* a burned out light bulb. "So that's his name," I thought, "the man I am to replace."

"Pleased to meet you," Flash said in a soothing baritone voice, his eyelids at half-mast. "Welcome to the Garden of Eden."

"Thanks," I replied.

The usual barrage of questions followed. "Where are you from?" "Did you attend college, and if so, where and when?" "When were you at Fort Sill?" "Are you married?"

As we walked, we talked until we reached a tent with its sides rolled up and stepped inside.

Flash turned to two specialists standing in the back corner of the tent. "Lieutenant Craig Pearce, these are the very best fire direction center operators the Army has." The two looked at each other and grinned. "Specialist Lane," he gestured to one of them, who stepped forward and shook hands with me. "And Specialist Lancaster." I shook hands with the second one.

"Well," I said, "it's good to be working with the best the Army has." They both smiled.

"As we process a fire mission," Flash resumed, "each of these men calculate the firing data at the same time, but separately. Then they compare their results—the 'double check,' we call it—and fire the rounds. As you know, this is where we will process the fire missions for you and any other FO out there who needs help."

I was familiar with the process, as it was the majority of my basic training, but felt pleased as I listened to his thorough review. "Your call sign will be Destroyer Niner-Three," he said in the vernacular of the trade. "Mine is Destroyer Two-Three." So, you request support by means of your trusty radio, and it comes here. You tell us what you want done—where you want the rounds to hit—we calculate what it will take to get artillery rounds from here—" He pointed to the guns and continued, "—to where you want them. I *know* that you know all of this from your training at Fort Sill, but it doesn't hurt to go over it."

We discussed how information was processed and sent to the guns and what they did with it.

"On some days, we fire as many as ten to twenty missions a day."

As if on cue, a fire mission came in over the radio. "Destroyer Two-Three, Danger Niner-Niner, fire mission, over." "Niner-Niner" was radio talk for Ninety-Nine, the caller's call sign.

Flash looked first at Captain Carlton and then at me. "You want to take this mission?" Flash asked as he turned to me.

I turned to the two specialists. "You guys want to work with a rookie?" They grinned and nodded. I turned to Flash. "Sure, let's do it."

"Be my guest."

"And what's your call sign?" I asked.

"Destroyer Two-Three," Flash replied.

"Danger Niner-Niner, this is Destroyer Two-Three," I said into the microphone. "Send your mission."

It felt like I had been trained at Fort Sill for months just for this mission. I sent information to the guns, processed what they sent to me, and made adjustments until the rounds hit the target. It went without a hitch.

When finished, I stepped to the back side of the board and shook hands once more with the operators. "I look forward to working with you."

I turned back to Flash and grasped his hand. "Do you like to play poker?" Flash asked as we shook. "When you are in town, instead of in the jungles, we can get together."

I grinned broadly. "Lieutenant," I said, "my Daddy Bud, my granddad, gave me advice as a young man. He told me that one day I would be approached by a stranger who would bet me ten dollars that he could stand ten feet away from me and piss directly in my ear. He said 'You'll take the bet and you will win the ten dollars, but you'll be left with piss running down you collar.'" They all laughed. "So, I'll hold off from the poker for a while.

"Thanks for the refresher training," I said.

"Never hurts to hear it again," he responded.

Captain Turner and I went once more to the mess tent, got two cups of water, stepped outside, and sat down in two plastic folding chairs. We had hardly done so, when a jeep pulled into the area. The driver got out and walked toward us.

"Just in time," Captain Turner called out to him, motioning for him to come. As he approached, Turner nodded toward him and said, "Here's another key man in this battery."

The new arrival stopped in front of us.

"Lieutenant Pearce, meet Lieutenant Terry 'Hangover' Hanover."

Five

"HANGOVER" HANOVER
FEBRUARY 2, 1966

The lieutenant twisted the right side of his mouth upward in a look of mock disgust. "It's '*Hanover*,'" he said, following a pregnant pause, as he turned to me. "Not 'Hangover,'" he concluded, as he looked at Captain Turner.

"Well, it was damned sure 'Hangover' after the night we left from San Francisco on the ship that brought us here," Captain Turner continued.

"Hanover," he said to me more sternly.

"Craig Pearce," I said, wondering what the rest of the story was.

"I understand you will be with Charlie Company, 1st of the 2nd?" Hanover asked.

"That's what my orders say. And I've read them at least twenty times since I got them."

"Have you met Lieutenant Allegretti yet?"

"Allegretti?" I asked.

"Yeah. Michael Allegretti. He's with Charlie Company."

"No," I returned. "I haven't been to my infantry company yet. We stopped here first."

"He is a great guy. He's the 3rd Platoon leader. Tell him that I told you that I could whip his ass any day of the week," he said with a broad smile. "We've known each other for a while. Mike and his wife and my wife, Sharon, and I lived next to each other in married housing at Ft. Riley. You'll like him. He's a super guy."

The Company Clerk came up to speak to Captain Turner. "Sir, you just got a call from Battalion for a meeting. Your presence has been requested." The Captain turned to Hanover smiling broadly: "Can you finish introducing the men and equipment to Pearce?"

Hanover laughed loudly. "Go to your meeting. I can handle this one a hell of a lot better than you can. You run along and do something else. We'll finish this up."

Hanover introduced me to the rest of the section Chiefs, the non-commissioned officers who oversaw each howitzer. Their pride in their work was obvious as they told me about what they did. He called to a sergeant in standard Army dress. "Chief, come over here. I want to introduce you to someone."

"Lieutenant Pearce, meet Sergeant Rankin. I get the credit for it," Hanover said with a smile, "but this man runs the battery."

He was wiry, and he squinted with his left eye as he talked in a high-pitched Southern drawl. "I'm from West 'by God' Virginia. Pleased to meet you, Lieutenant," he said, his voice coming across slowly as if he needed new batteries. It was obvious that he loved his guns. "My gals," he said as he patted one of the almost chest-high tires, "are the workhorses of the artillery. Yeah, there's bigger ones, longer range ones, but these are the workhorses. It can be hauled behind an Army two-and-a-half-ton truck, or it could be transported beneath a Chinook helicopter virtually anywhere." He stepped to the gun barrel and rubbed at a spot with a cloth he had pulled from his pocket.

"The normal sustained rate of fire is three rounds per minute, which can be increased to ten per minute for short periods. The total function of this battery is to take calls from forward observers like you and process your fire mission. "And Lieutenant Pearce, when we do finalize the adjustments, if you can get a Viet Cong to bend over, we can put one of these—" he said, pointing to a stack of howitzer rounds in the shade of a small tarp, "up his ass at 1,550 feet per second!"

"I'll remember that, Chief," I said as I laughed. "I don't remember any classes where we discussed putting 'bullets up the enemy's asses,' but I will certainly call you when I need it."

We were through with business, and Hanover turned to me. "Anyway we can help, just call." We shook hands. "Don't be a stranger. Come and visit us between operations. We like to keep up with what's happening."

He turned to leave and then turned back, staring at Captain Turner, who had returned to his chair in front of the mess tent. "And the name is *Hanover*."

"It is good to have you here," the captain said. No one here will agree that it is good to *be* here, but since misery loves company, it is good to have *you* here.

"You won't be with us much, but this battery is your home. You'll see a lot more of Captain Novak, Charlie Company's commanding officer, than you will us. I don't really know him too well, but he seems fine." He paused and studied my face. "You'll be in the field most of the time, tromping around the jungles." He waited for my reaction.

"That's what I understand," I said.

His eyes had never left mine. "Well, Darnell will take you to The Plantation to get you settled in. I know you'll be busy, but when you are back in this area, check in with us. Don't be a stranger."

As we drove away, I turned to look back, as everything behind me disappeared in the dust.

Six

SEARS AND ROEBUCK
FEBRUARY 2, 1966

As we drove through Phuoc Vinh on our way to C Company area, Darnell chattered. "This shitty place was put together to be a model city. At least that's what they say." He swerved slightly as he dodged an old man on a bicycle, splashing sewage water from a bar ditch away from the jeep.

"This is a model city?" I scoffed. "Surely you jest."

"Yes, sir," he replied. "You'll see a statue up here in a minute of the man who designed it."

"Well, it looks like somehow he fell pretty short of his mark. How many people live here?"

"Don't know," he replied. "Not counting our military—us, a couple hundred of Vietnamese, I guess."

It was a totally new world to me. "Are they friendly?"

"What do you mean by 'friendly'?" he asked.

"Have you had any trouble with any of them?"

"Here's my theory. These people—the barber, the sales people, the prostitutes—all of them, they're in this for themselves, yes, but they're in it for the VC too. The VC want them here every day, talking to you, talking to me, asking you how you are, how the war is going. The U.S. forces can't really prove it one way or another, so their advice is to treat them nice and don't trust them. The same ones smiling when they're taking your money for a folding lawn chair are passing information to the VC each night—your name, rank, unit, the color of your eyes—probably even the length of your what-you-call-it. And they are probably firing mortars at us after dark. My bet is that some of them *are* VC, and the rest are forced to provide money and info *to* the VC." He drove in silence for a moment, negotiating the street's right-of-way with a flock of filthy, white geese as they squawked and flapped their wings. "And by the way, we have to buy you a wash pan," he said as an afterthought.

I knew that Viet Cong was the common name for the Vietnamese rebels fighting against the South Vietnamese government, also referred to as Victor Charlie, using the Army's phonetic alphabet—VC, Cong, or simply Charlie.

"Charlie is the other team," he continued. "I don't trust any of the little bastards."

I turned to look at him. "You wouldn't fight to protect your hometown if someone came in shooting it up and trying to take it over?" I asked, just to test his mettle.

He turned slightly toward me. "Lieutenant, you've never been to Iowa, have you?"

We pulled over, and the conversation stopped as armored personnel carriers growled by, belching black diesel smoke. Dirty water and sewage stood, flowing sluggishly in a broad ditch next to me.

"Do you mind if I pick up my laundry?" he asked.

"Of course I don't."

We waited until the dust and smoke passed, and then he resumed the trip. In less than a minute, he turned in front of what appeared to be the largest building I had seen since arriving, and he killed the engine.

"And this, sir, is 'Sears and Roebuck.'"

The exterior was dingy, cream-colored stucco, with black-and-rust-colored stains running down the sides along cracks in the walls. Large shutters, badly in need of paint, hung on either side of four front windows, one tilted at an angle on its lower hinge. The overhanging clay-tile roof, held up by a series of square concrete columns, protruded past the walls and over the sidewalk.

I was surprised that the signs on the buildings were written using the Roman alphabet. I supposed it was another influence of years of French domination, beginning with Jesuit missionaries in the early seventeenth century to mid-1950s when that influence ended. In less than a minute, he turned to the sidewalk in front of the building. Cracks in the walls had been patched with off-colored stucco. Neatly lettered banners in Vietnamese that I assumed said something like "George Washington's Birthday Sale – Everything 15% off" were draped between the columns and tousled by a slight breeze. Against light from openings at the back of the store, I could see people, GIs in fatigues and Vietnamese in their typical black pajama-like clothes, moving around inside among tables heaped with what I assumed was merchandise.

I realized that the shallow V-shaped ditch we had crossed as we parked was a sewage ditch, running both ways from the jeep as far as I could see. Husky timbers, roughly fifteen inches wide and worn with foot traffic, crossed periodically, mainly in front of the shops, to provide passage over the ditches. A mangy brown-and-white dog stopped fifteen feet away, stared at me for several seconds, then lowered his head and drank from the ditch. The entire area smelled sour, like a mixture of spoiled milk and vomit.

I turned to stare at an old man who stood beside a small motorbike parked on the concrete slab in the shade just inside the entrance of the building. He was whittling at a small piece of wood and had watched everything that had occurred since our arrival. He looked closely at the piece of wood and brushed away shavings that were clinging to it.

Darnell stepped out, reached beneath his seat to remove a small brown bag, and then stepped onto the concrete walk that ran the width of the building. He was immediately swarmed by five screaming children, all barefooted with plain white, cotton shirts and black shorts. They smiled and squealed as they pulled at his fatigue blouse, shouting the entire time. The oldest, probably eight, was holding the youngest—a small girl—astraddle his hip.

"You'll need these," he said as he tossed me the paper bag. "Only two per kid" was his final instruction as he stepped away and walked inside.

I looked inside the bag and found caramel candy pieces wrapped in cellophane. In the same time it took the bag to travel through the air to me, the five arrived at my side of the jeep, all talking excitedly and holding out their hands and staring at me with large, pitch-black, unblinking eyes, each with unkempt matching hair. I pulled out a handful and gave two pieces to each child as instructed. They immediately began unwrapping the candy, shouting in what I assumed was Vietnamese. Their faces were dirty and chapped.

The youngest clung to her ride's shirt, her nose with two streams of mucous. Her bangs were cut in a straight line across her forehead, and her eyes, which looked like polished onyx, seemed to reflect the world. She turned away long enough to wipe a string of snot from below her nose onto her carrier's shirt, with ample evidence that it was not the first time she had done it. She accepted her share of candy from me, quickly wrapping a piece in each baby-fat fist, then turning her gaze toward me in a distrusting stare.

I winked at her. She twisted her brow in response, but she didn't move. I tore a quarter-size piece of paper from the bag, licked it, and stuck it on the end of my nose. They all stopped to watch, their cheeks bulging with butterscotch. Ebony Eyes was my target audience. I pushed my lower jaw forward so that it barely cleared my upper lip, and then twisted my left ear, blowing air upward past my nose at the same time and sending the paper flying upward, then fluttering through the air. They all laughed hysterically.

Ebony Eyes squirmed until the older boy put her down, proceeding to unwrap his second butterscotch. She fought her way through the forest of legs around her, retrieved the paper, and handed it to me. I repeated my act. Her laughter was delightful as she clapped her tiny pudgy hands.

Darnell came out carrying brown paper packages tied with string and a bright-colored "mattress" that resembled a lounge cushion.

"Go away!" he yelled, laughing. All the children jumped the ditch and ran inside...all except the baby, who waded through the stinking water and then turned to watch us leave.

"A housewarming gift for you," Darnell said, holding up the chaise pad. "The closest thing you'll find to a mattress. I went through a bunch of them, and this one had the least smell of wet feathers." He stuffed it in back, slung his right leg inside, and slid into the seat.

"Is that the Viet Cong's version of Madame Defarge?" I asked as I nodded toward the old man on the walk.

"What?" Darnell asked, turning to me and then toward the old man.

"You know, the French revolution? 'Tis a far, far better thing I do'?"

Darnell stared at me blankly.

"You know, In the *Tale of Two Cities*, the lady that knitted the names of people to be dealt with in the French Revolution. After your lecture earlier about the Viet Cong keeping notes on us, I thought you might tell me that that's what this character is doing. But instead of knitting the names of the people to be killed in the Revolution, he whittles them into that piece of wood he has been carving on!"

He stared at me for several seconds. "Sorry, sir, you've lost me."

"Charles Dickens?" I tried one last time. "Never mind. I should have known you wouldn't know what I was talking about. You *were* a football player, right?" I removed the cellophane and popped a piece of butterscotch into my mouth.

Darnell grabbed the bag and stuffed it behind the seat. "Sorry, sir, the candy is strictly for the kids."

Darnell shook his head slowly, backed out, and drove away. I turned back to see that the children had gone inside. All had left but Ebony Eyes, who once more waded across the ditch, toddling as fast as she could in our direction. Her hand was held up, still clutching the tiny piece of paper bag.

"Stop a second," I said, twisting in my seat and looking back. As I did, she fell and began to cry. The boy who had been carrying her ran from the building, chased by a woman who was yelling at him. He scooped the baby up and, dodging the woman, ran inside. She was screaming at him the whole time.

"OK," I said. "Drive on."

The vehicle growled and gained speed. "If you can't save 'em all, you probably shouldn't worry about trying to save just one of them, Lieutenant."

I sat back and just watched. A man in typical black dress and hat held a six-foot pole centered over his left shoulder, with straw baskets tied to each end, filled with vegetables that bounced with each step. Geese waded in the same ditch that ran in front of the store and honked noisily as we approached, dipping their long necks to pick up scraps in the water. They swerved away, complaining loudly across the ditch to avoid Darnell.

He pointed at a small building with a sign that read "Hot Toc." Three men, all barefooted and smoking cigarettes, squatted with their knees folded so that their rears rested on their heels and their armpits rested over each knee. Their heads turned in unison as we passed.

"'Hot Toc' is the word for haircut," he said. "Best barber in town. Price includes a neck massage. It's all done with scissors and razors. No clippers. And as a point of reference, as I'm told by those less scrupulous than me, that it is also the best 'boom-boom' parlor—or whorehouse—in town." His smile consumed his face, his eyebrows and cheeks rising as two deep dimples came into place. "You pay two bucks for 'short time,' five bucks for 'long time.' Pretty safe too, so I understand. I don't frequent the place, as I am a happily scrupulous husband and father from Iowa. Rumor is that the battalion veterinarian gives shots to them and keeps some sort of medical records on them."

"How *absolutely* romantic," I replied. "My dear, why don't you slip into something comfortable while I peruse your shot record?"

"I have also been told," Darnell continued, "that in front of the back wall of the main room, there is a big chest of drawers. They pull it out, and there is a square hole behind it. Crawl through, and you are with the ladies." He turned to me and grinned once more. "I can't confirm it, but that's what I hear."

As we passed the Hot Toc shop, a man stepped from the building and threw a pan of water into the ditch, tapped the pan against a sandbag, stared at us, and returned inside.

"There's the only cafe," he said, pointing to a rickety-looking open-air building, "but you don't eat there. Brigade medics have marked it 'off limits.'" He turned sharply to miss a dog that ran into the street, and then continued. "We call it 'The Ptomaine Temple.'"

We stopped at a marble statue of an officious-looking, overweight man in military dress mounted on a pedestal. "He's the one who designed this town," Darnell commented. "Don't you know his mother is proud?" The statue seemed totally out of place on a ten-foot high block of polished stone, surrounded on both sides with ditches filled with rancid water and shit.

"Sort of like our politicians: more impressed with recognizing his work than finishing it."

The town suddenly began to give way to dozens of canvas tents stretched over stout poles held up by ropes and pegs, all designed to accommodate ten soldiers each, all in perfect rows and columns. The canvas sides were rolled up

"And this, sir knight," Darnell said, "is where you now live. Welcome to 'The Plantation.'"

Seven

THE PLANTATION
FEBRUARY 2, 1966

At home in New Mexico, farmers judge each other's work by how straight the rows in their fields are. It is farmer's art, and the highest praise one could achieve is to have neighbors refer to him as a "straight-row farmer." As we drove slowly into The Plantation, it became obvious that the French cherished the same standards.

Every tree was placed to form perfect columns and rows and oblique lines, twenty feet apart, as far as I could see. It was obvious from some weeds and saplings that until very recently, this had obviously been a working plantation, probably operated by a French conglomerate somewhere. Even now, it was a tribute to the pride of French companies that had created it. I thought of the history books that Julie had given me. These people, filled with dreams, had fought nature and the elements to establish this plantation and won, had fought the jungles and won, only to be beaten down to a small number of families by a never-ending string of different Army uniforms, languages, and burning desires. As a farmer, I felt an unknown kinship with whoever had planted each and every tree in this plantation.

Darnell let out on the clutch, and we drove for a few minutes to a stop before an array of tents all in straight rows. We stopped in front of one that I recognized as the "admin tent." Given the heat, the sides of the tent were rolled up so that the tent really only gave protection from the rain. Almost everything there was olive drab: the two vehicles parked between rows of rubber trees, the tents, and the clothing worn by everyone there. We were greeted by the brightest thing I had seen: a flaming red bicycle mustache and matching hair, belonging to company First Sergeant Mitchell Flaherty O'Brien, as he stepped from the tent smiling. "Welcome to 'The Plantation,' Lieutenant," he said, saluting. "Our new forward observer, I am told."

"I've been told the same thing," I said, returning his salute and reaching to shake his hand. He turned his body slightly toward the tent area and said, "Well, it isn't much now, but we have wonderful plans for a school, a church, city hall..." His voice trailed off, replaced by a sly, closed-eyed grin.

"This is Specialist Wilson," he said, gesturing to a young man at a typewriter. "Our administrative whiz. Captain Novak, our company commander, is at headquarters at a staff meeting. Should be back in about an hour," Sergeant O'Brien continued. "In the meantime, Specialist Darnell will show you to the officer's tent—Lieutenant Swenson's old bunk." Then turning to me, he said, "And you have papers for me?"

"They're in my bag, I can—"

"No, no," he interrupted calmly, holding his palm out flat in front of him. "Just drop them off when you can. I'll be here through Sunday; then I have to meet Raquel Welch in Saigon." As he spoke, the tips of his fiery mustache rose toward his ears, and the grin returned as he closed his eyes. "Darnell will show you to the officer's tent."

Darnell shouldered the duffel bag, and I followed him along what he referred to as "Main Street," past the olive drab squad tents.

"Well, in the best tradition of the Army, the place looks neat, all raked and squared away," I said.

"It's not raked to look good," he said, displaying his impish smile. "It's raked to discourage ten-inch centipedes and scorpions...and sometimes snakes and other vermin from entering the tents."

He led me down Main Street, passing tents and soldiers who were attending to their chores. They paused briefly to size me up, the latest company oddity, and then quickly resumed what they were doing: cleaning weapons, rubbing preservative polish into boots, and raking leaves. There were no salutes as in other military operations, as snipers watched for that in order to identify officers.

We reached what Darnell referred to as the "lieutenant's tent," and Darnell walked to the side where the canvas had been rolled up and put my belongings on an empty wood and canvas cot.

It was what I had expected, having become familiar with such quarters through numerous training exercises. It was Spartanic and practical. Three aluminum folding chairs, laced with brightly colored plastic strips, stood, one each next to the occupied cots. Darnell spoke as he pointed to the obviously used cots, each neatly made with a camouflage-colored nylon and quilted blankets, one-quarter of an inch thick. He pointed as he continued, "Lieutenant Allegretti, there, Lieutenant Rose, there, and Lieutenant Wilson, there." It had dirt floors, which had been sprinkled with water and swept. Identical wooden foot lockers rested on artillery ammunition boxes, bringing them to the same height as the cot. On the top of each foot locker, except mine, an aluminum wash pan lay upside down, at the end nearest to the front of the tent. I turned as though to ensure that I had not missed anything. "All obviously coordinated to match the rest of the décor. How chic."

He read my thoughts. "Whenever you are ready, I can take you back to Sears to get sandals, towels, and a wash pan."

Two pieces of green nylon cord, roughly two feet apart, were stretched tightly from side to side across the rear of the tent, with army green socks, army green towels, and army green underwear draped on them.

Grinning, I turned to Darnell and said, "The decorator obviously went to a lot of trouble putting the color scheme together. I suppose I will have to ask the movers to hold up on sending my Van Gogh and the two Picassos. A pity."

"Only the best for our men in green," he said, smiling.

Two Coleman lanterns hung from the center cord of the tent, one at roughly four feet from the front, one at the center of the tent. "Want to step outside a minute?" Darnell asked. I did.

We walked to the shower at the rear of the company area, and he pointed to two small, box-like buildings made of artillery ammunition boxes. "That's the latrine—two holes. This is also referred to lovingly as Lieutenant Rose's library." Two benches ran across the inside of the building at knee height, each with an oval hole over a half barrel. "The shit drops into the two half-barrels beneath the holes. When they get full, they are dragged out and the crap inside is burned."

He turned slightly and pointed at three pipes that stuck up from the ground at an angle, three feet high. "Those are the pissers." He touched two cans full of white powder with the toe of his boot.

He pointed to a structure built of four-by-fours to hold up a platform six feet off the ground. On top sat three fifty-gallon barrels, each with a pipe attached to the bottom, which led to a valve with a chain hanging down and then to a shower head. "For the three or four days each day that we're not in the field, these are the epitome of chic! They also come with long lines of customers when we are in camp. Don't look for the hot water faucets...because there aren't any. So, you stand under the showerhead and pull the chain—no more than thirty seconds—to get wet. Lather up, and repeat the cycle to rinse off.

"Follow me," he continued. We walked to where we could see two more tents at the farthest point away from the latrines. "That is the dining area—the mess hall." Some crude tables made of discarded wooden artillery shell boxes, standing room only, stood in two neat rows. I surveyed the area slowly for several minutes as he remained silent. "If you are looking for a bus station, there isn't one." I laughed.

"Home for the duration," he said softly. "Anything else I can do to help you? I'm sure your head is spinning at the vast number of luxuries at your disposal. Do you need help unpacking?"

I ignored the offer and asked, "So Swenson was his name?"

"Sir?" he asked.

"The lieutenant I am replacing—his name was Swenson?"

"Yes, sir."

"And how did he die?"

"Killed in a jeep accident," Darnell said. "It rolled over on the road, about a mile outside the company area. He was driving."

"And you were in his section?"

"I was, ever since we left the states."

"So what was he like?"

"He was a great guy. Good at what he did. It was pretty pitiful."

After an uncomfortable pause, I said, "Check back with me in thirty minutes. You can bring me up to speed then."

"Will do," he replied, his broad smile returning. "If you need anything, just call the front desk." He turned and walked away.

Everything that I could call mine in Vietnam was either on my body or in the green duffel on the cot. Duffel bags were designed so that the top could be folded over a hasp and locked. I had always thought the whole idea of locking a canvas bag was ludicrous. It seemed like putting a door lock on a house of straw. I reached into my blouse and pulled a chain from around my neck. It held two dog tags with my name, rank, and serial number stamped on each, and a single key.

Less than two weeks before, I had had a sizable ring of keys, which, one by one, had left the ring as I began my departure. The post office box key went first, and then the room at the bachelor officer's quarters, the office key, my desk key, and finally—and most grudgingly—the key to my 1965 Mustang. I had considered it a "clever conspiracy" by the Army: a ploy for telling me that they did, in fact, own everything about me now. They had given me all of my clothing and boots and the cap on my head. Three weeks earlier, I had been required to take ten new sets of white briefs and T-shirts to the quartermaster laundry at Fort Bliss, Texas, to have them dyed olive drab, the Army's favorite color. Even that was part of the conspiracy. I had a billfold, but no driver's license (couldn't have any identification on my person except the dog tags that I wore on a ball chain around my neck), no family pictures in the wallet, and no personal items other than one small, plastic zipper case in the duffel bag. I had a razor, shaving cream, a toothbrush, toothpaste, a can of boot polish, and a comb.

I stared at the foot locker, a roughly three feet by two feet by eighteen inches deep box made of plywood and painted...in what else? *Army green paint!* I placed all of my clothing in the bottom compartment. I put a tray in next on wood rails five inches deep and arranged my toilet items in the left front corner. Then I picked up the photographs and put those of Julie in an airtight bag at the left rear corner of the tray and those of Angie in an identical bag at the right front. As I placed Angie's pictures, I couldn't help but laugh at the thought of a boxing ring announcer saying into the microphone, "And in this corner..." I closed it, fastened and locked the hasp with the padlock, and placed the chain with my key and dog tags around my neck.

Most of my remaining personal belongings had been turned into the company first sergeant to be inventoried and taken to the battalion for shipping back to my home.

My foot locker had been his foot locker until *that* fatal day when he went to work for the last time. He had put his belongings inside the foot locker and slept on the cot, which was now mine. "Sorry, soldier." I said softly.

I stared out. With the side tent flaps rolled up, I looked out at perfectly aligned rows of rubber trees stretching several hundred yards and a deep carpet of brown leaves.

I glanced at my watch. It was 3:00 p.m. "Be it ever so humble," I muttered aloud.

As I sat there, my thoughts turned to home and Daddy Bud, my maternal grandfather—an elf. He was a storyteller and a bit of a drinker of alcohol that he kept in dozens of partially filled bottles stashed in an old wood pile behind the barn. I grinned broadly as I thought of times when I had sat beneath his front porch, a structure roughly four by five feet and four feet high above the ground. It was surrounded by four o'clock bushes and formed my 'fort,' my fantasy world.

From here I would listen to him talk about anything and everything. He would give me advice, lectures, whatever he had on his mind. But he seemed to always know what I needed to hear at that given time. I knew if I needed advice, I could always go to Daddy Bud. And if I needed hope, he would tell stories of the Raincrow, and the mention of his name would place me in a trance. In New Mexico, growing up in a farming family, nothing was more important to us than rain. And if you hoped for one thing more often than anything else, it was rain. The Raincrow brought that hope and, hopefully, the rain with it. When times were tough as they often were, the mere thought of the Raincrow would brighten spirits, bring smiles to everyone, and make people realize that there is always hope for those who believed in him.

"Well, Daddy Bud," I looked up and said aloud, "There is definitely enough rain in this place. I sure hope the Raincrow followed me here as well to see me through. I'll take all the advice...and hope I can get."

I was brought from my reverie by a rustling noise at the front tent flap. I looked up to see the company clerk standing there.

"You're Specialist Wilson, right?" I asked, recalling the introduction from earlier.

"Yes, sir," he said, smiling. "Captain Novak is back from headquarters. He said he could see you now."

Eight

CAPTAIN ALVIN NOVAK
FEBRUARY 2, 1966

According to Darnell, Captain Alvin A. Novak had been the Commander of Charlie Company since it left Fort Riley, Kansas, in May 1965. I approached his tent and knocked on the tent pole at the entrance.

"Lieutenant Pearce," he said as he stood and stepped toward me. "Welcome."

As I approached, I saluted him and said, "Thank you, sir," and then we shook hands. Judging from my height, I estimated him to be just over six feet with angular features and a dark brown, quarter-inch crew cut. He wore heavy, black-rimmed glasses, which he pushed to the bridge of his nose with the middle finger of his left hand, opening his mouth slightly as he did.

"Care for a cup of coffee?" he asked, turning and gesturing toward a stainless steel pot that I recognized as standard mess hall equipment.

"No, thanks," I said, as he turned toward the pot and filled his cup. I noticed an elastic strap that ran from each earpiece of his glasses around and behind his head.

"Any problems checking in?" he asked.

"None so far," I replied.

"You've reported to your battery Captain Turner, right?"

"I have," I said, nodding. "I turned in my papers both here and there."

Facing me, he held a pencil by its point in his left hand and pressed it against his left temple, rotating it slightly. "So, tell me about yourself."

"Well, I was born and raised in New Mexico. I graduated from New Mexico State University in Las Cruces, New Mexico—a degree in accounting and a minor in structural engineering. I was commissioned there in January 1965. Then I reported to Fort Sill, Oklahoma, for nine weeks of my basic field artillery unit commander training. While I was there, I also received four weeks of reconnaissance and survey officer training. Then in April, I reported to the 7th of the 8th Field Artillery Battery at Fort Bliss, Texas. That's a self-propelled, eight-inch howitzer outfit. We did a hell of a lot of field training: bivouacs, fire missions, and all of that good stuff. Then last summer, July, I was sent to Fort McPherson for a month of chemical, biological, and radiation training. In late November, I received orders to come here, and here I am."

Novak cocked his head, lowered the pencil, and tapped it against the back of his other hand. "Family?" he asked.

"My folks are farmers in Southern New Mexico. We raise cotton, alfalfa, cattle, hogs—"

"Are you married?"

"No, sir."

He nodded slowly. "You'll probably find that a good thing over the next year," he said without explanation. "It makes life a lot less complicated."

As I studied him, I convinced myself that he couldn't be more than two years older than I was.

He stared at me over the rim of his coffee cup as he took a sip.

He smiled broadly and asked, "You're a virgin, right?"

I obviously looked shocked, at which he smiled even wider. "You've never been in combat?"

"Oh, yes. By that definition, I'm a virgin. No, I've never been in combat."

"Well, this coming week we'll have an opportunity to change that. I attended a briefing today about an operation we'll be going on in a few days. It will be short, probably a week. Aerial observers—helicopters—have spotted some VC supplies, bags of rice, and possibly ammunition, in what Battalion considers VC—Viet Cong—territory. We're going to go in and check it out and then turn it over to the Air Force to destroy."

"I've already admitted I'm a virgin. And I'll admit that I'm not as anxious to lose your version of virginity as I was when I lost my original virginity. But I'm ready."

Captain Novak continued. "You have a good team. Darnell and Raille, your recon sergeant and your radio operator, are both highly capable.

"Most of the operations we have done over the past several months have been what are called 'search-and-destroy' operations. These are designed to find and report evidence of enemy activity, supply dumps, explosives, equipment, food- fortified areas, and, as the name implies, we search for it and blow it up. And you are a key player for the 'blow it up' part. We also report everything we find to the intelligence 'spooks.'"

I frowned and cocked my head slightly. "Excuse me... spooks?"

"It's a nickname for people who sneak around looking for things—intelligence people. The process is designed to see what's out there and gather evidence." He raised the pencil to his temple once more and began to rotate it back and forth.

He discussed my three fellow lieutenants—the three platoon leaders—heaping praise on them. "Lieutenant Terry Wilson is our 2nd Platoon Commander, and he will be your sponsor—someone to show you around. His job, as such, will be to work with you and introduce you to the company and what we do. It's more honorary than anything else, but we are required by Battalion to assign someone. Have you met him yet?"

"No, Sir."

"Have you met Lieutenants Mike Allegretti and David Rose?"

"No, sir."

"Well, Lieutenant Wilson will introduce you around, help with any problems you might have with Battalion and that sort of stuff. Obviously, if you need anything, feel free to see me anytime. We are all available to help you get settled." He discussed the weather and how it would impact our combat operations. Finally, he paused and placed the pencil on the table. His mood changed.

"You will find that we are organized a bit differently than most infantry units. We have three infantry platoons, and that is normal. We are authorized to have a weapon's platoon also, but it has been detailed to Battalion for security purposes. It's some sort of an experiment, due to the open terrain and the fact that the infantry companies are away a lot. The bottom line to all of this is that it puts more of a load on you in the field, to make up for the loss of the mortars." He stopped briefly and stared. I didn't flinch.

"A little history," he said as he sipped his coffee. "The 1st Infantry was one of the first two divisions to come to Vietnam. Came over by ship. We left the states in late June on a Navy personnel transport ship—the General W.H. Gordon—in the September-October 1965 time frame. We started operating here in the Phuoc Vinh area in late October. So you see, we haven't been here much longer than you. We actually worked the area around Phuoc Vinh with the 1st Brigade in that time frame. I'm sure you'll get the rest of the story from your fellow platoon leaders.

"So far we have only had three casualties. All three were KIA—'killed in action'—one killed by a sniper and two by a land mines." He paused. "That doesn't include Lieutenant Swenson, the forward observer you are replacing, who was killed in a jeep accident. We've been responsible for protecting an engineer company quite a bit since we arrived here, fortifying the area. We've provided cover while they cut down trees and cane—bamboo, mainly— around the airfield. And we have had some firefights in the area."

He continued to stare at me, and after a long pause, he spoke in a businesslike manner, the smile gone.

"My responsibility is to the men of this company and to smash the enemy anywhere we find them. It isn't personal, but I don't know you yet. We'll take it easy when we get into the field—a few fire missions far enough away from us to get the hang of things, for you to feel comfortable that no one will be hurt. Is that fair enough?" He didn't wait for a response. "I know that at Fort Sill where you trained, that you shot up old, rusty jeeps, tanks, and truck bodies. This isn't Fort Sill, and we're not shooting at *old, rusty truck bodies* as targets on a practice range."

He paused for several seconds, tapping the pencil against the back of his hand. "And don't take this wrong, but please appreciate the fact that you are replacing a forward observer who I felt comfortable with. And you are an unknown quantity. Understand what I'm driving at?" After a pause, he continued, "I'll give you every benefit of the doubt. But if you ever feel uncomfortable with your job at any time—" He paused, and I sensed that he regretted what he had just said.

I took it as an invitation to talk. "Sir, I have a responsibility to this unit too. I trained at Fort Sill, just like Swenson. On the same range he did. I probably shot at the same damned rusty truck bodies he did. We 'cannon cockers' love to shoot at old truck bodies. I appreciate the concern, but I *can* do my job."

"I'm sure you can." He stared at me for several more seconds before he reached into his foot locker and pulled out a bottle of Jack Daniels and two Melamine coffee cups. He poured a healthy measure into both and then handed one to me. "I'm sure you can," he repeated, then raised his drink, and said, "To doing our jobs."

I held my glass up. "To doing our jobs...*well*," I said.

Nine

THE LIEUTENANTS OF COMPANY C
FEBRUARY 2, 1966

I left the meeting with Captain Novak to find Darcy Darnell waiting at the base of a rubber tree, talking to another soldier. They rose and walked over to me.

"Lieutenant Pearce, this is Specialist Mathias Raille, but everyone knows him as 'Panther.' He's our radio operator."

"Pleased to meet you, sir," Raille said in a soft, high-pitched voice that didn't seem to fit his tall, muscular frame.

"And I am to meet you. I'm looking forward to getting to know both of you.

"I had my first pep talk with Charlie-Six," I said. "It went well. He spoke highly of you two, and he discussed an operation we are going on later this week. I assume we are ready for it."

"'Ready' is our middle name," Darnell said.

"The two of you have a four or five-month head start of experience in this combat thing. I'll count on that to bring me up to speed."

I looked at my watch. "Let's get together in two hours. That will give me time to finish setting up my new home and hopefully meet some of the infantry officers. Where is a good place to discuss what tomorrow holds for us?"

"The Academy," Darnell said. "I'll meet you at your tent and take you there."

I walked to the tent where I had left my belongings. Two lieutenants were sitting on bunks inside when I arrived. Their conversation stopped as I entered, and both stood up and faced me.

"Well, Lieutenant Allegretti," one of them said. "We may have caught an artilleryman here. What will we do with him?" He stepped toward me and held out his hand. "David Rose. Everyone calls me 'Professor.' I'm in charge of 1st Platoon." He had a slender build, cropped blond and unruly hair, faint but noticeable freckles, and wire-rimmed glasses. He looked at me with his head slightly tilted to the left, the way a puppy might when expecting a treat, his brows slightly raised, and grinning broadly. We shook hands.

"Craig Pearce," I replied, as I shook his hand. I turned to the other officer and extended my hand. He was a giant.

"Craig, is it?" he asked. His hand looked twice the size of mine.

"Yes, Craig Pearce."

"Mike Allegretti," he replied. "I'm in charge of 3rd Platoon. Pleased to meet you. And welcome. 3rd Platoon," he said once more. Everything about him was oversized, including the ham-like hand that gripped mine.

"So," resumed Professor, "am I right? You *are* the new forward observer. Correct?"

"I am, and at your service."

"Well, it looks like you have already moved into the suite we reserved for you," he said with a broad smile as he put one foot forward, placed his right hand over his heart, bowed, and made a flowing gesture with his left hand toward my cot. Near each of their cots, an M16 rifle stood propped against their trunks, along with their standard Army helmets, ammo patches, a web belt, two canteens, and other accoutrements, all in deep army green.

"Your area has the view," Professor said, still smiling.

"You've really outdone yourselves," I said. "You've gone too far and too much trouble. You shouldn't have."

"Well, you know Uncle Sam," Professor said. "Nothing is too good for his boys. So, with that in mind, 'nothing' is pretty much what we get!" There was a slight pause, and then the inevitable questions began.

"Where are you from?" He asked.

"Hobbs, New Mexico."

"Is that in the United States?" Allegretti asked with a broad smile.

"And where did you go to college?" David continued.

"I went to New Mexico State University." I rattled off my college career and Army training: New Mexico State, Fort Bliss, Fort Sill, and Fort McClellan. "And then God decided you boys desperately needed me, so here I am."

"Married?" David asked.

"No," I replied. "I'm not."

"Any prospects?" he asked. "I mean, will we be blessed with the sweet smell of perfumed letters to freshen up this dump?"

"Well, yes," I answered sheepishly, after a pause. "Two, I suppose."

"Two what?" Professor asked again, his head reared back and his eyebrows raised. Allegretti stopped polishing the large boot that engulfed his left hand and turned his full attention to the conversation.

"Two possible prospects for marriage, I suppose," I replied.

He cocked his head to the left, examining me, and softly whistled.

"Mormon?" he asked.

"No. It's a long story. I was going with one, and we broke up. A couple of months later I met the second one, about three months before I left for here. And then, two days before I left, the first one called and said she wanted us back together. I guess I'm just slow making decisions." I realized immediately that I shouldn't have gotten this deep into this conversation yet.

"Well, then," he said, a grin spreading across his face, "you may find this little war a lot less risky for you than your personal life. And in comparison, mine is very simple."

Professor described his life: born and raised in Lincoln, Nebraska, he was a chemist and a disc jockey for a radio station, "with *one* wife and two daughters," he said emphatically.

Mike was next. "Born and raised in Worcester, Massachusetts. Married, one child, and *one* wife," he emphasized with a sheepish grin. I studied him as he spoke, his eyelids drooping as he resumed his boot maintenance.

"Well," I said, "judging from size, it's good to be on your side."

Suddenly, Professor sat up and looked toward the front of the tent. I turned to see yet another lieutenant entering.

"Well, if it ain't Colonel Beauregard, who has come home from the 'waar,'" Professor said in his best imitation of a Southern drawl. "Praise heaven."

The newcomer removed his baseball cap and sailed it at him, and then he turned and held his hand out to me. "Terry Wilson. Call me 'Bama' or 'your majesty,' if you so prefer." He was instantly likable.

"Craig Pearce. And I'll go with 'Bama' if you don't mind."

Bama walked to what I judged to be his "area," sat down on the cot, and stared up at me. "One fallacy about the entire military system," Bama continued, is that no matter how much training is presented, no matter how much practice is done, some men who wear the uniform are still uncivilized assholes. Sir, please allow me to apologize for First Lieutenant Rose." His Southern voice had the quality of mahogany: rich, smooth, and well-accented. And he looked remarkably like Mickey Mantle, with short-cropped, dirty blond hair. Mike and Professor were both grinning broadly. The show had started.

"You'll become accustomed, as time goes by, to the irascible rudeness of this individual," Bama said as he gestured toward Professor, "a quality that I have come to feel is simply a total lack of proper upbringing and no culture. The boy was raised in the Midwest and assumed the qualities of character from that region." Finally, the show stopped as he turned to Professor and laughed.

I looked at Bama. "And you must be 2nd Platoon."

"I must!" he replied. "My platoon sets the standards for these two lug nuts to follow."

Allegretti looked at me. He held his huge hands, tented together with the index fingers touching his chin as he spoke. "We were talking before this human whirlwind came in," he said, nodding his head in Bama's direction. "Allow me to continue." He had a soft baritone voice that brought to mind warm syrup—which seemed to match his swarthy complexion—and a weight lifter's build. "Yes, I only have *one* wife, but I am married," he said with a sly grin. "We have been sweethearts since the eighth grade and married after college." I mused at him referring to himself as a "sweetheart," but said nothing. He reached into his foot locker and pulled out a hinged five-by-seven picture frame. On one side of the hinged frame was a dark-haired beauty his age. She also looked to be of Italian ancestry. "That's Trish," he said, beaming.

"Wow," I said softly. "You are a fortunate man." The other side of the frame held a picture of a baby in what appeared to be a christening gown. "Is this a baby picture of your wife?" I asked as straight faced as possible.

His round face spread with a broad smile. "That's Mariana. Mari." The smile gradually faded. "She is three-months-old, born three months after I got here. I haven't seen her yet."

It was quiet for a moment, then Bama said, "Yes, and by God's good grace, she inherited her mother's good looks."

"Oh, and by the way," I said as I turned back to Allegretti, "I met Lieutenant Hanover at the artillery battery. He said to tell you 'hello.'"

Allegretti's smile returned. "Good old 'Hangover,'" he said as he, the Professor, and Bama laughed. "Bama and I were there the night he got that nickname, just before we left for here. He was so drunk that we thought he was trying to commit suicide rather than come with us."

As I listened, I decided that if in the beginning of our lives, we were allocated a certain number of words to be used, that at the rate he spoke, he would still have most of his left over when he died.

Once again Bama spoke. "Allegretti, please stand up." Mike looked at him blankly and then rose from his cot. He was broad-shouldered with the biggest, widest combat boots I had ever seen. Coal-black eyes were set deeply in a round, tan face beneath short, black hair and eyebrows that resembled small brushes. He watched Bama, obviously wondering where this was going.

Gesturing toward Mike, Bama said: "And on the other hand, I consider this fine individual, this...this Goliath, to be a perfect gentleman. My upbringing also helped me realize the difference between those individuals that I could easily cajole and those who could crush me with one thumb." We all laughed.

"Tell him where you went to school, Michael," Bama said.

"Syracuse University," Mike replied.

Bama continued. "And while you were there getting a double major in accounting and finance, what did you do for fun?"

"What did I do *for fun*?" Michael asked softly, his face a mask of confusion.

"What was your number one extracurricular activity, Michael?"

"Football," Allegretti said softly.

"Were you a punter?"

Mike slowly shook his head and said, "I was a linebacker."

Bama turned to me. "Not *just* a linebacker, Lieutenant Pearce. This man was a 'two-time all-conference' linebacker. And that," Bama said, turning back to Professor and hitting him on the thigh with his fist, "is why I show him the respect that I do." A smile creased Bama's face as he grabbed Professor's shoulders and gently shook him.

"So, did you all know each other before you came over?" I asked.

Professor answered. "Bama and Allegretti knew each other. I was in the same brigade but a different battalion. Their battalion commander looked around and begged the general to send me over to his group, and the General said, 'it is obvious that they need him—'"

Half way through the sentence, Bama had begun moaning and yelling, "Please, no more," until Professor stopped.

I watched Professor as the laughter settled. Unlike the other two, he had a slender build and the look of a sage, with eyes that sparkled through round glasses—the kind John Lennon wore—when he smiled.

"So, what's life like in lovely Phuoc Vinh?" I asked, as the laughter settled.

"Pretty much the same as anywhere else," Professor responded. "We eat three meals a day, mostly out of little green cans. Shit twice a day, mostly into *big* green cans. Is that what you mean?" he asked, smiling broadly.

"Well, it's a start, although I was more interested in the not-so-usual functions," I replied.

"Ohhhh," he said, stretching the word. "You mean our little war." There was a moment of silence, and then Allegretti responded. "So far we've been mainly gardeners. We've started here by cutting down trees, clearing fire zones around the base, providing protection as the engineers put razor wire around the airfield—things to make this area more secure. The last two months, we've been involved in small operations, going out each day around the area and all behind here," he said, motioning away from the tents around us. "The first shots fired at us after we got here came from a VC we started calling 'Bed-Check Charlie,' a sniper from down behind The Plantation. He shot at us two or three times a week—usually two shots just before dark. At first we would jump up and charge out after him. Then we realized that in two weeks, he hadn't hit anyone, and decided to leave him alone. We decided that his replacement might be a better shot. Now that we have the area around the brigade pretty well-protected with wire, bunkers, clearings, and Claymore mines, we've been going out on some longer two-to-three-day missions. And most of them have still been within ten miles of here."

Everyone sat quietly until I spoke again, after looking from one to the other. "And that's worked out pretty well for you guys?"

"We've lost three people and one wounded," Mike continued. The humor was gone, as was any hint of a smile. He looked at the other two for confirmation, and they simply nodded.

I pursed my lips and nodded. Again it fell silent, and again they stared at me, this time for almost a minute, before Mike spoke again. "Craig, it's okay to be a little antsy. We all were—still are. I was damned nervous when I got here. Most of the time, it is simply boring and nerve-racking. We spend hours having everyone cleaning weapons and putting them back together, and then tearing them apart and cleaning them again. Vietnam days are twice as long as Massachusetts days. You'll be fine." He looked once more at the framed pictures—dwarfed by his hands—folded and wrapped a cloth around it, and placed it back inside the locker.

It was quiet for a moment, and then it was Bama's turn. "The most terrifying thing we face here," he said, "we'll introduce you to right now." He looked at the others. "Let's get some chow."

As I passed Bama's cot, I touched the M16 leaning there. "Do I get one of these? Huh, please, Daddy. Huh? Do I? DO I!" I asked.

Bama glanced back to see what I was asking about. "Not until after we get the results of your psychiatric evaluation," he called back over his shoulder.

As we walked, I felt myself imagining that Christ probably hadn't drawn as many curious stares when he dragged the cross through town as I was at that moment.

Ten

HONING MY TRADE
FEBRUARY 3, 1966

I woke to the smell of coffee that permeated the area at 5 a.m. I dressed and followed the aroma to a slightly sagging tent, carefully stepping over the requisite ropes and tent stakes holding it up. A group of soldiers scurried around a collection of steel cookware on top of kerosene stoves, stirring and slicing as they prepared breakfast. A voice boomed out to one of the cooks, admonishing him to turn down under a stove unit, and then turned to me.

"Morning, Lieutenant. I'm Sergeant Zeigler," he said, saluting as he did. "I'm the mess sergeant, and this is my crew." He made a sweeping gesture at the scene before us, a collection of boiling pots emitting steam into the air and flat pans covered with frying bacon and scrambled eggs.

Miscellaneous items hung from a wire that ran diagonally from two of the tent's corner posts. Boxes stenciled in black letters describing the food contained inside were stacked on shipping pallets, and three specialists wrapped in white aprons scurried frantically to do what needed to be done.

"And I can bet that you were lured here by the seductive smell of my coffee!" Sergeant Zeigler said.

"Why, Sergeant, you silver-tongued devil. I never pass up a cup of coffee," I replied, smiling.

"Spangler," Zeigler said, turning to one of the cooks, "get a cup of coffee for the Lieutenant. Cream or sugar?"

"No, thanks. Just black coffee."

"This is quite an operation," I said as I walked to him and extended my hand. Zeigler smiled, wiped his palms on a towel stuffed beneath his apron string, and then shook my hand.

A cook approached me with a cup of coffee with vapor rising vigorously.

"We try," Zeigler replied to my comment, then turned and looked at a thirty-by-forty-inch cooking sheet of frying bacon.

Sergeant Zeigler looked at me. "Lieutenant Pearce, meet Lieutenant Colonel Urrutia," he said, cocking his head toward a tall, slender officer standing just outside the tent.

"Oh, good morning, sir," I said, moving my cup to my left hand and shaking his. "I didn't see you standing there."

"He smiled and shook his head. No problem, Lieutenant—"

"Pearce," I said. "Craig Pearce." For the first time, I noticed the cross on his collar. "Ah, you are a man of the cloth."

"I am," he responded.

"And I would imagine that as such, you are a busy man," I said, smiling.

"I have sufficient job security here," he returned, smiling. "There are very few men in Vietnam who don't want to believe in God and wish to talk to him."

"I suppose you are right."

He slowly sipped from his coffee cup. "I would take your voice to be that of a West Texan?"

"Close," I said. "I was born and raised in Southeastern New Mexico."

"Conservative family stock, I would suppose?"

"We are about as conservative as they come. We are farmers. We raise cotton, alfalfa, some cattle, pigs, chickens...and kids," I said.

"May I assume that you grew up with a Bible in your home then?"

"Oh yes. More than one. I was liberally exposed to life as a Southern Baptist at an early age—sang in a choir from a Broadman Hymnal choir book."

"Well, as you have already seen, I am one of the chaplains in the area. I am always available if you need me for any reason, like getting in touch with your family or helping you to resolve emergencies of any sort—for you or any of your soldiers. I have ways of cutting through red tape when we need to. I have some pretty 'high' contacts." He smiled broadly as he cocked his head upward and rolled his eyes toward the sky. I won't keep you. I know you are busy. So am I. On days before operations, the men like me to be there for last minute discussions." He sipped his coffee once more. "So, being from New Mexico—¿Habla Español?" he asked.

"Un poquito," I replied, nodding my head and recalling Spanish 1 and 2.

He drained his cup and sat it on a folding table. Then he turned to me, and we shook hands. "Vaya con Dios," he said in excellent Spanish. "It has been my pleasure."

"Y usted también," I returned with a smile.

I refilled my cup and then held it up in a toasting gesture toward the mess sergeant. "Good stuff," I said, then turned and left.

"Anytime, Sir, we're here pretty much from sunrise to sundown every minute of the day. We always keep a forty-cup pot brewing all night."

"Well, you've got your hands full. Thanks for the coffee."

As I walked away, he began yelling at a cook, admonishing him to turn over a rasher of bacon.

With a fresh cup of black coffee, I stepped away from the tent and faced a brave new world—my new world. I walked some distance away in order to observe the morning activities as soldiers were already dashing about the area. A boom box cranked on high was playing "(I Can't Get No) Satisfaction" by the Stones as soldiers cleaned their gear.

I walked the area.

Main Street was filled with NCOs overseeing the cleaning of the company's machine guns and mortars and men raking leaves away from inside the company area. Rifles were being stripped and cleaned under the watchful eyes of squad sergeants under a large square of canvas—a tent that I would come to know as "The Academy"—at the end of Main Street.

Near the latrine area, six soldiers had placed a ladder by elevated water barrels atop the shower platform. They had formed a line from there to a 400-gallon water tank trailer and were filling them.

The military latrines in Vietnam were fairly typical, consisting of fifty-five gallon barrels cut in half to sit beneath a framed stand with two toilet seats. Privacy consisted of four four-by-four posts buried in the ground to form a rectangle. The final touch was a canvas wrapped around three sides to form walls. I watched as a group of "lucky" privates carried the barrels from the enclosure to a clearing, a "burn spot" thirty yards away where they dumped kerosene into the barrels and set them on fire. It was a process that would be repeated numerous times until the only thing left inside the half barrel was a thin layer of soot, at which point the barrels were allowed to cool and return to the tent fly.

"This is as good as it gets, Lieutenant Pearce," I said softly. "Your life has come to witnessing shit being burned in oil drums as you have your morning coffee."

Later that morning, Darnell, Bama, and I went once more to town.

"It's a flea market," Bama explained to me, as Darnell pulled into a parking place in front of a urine-filled ditch for the second time since I had arrived, in front of Sears and Roebuck. He turned to me and said with a smile, "Literally a flea market."

Shrill squeals immediately announced the arrival of the same six children who received their caramel candy. I winked at Ebony Eyes, and she immediately buried her face into her carrier's shoulder.

Bama and Darnell had decided that I needed thong sandals, towels, and other supplies. We went inside. Darnell picked up an aluminum wash pan and was examining it when a woman appeared on the other side of the counter. She was withered and wrinkled with age and was probably four feet, six inches tall, and soaking wet she might have weighed eighty pounds. With her teeth in, she would have weighed slightly more. "How much is it, mama san?" Darnell asked her.

"Oh," she said with a smile as she looked at me. "This ees for new trung wee?" she asked in a mix of broken English and Vietnamese as she spoke.

Darnell spoke once more: "How much, please?" There was no smile, no humor in his reply.

She looked at the cross cannons on my collar. "Phao binh trung uy?" she asked, turning back to Darnell.

"How much, bitch?" he suddenly screamed at her, slamming the pan down on the wooden counter.

Startled, I looked at him. "Darnell," I yelled. "Take it easy, easy! What's the problem?"

"Lieutenant, she doesn't have to know your life history to sell you a damn pan." His nostrils were flared, and his teeth were clamped tightly.

"Step outside," I said in a calm voice. "Have a cigarette. We'll get a few more things, then we'll come out. Please." He cast a savage glance at the old woman and then left. I paid for everything that I had selected. Bama paid for two towels and a pillow. He spoke to the old woman and gave her some piastres.

I caught Bama's arm before we stepped outside and pulled him into a quiet spot. "What was that all about with Darnell? Why was he yelling at the old lady?"

"He was protecting you. She asked if you were a 'powbin trungwee,'" Bama said. "She was confirming that you were an artillery lieutenant, that you were a *new* artillery lieutenant, that you are with C Company, according to the numbers stenciled on the jeep you arrived in. And the other old lady, the one sitting behind her, was copying your name on a piece of paper—from your name tag." He thumped the strip of fabric above my right breast pocket with my name printed on it. "You just have to be careful what you tell them. By dark, half the town—and by inference—a good number of VC will know about you. The spooks tell us that these kids riding around on bicycles follow us sometimes to see which unit we go to after shopping. At sometime, somehow, the Cong know way too much about us. Darnell was just looking out for us—for you." I was stunned. "Either that, or she yearns for the thrills of your mature, masculine, virile male body."

I turned toward the jeep to see Darnell rationing caramel candy to the children.

Eleven

ARKANSAS RED, ENTREPRENEUR
FEBRUARY 3, 1966

From Sears, we went to a thriving business called Arkansas Red's Car Wash. The entrepreneur was an energetic individual known only as "Arkansas Red." He stood five-three, was totally Vietnamese, and most likely couldn't even spell Arkansas. The car wash consisted of rocks carefully placed across a stream to form a ford, as well as a shallow dam. As we watched, military vehicles would pull forward onto the ford, and what looked to be twenty or so Vietnamese with mops and buckets would wash it. I looked at Bama while Darnell attended to getting the jeep washed.

Bama simply grinned, closed his eyes, and said, "Quite an operation, wouldn't you say?"

"It feeds the whole family, or several *whole families,* I would guess," I returned.

"Sidelines are cold beer while you wait, and I'm told that occasionally a driver will take advantage of the 'Deluxe Wash', which includes a trip into the adjoining jungle with one of Red's Daughters."

I slowly shook my head in disbelief and stared at him. "You've got to be shittin' me!"

"Care to get in line and find out?"

"No," I said disgustedly. I started for the jeep.

"You've got to admit it's a hell of a lot better incentive than free air fresheners," Bama said softly to where the jeep was being toweled down.

We climbed in and drove forward to a small shed, resplendent with an Arkansas Razorback pennant tacked to the back wall where Red, perched on a tall stool in front, took our money.

When we arrived back at The Plantation, the company clerk called to us as we started to get out of the jeep. "Charlie-Six has called a meeting for 1430. He wants all of the lieutenants there."

"And what would that be about?" I asked Bama.

"Probably *about* thirty minutes," he said with a grin, "and probably about an all-expense paid tour to the lovely jungles of Vietnam."

Darnell turned toward the tents, stepped out of the jeep, and left. As Bama started to get out, I asked, "Can we talk about something?".

"Why, of course, darling. Anything for you." He slouched into the passenger seat. I slid in behind the steering wheel.

"The 'old man' and Lieutenant Swenson were close, right?"

He pursed his lips before answering. "They got along well," he said after a minute. "I never saw 'em pinch each other's ass, though. Why?"

"I felt like I was being measured against Swenson when I met with the captain earlier. I'm not sure I got off to a good start." I paused. "Like Swenson was a saint, and I might not measure up."

Bama looked at me directly. "I don't know. Swenson did his job. He was a professional. He was good at it. What can I tell you?"

"Well, after meeting with Captain Novak, I'm not sure that even Jesus Christ wouldn't have had a rough time replacing him."

"Look," Bama said, pulling up straight in the seat. "Everyone gets a little jumpy before his first operation. We never know what's going to happen. Do your job, and you'll be fine." He paused, then smiled and continued. "After all," he said, "it's only artillery. How difficult can it be?"

I nodded, and we walked toward the officer's tent. When we arrived, Bama turned to me, his grin forming. "And Craig, one more thing," Bama called after me. "Jesus Christ wouldn't have applied for an Artillery position. He had way to much class for that!"

At 12:30, Darnell and I sat in the shade of a rubber tree fifty yards from the officer's tent on piles of dried leaves, our backs against the trunk, beneath a royal blue sky. The air smelled of decaying vegetation and moisture.

"After the meeting, I'll get with you and Panther and tell you what went on. Right now I just want to ask you about what to expect tomorrow morning?"

"Well, first of all, you'll be expected to show up."

I smiled broadly. "I admit that that may be the toughest part," I said, "But assuming that I manage to do that, what's next?"

"The trucks will be here around 6:00 a.m. Panther will have the radio on by 5:30, and he and the radio operators will go through communication checks for fifteen minutes to each other, to Battalion, to our supporting artillery battery. That's routine. I assume he's already picked up an extra battery. At 6:30, we leave for the airfield. The choppers will arrive just around 7:00, we'll all check our flies, and we'll load and leave." He held his hands palms upward and pursed his mouth. "Simple as that," he said.

When I didn't comment, he continued. "One of the platoons, not sure which yet, will leave first. They take turns at that. They will be the first to reach the LZ when we—"

"LZ?" I interrupted.

"The landing zone—our destination—where we will start," he returned.

"I know what that is, but don't use abbreviations when it is just the two of us, at least until I get familiar with things. Just don't assume that I know all of the language. I suppose I know most of it, but humor me."

"Yes, sir," he said, "and they'll set up a perimeter, the spot from which our stroll will start. On the average, a chopper will hold seven, maybe eight, men with equipment...and maybe a machine gun on the side of the chopper. Figure eight choppers per platoon."

He paused.

"OK, go on."

The 1st Platoon will still be loading when the second slip—" he paused. "—a slip is a group of choppers—will be on the ground to pick up the second, then the third, and finally yours will come in, and you and Charlie-Six will load. Everyone will be in the air in about ten to twenty minutes, depending on the flight distance. Usually, you, Panther, and I will be with Charlie-Six in his back pocket. Also, two radio operators, Specialists Swizzledick and B.J. Tucker, and the medic—everyone lovingly calls him 'The Butcher'—will be on the last chopper."

Another pause, and he continued. "You'll be given maps at the briefing this afternoon." He paused again.

"As far as the maps go," he continued, "they're a mixed blessing. We have to have them, but they aren't always accurate. We're taught to locate terrain feature that we see on a map, with the same feature on the ground, like a mountain. Trouble is that first of all, there aren't that many recognizable terrain features. It is mostly flat and green. We could walk right past the Statue of Liberty and never see her because of the trees. The other thing is that some of the maps are based on maps the French used when they were here.

"The LZs are usually about a couple of acres. The choppers carrying the first two grunt platoons—" he paused and said, "—infantry platoons—will sit down and unload, then move out a couple of hundred yards and set up a perimeter to cover the rest of the landing. We'll come in with the other two platoons, and they will immediately get ready to move out. Barring any reception committees, we'll do one more communication check and be on the move from the LZ in, at most, ten minutes. Panther will check in with the artillery battery that is going to be supporting us and let them know we are on the ground...and inform you that he has done that.

"Around then, Charlie-Six will tell the point platoon to move out, followed by the next platoon, then us, and then the last platoon. Lieutenant Swenson usually always stayed with Charlie-Six. I assume you will too. So will Panther and me."

"What about support? Which battery will be supporting us?"

"It will most likely be the one we visited yesterday, Alpha Battery. If it is anyone else, you'll find that out at the briefing. Charlie-Six will give you the call sign and radio frequency so we can communicate with the battery at the briefing. It's classified for obvious reasons. We have worked a lot of missions around the airfield, and in those cases we most always had been supported by Alpha Battery-our battery—from right here in Phuoc Vinh."

"That would be Destroyer Two-Three?" I asked.

"That's correct," he affirmed.

He paused long enough to pull a pack of cigarettes from his blouse pocket. He held the pack out to me. "Do you smoke?"

"I've never touched the stuff. Don't use the stuff," I said.

He laughed. "You will," he said, as he removed a cigarette from the pack and tapped the filtered end on a Zippo lighter several times before lighting it. "And within two months, you'll own a Zippo lighter too."

He inhaled, closed his eyes, and then exhaled, beginning to speak as he did. "Another thing," he continued. "We aren't supposed to fire into rubber plantations. Seems to piss the French off. We don't fire into cemeteries either. The only exceptions are if we are fired upon first from either of those places. Then we can return fire." He paused and smiled. "It's funny, but we sometimes sleep in cemeteries too, because Charlie won't fire into them either."

We both watched as a breeze picked up leaves and scattered them. "No wallet on operations. You won't need it. You don't have anything in one anyway. If you have to show proof that you are twenty-one, I'll vouch for you." He smiled and paused for another drag.

"Mail comes to the field fairly regularly, about noon when it does. If you have letters to send, get them to the company clerk by nine o'clock. We'll be re-supplied by Huey's about every afternoon while we're in the field, depending on the weather and whether or not we are under fire. If you get letters, you can keep them with you, but you're advised to tear all of the addresses off first thing when you get them and destroy them. Don't want Charlie Cong writing to your gal."

We were silent for a couple of minutes as I mulled over what we had covered. Then I asked:

"What does 'Viet Cong' mean in English?"

"I think that the direct translation is 'prick,'" he replied.

"OK, continue," I said.

"As short as the operation is, as I understand it, chow will be all C-rations. We're supposed to crush and bury the cans or stash them in the bushes as much as possible. That's just another thing that Charlie has figured out how to use against us."

He picked at a bit of tobacco on the tip of his tongue. "Other than that, we walk, we sweat, and we cuss."

He became serious. "And Lieutenant, I apologize about the incident with the old woman at Sears and Roebuck." He sat silently for almost a minute. "She may be one of them. She may not. I just didn't like her probing." He looked at me. "But in the morning when we climb on the choppers, the VC somewhere will know that we just saddled up and left town with a new trungwee named Pearce."

"I appreciate your concern. I didn't realize what was happening with the old women. It looks like you already have my back! Thanks."

Twelve

A MEETING WITH FELLOW OFFICERS
FEBRUARY 3, 1966

Darnell and I joined Panther, and we picked up lunch from the mess
tent and found a quiet spot where we sat down to continue our discussion.

We discussed types of artillery ammunition, from those designed to
explode above an enemy to those designed to explode when they hit the
ground to those designed to light up the sky in order to see the enemy at night.
We discussed rumored problems reported concerning the M16 rifle, and they
assured me that they were unaware of any problems, as long as the rifles were
kept clean. I asked Panther what he considered his responsibilities to be for
our section. He looked at me with a questioning frown, as if he didn't know
what I was asking.

"Start with the radio. Your main duties are with that, right?"

"Yes, sir. I operate the radio—the one that we use to stay in contact with
whatever artillery battery is supporting us. Is that what you mean?"

"A good start," I said, "but continue."

"I keep it clean, make sure that we always have a good battery in the radio, and I carry a spare one." He paused and pursed his mouth as he thought. "And I help the other radio operators out sometime. Oh yeah, I maintain your jeep. And I'm the designated driver."

"Have you ever called in a fire mission?" I asked him.

"You mean where I located a spot on a map and call an artillery battery and coordinated with them to get artillery rounds to hit it?"

"Yeah, that's a fire mission. Have you ever fired one?"

Panther shock his head. "No, sir, not in combat and 'for real.'"

"Well, we will work on that," I said." I turned to Darnell. "What about you?"

"I'm handsome, quick-witted, a woman killer...what else is there?"

I grinned widely as Panther hit him on the shoulder. "Answer the man."

"Lieutenant Swenson was the only officer I ever worked for in Vietnam. And for him, I helped with artillery fire missions a little. Never really called one in, though...not a real one." He became quiet and stared at me.

"Could you call in a fire mission if you had to?" I asked.

"Yes, sir. I've had the training...just not much actual experience."

"We'll work on that," I said, nodding. "And what do you see my responsibilities to be?" I asked, looking first at Darnell and then at Panther.

Darnell spoke after a few minutes. "You're 'the man.' Obviously, you are the one who calls in fire missions when we get hit—when we come under fire." We sat quietly. Finally Darnell spoke. "And what do you see your responsibilities to be, if I may ask?"

"They're all the same, for all three of us. If something happens to me, the two of you will be 'the man' or 'the men.'" They looked at each other and then the ground. I looked at my watch.

"I have to meet with Charlie-Six when he gets back from Battalion. We'll continue this after that. In the meantime, do what you do. That's enough for now."

Panther stood and looked at me. "Is that it?"

"Yeah," I said, "do whatever you have to do and then whatever you want to do after that."

"Is there anything else?" I looked at one and then the other. As if to answer the question, without warning, rain began to fall. We jumped up and ran, Panther back to the mess tent and Darnell and I to The Academy.

We brushed the water from our uniforms and sat staring toward the mess tent. Darnell was gently rolling a Winston Cigarette between his thumb and forefinger and staring at the ground. We sat silently as raindrops that sounded like the size of limes pounded against the canvas above. It went on for several minutes and then stopped, Darnell's face a mask of melancholy. Random drops dripped from the canvas cover as a reminder that the rain had actually occurred. He looked up at me. "Sometime—not now, but sometime—I want to tell you about my bridge," he said, looking up at me. He drew several drags from the butt and then crushed it out on the dirt floor.

"You set up the time, and I'll listen," I replied. He nodded, crushed the remaining tobacco from the paper, and rolled the remains into a tiny ball.

At 2:30, the officers met under The Academy tent. It was used for the entire company as needed. Furnishings included a crudely built table made of the boards from artillery ammunition boxes, which stood at the center with legs formed like x's, and benches on either side. Through a hole in the table top, the center tent pole ran upward, serving as the main support. The corners of the tent rested on four poles, six feet tall, where ropes ran from there to tent pegs in the ground eight feet away.

Charlie-Six began the afternoon meeting, a simple one, where each officer was asked if his platoon was ready and if everything was set to go. The discussion was positive, with only small issues.

"We can go in twelve hours?" Charlie-Six asked. Everyman looked around and then nodded their heads.

"That's what I want to hear every time I ask that question."

Charlie-Six looked at Bama. "You ready?"

"As ready as a ninth-grader in a whorehouse," Bama replied, smiling.

"So you'll have the supplies?"

"I will," Bama said softly, "at sundown."

Captain Novak scanned the faces and, without a word, turned and walked away.

"What was that about?" I asked.

"Be at the tent at 6:00. You'll see," Bama said with a smile.

I sat on my chair just outside the officer's raised tent, reading my mail. I was particularly interested in a letter that had been folded inside the letter from my brother. I laughed at the fact that my last credit card gasoline bill from a major oil company, which had obviously not gotten my forwarding address, had arrived. They were threatening me for non-payment. I folded it and placed it in a letter I had written to my brother, asking him to pay it for me. "Or, better yet, tell them to come and get me, please."

I looked up to see Darnell coming my way. He had pictures of his family, two beers, and two wedges of chocolate cake from the mess tent. Somehow, in Vietnam, the combination of these items didn't even seem strange.

"I wanted to show you these since you've never seen my bridge."

"You have a bridge?" I asked.

A wry grin came over his face. "Well, I spent so much time there growing up, that if you ask anyone there who owned it, they would say me." He paused as he stared at a picture, then spoke. "This is Amanda." He placed the picture of his wife on the table.

I looked at it for several seconds. "Now-now remind me again, you had to drug her in order to get her to marry you. Isn't that right?"

He smiled as his lower eyelids filled with tears.

"It was something like that. And this is 'Winnie the Pooh,'" he said as he handed me the next one. She was standing on the side railing of a bridge in pink overalls, her hair in twin ponytails on either side of her head. "Amanda was holding her as her mother took the picture. She is my pride and joy." This time, the eyelids emptied.

There were twenty-two more photos, each with loving comments and stories, and each with different views of the family on the bridge.

At dusk, I approached the tent. Bama emerged holding an expensive-looking wooden mahogany case, trimmed with thick brass feet, hinges, and a lock. Allegretti was behind him with a bottle of Johnny Walker Black Label Scotch. "It's time," he said, "come on." With that, we turned and left.

As we crossed Main Street into the rubber plantation, we were joined by Captain Novak and Professor Rose. We walked twenty-five yards into the woods that joined The Plantation. Allegretti brushed the leaves away to clear a spot and placed a folded C-ration box on the ground, and Bama sat the case on it. He unlatched and lifted the lid. Inside, in a compartmentalized box lined in thick, red velvet were six heavy highball glasses, the quality of which matched the case. Bama removed five of them, one at a time, and each of us stepped forward and took one. I was the last to get one. It was obvious to even me that they were heavy crystal. I held mine to the light and stared at the colors. They seemed totally out of place.

"You got these from the mess tent, did you?" I asked Bama, as I hefted the glass.

"Yes, sir," he answered with a smile and his usual drawl. "They're kept in the same cabinet that the cooks keep the sterling silver."

Bama turned to me. "Pearce," he said, "this is something we've done since Thanksgiving. I asked my mother to send these glasses, heirlooms of my family for 'God-only-knows-how-long.' With a little help from an uncle who is a U.S. Senator and a mail service eager to deliver, they all arrived quickly and safely. So, for each operation, we have one glass of the finest scotch the Post

Exchange at Battalion has to offer and toast our futures—our long and profitable futures."

I obviously looked somewhat confused.

"It's okay, Pearce," Allegretti spoke. "We're not going to burn a cross or anything like that." As he spoke, he opened the bottle, poured three fingers in each heavy crystal glass, and sat the bottle on the ground beside the wooden box. I held the amber liquid up to the light, and it danced inside like a fire.

"Gentlemen," Charlie-Six said as he raised his glass and proposed a toast. "We know our jobs and will do them well. We will all go home to those who love us. So, to all of us, may our futures be bright."

"Here's to bright futures," We all said as we stepped forward and gently brought our glasses together, responding in unison: "To bright futures." I repeated the toast belatedly, still learning the process.

Six turned to face Allegretti. "To the true gifts that only God can give us, here's to families," Allegretti said as he raised his glass.

On cue, we all echoed, "To families."

It was Mike's turn to raise his glass. "To wives—" he said. A full smile appeared across his face as he turned toward me. "—and lovers. May we only have one of each at any given time." Everyone looked at me and sheepishly grinned. By his confused look, it was obvious to me that Captain Novak didn't know what this toast was about, but he raised his glass and drank anyway.

"To wives and lovers," the group repeated.

Professor turned to face Bama. "There is no question," he said as he raised his glass to the Infantry. "*The king of battle*."

We repeated "the king of battle" and drank. Then Bama turned to me.

They all looked at me. "Well then, let's toast the Artillery," I began. "To *the queen of battle*, without whom the king would never know where to place his balls!" Another round of clicks as the crystal glasses touched.

Once more, Charlie-Six spoke. "And finally, let's toast to the upcoming days of this search and destroy mission. May we all soon be able to cross it off our calendars."

We all drained our glasses, placed them in the box, and walked back to the tent.

The evening was filled with the other officers dashing off to remind a platoon sergeant to check on some last minute detail, or writing letters home, or silently reading. Finally, with the precious bourbon still working its magic, I lay down on my bunk. As I lay in the dark, the smell of the canvas preservative heavy in the air, I tried to imagine what would happen the following morning.

I drifted off to sleep thinking of Julie and her surprise call to me the day before I left the country. I would have given my next check to hear her voice tonight.

Thirteen

AN ARRANGED MEETING WITH A GODDESS
FEBRUARY 3, 1966

In mid-April 1965, I received a call from 'Cha-cha' Chandler and
Trace Tingle, friends since junior high school, insisting that I drive up
from Fort Bliss, Texas, to Las Cruces, New Mexico, for dinner. The two
of them had gone together since the seventh grade, and not counting
slight periods when they had had spats, neither had ever dated anyone
else. Then we all went to college at New Mexico State University, with
Trace and I rooming together the first year. Then he and Cha-cha moved
into an apartment.

"I have the best proposition a friend can make to you," Cha-cha said
slowly.

"Whoa, girl, does your husband know that you are propositioning
me?"

"You wish! But this one may even be better than me!"

"Don't taunt me, girl. Talk."

"Well, there is this fourth grade teacher at my school—"

"Wait. It's not another date with the art teacher, is it? That woman is wacko."

"She's not wacko, and it's not her. This one is like a flash bulb—bright and hot."

I paused briefly. "Trace, are you on the line?" I asked.

"I'm here, buddy."

"Is your wife lying to me?"

"Well, in this case, she's not," Trace said.

"OK. So here's the scoop," Cha-cha continued. "We are all—including you, Craig Pearce—going to have a double date for dinner."

"I'm not sure, I—"

"I'm *not* asking. I'm telling you. She is definitely too good for you, but *you need to meet this lady*."

"Cha, I love you, but I don't—"

"*Not* asking. I'm telling you, numb-nuts! Besides, your social life sucks, and you need to get out more. Playing with yourself while watching cartoon shows isn't good for you."

"I'm in the middle of some field training exercises now—"

"*Not* asking. Don't want to hear it."

"Trace, on a scale of one to ten?"

There was a slight pause before he spoke. "I'd put her at a fifteen," Trace replied.

"Whoa," I said, "I thought the scale ended at ten."

"See, numb-nuts!" Cha blurted out. "Even my husband agrees. You *will* be here at 7:00 this coming Friday. Meet at our apartment. So help me, Craig, if you mess this up—"

"For you, Cha, the 'matchmaker,' I'll give you one more chance."

When she walked into the living room at Cha-cha's apartment at seven o'clock, I began to melt. She was what Webster had had in mind when he defined beauty. She wore a sleeveless beige dress, which set her hazel eyes on fire. Her light brown hair, in a bouffant style, was lightly frosted and perfectly set. And she had on camel-colored high heels. A short, suede jacket was draped over her shoulder. She carried her knockout body with grace, like a model.

She hugged Cha-cha, and they spoke for a moment. Cha-Cha took her wrap and hung it in an entry closet, and then she led her to me.

Cha turned to Julie, and then to me. "Julie and I have been friends for a long time. Julie Mayes, I hate to do this to you, but this is Craig Pearce. And he needs a lot of work."

She smiled. "Pleased to meet you, Craig. I've heard a lot about you from Cha."

"Well, I can only hope that you don't believe what you hear from this evil woman," I said, nodding toward Cha.

Trace offered grace at dinner. "Bless these friends, bless this meal."

I silently offered my own: "Thank you, Lord. Thank you, thank you."

As we had after-dinner drinks, Cha kicked me under the table. "Craig, you're staring!" We laughed and enjoyed one of possibly the greatest evenings of my life.

A week later, minus the Chandlers, Julie and I had a proper date. I picked her up at her apartment in Las Cruces. We ate dinner at a quaint, legendary Mexican restaurant in Mesilla, New Mexico—La Posta—and talked over Margaritas, guacamole salads, and huevos rancheros.

We sat on a bench in the square and talked. Our conversation became a game—a game of getting acquainted—and it jumped from one subject to the next. "OK," I asked, "if you had to pick one book, what would it be?'"

Her eyes narrowed as she stirred her icy green drink with a swizzle stick for almost a minute. Finally, she blurted out: "*To Kill a Mockingbird.*"

"OK, not bad. Mine would have to be *Dr. No,*" I immediately proclaimed.

She smiled and shook her head. "What a *totally* unsophisticated choice. Oh well," she said, "at least it wasn't *Tarzan.*"

"What about your favorite movie?" I asked.

She wrinkled her face and thought for almost a minute. "My favorite would be..." She pursed her lips and shifted her gaze to the sky. "A *Summer Place.*"

"And who was in it?"

"Sandra Dee and Troy Donahue!"

"OK. Well done," I said.

She looked at me and laughed. "Now it's your turn."

"This is easy. It would be *Thunder Road.* Robert Mitchum. No question."

Her mouth fell open slightly, and she shook her head. "How romantic," she said sharply. "How very romantic. Are you kidding me? *Are you kidding me?*"

"No kidding. I loved it. Although, I could also go with *Giant.*"

She slapped the bench. "Dammit, I change my mind. That's mine as well. Elizabeth Taylor. Rock Hudson. James Dean. I love it!"

The night was filled with the tantalizing smell of chili peppers and a chill breeze off the Rio Grande and honeysuckles that clung to adobe walls. We strolled through art shops, walked around the historic square, and paused to listen to a mariachi band. We sat for a while to admire the Basilica of San Albino established in 1852, an historic landmark with its ancient bells.

I took off my sports jacket and draped it over her shoulders. We went through little shops in brightly painted adobe buildings filled with Native American turquoise squash blossom necklaces, beautifully hammered silver bracelets, pottery, and collector quality kachina dolls. We walked back to the car holding hands. I stopped to open the door. A miracle occurred for me as we stood there and she snuggled closer and pulled my arm around her. "There are far more stars in New Mexico than anywhere else," I said. She looked up and smiled, and we kissed.

As I drove back to El Paso that night, one thought ran through my mind: I desperately wanted this lady in my life. "Please, God, don't let me screw this up," I said aloud.

Four nights later, it was just the two of us once more. She fixed dinner at her apartment, and I brought wine, and the conversation continued. As we talked, I was amazed that this lady was interested in a lot of the same things I was. I was thrilled that she actually loved cars. She *knew* cars. In fact, she had helped her brothers—four of them—rebuild a 1956 Chevrolet two-door hardtop. We discussed carburetors, and she immediately declared that in the category of 'Best Carburetors,' Rochester won hands down, and the most exciting engine would have to be the Chevy 409. She laughed softly, and it was music. As it died down, she moved closer and put her head on the nape of my neck and folded her legs on the couch. We didn't speak. She looked up at me, and we kissed.

My world was fine! My world was magnificent.

We had our two-month anniversary celebration with Cha and Trace at our favorite steakhouse in El Paso.

"So, you are making bulletin boards and reading to the kids now, Mr. My-*life-is-too complex-right-now-to-go-out-with-anyone*?" Cha-Cha chided, as a second round of piña coladas arrived.

"OK, you won that one. Here's to that," I said as I raised my drink above the center of the table, and we toasted.

"He may even make the honor roll this six-week period," Julie said. "And he's even going to a third grade choral program this coming Wednesday."

"How domesticated can you get," Cha almost screamed as she began to laugh.

Back at Julie's apartment, we danced. We finished a blender of drinks. And she and I shared the most wonderful, most meaningful sex I had ever known.

I had to call Julie three days later, just before the program at her school that I had promised to attend. "I can't make it to the choir program tonight."

"What, why?" she asked.

"We just got called out for a surprise tactical inspection. We'll be up all night, inspecting every vehicle. Sorry."

"What is it? What does it mean?"

"It's nothing. Every once in a while, totally unannounced, our battalion just has to have an inspection to ensure that every tool, vehicle, every log book, every nut and bolt, and all of the rest of the supplies and materiel are in top shape. We even have to count lug nuts on the trucks! It's deemed to be critical in the event we get called up."

"Do you think you are?"

"Are what?" I asked.

There was a pause. "Do you think there is a chance that you are going to be called up...to war?"

"No, I don't, for the simple reason that we are not at war with anyone. It is just something we have to do on an unannounced basis. To ensure that the unit is in top shape, we get inspected. They've been doing it this way since the Civil War."

There was a long pause. "OK, soldier. Come to me when you can. I love you." She hung up.

The next evening, I drove to Las Cruces and picked up Chinese food on the way to her apartment for dinner. Conversation was sparse. I watched her sip her wine and peck at her meal. Finally she steered the conversation, once more, to my job. "How often do things like last night happen? A lot? Once a month? What?"

"Several times a year, I suppose," I said.

"And you have to be there."

"Yes. I have no choice."

"So, that's more important to you than me?" she said with a nervous giggle.

I leaned forward in my chair. "No, not at all. That's a ridiculous question. You know—"

"But I don't know," she said, her smile fading. "So, if we _were_ at war, could you be called to go?"

"Yes, yes I could. That's my job. Those are the clothes I wear. But we don't have a war going on."

"What about Viet-Viet-whatever it is?

"There's no war there. Vietnam is a crappy, backward little country and not a threat to the U.S. There is not one U.S. Army division over there. Just last week, Ronald Reagan said that 'It's silly to talk about how many years we will have to spend in the jungles of Vietnam when we could pave the whole country and put parking stripes on it and still be home on Christmas.'"

Awkward silence followed for several minutes, with me staring at her staring at a mug of coffee. I took her cup and placed it on the end table, and then sat beside her and took her in my arms. Neither spoke for several minutes. "Let's take a trip," I said, "School is almost out. I have leave time, and vacation time is coming. We can go to San Fran or Yellowstone. Or better yet, both. Would you like that? I walked into her kitchen and returned with a calendar and two glasses of cold wine, and I dropped beside her.

"How about there," I said, touching a square in early June. "Say, from the fourth through the eleventh? I sat forward on the couch and stared back at her. "Hell," I said, "we can do both of them. And I promise I won't take my sergeants with me!"

A tear ran down her cheek, and she laughed softly. She stared at me for several minutes, then stood and walked toward her bedroom.

I had to admit to myself that it was one hell of a lot better than counting lug nuts.

I took a week of leave in June, and we leisurely drove to San Diego and spent the night in a small hotel on the Pacific. We walked along the beach, laughing at seagulls as they ran along the foamy water's edge. The next few days, we went to San Francisco and had lunch at a five-star restaurant. One afternoon we spent "wine-label hopping" in Napa Valley, from one vineyard to another, sampling far too much wine. And then we went to Yellowstone. We stopped frequently to smell the air closest to heaven and fed bears from the window, parked next to a sign that said "Do Not Feed the Bears." We stayed at what was called a boutique hotel.

We ordered hors d'oeuvres and cold, ridiculously expensive wine and sat in a large porch swing outside our room in fluffy robes, a down comforter, and furry house shoes, watching as God painted a most magnificent sunset.

"I do love you, Craig," she said as she stared at the setting sun. "I love and respect all that you are. I have never known anyone I have loved as much."

"Have any of your brothers threatened to beat me up yet?"

She laughed, turned, stretched her neck upward, and kissed me...one of her patented 'before-this-kiss-is-finished-I-will-own-your-soul' kisses. It lasted for at least two minutes. She owned me!

Once back in El Paso, the questions became more prevalent, the concern more real. I didn't have the answers. "A war can start in one second. Pearl Harbor is the prime example of that. And I could be on a ship or a plane to anywhere in the world in less than a week. I signed a contract my junior year that when I graduated from college, I would be commissioned as a second lieutenant and would serve two years in the Army. Otherwise, I could have been drafted any day of my junior-senior year and never finished school. There were no wars going on, and I assumed it was a safe bet. I have no choice but to do my time, then it will be over."

In mid-July 1965, I arrived at my apartment, and she was not there. There was a note on the bar next to her key. "Craig, I need some time. I have some things to do, one of which is straighten myself out. It's not you, it's me. Please give me some time to figure out what the hell is going on in my mind—who I am. Please give me a week." After seven miserable days,

I went to her apartment. She answered the door and let me in. It was a short meeting. We talked, then we yelled, and then I left.

The next time I called her apartment, the phone number had been changed. I called Cha-cha, and she cried, but didn't have the number. Finally, I decided it had to be me. I gave up my apartment and moved back into the bachelor officer's quarters at Fort Bliss. Everywhere I turned, I met blank walls. Cha-cha stubbornly insisted that she couldn't—or wouldn't—tell me what was going on, and there were no responses to letters sent to her apartment.

It was over. I quit trying.

On January 29, 1966, less than forty-eight hours before I was to leave for Oakland to depart to Vietnam, I got a call from Cha-cha. "The two of you are going to give me a damned ulcer," she said.

"What 'two of us' are you referring to?" I asked as I felt the hair on my neck rise.

"Julie called. She wants you to call her."

"Who?!" I screamed into the receiver.

"You know who, jackass!"

"Well, it's a hell of an interesting time to do it. I leave in thirty hours for 'Nam. I am living in the bachelor officer's quarters. I'm not supposed to leave post. What is it about?" While I sounded tough, my mind was racing, screaming inside my head.

"You'll have to ask her. She's staying at her parents' place in Las Cruces. Have you got a pencil and paper?" I was back in less than a minute, and she rattled off the phone number.

"What does she want?" I asked.

"Call her and find out, you ignorant cannon-cocker," she said with a chuckle.

I called, my stomach pumping acid as I dialed the number. Mrs. Mayes, Julie's mother, answered the phone. "Hello," she said.

"Good afternoon," I said as calmly as I could. "I'm Craig Pearce. How are you?"

"Hello, Craig, it's good to hear from you." How are you?"

"I'm fine. I'm trying to reach Julie."

She responded guardedly, the voice of a mother protecting her child. "Well, yes...yes, Craig, I know she is trying to get in touch with you, but she's away from the house right now. She and her father are in the fields checking on cattle."

My mind raced. There was no way that I had time to do anything. "Would you tell her that I called, and ask her to call me as soon as she gets back?"

"I will," returned the soft voice. "I expect her back within the hour. And Craig, be careful over there."

I folded my T-shirts, socks, and shorts and placed them in the duffel bag that I would take to Vietnam. Then I took them out and did it again. Finally, the phone rang two hours later. "Don't hang up," came her voice even before I spoke.

"Julie!" I shouted.

"Please don't say anything."

My heart froze.

"Julie...is it really you?"

"Yes, but don't say anything, dammit. Not just yet. I need to say something."

My heart was hammering.

"Julie, I've been going nuts trying to—"

"Dammit, shut up. Would you let me talk?" She had begun to cry.

There was a long pause, and then she spoke. "Not having you is the most horrid thing I can think of. I can't stand it. I have thought of you every day." There was another pause. "I've decided. Having you and knowing that I might lose you to some silly ass war—*might* lose you—at any time is better than not having you at all. Cha-cha says that you leave in the next couple of days. Is that right?"

"Julie, I—"

"Just answer the question, please. This is my phone call. Are you leaving in a couple of days: yes or no?"

"I leave for Oakland tomorrow evening at 8:00 p.m. Until then, I am pretty well restricted to quarters."

My heart was pounding. After what seemed like five minutes, she spoke.

"Craig, I love you."

My first thought was a flash of anger. "Well it's a pretty crappy time to tell me that."

"I know," she said, "I have been foolish. I have squandered all this time since I walked out on you. Crying has become a past time for me." She covered the phone mouth piece. She was sniffling the next time she spoke. "I am a betting woman," she said softly after a pause. "I bet that you will return...and that you will be ok. I know that you will return...and I'll be here." For the first time, she began crying uncontrollably.

"Julie...dammit, I have tried to contact you for the past six months. You changed your number and threatened Cha-cha if she gave me the new number. I have done all—'

"I know, Craig. I'm so sorry—"

"No, Julie, you have to listen. I have been seeing someone else. I met her four months after you left me."

There was a long pause. "Is it serious?" Julie asked at last.

It was a question I had not pondered. Was it serious?

After a pause, Julie spoke again.

"Craig, I deserve that. I've been a jackass. I know that by far and away, the number of soldiers that go to Vietnam return home, and that when they do, it is to lovers at home. When you come back, I will be here. I love you. I *won't give you up. I can't give you up.* I will do all I can." There was another pause. "And Craig, this new girl has a fight on her hands. *You are mine.*"

Fourteen

JOHN WAYNE WOULD HAVE BEEN PROUD
FEBRUARY 4, 1966

The clearing was flat and grassy, with a small pond covered with green moss along the outer edge of the tree-lined perimeter. As I drank the coffee in my canteen cup, I watched small gray birds drop from the trees to the water, their eyes on me except for when they quickly stole a sip and then flew once more back to the foliage above.

Small fires for coffee were approved, and I cherished the first sip. The staff meeting was short.

Darnell, Panther, and I ate in silence, except for the occasional sounds of the radio. I was eating white bread and jelly from a small C-ration can. I watched Charlie-Six talking on his radio twenty feet away. He finished and walked to where I was.

"The group of concentrations that you plotted around the truck and the other crap there won't be fired tonight. We will only fire the ones around the area where we settle in. We should be—"

The sound was one of the most recognizable, terrifying sounds of the war: the flat cracking "clack" of a mortar being fired somewhere on a hill to our northeast. I glanced at the second hand on my watch. I had roughly eighty seconds to get a shot of artillery to the spot where the mortar was located. "Incoming!" a voice yelled, as everyone moved for cover. I was up, trying to determine from where the sound had come. Mortar rounds fly in an extremely high arch, taking time to arrive. As I searched the hillside, another one was fired.

"It came from there!" I yelled, "from up that draw!" I stared at the map, with Darnell looking over my shoulder. "Here," I said more calmly. Charlie-Six was at my side, listening as I called in artillery support. "Destroyer Two-Three, this is Destroyer Niner-Three. Fire mission!"

"Destroyer Niner-Three, send your mission."

I gave him the necessary information, and in a minute, the rounds were on the way. They hit a little too far to the northwest, beyond where the mortar was, but close. I adjusted, and in less than a minute, twelve rounds would be on the way to a point up a ravine where the mortar was firing.

"Roger, wait," came the voice. Charlie-Six nodded in agreement. This part was my game, and he seemed ok with that.

My rounds began to hit. They were music. One more adjustment, and I called for a volley from the artillery battery to our northeast. It hit where I wanted it to, and I called for eighteen artillery rounds to hit farther up the draw from which the mortar had fired. We waited, on the likelihood that the Viet Cong would retreat up the draw from which he had fired and over the ridge above.

The second VC mortar round hit, still with no casualties. "That will be your last one, Charlie," I said softly.

When finished, I called for eighteen more, farther up the draw.

There were no more mortar rounds. I waited and listened. I had either hit the VC mortar position or scared him into leaving. A big part of the value of any forward observer was the "scoot" factor: "scare crap out of them."

Charlie-Six had directed Allegretti to check out the damage, and we watched as two of his squads worked their way up the draw.

Within ten minutes, he called in. "A hell of a lot of torn up trees and ground, and we found what remains of the mortar. There is quite a bit of blood and a human hand. If he's still alive and wasn't left handed before, he is now. That's about all, over."

"Nothing else?" Charlie-Six asked.

"Yes. There are some well-traveled trails going to the northeast. It might be something to consider. They are pretty well-beaten down, so the traffic has been recent."

"Come on in. I'll report to Battalion."

"Roger," Allegretti said. "We've started down now."

Charlie-Six reported to Battalion. He called us together. "The word came down that we are to dig in for the night. In the morning, Professor, you move to—" He gave a set of map coordinates and waited until we found the location. "Intelligence is itchy about the mortar fire today. They think that we have made someone very nervous. A chopper pilot flew over and reported what looks like supplies of some sort to the east of where the mortar fired. They are covered with camouflage netting.

"Just a few quick words about what happened earlier. First of all, Allegretti, your response was excellent. You moved out quickly and found the mortar nest. Bama, Professor, your reactions in setting up a solid perimeter were also done very well." He turned to me. "Lieutenant

Pearce, your reaction was excellent. It was quick and accurate. Good jobs all around. Get back to your units and prepare to move out." He turned to me with a wry grin on his face. "You might work out."

"You don't know how lucky you are to have me," I returned.

Instructions came just after sunset that evening. Battalion had decided that Bama and his platoon, along with me, Panther, and Darnell, needed to look the area over and get back to them first thing in the morning.

By 10:00 the next morning, after following the trail and stumbling through the jungle, Bama, his party, and I were at the clearing. Bama called in to Charlie-Six, "It appears to be big. There are tons of bags of rice, what looks to be rifles, cases of artillery ammunitions—I guess to be used in bomb-making—a lot of shit. There are some stacks of jeep tires, and even an engine. They've put a lot of netting overhead, hoping it wouldn't be seen from the air. There are a lot of C-ration boxes, unopened. Wait a minute, Pearce wants to talk to you."

"Charlie-Six?" I asked.

"Yes?" he replied.

"And the coup de grâce," I began, "is that there is a rusty, old truck stuck in the woods."

"A truck?" Charlie-Six asked incredulously. "What kind of a truck?"

"It looks like something from the Ford Model A era, but it is definitely foreign. French, I would guess."

There was a pause. "How in the hell did it get there?"

I felt the grin grow on my face. "Valet parking, perhaps?"

"Come back to camp, smart ass."

"And Charlie-Six," I said, "I suppose that the Artillery gods gave me one more truck to shoot at!"

We escorted two intelligence officers and Charlie-Six over to the site later that afternoon, and they concurred with our evaluation: it had been a substantial Viet Cong supply site.

"By my calculations, we are about five kilometers from the target," Charlie-Six began after breakfast the next morning. "The Air Force will be here sometime around mid-morning. We'll set up a fortified area around this clearing. We have a light observation helicopter coming in. The pilot is T-Bone Thornton—"

With the sound of the name, Bama spit coffee down his shirt and began to laugh. He was instantly joined by Allegretti.

"You mean *the* T-bone Thornton!" Bama snorted, still laughing.

"One and the same," Charlie-Six said, sharing the laughter. "He is the Army chopper pilot for the mission. He will be here around ten. Pearce, you will accompany him and coordinate with T-Bone and the Air Force."

By 0700, the clearing in which T-Bone would land was secure with all three platoons forming the perimeter. The spot was grassy, but without trees, and in one corner was a scum-filled pond.

Observation posts were in place thirty to forty yards out around the position. A solid piece of ground suitable for the landing had been identified, and Darnell had three yellow smoke grenades to be used in marking the spot when T-Bone arrived.

We were set. At twenty past nine, the faint sound of an Army light observation helicopter, an LOH, was heard, followed by the radio. "Destroyer Niner-Three, this is Delta Three-Three, over." It was T-bone.

"Delta Three-Three, this is Destroyer Niner-Three, over."

"Roger, Niner-Three. Throw smoke."

Darnell ran into the center of the clearing, pulled the pin on one of the yellow smoke grenades, and dropped it in a patch of dirt that had been swept clean. It popped, and bright yellow smoke began to rise in a thick cloud. "Delta Three-Three, observe yellow smoke," Darnell said into the radio.

"Got it," was all T-Bone said. We listened as the sound of the flashbulb grew closer. It derived the nickname from the fact that the cabin was round, with most of the front made of clear Plexiglass, giving the appearance of a Kodak flash bulb from a distance. In minutes, he was visible and landed thirty feet from the dying smoke grenade, scattering the remnants of the yellow cloud.

I ran to the passenger opening of the chopper—there were no doors—and crawled into the cabin. There was an armored body vest lying on the seat, and I picked it up and began to put it on. He touched my arm, and I looked up to see him shaking his head *no*. He took it from me, folded it, and placed it back in the seat where it had been. I climbed in, sat on the vest, strapped the seat belts across my chest, and placed my helmet between my legs.

Once I was buckled in, he handed me a set of earphones, which I put on. "Can you hear me?" T-Bone asked as he held up the line that ran to the radio. He clicked the switch several times. The intercom, which could only be heard by the two of us, was working.

I nodded. "Welcome aboard," he said, as I finished adjusting my belts.

I turned to him. "Thornton," he said as he extended his right hand. "Call me T-Bone."

"Pearce. Craig Pearce. Call me Craig," I replied.

"Welcome to my world," he said with a grin, as the ends of his red mustache rose.

We lifted slightly, hovered for several seconds, tilted into an angle with the ground, and rapidly began our ascent to the tree line. In seconds, we were well on our way.

I estimated him to be five-ten, with flaming orange eyebrows that extended above the top of his mirrored aviator sunglasses and a matching Yosemite Sam mustache that covered his upper lip. It was mid-morning, and he held a plastic cocktail stick between his lips. "Sorry about the confusion with the flak jacket, but up here we sit on flak vests. If you are going to get shot in this chopper, it will most likely be in the ass, not in the chest." He smiled broadly as he turned toward me.

The rush of cool air through the open cockpit was delightfully refreshing, and I felt the sweat of my body begin to disappear. I marveled at the vastness of the sky and the mixed textures of the shades of green below us.

"We are about fifteen minutes away from the target," he offered, as if reading my mind, and handed me a small clipboard with a piece of paper with coordinates of the target scribbled on it. "That's where I was told we would be going. Does that check out with you?"

I compared the numbers. "Roger. That's where the action is to be."

Within minutes, I spotted it. I pointed and spoke into the intercom. "There it is."

"Good call" was all he said.

"We'll just move away some, in case there is a trigger happy Viet Cong down there. As early as it is, I feel confident that we can find a good seat to watch the show."

"Do you have any idea what's there?" he asked.

"I do," I returned. "We were in there yesterday. There is a considerable amount of supplies and ammunition." I told him about all that we had found. "There is even an old—*really* old—truck there."

"A truck?"

"A truck," I confirmed, "just sitting there rusting away. In short, there's a shitload of other stuff in there."

"Ooh," he said as he turned toward me. "I love to watch the good guys destroy 'shit loads' of anything cherished by the Viet Cong. Have you ever coordinated an Air Force mission?"

"Well, I've had a lot of aerial missions from Army helicopters," I said.

"Well, this is way different, but it's pretty simple," he said. "We give them the coordinates and watch them blow the target to hell. Then we move in and confirm that the mission was successful. If it wasn't, we do it some more."

The map was amazingly clear from our height. Landmarks could be instantly identified. I watched as the tiny shadow of the chopper rushed over the landscape below. I found the red X on the map that marked the target. In seconds, the truck was visible on the ground. I pointed and spoke into the intercom. "There it is. Look!" I shouted like a school boy. "The truck, just to the left of that dominant tree in the middle."

A grin formed below his visor. "I can only imagine how fast he must have been going when he left the highway!"

Fifteen

IT'S ALL ABOUT T-BONE THORNTON
FEBRUARY 6, 1966

T-Bone's radio crackled, and he spoke into his handset, nodding his head several times. He then flipped the radio back to intercom and spoke to me. "The jet jockeys are about twenty minutes out. They said they will advise when they start their final approach. We can listen, but not talk unless we are asked to." He changed the frequency on his radio so we could hear the Air Force chatter. There was crackling and heavy rushing noise, then radio traffic, obviously between the jet fighters and a control tower. The only thing that made sense to me was "fifteen minutes out."

T-Bone moved to a spot where we could watch, suspended well out of the way.

"Charlie-Six, this is Destroyer Niner-Three, over," I said into my radio. In the clearing, Swizzledick ran to Charlie-Six's side and handed him the handset.

"This is Charlie-Six."

"We're at the sight. The payload is on the way. Won't be long now, over."

"Is everything okay?"

"As far as we know, everything is fine," I said. "Stand by for the Fourth of July."

T-Bone pointed at a flock of long-legged storks, seemingly unaware of our presence, as they flew across a background of massive thunderheads in the distance.

We hovered at a spot directly above the target and well above the jet's approach. In minutes, they would be in view, well below and to our right.

T-Bone received a call on the frequency that he had been told to use by the Air Force and nodded his head. He switched once more to the intercom. "They're about ten minutes out. Do your thing," he said to me. "There are First Lieutenant bars in your future."

T-Bone was on the radio once more with the Air Force Coordinator. "Observe yellow smoke" was all he said.

The jet pilot's voice came on. "Roger, wait."

I pulled the pen from a yellow smoke grenade and dropped it outside the chopper and then immediately repeated the process for a second one. We watched as hints of rich yellow trickled through the jungle canopy, then expanded into billowing, velvet-like clouds.

T-Bone pointed and spoke. "There," he said. I caught a glimpse of silver on a background of white clouds.

"I got it," I said. I looked down to see the smoke continuing to stream from the grenades and into the sky.

The lead pilot's voice came over the intercom of the chopper. "We have you, payday, in three to five minutes." In seconds they passed below and in front of us, then banked away and climbed, and were once more out of sight.

"It's *showtime*," T-Bone said.

"Charlie-Six," I said into my radio headset. "It all happens in a few minutes, over."

It was still.

"They'll pass in front of us on the final approach," T-bone said, "any minute by my estimation." I moved the mouthpiece on the helmet, chewed on a filthy fingernail, tearing a sliver away, and spit it out as I scanned the clouds before us, imagining what was about to happen.

"Four minutes," T-Bone said. "Don't blink your eyes, or you will miss the whole thing."

"Three minutes," he said, turning to me.

I called Charlie-Six. "Payload in less than three minutes," I said, giddy with what was to happen.

T-Bone's radio crackled. He took the message. "They are in their final approach."

"Two minutes," T-Bone said. I glanced at my watch, then locked my eyes on the cloud from which they had come earlier. I looked at the faint remains of the column of yellow smoke, like a giant finger pointing directly at the target.

"It is *show* time," said T-Bone, moving the swizzle stick around in his mouth. My eyes watered as I realized that I hadn't blinked in what seemed to be hours. I stared at the huge cloud from which they would come and marveled at the serenity.

They came silently out of a cloud that swirled behind them as angel wings, and the sun flashed off of their silver bodies like lightning bolts from Thor's hammer. They plummeted downward and then rose, followed by a hideous explosion as the sound caught up, leaving strings of napalm fire that careened into the target. Secondary explosions rose from the greenery below as the munitions ignited, and I felt the chopper jolt. Then all was still and quiet except for the noise of T-Bone's chopper, as gruesome strips of black smoke curled into the sky.

In three more minutes, the two jets swept by once more and dropped a second dose of explosives and a fresh wall of flame on the same spot.

The jungle at the target area was an inferno, punctuated by munitions on the ground, as the napalm and high explosives exploded in the immense heat and threw fireballs, as though some mythical beast was clawing to escape from hell.

T-Bone's red mustache rose on each side of his mouth. "Horse shit!" he screamed into the intercom. "You got to love this, it's awesome!" He showed the excitement of a young boy when he discovers that his science project worked.

"Charlie-Six, this is Destroyer Niner-Three, over."

Once more, Swizzledick answered and handed the handset to Charlie-Six. "It looks like they got it all. What a hell of a sight. It makes my artillery look like firecrackers!" I screamed into the microphone.

I reached to shake T-Bone's extended hand. He released it, thanked the jet jockeys over the radio, banked sharply, and headed toward the scene for a closer look.

We hovered for ten minutes as smoke clouds continued to rise. He circled as close as he dared, as we verified that the target had been obliterated—a destroyed patch of jungle with ruined, twisted items that had been there. Occasionally, even after fifteen minutes, a round would cook off, but the frequency of that was tapering away.

Thirty minutes later, Professor's platoon arrived at the scene for an eyes-on-the-ground assessment. "Charlie-Six, this is Destroyer Niner-Three. We're here, and we pretty well combed the area, at least all we could see without walking any closer into the center of destruction."

"And what's your opinion?" Charlie-Six asked.

"My opinion is that it's one big mess of ruined equipment and tons and tons of burned rice covered in school boy's snot. They did a hell of a job on it."

"Roger, Niner-Three. You come on home."

The chopper had hovered in the air as Professor walked around the edge of the destroyed area. I watched him talking into the phone and finally head back to the camp.

As we turned to leave, T-Bone took a call. He nodded and then said, "Wait one," as he turned to me. "Battalion has some more targets they want us to take out. They've asked us to do another fire mission northeast of here, something the intelligence people have found. They've already contacted your captain."

"Well, it sounds like a done deal," I replied.

I called Charlie-Six. "The mission was a success," I said. "T-Bone has been directed to conduct another fire mission. A target of some sort has been spotted not far toward Phuoc Vinh."

"Roger," Charlie-Six said. "I got the call. Get back as soon as you can."

"And Charlie-Six," I said, "artillerymen around the world can celebrate tonight. The rusty, old truck was completely destroyed."

We flew with our backs to the sun, looking into a brilliant palette of every shade of green imaginable beneath us. Light flashed as the sun hit upon a curve in the river... and was then gone.

Sixteen

A COUNTRY BOY'S BAPTISM
FEBRUARY 6, 1966

"We should be at the target site in a few minutes," said T-Bone.
"According to the intelligence guys, it's a group of low buildings with
camouflage netting over them. They received information from a long-
range patrol. I get a lot of this a lot of times from intelligence spooks, or
Rangers, or whoever."

"And where are the guns?" I asked. "The ones that will be supporting us."

"It will be the eight-inch battery in Phuoc Vinh."

In ten minutes, we arrived at the new site. It was a group of huts just as
they appeared on our maps, small black squares around an abandoned larger
square. There were huts built at the sight of an earth dam, which still held
water from a small creek. To the east, fresh tracks led into a small jungle

clearing. T-Bone got low enough that we could make out criss-crossed tracks and a building covered with sheet metal and netting.

"I'd say that's it," he said, turning to me. As he spoke, there was a metallic "clank" on the right landing rudder. He banked immediately. "Nobody shoots at my chopper!" he yelled. "You sorry little bastards!" he yelled into the wind passing his open window.

I had already started calling in the mission to an eight-inch howitzer battery, Destruction Two-Three, sitting in Phuoc Vinh, Charlie Company's home base.

"Destruction Two-Three, this is Destroyer Niner-Three. Fire mission, over."

A voice returned in less than a minute. It was a new voice, one I had not heard before. "Destroyer Niner-Three, this is Destruction Two-Three. Send your mission." It was as simple as the act of ordering a pizza, and it would require few adjustments as everything on the map lay before me. I gave him the mission, and in three minutes, he told me that they were on the way. As this was being done, T-Bone flew higher and farther out to a point where we would be safe when rounds came.

An eight-inch round was almost two-and-a-half times the size of the 105 howitzer round. They hit, in a commanding display of fireworks, and were immediately followed by secondary explosions, most likely ammunition buried in tunnels. Within six minutes, new craters existed over what I estimated to be over several acres. Whatever had been there no longer was.

"What a team!" T-Bone said. "While we are this close to Phuoc Vinh Field, I am going to fuel up. Care to get a bite to eat?"

"How long will we be there?"

"Forty-five minutes, I guess."

"If you don't mind, I'll take a rain check on the meal, but I would like to 'freshen up' a bit. I can have one of our cooks from our area pick me up and then meet you at the field in forty-five minutes."

"Sounds like a damned good idea—the shower part, I mean—my olfactory nerves are burning."

In twenty minutes, we landed. The company jeep was there with one of the cooks behind the wheel.

When I arrived at The Plantation, I went to Sergeant Zeigler's mess tent where the cooks were receiving and unpacking crates of food. He looked up and came to me. "Can I help you, Lieutenant?"

I shook his hand. "I hope you can. I need some things if you could get them over the next fifteen minutes." I rattled off a list.

"Let me see what I can do," he said, a broad grin on his face.

"And you probably won't get any of it back."

Still smiling, Sergeant Zeigler said, "I don't know what you are up to, but you have spunk."

I had forgotten what a miracle a bar of soap was. I showered, then shaved, and went back to the tent. The items were on my bunk.

I donned my only remaining clean, starched set of jungle fatigues, pressed by the cleaners at the Fort Bliss Laundry. I combed my hair and doused a hefty dash of Old Spice on my face and upper body. I pulled out a red T-shirt that I had brought from the states. Red was the color for the artillery, and the shirt had been used for intramural basketball. I cut it in half and fashioned an ascot around my neck. I put on my second pair of spit-polished boots, which had yet to see service in Vietnam. I donned a pair of shades and put a clean helmet cover on. Sergeant Zeigler satisfied one more request. He provided a dowel pin, eighteen inches long, to serve as a swagger stick. I was ready. The last item was two cold bottles of Vietnamese "33" beer.

Ziegler drove me to the airfield where T-Bone was checking over his chopper.

He looked at me and smiled. "You are gonna start your own war, young man. You may not be very smart, but you've got balls."

As we flew back to Charlie Company, I keyed the intercom mic. "So what exactly did I contribute to this mission?"

"Confirmation of the target," he replied. "And if a second shot from the Air Force had been needed, you would have had to give the locations. Or if we needed to use conventional artillery, like the second mission, that would also have been your call and your fire mission." He turned to me and then continued. "You're not the only one who has done this. Top brass wants artillery forward observers to have the same experience you did. And there is no added expense for me to pick you up on my way to the target."

We continued in silence until the chopper landed in the clearing, with the pond on the far edge. I held out my hand to shake with T-Bone. Instead, he began killing the engine. He climbed out as I did, and he walked around to my side of the chopper. Then he shook my hand and held it. "I can understand why I missed the Alamo, why I missed D-Day, and why I missed Gettysburg. I understand why I wasn't at Okinawa or Bull Run." His smile was at its maximum. "I don't know what you are up to, but I'm *not* going to miss it."

I spotted Charlie-Six and the lieutenants sitting on their helmets forty yards away. I handed my steel helmet to T-Bone. "Take care of this for a few minutes," I said. I donned my mirrored sunglasses and a red baseball cap with yellow lettering that read "Wars are won by the Artillery." I slapped my calf with my swagger stick against my stiff starched trousers and began to walk, not toward the group, but in a circle around them. Professor stood, yelled, and motioned for me to come to where they were. I ignored him and continued the walk around them until I was upwind, and I turned and sauntered toward them. I stopped five feet away. They were a filthy lot, like cavemen.

"What the hell are you doing?" Charlie-Six asked.

"Sir, I can understand and accept my role as a forward observer and a gentleman, and even the fact that I have to associate with infantrymen. But just because fate has dealt me this hand where I have to be around filthy, stinking animals, doesn't mean that I have to become one."

Silence reigned for several seconds as they all stared.

I would never have believed that Michael Allegretti could have moved as fast as he did. I turned to run, but it was no use, as he dove and grabbed my left ankle, dropping me to the ground. Bama grabbed my arm, and Professor wrapped his arms beneath mine and locked his hands over my chest. Within seconds I was carried to the pond, which was covered with scum and moss. "On three," Allegretti said.

I sat up in the foul-smelling water, covered with moss and pond scum, to riotous laughter throughout the camp. Gnats swirled about my head, which was covered with clumps of mud. Laughter filled the entire camp. I joined in.

Allegretti was the first to step into the knee-deep water and extend his hand, still laughing wildly. He was joined by Bama, and they pulled me out.

I looked up to see T-Bone Thornton howling madly as he joined everyone else in camp. He shook hands with Charlie-Six, Bama, and Allegretti, and then introduced himself to Professor. He turned to me and grasped my hand. "I've worked with a lot of outfits since I got to 'Nam, but this is a tough bunch, and this was the only time since I got here that I have witnessed a Vietnam Baptism!"

I bathed in a helmet full of fairly clean water and put on dry, if not clean, underwear and dirty fatigues from my pack.

Just before dark, Charlie-Six called a meeting. "We have a change of plan. We are to move from where we are now to the coordinates that I gave you earlier, by noon tomorrow. Our mission is to hopefully drive a group of Viet Cong into an ambush site manned by Bravo Company. We will start tomorrow at 0630. I will have final details by morning. Anyone have any questions for now?"

"Yes, sir," Allegretti asked, "what's that smell? It's like horse piss!" He turned to me, and we all laughed once more.

Allegretti continued. "You're okay for a country boy," he said. He cocked his head. "'Country'—yeah, that's what I'm gonna call you from now on."

Charlie-Six turned back to the meeting and me. "How was it?" he asked.

"What," I asked, "my Baptism or the fire mission?"

"Well, both," Charlie-Six said, smiling.

"Damned interesting," I returned, and described the Air Force assault.

"Well, it's still the 'boots on the ground' that win the wars," he said. "Anybody have any more questions?"

Bama broke the silence. "Do you mean questions about the operation or questions concerning morale issues?" he asked in a serious tone, with a somber look.

"About whichever one is bothering you," Charlie-Six answered, as a frown of concern filled his face.

"Well, sir, I guess I have a 'morale' issue."

Charlie-Six looked up with a shocked look. "Well, spit it out!" he barked.

Bama took a deep breath as he stared into his coffee cup. He looked up, his eyebrows bunched. "When we get back to camp, would the captain be considerate enough as to have a detail go through Lieutenant Pearce's belongings and confirm whether or not he has any more 'stiff starched, state-side laundered' fatigues still in his possession...and if so, have them burned?"

There was a moment of silence before we, including me, all erupted into laughter.

In the clearing where Darnell and Panther sat talking, I spread my wet clothes out over a bush to dry. I combed my hair and walked to where they sat, eating from C-ration cans. Darnell pointed to where my pack lay. Something pale yellow lay on top of it. I picked it up. It was my first letter from Angie to me in Vietnam. I held the envelope to my nose and inhaled her Chanel No. 5. I pulled out my knife and carefully slid the blade along the inside of the envelope. There was a letter and a photograph: a photo of Angie in a bathing suit and high heels, her back to the camera as she looked over her right shoulder. Her hair had been curled and piled on her head. It was identical to the pose made famous by Betty Grable in World War II. "This picture is my idea of what a GI wants to see today—my version." I removed my boots, leaned back against my pack, and began staring at the photo.

The sky was clear, and shortly after dark, the moon rose above the crest of the jungle. I picked up the letter, laid it over my nose and mouth, and breathed in the fragrance. I realized how badly I wanted—needed—to be with her. I immediately wondered what I would do when I finally heard from Julie. Then in the deep recesses of my mind, a soft voice came to me: "You are going to burn in hell, young man."

Seventeen

GAS MASK INSPECTIONS
FEBRUARY 10, 1966

At the request of Charlie-Six, I gathered a work detail to inspect and clean gas masks for possible use in upcoming operations. We met at The Academy. The work crew consisted of two men from each platoon and two from the company command group. The two from 1st Platoon were both named Williams. Panther had told me earlier that they were inseparable. PFC Afton Williams and PFC Benjamin Williams were referred to as "A. Willy" and "B. Willy." Allegretti had "offered" up Wayland Dieters and Roller Coaster Randolph, and Bama's contributions were one he described as a "Chicago thug" named "Chicago" Mueller and Jacob "Creepy" Somers. Swizzledick had been provided to control the inventory, and B.J. Tucker and Darnell had volunteered. They had all been instructed to bring their plastic ponchos to work on.

"Good morning. I am Lieutenant Pearce. I am attached to the company as an artillery forward observer. I was asked to do this because of the fact that I have also been trained as a chemical officer. The company received forty-five more gas masks last week, and today we are going to check them out to determine what condition they are in. Added to the ones the company already has on hand, this will bring us to enough for every man.

"The intelligence people have told us that over the next months, we will be working in an area where there is a high probability that we will take them with us one or more missions along the Cambodian border. There have been reports that the Viet Cong have already begun using tear gas, specifically the same type we do, CS-4, in and around networks of tunnels they've dug, and that the probability is high that tear gas will be used even more on upcoming missions, so we'll need these." I held up a mask. "Some of you might even be asked to go into tunnels." Everyone turned and stared at "Creepy" Somers, the company "Tunnel Rat," who quietly sat with a twig between his lips. "Are you the one?" I asked.

He nodded. "Yes, sir." While not an official position in an infantry company, each one had identified someone who would be called upon to go into tunnels when gas was in use. "What attracted you to tunnels—to going into them?" I asked. He was short and slender and seemed to fit the bill.

"I grew up in West Virginia. Started going into mines when I was ten," he answered.

"What kind of tunnels are we talking about?" A. Willy asked.

"Tunnels in the earth," I replied. "Tunnels dug by the VC with entrenching tools, some of them hundreds of feet long, from what our intelligence people have told us. Some are concrete-lined and high enough to stand up in. Some of the areas we will be going to along the Cambodian border are well-developed with underground bunkers, some built as long as six to eight years ago. They include bunkers three stories below ground, some made with train rails, which were carried into the jungles by hand. And there are miles of tunnels running between them. One of the best ways to flush them out is with tear gas. The problem is that when we use this stuff and throw it into a tunnel, it often travels along and eventually comes out somewhere else—anywhere there is a hole—and you might be standing next to it."

B. Willy raised his hand.

"Private—"

"Williams, sir," he continued. "Private B. Williams."

"Go ahead," I said.

"Tear gas—that shit is bad, ain't it. I've been in that."

"No, no," came a voice from the back. "You are thinking about the time you farted in your sleeping bag and it brought tears to your eyes."

I waited a moment for the laughter to die. "Settle down," I said calmly. "As a matter of fact, all of you have had training with tear gas, and yes, it is bad—not necessarily lethal, but unbearable when encountered without a mask. And that is why we will most likely need these." I held up the mask. "This is the M17 Field Protective Mask, or as we like to call it, the 'gas mask.' This is the one we will use. It is highly effective in protecting you from agents you might come in contact with. Williams—"

They both snapped their faces toward me, responding with "yes, sir," almost in unison.

"Would the two of you mind passing these out to everyone? One each."

I watched as each person received one and then yelled, "GAS!" True to how they had been trained, each held his breath and pulled the mask out of the cases, slipped them over their faces, and adjusted the straps; and with the heel of their hand, pushed against the intake structure in front, thus clearing it. In seconds, each was breathing normally.

I had my mask on also. "Can you hear me?" They responded in a mixture of voices and nods. "Good. If we find problems, they will most likely be a busted intake valve, a tear along the seal at the edge of the mask, or a cracked lens. Another common problem is what is known as rubber-rot."

"Our job today will be to check them out. Do your job well, because the one that you say 'is fine' may not be and might be the one you end up with.

Hold your hand over the intake valve and try to breath." Each held the butt of his hand against the mask under his chin. His fingers extended toward his nose and blew out, forcing the air in the mask out. "If you can, that is a good indication that the mask is working. Take them off. Do you have any questions?"

No one spoke.

Together we identified the parts of the mask—the seals, valves, straps, and the soft rubber surface—stepping through the process to ensure that each was in good shape. We checked the canvas case and discussed what to look for there. Are there any questions?" No hands were raised. "OK, then as you finish cleaning and inspecting the masks, I want you to take them to Sergeant Darnell or Specialist Crane. They will inspect the mask and accept it or mark it as unserviceable or defective. So, I'll ask again. Do any of you have any questions?" No one spoke. "Then let's get started." We went through the process together, step by step. Then they were on their own. Once finished, they began to take them to Darnell and Swizzledick to be checked.

In the finest tradition of the Army when two or more soldiers meet, conversations started as they worked. This was no exception. Subjects on everything, except what they all currently did for a living, began. An argument grew between which was the better league, the American Football League or the National Football League; how long a person could hold his breath in a gas attack; and if it might become possible in an emergency to breathe through one's ears, with the proper training, of course.

"What proper training could there be?" Darnell asked, looking at Dieters, who had asked the question, an obviously timid man with a silver chain and cross around his neck.

"I suppose the Army is working on the idea," he said, sighing softly as he pulled gently on a rubber valve.

"Probably have a better chance of inhaling through your ass," Swizzledick offered with a grin.

They argued fiercely about the virtues of Raquel Welch and Sophia Loren, lacing their conversations with words describing bodily functions: about the various virtues of long legs in six-inch heels, of well-rounded bottoms, and small pert breasts that held their shape or huge breasts that hung like water balloons.

"What turns you on, Lieutenant?" Mueller asked as he rubbed a damp rag over a stubborn spot inside his mask. He never looked up. And no one spoke.

"Why that's simple, Private," I said. "I want to serve my country in a manner that will make my family proud." For seconds, everyone stared at me, their attention to the masks, suspended. "And to frequently recall, memories of the night I spent with Raquel Welch." There was silence and slack jaws though the circle. Then they all laughed.

"Do you have a secret favorite song?" Darnell asked.

"Of course. Everyone has a favorite secret song."

"And what is it?" he asked, staring at me.

"It's secret, of course."

"I'll know it in two months," Darnell said with a grin.

The conversations split into two categories: one continuing to define the perfect mate, the other turning to slingshot dragsters and "Big Daddy" Don Garlits.

Finally the job was done. We had identified five masks that were damaged. I thanked the group as they rolled their ponchos and drifted away.

Panther, after servicing the radio, approached with another soldier. "Lieutenant, this is Wayland Dieters. He is my friend." The two of them made a "Mutt and Jeff" pair, with Dieters being at least eight inches shorter. I reached out and shook his hand.

"Yes," I said, "Pleased to meet you. And thanks for your help. Where are you from?"

"West, Virginia—Gassaway, West Virginia—farm family. I didn't like that kind of work. That's why I left. It's been almost a year. I was..."

As he continued to speak, my mind wandered. I realized that in spite of combat boots, fatigues, swagger, and a rifle, they were all still just boys.

And those boys would be there for the main act to start tomorrow. As far as I knew, everything I had to do, I had done. We had identified five damaged masks.

Eighteen

ROLLING STONE
FEBRUARY 11, 1966

For me, the war started in earnest at 5:30 a.m., February 11, 1966, with the beginning of Operation Rolling Stone.

I stood with Professor in front of the captain's tent, watching the activity around a line of two-and-a-half-ton trucks that sat idling, belching black smoke from their upright exhaust pipes. Loaded with the men of Charlie Company, they would depart for Phuoc Vinh Airfield in the next fifteen minutes. We watched as soldiers ran back and forth between the trucks and their tents to retrieve articles, as squad sergeants questioned their intelligence, their parentage, and their worth to the Army. A sergeant had one soldier backed up against the side of one of the trucks, his finger in the soldier's face. Finally he yelled for the soldier to get on the truck, and then Professor continued.

"The Viet Cong have two basic missions. The main one is to kick us the hell out of their country. The other is to gather supplies—guns, bombs, and bullets—necessary to do that." He pulled an apple from one of his cargo pockets on his trousers and polished it on his shirt, then resumed. "Our mission is to destroy the Viet Cong and their supplies." He paused and chewed a bite of the apple.

"So, simply put, that is all that this war is about," he said, speaking from one side of his mouth. "Mission one for the U.S. is for them is to build armies and provide them with guns, rice, and bullets. Mission two is for us to destroy their armies and deny them the material they need to wage war. That, my friend, is what we call 'conflicting goals.'

"'Big Bill' Westmoreland and his disciples have already started pushing the Military Assistance Command, Vietnam (MAC-V), to move to become a more aggressive Army. He is calling for a more mobile approach to the war. That requires better roads, more helicopters, and better communications. What that translates to, for us here and now, is that we are going on this mission to provide security for engineers as they build those better highways for better mobility, from Phuoc Vinh to Lai Khe. Does that sound like a good idea?" he asked as he bit into his apple once more.

"Well, of course. The ability to transport men and equipment is vital," I said.

"Ah, your Military History at wherever-the-hell College you attended would be proud of you. But here's the problem." He wiped his mouth on his sleeve. "At the same time that our goal is to protect engineers, Ho Chi Minh's Viet Cong's Army mission is to *disrupt* security for engineers and destroy these 'newly built better highways' as quickly as they can." He closed his eyes and smiled.

"So, they destroy them as fast as we build them?" I asked.

"Well, maybe not exactly *as fast as we build them.* As long as there is protection for what we build, they have problems destroying them. Once we leave, however, they will blow the highways all to hell, and we chase them through the jungle!"

"So what do we need to do?" I asked.

"We do what 'Big Bill' Westmoreland says to do. The Viet Cong do what Uncle Ho says to do. That is why there are battles, and that is why we are here today—the glory of the United States Army!"

"All of the top brass seems to be calling for larger assaults by brigade-size armies. And as it stands, this operation—Rolling Stone—is shaping up to be one of those prototypes, with two full brigades working the same area—that's us."

"So how do you interpret that? What does it mean?"

"It means a hell of a lot of infantry and artillery in the same space. We'll probably be shittin' in each other's mess kits before it's over." He pulled a copy of *Stars and Stripe* newspaper from his hip pocket. "I quote: 'The 1st and 2nd Brigades of the 1st Infantry Division will begin conducting preliminary operations north and west of the Michelin Rubber Plantation.'" He paused. "The article didn't say anything about the handsome, fearless Lieutenant David 'Professor' Rose, however, so I question the editorial credibility, I suppose." He stopped and yelled at a soldier who was walking brusquely toward his truck. "You don't have a canteen in your left pouch. Get it. Di di mau."

"And that means?" I said, turning to him.

"What?"

"What does 'di di' whatever mean?"

"Oh, politely, it means haul your ass." The young soldier turned and ran towards the tents. With that, Professor continued.

"But back to my lesson. Here is the total story of what we face. Uncle Ho, Ho Chi Minh, has publicly declared that he can forfeit ten men for every one of the United States and still win the war." He stared at me as it sank in. "How can we fight a commitment like that?" I didn't answer.

"Until someone yells 'uncle.'"

Soldiers were darting around, running back and forth from the trucks and their areas to get something they had forgotten, choreographed in most cases by a yelling sergeant. A private walked past me toward the command tent, with "God is my *Pint* Man" crudely printed on his helmet. In minutes, he came back by me. "Point" was misspelled on that side of the helmet also.

Professor smiled at me, his eyes barely open as he responded to my question through a mouth full of apple chunks: "With you and me, anything can be achieved." He tossed the core into a bush and moved to his platoon area.

Darnell approached with three men, one of which I had seen hanging around the command tent the previous day. "Lieutenant Pearce, you've already met Swizzledick."

The young soldier stuck his hand out, and we shook. He then turned and hit Darnell on the arm and softly said, "Asshole!"

Darnell continued. "And this is B.J. Tucker, the radio operator for the company's internal network. He is how Charlie-Six talks to the three platoon leaders when we are scattered out." The young soldier extended his right arm, dipped his head, and smiled as we shook.

"Nice to see you again," I said.

"And finally, Specialist Boucher here is our medic. Everyone calls him 'Butcher.' A hell of a way to instill confidence, wouldn't you say?" I shook his hand and nodded.

"Get used to them," Darnell said. "We're gonna be together a lot."

By 0600, the men stood at ease in loose platoon formations, their gear at their feet, quietly swapping tales and occasionally bursting into laughter. Each smelled of insect repellant, which covered exposed skin with a shiny glow. At 0615, the voice of First Sergeant O'Brian exploded from a megaphone, a smile on his face. "It's time, maggots. Get your sorry asses loaded on the trucks. This isn't a picnic. Knock off the chatter, and watch what you are doing. It's a great day to win a war." He stood watching and turned toward one of the soldiers with specific guidance. "Close the gap. Watch where you're going. Stumble and fall, and I'll drop kick your ass into the truck." Similar comments rang out from the platoon sergeants.

Men climbed aboard, roughly twenty per truck, and sat on wooden slatted benches, which folded down from the sides of the bed, facing across the truck bed at the similar row of men on the other side. Each man had his pack behind his legs beneath the bench on the flooring in front of him, their rifles standing upright between their knees. The diesel engines clacked noisily, spewing thick, black smoke as they idled.

Captain Novak, Swizzledick, B.J. Tucker, and one of the company cooks—a soldier along for the ride who would return the vehicle back to camp after going to the airstrip—were in the lead jeep. The second vehicle was mine, with Darnell, Panther, and another cook with the same task.

Six nodded to B.J. Tucker, who pulled onto the dirt road, headed for Phuoc Vinh Field with my jeep right behind. Immediately the trucks began to move forward in awkward, bouncing motion as they gained speed.

Within ten minutes, we arrived at the airfield, and everyone quickly dismounted and formed into their regular squads, ten men each in rows, three squads per platoon, and three platoons. Everyone was counted once more.

"The choppers will arrive in groups," Darnell was telling me, "called 'slips,' with six, maybe seven, choppers per slip. Each slip will carry one of the platoons to the destination. Given the average weight of a man, a helmet, a rifle, and sixty to eighty pound packs for each soldier—and other bulky equipment like machine guns, machetes, extra ammo—were talking six to seven men per chopper. Forty men to a platoon, that takes roughly..." He placed the end of his index finger against the end of his thumb and rolled his eyes upward for an instant. "That takes six to eight men per chopper, give or take a bit." Darnell grinned. "So by my math, we require four slips, counting the command group—you, Panther, me, and the medic—for the entire company." He drew from his cigarette, blew out a cloud of smoke, and pinched a bit of tobacco from the end of his tongue.

I looked at him and smiled. "Don't do calculations like that. You might hurt yourself." He laughed and hit my shoulder.

Conversations were soft, with occasional laughter. The men remained clustered in platoons, mumbling, most of them smoking.

Panther nudged me and pointed into the sky at silent dots, accompanied in minutes by the faint popping sound of propellers slapping the moisture in the air. They grew larger and louder as they approached, angling toward the air strip. The men of Bama's platoon began grinding their cigarettes into the laterite strip, hoisting their backpacks over their shoulders, fastening web belts, donning radios, and lifting their M16 rifles across their chests.

The *whap, whap, whap* sound of the chopper's blades slapping the moist morning air grew in intensity as the aircrafts drew nearer. Then, like prehistoric insects, they hovered and softly touched down, dust rising in curls from the ground around each ship. I looked inside at the pilot of one of the ships—a major—his eyes covered with a shaded visor, adding even more to the eeriness of the scene. Dust continued to rise as Bama's men climbed on board. Each ship had a cartoon bulldog, the mascot of the chopper unit, painted on its nose. Platoon sergeants yelled, unheard from where I stood, as soldiers quickly boarded. Bama and his group were the last of the first slip to climb into their ships. Then all six rose, teetered, and leaned into the direction of the flight; and in ninety seconds they were gone, shrinking in size as they rose.

The next slip landed, and Professor's platoon loaded onto six of the ships. Six, Swizzledick, and I sat on a bench seat across the last chopper. Darnell was on the floor in the space between the co-pilot and me. Panther and B.J. were in vacant machine gun pockets behind us in the side of the ship. Though I wouldn't see it, Allegretti's platoon followed.

I looked to see the streets of Phuoc Vinh below. Charlie-Six's jeep and mine were being driven back to camp by the two cooks from the company. Sears and Roebuck passed beneath us, and I couldn't help searching for Ebony Eyes. The myriad of tents of the battalion passed beneath us—the admin area with its American flag; a group of medical vehicles at the hospital, each with a white cross on a red circle painted on its hood; and finally, the maintenance tents with soldiers bent beneath hoods on various vehicles.

I recognized the string of trucks that had delivered us to the airfield as they passed the statue of the pompous-looking father of the city and through the gate in the razor wire opening.

I could see one of the chopper slips out the right side door. Beneath us lay a lush bed of green, traversed occasionally by streams and rice paddies with their grid-like fields of berms.

Suddenly I realized that it was cool, as wind passed through the openings of the chopper, drying the sweat that had collected over my body.

Fifteen minutes later, the co-pilot looked over his shoulder toward Charlie-Six and pointed toward a patch of grass large enough to land the choppers in the distance. He held up his gloved fist and gave a thumbs up signal to Charlie-Six. The pilot held up his fist and extended his fingers into the air. We would touch down in five minutes.

The ship banked and curved toward our destination, and I could now see what I assumed to be the clearing, the landing zone. We landed and hurried from the aircraft. I immediately spotted Bama's platoon running for the high wall of jungle where they would form an impromptu defensive ring around the area. Sixty feet, fifty, forty, fifteen, and we hovered for only seconds and landed. Charlie-Six patted the pilot on the back as we left. We vacated the ship in thirty seconds, and it began to rise as Professor's slip dropped into the clearing to our right. Within less than a minute, the only sound was the ringing eerie silence. The radio operators began their communications checks, ensuring that we had contact with Battalion and, in Panther's case, the artillery battery that would be supporting us. He turned to me and gave me a thumbs up signal that everything was fine. I oriented my map, quickly identifying the point on the perimeter at which we would leave this clearing into the jungle in a matter of minutes. Charlie-Six was on the radio with Bama. The command group joined Professor's group and moved into the wall of foliage. The choppers were gone.

It was deathly quiet.

Nineteen

STEPPING INTO A WORLD I NEVER IMAGINED
FEBRUARY 11, 1966

Triple canopy jungle rose above us. Hardwood trees, what I took to be mahogany, with bark like the skin of elephants, towered hundreds of feet to reach the sky, held there by trunks up to a yard in diameter. At a lower level, trees of different species that would never reach those heights had evolved larger leaves to absorb what sunshine managed to fall on them. Beneath that, spindly trees formed their own layer. Stout vines curled around everything everywhere, as if determined to pull their way to the sky. I realized that I knew little, if anything, and most likely nothing about any of them. Patches of tiny life, like algae and moss, clung to trees. It was a greenhouse: dank, dark, and musty like a deep cellar. Humidity and heat had worked together to turn those plants that failed to reach the sky into black compost that covered the floor, where the only signs of life I could see were ants crawling over the vegetation. As I watched, ants began to drop from above and land on my body. I flinched as one stung me. I crushed it, and a smell like vinegar came to me.

The platoons formed a defensive circle just inside the jungle, and the platoon leaders closed on the command group. Darnell was behind Panther, who was just behind me. I heard Panther on the radio, ensuring that we had radio contact with the outer world. I glanced at him, and he held up his fist and raised thumb.

Charlie-Six's helmet was beneath his left arm, and I recognized the black, elastic glasses strap that wrapped the back of his neck.

No one spoke. I realized how an infant must feel, with something new to learn with every step. There were no exotic birds, no noises...just silence, broken only by slapping sounds of men killing insects and the occasional sound of the radios. I smiled as I remembered Darnell telling me that the "vines in a jungle will grab you and hold on like a Saigon whore," as I stumbled over one, barely managing to keep from falling. I also recalled him telling me that he had only heard about "Saigon whores" and "could neither confirm nor deny their existence."

We moved out, one of Professor's squads leading the way well ahead of the rest, in case of an ambush.

We had gone about 1000 meters, by my estimation, since we left, and Charlie-Six called a halt for a meeting. "Ask the lieutenants to join us." In minutes, we were looking once more at our maps. The radio operators had dropped immediately, rolling onto their backs in order to rest the packs and radios against the ground. In fifteen minutes, after our locations were confirmed, we were up and moving again.

In another hour, we had gone another 500 meters by my estimate. The point men hacked at vines and saplings in what seemed at times to be mostly impenetrable forest and undergrowth that tugged at our packs, legs, and arms, as we hacked at giant ferns covering the ground. There had been very few clearings, just poorly marked trails and decaying vegetation covering them.

Every group of trees seemed to look like every other batch. We had been moving for about four hours, and already the straps of my web belt had dug into my shoulders. Continuous streams of sweat ran into my T-shirt and shorts.

Charlie-Six turned and motioned for me to come to where he was. Without a word, he held out his map with an "x" drawn on the plastic cover.

I consulted my map. "I agree" was all I said. He stared at the map, which was totally jungle green and, judging by the contour lines, totally flat. There were small clearings that could be seen on the map, verifying our location as we came to them. That, and the process of counting steps along lines of the compass to get where we were, served as the only tools we had to confirm our locations. We were still four to five hours from our destination for the day.

We stopped, and cans of C-rations were pulled from cargo pockets on the legs of their trousers. Can openers on the dog tag chains were quickly used to open and gorge the food inside. Men stepped away from the trail several yards and relieved themselves, cigarettes were lit and inhaled, and canteens were refilled from a stream.

The lieutenants arrived—frazzled, sweaty, and smelling like rotten meat—and joined Charlie-Six and me. They quickly laid out clear plastic map cases, folded in roughly ten-by-ten plastic packages, and then pulled out C-rations and began devouring the contents.

Charlie-Six turned to Allegretti. "You'll have the lead to the final destination. We will come to a small stream—not much of one. but enough for our needs—in about forty-five minutes. Just beyond is a small clearing on a rise. That will be company center for the night." He waited patiently as the lieutenants found where he was talking about. He held up his map package and pointed to a narrow, blue line with his grease pencil. This is the stream. He turned to Allegretti. "Once there, fan out and dig in. Allegretti, you take from twelve to four on the clock." It was a reference to an imaginary clock, with twelve o'clock at the northern part of the clock, down to four o'clock. "I want at least two listening posts about another twenty yards beyond the company line. Professor, you will do the same from four to eight on the clock. And you, Bama, will have eight to twelve on the clock. Dig in when you get there." He looked at each man.

"Lieutenant Pearce, we'll get together to mark potential firing points around our current positions. Get with me after this meeting, and we'll decide where we want them.

We arrived at the new destination in an hour, the vegetation along the way becoming even more difficult to cope with. In thirty minutes, defensive positions had been made for everyone in a hole or behind a log or fallen tree. In thirty minutes, the officers were back together for a short meeting. In forty-five minutes, I got with Charlie-Six, who approved a list of targets. The targets were ten spots, which, in my mind, might be areas of concern: a dry stream bed that provided protection to VCs that might be inclined to sneak up on us, two spots for mortar emplacements, three in ravines where enemy soldiers might be approaching us, and four more located in heavy jungle. I had asked the artillery to do all the calculations needed to hit these areas of concern and give each one a name. If I needed artillery fire quickly, the supporting battery would already have the data for the guns, thus shortening the reaction time.

The next layer of protection for the campsite was a ring of Claymore mines in an arc fifty meters away from the perimeter. If needed, if detonated, each mine would explode, casting 700 one-eighth-inch steel balls per mine, away from us, up to 100 meters into the jungle.

We were in for the night. It was time for each soldier to see to his body. Poor excuses for baths were taken in steel helmets filled with water from the stream. Until sundown, C-rations could be heated over small fires. After that, everything had to be eaten cold. Then, at 1900 hours, the officers would meet once more with Charlie-Six.

"OK, here's the scoop," Charlie-Six began. "Our next objective is northwest, fifteen hundred to two thousand meters." He read off the coordinates on the map, waited patiently while everyone found the location, and placed a small grease pencil "x" there.

"A chopper pilot recently spotted something there, says he saw small patches of what looked to be canvas and camouflage netting—American camouflage netting," he said disgustedly. Whatever it was, it was enough to arouse Battalion's curiosity to the point that we have been asked to investigate. Intelligence officers suspect, given the size of the cache, that if he's right, there may be guards, so we will approach as if there are." He looked at each of us. "At 0530, we will go over there and take a look. The order will be you first, Bama, followed by Allegretti, and then you, Professor. When we reach a couple of hundred meters, Allegretti and Professor will form an arc facing the target. Bama, your platoon will move in to get a closer look. We'll have more information at first light and will fine tune this plan then.

"Lieutenant Pearce," he said, turning to me. "Let's lay out some artillery firing points in that area in case we run into trouble. Stay with me after the meeting, and we will coordinate that. Do you have any questions?" There were none. "See to your men and get settled for the night. We will move out before first light in the morning."

Everyone shook their heads in agreement. He looked at each one of us. "OK, let's do what we're trained to do."

Charlie-Six turned to me. "First, let's set up some artillery around our position for tonight." As the others left, I handed Charlie-Six my map, with small red x's surrounding our position. He looked at it for several minutes. "These look good," he said, looking up at me. "Coordinate them with the battery."

"I already have, subject to your approval, of course."

"They look good," he said dryly. "We'll get together at first light to lay out artillery for our trip to the objective."

Beneath a poncho draped over our heads, by flashlight, Darnell and I studied the map from where we were to where the target was. We identified each trail, each stream, and any rises in the terrain with a small "x"—any place that might be a good ambush for VC—and wrote a list of map coordinates. The x's represented potential ambush points along the way and around the points we were to investigate. I would ask the artillery battery some five miles away to arrive at the information that would be needed by the howitzer crews to drop rounds on any or all of the x's. They would be in place by the time we moved out the next morning.

I had also assigned identification numbers to each of them. In case of an attack, I could call for rounds on the nearest one, reducing the time it took to get artillery rounds on the way and shortening the process considerably.

I moved to where Darnell and Panther were eating. I took the radio and called Destroyer Two-Three, Flash Gordon, the voice of Alpha Battery. I gave him the coordinates, and with each one, he gave me a designator number.

I was hopefully finished for the night. My body was ready to shut down. The tendons across my upper shoulders throbbed from where the eighty-pound pack and load had ridden all day. There was a ring along my head from where my helmet had sat that burned intensely. And the pressure points where my boots had rubbed screamed to be relieved.

I removed my boots, pack, and blouse. I opened a green C-ration can with "beans and franks" stenciled in black block letters on top, pulled out the plastic fork, and took a bite. I studied the map once more and then leaned back on my pack. It would be an hour before Panther would wake me for my first share of the night watch, to be followed by Darnell, and so on through the night. In less than five minutes, surrounded by my reeking body odor, I fell asleep.

At dawn, after a night of little sleep, I woke. I pulled on my boots. My foul-smelling fatigue shirt was stiff and clammy from yesterday's sweat, with white rings of salt formed by the sweat looped beneath the armpits. The left hip pocket had a dark stain on it from something I had obviously sit on or in.

In the time it took me to wolf down my C-ration meal, crush the can, and hide it beneath the thick mulch adjoining the trail, we met once more with Charlie-Six.

Morning came as a sauna, with beads of perspiration already glistening on everyone's face, and once it was wiped away, it reappeared immediately. "I seem to be the only one here," quipped Panther, "who isn't red in the face." There were no smiles, just the placid expressions of beasts of burdens. My green towel was soaked. I realized that I had already emptied one of my canteens, and I walked a short distance to the small stream we had been skirting the previous day. I unscrewed the lids of both canteens and watched the bubbles erupt as I held them beneath the clear water. Once full, I removed the lid from the bottle of quinine tablets—a water purifier—from my web belt and placed two of them in each canteen. I stood there and let the cool water seep into the ventilation holes in my boots.

The stash that we were told to investigate turned out to be overrated, with primarily empty ammunition boxes.

Every man was tired and sweaty. Each smelled of Army-issued mosquito repellent. Each one's face was smeared with dirt and black camouflage.

Charlie-Six reported to Battalion to tell them that the reported site was a bust. There was nothing there but trash. When he finished, he turned to Tucker. "Tell everyone that we bed down here".

That night, in a clearing beneath a star-filled sky, I dreamed of Julie.

Twenty

ANGIE
FEBRUARY 11, 1966

I began to read the letter once more. "Well, hot pants, how goes your war? I hope you are safe. Write as soon as you can and tell me what it's like. I just bought a book from the PX — on South East Asia. There is a map. Let me know where you will be located — if you can." The rest of the letter was about work and small talk about friends. "Pauline asked about you — said to tell you 'hello' — My car is acting up — Larry and Ramona are expecting. I love you, hot shot." I folded it and returned it to the envelope after stealing one more sniff.

I dumped the contents of my pack onto a grassy spot. Except for one more clean set of underwear and one pair of socks, everything there was dirty. I rolled and placed the items back into the pack, the dirty items on the bottom and the clean clothing on top. I laid Angie's letter in next.

I picked up the letter and looked at the postmark, and then I counted on my fingers. It had taken six days to receive it at the company tent and another day to catch up with me here. If I asked her a question in a letter mailed today, I concluded, and everything went ok, it would be at least eleven or twelve days before I got a response. I was twelve days out of sync with her and her world. I laid the letter on top of the clothing once more.

I had met Angela Marie Wilson, Angie, in mid-August 1965 in the Fort Bliss Post Exchange, the Army's version of a department store. I was looking for shaving cream, and as I turned into one of the aisles, there she was, talking to a customer not twenty feet away. I stared for a moment and then turned and picked up a box from one of the shelves, pretending to read the label. She was gorgeous. She took a product from an elderly lady and pointed to something on the side. She had more curves than a mountain road, tan legs wrapped in clinging nylon, and a fashionable fitted skirt that ended just above the knees. It fit like body lotion.

Finally the customer nodded, said something, and left. Angie turned to walk away, and I called out. "Miss, could you help me, please?"

"Of course," she said, revealing perfect white teeth. "What can I do for you?"

"Oh, if you only knew," I thought, as I made a mental note of deep blue eyes with flecks the color of sunset.

"I was wondering which of these products would be best for me." I handed her a small box.

"How old is the child?" she asked, turning her attention from the box to my face.

"What child?" I asked, totally unaware that I had handed her a box of baby aspirin.

"The child you are buying these for."

"Oh. That child. Uh, yes, of course. He—she is four—no, five months."

She stared at the box as a smile formed on her face, and then she turned it over with delicate hands, beautiful nails, and *no* ring. "You need to make sure that your doctor doesn't have an issue with this medicine at this age. It could be a problem. Aspirins are acidic." Handel would have envied her voice. Then she was staring at me, and I realized that she had stopped talking.

"Uh, yes," I said, "Of course. Acrid—acidic."

She smiled and handed the box back to me, brushing my hand as she did. "Will there be anything else?"

"Uh, yes...uh..." I snapped my finger. "Of course. Shoe polish. I need shoe polish." I followed her, inhaling her perfume, and watched the rhythm of her body. We almost collided as she stopped and handed me a bottle of white polish.

"Will there be anything else?"

"Your name," I blurted out, immediately feeling like a seventh grader. "Well, you have been so helpful that I wanted to know your name so that when I come back, I would know who to ask for."

She grinned broadly and ran the tip of her tongue across the lower edge of her upper teeth. "Right," she said, nodding her head slowly. "It's Angie, but *I'm* not for sale," she said with a grin as she turned to leave. I called after her. She was like a fisherman setting her hook.

"OK, Angie, I need one more thing."

Ten minutes later I left with a bottle of baby aspirin for a man who had no children, two bottles of white shoe polish for a man who had three pairs of black combat boots and two pairs of black shoes, and a twenty-five dollar steam iron for a someone who had never pressed anything more complicated than a handkerchief in his life.

I went back to the PX twice more over the next two days before finally hitting a time when she was there. I literally stalked her, standing behind stacks of men's sweaters and irons and at the end of long rows of shelves, observing her over racks of clothing. Finally, she was alone.

"Hello," I said, and she turned toward me. She stepped back, clutching at her throat for an instant, and then she smiled. "You startled me."

"I'm sorry, I—"

"It's fine," she said. "How's your child?" she began with a knowing grin.

"Fine, just fine," I replied.

"Really," she said sarcastically, tilting her head as she softly bit her upper lip. "And you finally decided how old he—she—is?" The smile grew, pulling back to reveal the sexiest mouth I had ever seen.

"Yes. He-he is two. And fine—"

"And your wife?" she asked.

"Wife?"

"Yeah, you know, those things that little children like your son come out of?" She stared into my eyes.

She came closer to me and picked a piece of lint from my shirt. "Relationships have to be built on trust and honesty," she said as she raised her eyebrow. She leaned over slightly and pulled up my left hand, studying the ring finger. "OK. No white lines where a ring could have been. That's a good sign."

She stared into my eyes for several seconds, still holding my hand.

"So here's the deal. If you can control your white *lies*, we might meet some evening somewhere other than Aisle 7 in this PX. Is that what you are wondering about?"

I smiled. "Precisely. That would be very nice."

Suddenly her smile was gone, and she stared at me.

"Honesty is the key. So, let's try this one more time. Tell me about your wife?"

"Excuse me?"

"Your wife. You know—"

"Huh, yes, no. I don't have one," I grunted, shaking my head.

"Tell me about your son."

I stuttered and smiled sheepishly. "Why, I don't have one of those either."

"What about a daughter?"

I shook my head vigorously. "No. I don't have a single one."

Her smile returned.

Two nights later I picked her up at her apartment to go to the officer's club for seafood night. She wore a beautifully fitted, strapless, satin cocktail dress, which could have been designed by the devil himself. And from the time we entered until we sat down, she turned every "horny head" in the dining room.

Twenty-One

We were in the fifth day of my second operation, Rolling Stone: four miserable days of clouds of gnats and heat. My pack straps cut into my shoulder, most of my clothing was wet with sweat, and every muscle in my body burned. I smelled like spoiled cheese. I worked diligently to keep track of where we were on the map. The maps we used in training had lots of recognizable symbols that could be used to determine where we were. There were black squares for schools, houses, and churches; there were red lines that identified roads; and there were contour lines that identified hills and mountains. The map in front of me now was mostly two colors: light green and dark green, the colors of jungles. I used my compass to know which way we were going and tried to count steps to determine how far we had gone on the compass line, until we came to a rare stream. Charlie-Six stopped frequently, and we compared notes as to where we were. I smiled each time this happened, and I reveled in the thought that "he needed me."

As usual when we stopped, everyone dropped their packs and followed them to the ground. Charlie-Six motioned for me to come join him. "I put us here," he said, pointing to a small "x" he had drawn on his map. He removed his glasses, brushed them against a filthy scarf he wore around his neck, and then held them up to the light. He shook his head disgustedly and put them back on.

"I concur," I said.

Location was absolutely critical. If I had to call for artillery, I needed to know where everyone in the company was, in order to avoid calling rounds in on top of us.

And so went the time, with us moving through the jungle, stopping to compare notes occasionally, and wishing we were somewhere else. At 1700, we stopped for the day.

Darnell and I identified positions where we might need to drop artillery during the night and called locations to the artillery battery to be plotted.

Thirty minutes later, I had done my job and was preparing the Army's version of a delicious meal of nondescript meat and potatoes packed in grease.

I had placed my pack against the base of a broad tree so that I could lie down with my feet facing north. It was a trick Darnell had shown me. If anything happened in the night, I would be oriented properly, facing toward the north as soon as I sat up. I removed my boots, stuck a stiff stick in each one, and leaned them upside down against a tree. This would help to keep scorpions out of them. I rubbed my feet. I had read somewhere that there were around twenty-five bones in each foot, and I could feel every one of them. I knew that I could feel pain in each one as I rubbed them deeply and decided that each bone had somehow been damaged today. I wiggled them. Everything worked. I removed the fatigue blouse and immediately realized that it smelled like some unknown animal. I spread it over a bush beside the tree to dry. I walked to a small swamp-like stream, placed two quinine tablets in each of my canteens, and held them beneath the surface of the water until they were filled. I wet a small, army green towel and washed my upper body, face, and head, then returned to where the evening's conversations between the radio operators had already begun. I hung the towel over a small bush, knowing that it would still be wet the next morning.

I could never remember a time when it felt so good just to sit.

The sounds of low voices in conversations ten feet away and the soft rushing sounds from the radios were the only things to be heard.

"OK," Darcy said, as I tuned into their conversation. "Who says asses?" There was a pause, then two soft grunts. "Two," Darcy said softly. "Now, who says boobs?" Another count, then Darcy said: "Two. So, I am the tie breaker, and I say boobs. Boobs win!" There came muted sounds of movement and laughter. These men would take turns manning Charlie-Six's radio and mine throughout the night.

It was silent for almost a minute. Finally one of them, B.J. Tucker, spoke softly.

"I saw a woman once who had three of 'em."

"Three of what?" a voice questioned. I recognized it as Swizzledick, Charlie-Six's radio operator.

"Three tits!" returned B.J. Tucker.

Swizzledick chuckled softly, finally saying, "You lying sack of shit. You never in your sorry backwoods life ever saw a three-titted woman!"

"I'm not lying!" Tucker sputtered. The others were laughing softly. "It was at the Mecklenburg County Fair. She was in a tent."

"First you make up a story, and then you make up a town to support it. And you think that that 'reference' is proof enough that you *did* see a three-titted woman?" asked Swizzledick. "Here we are in the jungle, and your word is all you have to offer as proof? As far as I know, there may not even be a place called Meckelbrub, or whatever you said. And this all happened at a hick fair?" He paused a moment, then continued. "It was probably a cantaloupe."

Tucker responded quickly. "What was 'probably a cantaloupe'?"

"The third tit, you hair brain. The third tit was a cantaloupe."

B.J. Tucker barked a short laugh. "You think I don't know a cantaloupe from a tit?" he returned softly in a high pitched voice.

"Yes!" came the reply. "That's what I'm saying. And as supporting evidence of your lack of knowledge concerning the human anatomy, I further testify that you don't know your ass from a hole in the ground either!" Tucker started to speak, but was cut off. "Some con man painted a cantaloupe pink, probably with a grape for a nipple, stuck it in her bosom, and every redneck in Meckelbrub County went home with a hard on!"

Everyone was too busy softly laughing to hear him.

Theirs was a never ending, normally meaningless conversation.

"OK, listen up," Swizzledick said, becoming serious. "I have a friend who works at Battalion. He says that we are going to a place on the Cambodian border with rubber plantations, and they're all owned by rich Frenchmen and their families. He told me about a blonde who sunbathes in the nude. Playboy quality stuff, in the nude." He stared around the circle to see if he had their attention. He did.

"He says that she rides a huge horse through the fields and into the jungle with nothing on but a man's open shirt. She goes to her secret spot, hangs the shirt on a tree, and spends the weekend completely nude. And she's French. And we *all* know what *that* means. My friend says that our battalion, and us, will be moving there in the next operation, by the end of the month."

It was silent for a moment. "We have to get some of that," the Butcher said.   I stared into the canopy above. There might as well have been no stars, as light could not filter through the layers of jungle. There was no movement of air, leaving me with the smell of my body and clothes.

"It is 7:30 tomorrow morning in Las Cruces, New Mexico," I thought. "Julie had gotten up an hour ago. She had showered, put on her makeup. She would be wearing something conservative, something comfortable: a cotton blouse, or light sweater, a skirt, and low-heel shoes...something she could wear to herd twenty-five grade-schoolers through the day.

Her light brown hair, short and wavy, would bounce with each step as she moved about the apartment, dipping with each long stride. She would smell heavenly, with a hint of Windsong. The coffee cup, a Winnie the Pooh cup I had bought for her in San Francisco, which she had put in the sink just a few minutes ago, would still be warm, still with a lingering hint of oolong tea and with a perfect print of her lipstick on the rim. I concentrated to see her eyes: almost purple, with flecks of hazel, and as deep as the universe. I breathed a deep, exasperating sigh. 313 days," I thought...

I was momentarily startled at the explosion to the northeast and then settled back. It was one of my artillery bursts that I had scheduled earlier that evening. Concentration number CD 11 had fired. This would happen five more times during the night.

"Settle down, Angie," I smiled, as the noise faded. "I love you too." *You will die at the hands of two beautiful ladies if they ever meet*, I thought to myself.

Darnell and Panther came over and bedded down within ten feet of me. They were quiet, content to just sit and feel the night air. Darnell offered a cigarette. I looked at him and smiled. "Sergeant," I said, "you are a piece of art. No, thank you. I don't smoke, and you know it."

Swizzledick was still holding court with the other operators, talking so softly he could barely be heard over the rushing noise of the radios.

"The man never shuts up," Panther said.

"OK, so tell me where he got the name. There's a story screaming to be heard there," I said.

"What name?" Darnell asked.

"Swizzledick," I replied. "Where did that come from?"

Panther lay back against his pack, laughing softly.

"You want the long version?" Darnell asked.

"Might as well," I replied. "I'm not going anywhere. Sure, give me the long version."

Darnell drew deeply from his cigarette and began the story.

"Before we left Fort Riley to come over here, a bunch of us went to a dive to celebrate one last time. Well, the highlight of the evening—other than getting smashed, that is—was a new waitress. When Swizzledick saw her, he licked the end of a dirty finger and jabbed it into the air, making a sizzling noise." Darnell drew a sip of cold coffee from his cup and resumed.

"She was our waitress. She was hot. Well, later in the evening, she stopped by to see how the drinks were holding out." He shook his head slowly. "She *was* a looker. Had to be Penthouse threefold material, and Swizzledick had been hitting on her all night. 'How are you guys doing,' she asked. 'Do you need another round?'"

"Well, Romeo over there," he continued, as he pointed toward Swizzledick Crane, "pulled the swizzle stick out of his glass and slipped it between his lips in his best James Dean impersonation, winked at her, and said, 'How would you like a little excitement?' She sat her tray on the table beside me and walked around, stopping next to him. 'Well, private, I—' she began, only to be interrupted by him. 'Specialist,' he said with a grin. 'I'm not a private. I'm a specialist. Spec 4, to be exact.' She leaned down in front of him and smiled. 'Well, I'm a specialist too,' she said softly."

Panther laughed and slapped his leg, and Darnell continued. "She opened her mouth and ran her tongue across the bottom of her upper teeth. Then she said, 'First of all, I really appreciate the offer. I really do.' She pulled his swizzle stick from his mouth and slid it between her lips. 'But I make it a habit not to engage in activities with men who can only offer little excitements.' Then she pulled the swizzle stick from her mouth and held it lengthwise between her thumb and forefinger, contemplating its length. She cocked her head and evaluated it, then turned her gaze to his crotch, spread the finger and thumb of her other hand about three inches apart, and brought it next to the swizzle stick. 'And secondly,' she said as she slid the stick back between his lips, 'it's impolite to talk with your dick in your mouth, Swizzle*dick*!' Her boobs couldn't have been four inches from his face. And he just sat there." Panther doubled over with laughter.

"And *that*, sir, is *that* story."

A drizzling rain that had fallen since midnight stopped, leaving eerie, ghost-like white wisps of clouds floating among the branches above, as morning light began to filter down. I pulled my poncho from over my body, shook away the rain drops, rolled it up tightly, and tied it to the bottom of my pack.

Darnell and Panther sat before me as I began to discuss the day. Panther handed me a small lump of white clay, which I recognized as C-4, a highly volatile explosive used by engineers.

I had already learned what it was for, at least to infantrymen. "Oh, thanks," I said cheerily. I took one of the empty C-ration cans from my morning meal, cut the top and bottom out to create a stove, and placed it on two small sticks laid about an inch-and-a-half apart. In one of my canteen cups, I emptied an envelope of instant coffee and poured in roughly a cup of water. I rolled several pieces of the C-4 into beads, about the size of pencil erasers, and kept them in my hand. Panther and Darnell looked on as if evaluating my progress. I removed a flap from the C-ration box and set it on fire, sliding it beneath the cup. Then I began to drop C-4 "gumballs" into the flame. Each time, they flashed brightly, releasing considerable heat and dimming only after fifteen seconds. Each time as it dimmed, I flipped another into the flame. Finally, I touched the side of the aluminum canteen cup and found it sufficiently hot. I stirred the coffee and put the cup to my lips. Deprivation can be a wonderful ally. Since my first attempt at making the concoction that I now held in my hand, two things had happened: I had improved my ability to make instant coffee considerably, and I had reduced my standards even more. It was fairly warm and soothing.

"It's better with a cigarette," Darnell said as he offered one to me.

"No, thanks," I said with a smile. "Maybe next time."

I returned after the morning briefing with Charlie-Six and was joined once more by Panther and Darnell. "We move out at 0700. We have two villages to look at today," I said. I placed the folded, plastic-covered map before us and, using the end of a plastic C-ration spoon as a pointer, touched groups of tiny black squares. "Here and here. Charlie-Six expects it to be fairly straightforward. If all goes well, we should make it to here by this afternoon," I said, pointing to where two streams joined in a deep green spot on the map. "That's where we plan to 'circle the wagons' for the night, and we'll be back in Phuoc Vinh by early afternoon."

We stepped off at the designated time. It seemed to be the same trees that we had passed the day before, the same streams we had sloshed through, and the same hungry mosquitoes and ants. It was the constant pressure to ensure that I knew where we were on the map in the event that artillery support was needed. It was the drudgery of pulling free from clinging vines in order to take another step. And it was the same realization that at any moment, "Charlie Cong" could change my life.

We saw signs of what we took to be enemy activity, and we surmised that only because this was mostly jungle inhabited and traveled by the Viet Cong. There were non-U.S rifle shells, propaganda, and freshly opened C-ration cans. At one point, we found a discarded North Vietnam military shirt, rifle shells from a variety of weapons, papers with writing on them, and footprints.

We found ashes of a small fire. There had been no contact with the enemy, nor was there the next day, but they were there.

That evening, on the eighth day, Charlie-Six gave us the word. Tomorrow afternoon, the choppers would arrive to take us back to The Plantation. When I got back to camp, three letters awaited me: one from Mom, one from Angie, and one from Julie. I decided that they would wait until after my shower.

The Plantation had become home. Panther pulled into the camp and we unloaded and cleaned our weapons. We showered, shaved, and scrounged meals from the mess tent.

Thirty minutes later, I met with Darnell and Panther to discuss the previous operation. Darnell held out a packet of cigarettes, one extended past the opening, to me. After a few seconds, he jerked it back, saying "Oh, darn it, I forget. You don't smoke, do you?" Panther shook his head and laughed softly.

We talked about the last mission, which had been a search and destroy. It had been pretty much nothing.

"Panther, what did we do right?" I asked him.

"We didn't get our asses shot." We laughed.

"Darnell, what do you think about this?"

"I think the idea of you letting me and Panther fire live missions is coming on well," he said. "I feel more and more confident every time I do that. I'm not as good as you, yet," he said, looking up at me. "But I will be. I will be."

"I'm sure you will."

The discussion quickly finished, and Panther asked permission to go see Dieters.

"Of course," I said. "Tell him we said 'hello.'"

Darnell sat quietly for five minutes.

"What's eaten at you?" I asked.

"A letter," he said. He pulled a stack of photos out, of Amanda and his daughter and of others. He pointed out his father cooking on a portable barbeque grill, his mother holding his daughter and pointing to a butterfly. He was quiet for several minutes. "We used to spend evenings like that, a lot."

He held out a picture, and I took it. "When we get home, I'm gonna come see you and that bridge."

He showed me pictures from the river and the fields. "That old bridge was my amusement park. Two friends and I spent ninety percent of our time there."

"When our football team won district, fifteen of us climbed up on each side of the bridge." He pointed at the top of one of the spans. "In nothing but our jockstraps. The captain said that he would 'count to three and then all of us would jump.' Just as he started, Mrs. Hassenfelder, who must be as old as Methuselah, started to drive across the bridge and saw us standing up there. She couldn't have been doing fifteen miles an hour, but she swerved and hit the end railing. She wasn't hurt. The funny part was that the judge advised that she 'keep her eyes on the road and not the scenery,' in cases like that."

We sat quietly, and then I spoke. "When this shit is over, I'll come there and we can get drunk together. A deal?" I asked as I extended my hand. "I might even steal your beautiful wife and baby."

"Damn right, it's a deal. I'll even get the mayor out for a photo of the three of us." He continued. "So, this morning, what is your favorite song? If I guess it, will you tell me?"

"I suppose, if it's that important to you."

"I say it's 'When a man loves a woman.'"

"What," I said, caught off guard, and then a smile came. "Nope. Not even close."

We both stared at the sky. In two days, the process would be repeated: the trucks, the choppers, the heat, mosquitoes, and unbearable homesickness.

Twenty-Two

THEY CAME AS GHOSTS
FEBRUARY 27, 1966

They came as ghosts, to a point some ten yards before the jungle gave way to a collection of crude huts, a small village. An early morning haze hung in the jungle five feet above the ground, like spirits. Bama raised his hand in a fist to signal the squad behind him to stop, remaining hidden in thick foliage. He quietly moved toward the clearing, his radio operator behind him, stopping short to remain concealed in the thin brush, but able to observe the scene before him. He knelt on one knee, folding the other leg like a chicken's wing as he did, and began studying the hamlet before him.

He methodically scanned the collection of thatched structures that formed a ring roughly forty yards in diameter around the village common area. The surface of the damp dirt had been packed to the consistency of concrete over generations, and it had obviously been recently swept, most likely a daily chore for the women, and it shined beneath the thin layer of dew.

He counted ten huts—hooches—all about eight feet high, with frames and rafters bound together by leather straps. The roofs were made of layers of palm fronds, while the walls and floor coverings were made of tightly woven mats of the same material. Each dwelling was surrounded by adjoining pigsties, chicken roosts, and neatly groomed, grayish-green gardens with rows of vertical poles laced with what looked like bean vines of some sort.

It was eerily still.

Ten yards away to his right was a circular concrete pond, approximately eight feet in diameter, with what he guessed to be a four-inch thick concrete rim that rose a foot above the packed earth and encircled the pond. It was apparently a holding tank for fish for the community, as evidenced by the rancid, piscatorial smell of murky water.

A ceiling of heavy fog rested above the village, increasing the eeriness of the scene, and intensified the odors. The entire area was roughly ringed by the jungle.

Bama flinched at a movement: a bantam rooster that strutted from behind one of the structures, stretched his neck, and then crowed, cocking his head from side to side. He flapped his wings violently, fluffing his collection of bright red, orange, yellow, brown, and black feathers, as if shedding the night from his body. The only reaction was a high-pitched squeal from a startled pig somewhere behind one of the huts, toward the opposite side of the clearing where Allegretti's platoon was positioned. He seemed unaware of Bama's presence as he strolled confidently in a display of arrogance, as though proclaiming himself the village constable.

For the past half hour, 1st and 3rd Platoons, Professor's and Allegretti's, had stealthily made their way around the village to form a ring thirty to forty yards away from the huts of the village.

Everyone was in place.

Bama, still focusing on the dwellings, reached his hand over his right shoulder for the radio handset. It slid into his hand. He briefly depressed the call button, silencing the rushing noise of every radio on his frequency for an instant, and then placed it against his ear. He waited for several seconds. Twenty yards behind and totally obscured by the jungle, B.J. Tucker turned at the signal and handed the radio handset to Charlie-Six. The radio was once more silenced, and Charlie-Six softly spoke one word: "Dance."

Bama rose and moved back to where the second of his three squads waited. Making eye contact with the team leaders, he simply held up his hand like a pistol and then pointed it into the village.

This was the second day of a search and destroy mission, designed to "find and identify enemy soldiers and supplies, force them into combat, and destroy them."

Bama's first squad stood and passed by him, the brushing of their boots no louder than a whisper as they stepped from the jungle onto the hard surface of the square. They had shed their packs out of sight in the brush, allowing them to move quietly toward the ring of dwellings. There were two teams of four men each and the squad leader. Each man's face was smeared with camouflage paint. They separated, approaching the ring of huts in opposite directions. At their appearance, the rooster exploded into a cacophony of screams, wildly flapping wings, and thrashing legs as it ran from sight. He was immediately joined by a choir of several pigs located out of sight behind the huts.

Bama continued to kneel as the increasing light defined huts, pig pens, and chicken roosts, all intermixed with shadowy vegetation.

The air was heavy and moist, smelling of smoke and recently cooked meat, of grain, of tilled earth, and of human and animal urine and waste. One of the pigs, startled by the soldiers, screamed angrily at the intrusion.

Randomly located banana trees stood in silence as witnesses to the scene. Their slotted yellow and lime green leaves and short, green bunches of fruit were perfectly still. It was once more silent except for the continued fussing of the rooster, the startled squeals of several pigs, and the occasional soft shuffling sound of boots brushing against the packed surface.

A foot-high clay statue of a woman with extremely distorted breasts stood on a small mahogany bench at the entrance to one of the homes, ringed at its base by fresh flowers. Someone had recently been there. The rooster had calmed and seemed content to imperiously strut, cocking his head to watch the intruders.

The search continued, each team moving silently from hooch to hooch, M16 rifles held diagonally across their chests. At each hut, two men moved to the two back corners of the hut, and two remained at the front. Each scanned the area, and once satisfied that it was clear, nodded to the team leader. The lead soldier of the group needed to do nothing more than to stoop and stick his head past the door frame of each structure in order to see it was empty. In every case, he stepped on the sleeping mats that covered the floor, patting them with his foot to ensure there was solid ground beneath. Small, black metal pots and pans hung from pegs driven into one of the back corner posts. As they progressed slowly in response to hand signals and gestures, both teams seemed to float from one hut to the next. There were no conversations, no humor, and no talk as we moved.

In fifteen minutes, the search was finished. The leaders reported to Bama as he motioned to Charlie-Six to join them. He turned to me and motioned me to join him. We did so in seconds.

"Well?" Bama asked.

"Someone has been here within the last six to eight hours," the team leader said. "There's the recent smell of cooking and smoke, and one of the fire pits is still slightly warm. Other than that, there is no sign of hanging laundry or cooking fires and no activity."

"Was there anything else?" Bama asked.

"There were flowers—they looked a bit wilted—on a mahogany bench in front of one of the hooches. It had a clay effigy of some sort, a naked, fat woman with gigantic breasts almost down to her knees and a huge stomach."

Bama grinned broadly and patted the speaker on the shoulder. "Try to control your urges, Specialist Davidson. No arousal. This is serious business." They all laughed softly.

It occurred to me as I knelt next to Charlie-Six that there were no birds, not even sparrows. Nothing flitted from rooftops to the ground and then off again, carrying feathers or bits of straw for nesting or worms pulled from the dung heaps for their offspring.

The soldiers had found nothing of concern. I moved toward the center of the courtyard where the fish pond was. Huge, brownish-green, carp-like fish, highlighted with pale yellow patches like saddles over their spines, drifted slowly in circles, oblivious to what was happening, as snails at water level moved about their morning routines.

In twenty minutes, Charlie-Six and the platoon lieutenant leaders were kneeling in a circle around a map that he was discussing in the growing light. He looked around the circle. "First of all, that was good work this morning. Pass it on to your guys. They showed great discipline. Very professional." He lifted his glasses from his ears and let them drop to his chest, suspended by the black elastic strap.

He leaned over the map. "When we finish here, we'll move to here. he gave the map coordinates." He jabbed the map with a dirty finger adorned with a black crescent nail. He waited as everyone identified the spot to which he was pointing with a grease pencil.

"Late yesterday, a chopper pilot reported something east of here, said it looked like something covered with sheeting of some kind—tarps or cloth, maybe netting. He also reported what appeared to be some equipment— machinery. Well, all of that aroused Battalion's curiosity, so our plans have changed slightly. We are going there next, probably in thirty minutes.

Professor, you will lead when we leave." He looked up to see the 1st Platoon leader nodding. "Allegretti, you will follow. And Bama, you bring up the rear. Anyone have any comments?" Charlie-Six asked. There were none.

"Tell the guys not to destroy anything in the village—to leave everything alone. This doesn't seem to be a major threat to the free world." He turned to me. "Pearce, you have any comments?"

"No, sir," I said.

Charlie-Six continued. "When we leave, I want to move—"

Two voices yelled, "Grenade!" I turned in time to see an object flying through the air. Three rifle shots exploded to my left in the village area, accompanied by shouts. My first thought was that the object was a small green squash, until it bounced on the packed clay of the square with a heavy thud. I lunged to my left and landed beside the fish tank, as Darnell and Panther crashed to the ground beside me.

I looked up in time to see a lanky soldier, seemingly suspended in the air above the grenade, falling to earth and landing on it, amid the clanks and rattles of the equipment attached to his body. His rifle pinwheeled through the air and clattered noisily as it hit the hardened surface several yards away. All of this had been accompanied by warning shouts, squeals from the pig, and shrieks from the rooster as it ran for cover.

Adrenaline instantly charged my body, and bile rushed upward into my throat. Stone silence followed for several seconds, quickly yielding to shuffling noises as soldiers began to survey the area once more. I spied two of Bama's men, members of the search team, lying beside one of the huts, concentrating on a black clad body before them as Darnell spoke softly into the radio: "Destroyer Two-Three, this is Destroyer Niner-Three. Fire mission, over." I visualized the artillery battery five or six miles to our east scrambling to make ready to provide fire support for us. I heard the response on Panther's radio: "Destroyer Niner-Three, this is Destroyer Two-Three. Send your mission."

"Destroyer Two-Three. Wait, out."

"Roger, Niner-Three. Ready when you are."

"Roger," Panther repeated. It was our way of telling them that we weren't sure what was happening and asking them to prepare to provide artillery support, should it be needed. I envisioned the turmoil in the battery, as the chief of the fire battery ran into the howitzer area, yelling: "Off your lazy butts and get out here, or I'll have enough of everyone's ass to feed the division," as tarps were jerked from ammunition stacks, folded, and placed out of the way. Equipment was readied, and men ran to their positions in varying stages of dress, in preparation for supporting us.

Charlie-Six was speaking softly on the radio ten yards away. I could barely make out what he was saying to Allegretti and Professor, who were still in their positions around the village. "We have one dead, assumed to be Viet Cong. No casualties for us. But we have a situation. One of our men is lying on top of what might be a grenade here. Hold your positions and stay alert." The final warning had probably not been necessary, I thought.

The original search teams were moving once more from hut to hut, beneath the slightly dancing shadows of the banana trees. They were once more examining every hut, chicken roost, bean pole, and pigsty, to the extent of jabbing sticks into dung heaps to ensure that they concealed nothing. Within several minutes, they came together at the far side of the compound, the senior sergeant yelling, "Clear!" as he stared at Bama, who acknowledged him with a thumbs up signal.

It was eerily quiet once more, an intense vigil by everyone, as nerves stretched like guitar strings. The silence felt as complete as the closing of a coffin in a church funeral.

In a sudden motion, Bama rose, threw off his pack, and tossed his helmet aside where it bounced away like a bowling ball, spinning as it did. In seconds, he knelt beside Terry Grayson, still lying on the grenade.

His creamy voice was amazingly calm. "I don't want you to move. I don't even want a flinch from you. OK?" Bama asked. He could see the terror in the soldier's watering eyes as Grayson looked up, his face ashen gray with the exception of blood oozing from his nose. Bama spoke softly, as if ordering a cup of coffee. "It's Terry, right?" Bama asked, smiling as he stared into the soldier's terrified eyes.

It took almost a minute for the soldier, seemingly confused, to decipher what he had just been asked.

"Your name," Bama asked again. "It's Terry, right?"

"Yes, sir, Ter-Terry-Grayson."

"Are you hurt?"

The young man's head turned as if he were trying to see where he was. "I...No, I don't think so. My ankle. I think I twisted my ankle."

"OK, just lie still. Butcher's on the way." Bama placed his hand on Grayson's shoulder, the same effect as anchoring a boat. "That was a hell of a brave thing to do, you know that?"

Grayson stared at Bama's mouth, seeming not to understand what language was coming from it. Then his eyes began to dart about once more.

Finally, he seemed to remember English. "I just-just-didn't-I-I couldn't..." Sweat was running profusely down his face. He was trembling.

Butcher ran from the jungle, already unbuckling his aid kit, and squatted beside Bama. He immediately began gently probing. "Are you hurt?"

Grayson turned to him. His tongue rested on his lower lip. "Hurt? I-I twisted my ankle when I hit, and my knee is hurting. I bumped it pretty hard."

Butcher began to probe Grayson's body.

"Where are you from?" Bama asked softly, calmly, his voice the texture of cream gravy as he put his hand on Grayson's shoulder.

The young man's eyes darted wildly, as if the question had been asked in Yiddish, as he seemed to continue inventorying everything around him. "Be-Benson, Arizona."

Butcher looked toward Charlie-Six, who was fifteen feet away wiping the lens of his glasses with a sock. The medic held his hand above his head and made a rapid circular gesture.

Charlie-Six turned to B.J. "Call in a medevac chopper," he said, then turned back to the trio.

Butcher pulled a packet of gauze from his bag, poured water from his canteen from it, and wiped sweat, grime, and snot from Grayson's face.

"He's on a grenade," Bama said softly to the medic.

The Butcher continued to probe the frightened soldier's body, speaking softly and clearly. He turned to Bama. "I don't see anything here, but you have to get him off whatever is underneath for me to finish. Can we turn him over? I have to get his clothes off. Whatever you do, you have to do it quickly. He's going into shock."

"Aren't we all, Doc," Bama said softly as he grinned.

"I have to cool him down and examine him better and quickly." He poured water from his canteen onto Grayson's body.

"OK. Here's what we are going to do, boys," said Bama. He turned to Butcher. "You step back, but not too far away. There," he said as he nodded his head. "By the pond. I'll need you. Gather whatever you need, and be ready to work your magic." He turned to Grayson. "Terry, you and I are going to get up and walk away from this."

As an afterthought, he turned to Butcher. "He's yours in three minutes."

"Yes, sir," the medic said as he turned and scurried to the pond and began laying out items from his bag.

"Breath normally, Terry. We're gonna get you out of this mess," Bama said softly and calmly. He paused for several seconds. "You believe that, don't you?" As he spoke, he searched the area looking for someone. His search stopped at Panther. "You," he said softly. Panther pointed at his chest, then in less than a minute, he shed his shirt and pack and was kneeling next to Bama.

"OK?" Bama asked once more.

"Ye-yes, sir," the soldier said. Slobber was oozing from the corner of his mouth as a pool of urine crept from beneath him on the ground. Tears had begun to flow.

"Terry, you know Panther, don't you?" Grayson glanced at Panther, then back.

"Yes, sir. I know him."

"Well, here's what we are going to do. We're going to pick you up and move you away from here. Clear?" He turned to Panther. "Clear?" he repeated.

"Yes, sir," Panther said softly, nodding rapidly at the same time.

"OK, Terry, when I tell you to—not just yet," Bama said, "but when I tell you to, I want you to do a perfect push-up."

Grayson's eyes rolled, and his face instantly knotted as he turned toward Bama. "Do what? We're gonna do what? If I—"

Bama's hand was on his shoulder again as he interrupted, a shushing sound flowing from his pursed lips. "Take it easy, man. Easy."

"But if I move, it will go off. It's just layin' there, waitin'-wa-waiting to go off." Grayson's voice was rising to a high pitch, and his lips were quivering.

"Nothing is gonna go off. Relax. I've done this with other soldiers before, lots of times," Bama lied as he spoke.

Grayson turned his face—a mass of dirty wrinkles—toward him and stared, his expression equal parts of fear, confusion, and hope. Everywhere his fatigue shirt touched his body, it was dark green with sweat.

"We're gonna do a push-up," Bama said in his soft, creamy drawl.

"A push up?" Grayson almost screamed, his brow twisted and his lips trembling. He started to mumble. Each word he spoke seemed less firm and stable than the one before.

Bama smiled slightly. "Relax. Surely to God, you remember how to do push-ups, as many as you did in basic training?" Grayson moved his hands beneath his shoulder, his elbows extended upward like a grasshopper.

"Whoa, whoa," Bama said quickly, "not just yet. When I tell you to. OK? Relax!" Grayson nodded, but remained in position. Everyone else had stepped back and away to minimize confusion.

Bama turned to Panther. "I will straddle him and help lift him up by his arms. When I do," he began, his eyes locked on Panther's, "you are going to look under him to make sure the grenade doesn't move...that it isn't caught up in his clothing. And it won't be. Then you get behind me between his thighs and grab his legs. On my word, 'go,' we'll lift him up and walk to other side of the pond."

Panther, obviously only slightly less rattled than Grayson, nodded and moved into position.

Bama stood, slid his hands beneath Grayson's armpits, and wrapped them around his chest. "Panther, you ready?"

"Yes, sir," Panther replied, kneeling five feet away where he could see under Grayson once he was lifted.

"OK, Terry, let's do this." As he spoke, the upper body rose, and Bama lifted him.

"It didn't move," Panther said hoarsely, "It's right under his heart. You're clear. It's not hung up on anything." He spun around and stepped between Grayson's legs. They lifted him and crab-walked to the edge of the pond where they lowered him, turning him gently as they did, onto his back.

The Butcher was immediately on the ground beside him, looking into his eyes, examining his nails.

Grayson was crying uncontrollably.

The Butcher was slashing at pack straps with a scalpel, like a surgeon, as he removed the pack. "Swizzledick," he called out, "do you have a Dustoff chopper coming in?"

"Yes!" came a yell from behind him. "They are on the way."

Butcher's attention turned to the clothing, carefully making long slashes until the fatigue pants and shirt lay in wrinkled heaps. One more cut, and the T-shirt opened like a vest. As he worked, he yelled, "Get me some water—

fresh water, not that piss in the fish pond." He handed the scalpel to Panther. "Cut the shoe strings and get the boots off. And the socks. As he spoke, Butcher allowed drops of water to trickle from a canteen into his patient's mouth.

"Medevac chopper's on the way!" yelled Tucker. "Ten minutes out at the most." Butcher sat back, allowing his hand to rest on Grayson's shoulder, as Charlie-Six knelt beside him.

"Pulse is still up a bit, but not racing. He's coming down. Breathing is slowing. He's sweating, but who isn't. It has to be over a hundred degrees in this shithole. There are no signs of injuries that I saw, other than a skinned up knee. His eyes are dilated some, and there is some coloring under the top of the nails. He's in shock." As he spoke, he continued to slowly pour water, which had quickly been supplied in dozens of canteens, over the patient's nearly nude torso, into his armpit and crotch area, as two privates from Bama's platoon held a poncho over him for shade. B.J. turned and called for more water, which arrived in seconds.

"He's scared shitless, nervous, but that's subsiding," he said to Charlie-Six. Then turning to Grayson, he wiped his forehead with a wet cloth. "Slow, normal breaths. Slow and even. That's it. We're home free, Terry."

Charlie-Six stared at the medic for a moment and then grasped his shoulder. "Good work. I'm proud of you."

As he spoke, we began to hear the soft, flat, clucking sound of the medevac chopper's rotors. In seconds, it cleared the tree line to the north, a giant white cross on its nose. It eased slowly toward a spot that had been cleared. Palm trees thrashed wildly in the furious down blast that raised grit all around us. I had an image of Thor, his fearsome hammer in his hand, descending to Earth. We could hear nothing else. Then the chopper powered down, and the breeze calmed.

A medic jumped down and rushed to where Butcher sat hunched over his patient, shielding him from the down blast. The new arrival shook Butcher's hand. I watched as the two of them talked, unable to hear them from where I was, like a silent movie. A third medic, accompanied by two volunteers from Professor's platoon, scurried up with a stretcher that was placed next to Grayson. The two new medics gently lifted and placed him on it. I watched as the two volunteers and the medics assumed their positions at the four corners of the stretcher. Then the senior medic screamed the words: "Three-two-one." They lifted their new patient to waist height and moved to the chopper. In seconds, it was fastened securely in place on the inside back wall of the aircraft.

The senior medic inserted a hypodermic needle into Grayson's thigh and slipped it out. He shook hands with Butcher and mouthed something to him, smiling as he did, and patted him on the back. The pilot gave Charlie-Six a thumbs up, and Charlie-Six saluted him. The ship rocked and shuddered. Within seconds, Thor rose, once more in control and oblivious to the weaklings around him, blowing down three of the hooches as he did and sending the hurtling rooster through the air.

Twenty-Three

MAMA-SAN, COME BURY YOUR SON
FEBRUARY 27, 1966

Darnell had already called Flash Gordon and cancelled the fire mission. I glanced across the clearing at the hooches where two soldiers were standing in front staring at the ground. It was a moment before I realized that an arm in a black sleeve extended from the doorway. I rose and walked to the hut where the body was. He was a boy. A rare breeze tugged at his black hair. Two pools of blood, syrupy and dark, had bled out of his chest and pooled beneath his body, forming the shape of a gruesome pallet.

I looked at the rifle by his side. It was an antique, probably French, I guessed. A group of rounds had been laid out beside him. I recognized two as shotgun shells and four cartridges, only one of which looked like they would fit the rifle. "Fourteen, sixteen-years-old?" I thought.

I rose and walked behind the hut and vomited.

A squad sergeant and two privates from Professor's platoon stopped next to Charlie-Six. "We're done, Captain," the sergeant said, pointing toward the body, neatly wrapped in a poncho and tied with several fatigue belts.

"Good job, Sergeant Mansfield," Charlie-Six said. "Thank you, guys. I appreciate it." There was a short chorus of "yes sirs," "no problems," and other comments, then the threesome left to join their platoon.

"OK. We move out in five minutes," Charlie-Six said as he handed the handset back to B.J. Tucker after speaking to the platoon leaders. He turned to me. "In all the confusion, you might not have heard. The VC was hiding in a spider hole with a thatch shield covering him, behind one of the shanties. Search team must have walked within five feet of him on their search. There was no way they could have seen him. The problem with these people is that if they don't want us to see them, we won't."

Allegretti's platoon was first to move out, and they plodded across the village square through the banana trees and began disappearing into the thick growth on the north side.

As they passed, Allegretti stepped away and patted Bama on the shoulder. "Nice job."

"Superior Southern knowledge, son," came the reply. He received a gentle slug on his shoulder, and then Allegretti smiled and rejoined his platoon. With their heavy packs, they resembled a caravan of camels from an Errol Flynn movie, weighted down beyond reasonable expectations and swaying as they walked beneath their loads. In seconds, they began to disappear into the foliage and the jungle.

Professor's platoon was next. As they passed, moving slowly and silently, Professor stopped by Bama. "Good work for a Southern boy," he drawled heavily in his best Southern accent and patted his head. "How did you know how to do all that with Grayson?"

Bama closed his eyes and tilted his head back. "It was simply superior Southern knowledge and intellect, old son. Nothing less. Just another product of the University of Alabama." Professor shook his head. "Well, you looked good anyway," he said as he re-joined his platoon and stepped away, moving with the dirty grayish-green line of men passing by. He walked quickly to one of his men, grabbed a pack strap and worked a twist out of it, slapped the young trooper on the back, and joined with his caravan.

A soldier I knew only as Chalmers walked to where I stood. "Rough start for the day, wouldn't you say, Lieutenant?" He was tall, six-three or six-four, with coal black hair and black whisker tips that pushed through his powder white skin, giving his face a bluish-gray hue. "Another young man," I thought, "aging way too fast." The only outstanding color in his face was in his deep blue-gray eyes, the hue of winter sky. They framed a large, narrow nose, crooked like a hatchet. The sniper turned to stare at Charlie-Six twenty feet away. Charlie-Six had told me that the soldier had been trained as a sniper, won competitions, and served with a special forces unit before asking to be transferred to a "regular" infantry outfit.

"So you're a sniper, right?" I said.

"Was a sniper," he replied. "I didn't like it."

"Oh?"

"No, sir. It just wasn't for me."

Charlie-Six motioned for us to join him where the grenade was. I walked with him and stood as a curious bystander.

"Fucking antique. Probably Chinese," Charlie-Six said, staring at the grenade. "Can you shoot this thing at a safe distance, say, seventy-five feet? Say, from that line of banana trees?" he asked, looking up at Chalmers. He pointed at the spot where the soldiers continued to disappear through the long, green leaves into the jungle.

The soldier knelt and looked at the grenade that had been thrown, for almost a minute, never touching it. "Yes, sir, I can. But I have a question." He motioned for Charlie-Six to kneel and then said, "Please."

"Yes?" Charlie-Six replied, with his eyebrows lifting.

"There are two dots on the side of it—bumps, I'd say," Chalmers said, pointing.

Six knelt and studied them. "OK. I see them." They were the size of a match head and dirty white. He turned back to Chalmers. "So?"

"At that distance, do you want me to hit this one or this one?" As he spoke, he moved his finger from just above one to just above the other, careful not to touch anything, a smile growing on his face.

Charlie-Six looked up at him and grinned. "Does it matter?"

"To me it does," Chalmers said. "I need to keep my reputation clean."

"Oh, I see," Charlie-Six said, with a grin of his own. He pointed at one of the white dots. "That one," he said, his smile growing.

Charlie-Six, Bama, and I watched as Bama's platoon passed into the jungle.

"Showtime, Sergeant," Charlie-Six said, turning to the sniper. "Are you ready?"

"I was born ready." He looked at Charlie-Six and then at me. "If you will move back some more." We did. He raised his rifle and steadied it against a banana tree. It barked as the grenade jumped from the ground and clattered fifteen feet further away. Charlie-Six started toward it. It was twisted and split.

"Let's go," he said.

"Not just yet, sir," Chalmers said, motioning with his hand for Charlie-Six to stand where he was. A quizzical look came over Charlie-Six's mouth, but he did as instructed.

Chalmers walked to the grenade and stared at it. He stepped back thirty feet and raised the rifle once more, inhaled, held his breath, and fired again. The grenade jumped again and landed in two pieces. He turned to the captain.

"I needed to hit the other dot too, just to make sure." he said. "Will there be anything else?"

The two of them walked over to examine the remains. It hadn't exploded. "A dud," Charlie-Six muttered.

He patted Chalmers on the back, and they walked to where I was standing. "Good shooting. But you need to work on your confidence, soldier," he said with a wide grin as he patted him on the back one last time. Chalmers touched his forehead with his index finger and jogged past Bama and me to the disappearing column.

The last of Bama's platoon disappeared into the palm trees like silent zombies, followed by Bama and Charlie-Six. I looked once more toward the hut where the body lay, carefully wrapped in a plastic poncho. The ancient rifle lay a short distance away, the barrel bent at an angle.

"You should have been playing soccer," I said softly, then turned and followed the company into the lush green wall as rain began to tap gently against the giant banana tree fronds.

I deeply missed home, my family, and the gentle, caring world that held the *Raincrow*. I wanted to hear their voices and see their smiles.

Twenty-Four

THE PHILOSOPHERS
FEBRUARY 28, 1966

My life had been lived in a simple world. I had been raised on the flat plains of West Texas and Southern New Mexico in a peaceful, agrarian lifestyle of Sunday morning gatherings, of planting, branding cattle, and the necessity of constantly irrigating water from beneath the earth's surface in order to coax cotton and alfalfa from the ground. It was a hard life of branding, vaccinating, and butchering. Excitement consisted of two to three movies a month, gathering at the one small high school for Friday night football games, and gatherings over fried chicken dinners with neighbors. These were things that formed a fine life. It was a life of God, country, and the American Way!

I now sat in Bermuda shorts in the shade of a rubber tree, my right foot resting on my left knee, a thong sandal dangling from it. Most Americans knew nothing of what I was doing. They went about their lives, the majority of them unable to even pinpoint Vietnam on a map. I sat alone. Rain had fallen less than an hour earlier, leaving cool evening shadows, now being tossed about by a gentle breeze. In my new world, this was as good as it got.

On March 2, we would leave on our next mission: Operation Hattiesburg in Tay Ninh Province, somewhere near the Cambodian border. But for now, it was down time.

Darnell had already obtained a map of the general area of the next operation and placed it in the clear plastic map case. Although, we had not been given the exact location, as that was classified and would most likely remain that way until the next day. We speculated as to where we would go. The only thing that our guesses had in common was deep dark green spots on the map: triple canopy jungle.

I had already worked with Darnell and Panther to get everything, ready for whatever came next. We had talked about the mission we had just completed and discussed "what we did well, and what we could have done better."

We talked about the last mission. "That's what I love to see," Darnell said in a soft, sarcastic voice. "Bugs the size of chickens, snakes you could play jump rope with, and blood-sucking insects." He shook his head and took a deep breath, then continued. "Dear mom, you can come get me as soon as possible. Camp just isn't much fun anymore."

Well, that's all I've got," I said. "Plan to meet again after Captain Novak's meeting with Battalion."

I was joined by the other lieutenants to watch the antics of the company soldiers and enjoy the few beers we had been given. The afternoon provided a series of foot races being run about thirty yards away, and I had taken a mild interest in it since Panther seemed to be one of the stars. The man was fast. Allegretti and Bama arrived with two six-packs of beer, and in less than fifteen minutes, Professor came with one more. The conversations began.

"Listen to this," Professor almost demanded without looking up from the dog-eared *Newsweek* that he was reading. "Ammunition alone costs the U.S. $200 million a month. In 1965, U.S. forces in Vietnam fired one billion rounds of small arms ammunition, 89 million airborne machine gun rounds, five million rockets, seven million air launched grenades, ten million mortar and artillery shells, and two million air-dropped bombs. Guam-based U.S. Air Force B-52s have been modified to carry 108 bombs of 500 and 750 pounds each and have flown some 200 raids to date at a cost of $500 million." He sipped his beer, then swatted at some creature that had crawled across his foot. "Now get this...are you ready?" He looked at his audience. "Amateur statisticians have computed the cost of killing one—*that's just one* VC—at $375,000!"

He continued to pontificate as Allegretti wrote letters. "Death is one thing we all know will happen. And there is nothing we can do about it." He took a long drag on his beer and then continued. "You could have a three-story-high concrete building built underground, with walls three feet thick," he said as he belched like a bullfrog. "You could be inside, isolated from disease, with the finest doctors and the best drugs on earth inside with you, with every precaution in the world; and if it was your time, you would die." He belched once more as his chin dropped to his chest. "Or, you could walk across a battlefield, naked as a jaybird with an American flag draped across your ying-yang; and if it is *not your time* to die, you won't!"

It was quiet for a moment, until Bama spoke. "I don't know. Something troubles me about your hypoth—" he said, belching loudly, then continued, "your hypothesis. I'm not sure I can go along with it," Bama said after a pause.

Although Professor's head turned quickly toward him, he seemed to require several seconds before he could focus on Bama. "You don't agree with that," he said in a high-pitched voice. "You don't like my theory?"

"Oh, I suppose the theory is okay. What I'm concerned with is that I don't think I have enough 'ying-yang' to drape a flag over." Allegretti immediately burst into laughter, spitting out a mouthful of beer.

Everyone was silent for several minutes. Bama whistled softly. "I wonder if Uncle Sam would consider contracting some of that money out to four handsome—" he paused as he looked at Professor, then continued. "Well, three handsome ones and one barely pretty one," he said as he turned to stare at Professor, "to do some 'freelance' work." We could go freelance and charge, say, $200,000 each. That would save the taxpayers...$175,000 each." He drew from his third bottle. "We could bring in pelts, like wolves. No, we could bring in ears—yeah, ears—$150,000 for a pair of ears. If we killed just ten a month, that would be..." He stared at the trees above as he calculated.

"1.5 million a month," Allegretti interjected.

"Professor, why don't you write it up for consideration, and we will send it to the Pentagon."

The sporting event had turned to football that was being played with a rolled up pair of fatigue pants. I touched two unopened letters that had come in that afternoon: one from Angie and one from Julie. They were beneath the left sleeve of my T-shirt like pieces of candy that I intended to make last all night.

Interest turned to a bayonet-throwing contest. The top flap of a C-ration box had been nailed to a rubber tree, and soldiers were taking turns throwing at it from varying distances. Cheering went from catcalls when any contestants achieved any success at all to riotous laughter for those who missed the tree completely.

"I'm glad they can shoot better than they throw knives," Allegretti said. Then Mueller arrived at the throwing line.

"It just got professional," Bama said as he pulled himself up in his chair.

"He's the one from Chicago, right?" I asked.

Bama nodded as he continued to stare.

"What's his story?" I asked.

"A thug from Chicago. Gang fighting. Robbery. It got bad enough that a judge gave him the choice of going to jail or joining the Army. He supposedly told his honor that Vietnam had to be safer than downtown Chicago and he would take the Vietnam offer."

"Sort of cheapens a college degree. I go to college for four years to get my bachelor's degree and to get into the Army, and he gets in by breaking the law," I said.

We watched as the finalists, five soldiers, took turns at sticking a bayonet into the target in the tree from what looked to be fifteen feet away. The results so far had been mediocre at best. Then Mueller stepped up to the line with a bayonet. He stared at the ground in front of him and then turned his eyes toward the target. He leaned back and took a breath, then sprang forward like a cobra and released the knife, which could not be seen again until it hit the center of the target with a thud. Hoots and yells followed, then it quietened. Mueller walked to the tree and removed the knife. He walked past the original throwing line another five feet and repeated the event with the same results.

It was quiet with a cool breeze. Each of us had consumed four beers to calm our minds and squelch the conversation. I held my last beer to my forehead and stared at the trees above, its branches waving and whispering as if just to me alone.

Professor looked up at me. "Why the somber face, Pearce," He asked. "These days are the good parts of this war, to be enjoyed."

"I can't seem to get past the incident in the village, with Bama, Grayson...and the boy with the rifle and grenade."

Everything became quiet for a minute or two. "What about it?" Bama asked softly, as he worked to stare at me.

"Excuse me?" I asked.

"You said, 'the *boy* with the rifle.' What about him?"

I shrugged my shoulder. "He was just a kid," I said.

"Bullshit," Bama said, pulling himself up in his chair as he continued to speak in his soft Southern drawl. "He was an enemy soldier—a soldier by three distinguishing characteristics. One, he had a grenade. Two, he was in the process of using it against us. And three, he chose to use it against my platoon."

"OK, I get that. But he was so young," I said, my voice rising slightly.

"I have a whole platoon of *boys*. Odds are that some of them lied about their age to get in. Angel Ramos can't be a day older than sixteen." He slurred slightly and finished the contents of the bottle in his hand. He stood and looked at me. "You have your concerns in the wrong place, Lieutenant Pearce. That son of a bitch was out to get my soldiers." He spit on the grounds and cleared his throat. Then, without looking up, he said in a hoarse voice: "Get your mind in the game."

"Easy, Bama, calm—" Allegretti said softly.

"Stay out of it, big guy," Bama said. "We pulled the trigger on *an enemy soldier—a soldier*—and he died. If you aren't willing to do the same thing, you are in the wrong part of the world." He threw the empty bottle against a tree and then turned once more toward me. "If you aren't willing to pull the trigger, you shouldn't pull the paycheck. Make up your mind." He staggered into the darkness and was gone.

The next day, Darnell, Panther, and I went to Alpha Battery for lunch. My head was splitting, and my mood had bottomed out. I was still mad about Bama's reaction the day before. It was good to sit with Flash Gordon and talk. We discussed basketball and sports cars. We talked about movies and actors. We talked about luxurious meals we had eaten.

We were back at The Plantation by 2:00 p.m., and I went to the tent. I was alone there. I read the last two letters I had received from Angie and Julie, for the third time. The perfumes weren't the only things that seemed to be clashing.

His voice came from outside the raised side of the tent behind me. "I was drunk," he said in his heavy Southern drawl. I turned to see Bama.

"We were all pretty well tanked," I said.

His expression was somber. "I don't even remember what I said." He looked like a stray dog, a creature with soulful bloodshot eyes. "Do you remember what I said either?"

I pursed my lips and raised my brows. "I wasn't any better off than you were. I probably spouted off too much too. I'm afraid I don't know what I said." I turned to stare at him.

"Then, we're okay?"

I rose and walked around my bunk and out of the tent.

"We're fine. Some lines were crossed, but that's part of the insanity we have all contracted." He stuck out his hand, and we shook as he pulled us together in a stout embrace.

"I apologize for the unpleasant situation," he said. "I'm sorry. The incident hit all of us. It was unpleasant and my fault."

I pulled away, my face twisted, as if looking deeply into my brain. "What are you talking about? I don't remember anything unpleasant," I said, as a grin came to his face.

He smiled broadly at me. "You know," he said softly, "for an artilleryman, you are okay. Thank you." He turned and walked away.

"Oh, and Bama," I called out to him. "If I lose control of a fire mission sometime in the future and send an artillery round your way, I'm *sure* it will be an accident. And I'm sure I won't remember a thing about it after I sober up."

"Fair enough," he said as he pulled two deep dimples into his cheeks.

I took a long walk around the compound later that day and consumed two cups of coffee. Finally, my head cleared to a point that it was once again somewhat normal.

Twenty-Five

THE CURSE OF BEING A SOLDIER
MARCH 3, 1966

Our choppers landed two days later, southwest from Tay Ninh, and within two hours we had made our way to a point surrounded by thick jungle. A perimeter was set up. I called the artillery unit that would be supporting us, one I had never worked with, and identified seven targets to be fired at throughout the night. We had dinner from little green cans. I took the first hour watch, monitoring the radio. An hour later, Darnell took his turn on the radio.

The call came in around 3:35 a.m. I heard B.J. Tucker's voice. "Wait one—" he said softly, as he scurried to where Charlie-Six was sleeping, leaning against a tree. There was a muffled conversation. Tucker nudged Swizzledick as he passed, waking him. When I joined Charlie-Six, he was on the radio.

"Hold your light on my map." He then returned to speaking to the radio. "We can be ready to move out in twenty minutes. Roger, out." He turned, glanced up at me, and turned to Tucker. "Wake the lieutenants and tell them to be here in five minutes. Oh...tell them to have their platoon sergeants get everyone ready to leave in fifteen minutes." He stopped in front of me. "Where's your map?" I handed it to him, and he marked a small "x" on it and handed it back. "Call Battalion and find out what artillery is in that area where we are going. And when we get there, make contact with them."

We sat in our usual circle with all of the lieutenants, the radio in the center with the speaker on. Charlie-Six made the call, his face stern in the light beam.

The S3, the operations officer from Battalion, was on the radio. "Bravo Company was hit two hours ago. Hit hard. They managed to get to the top of a rocky hill and hold the VC off. We don't know how many were killed, but it was pretty bad. Except for the artillery still dropping rounds at the base of the hill, the shooting has stopped for now, but the company is vulnerable, especially around dawn. Your company is the closest, and I need to have you there quickly. We don't know what will happen. Here's the problem. It's a rough damned mountain. The terrain is steep and rocky, with big friggin' rocks. That's the only thing that saved the company. They made their way up with their wounded and were able to defend themselves. When can you get there? There is still VC activity in the area, but we have choppers flying around the area to keep things calm."

Charlie-Six spoke. "We haven't had a chance to really study the map yet. The terrain looks rough. I'll say we can be there in one hour, two at the latest." He paused. "It's 0400 now. We'll be there by...0530."

"Cut every corner you can. I'll have more info for you as the morning goes on."

Charlie-Six spoke. "Well, you heard it, and you know as much as I do. Professor, you lead, followed by you," he said, pointing at Bama. "And then you, Allegretti. Cold C-rations as we go." He turned once more to Professor. "We leave from where your position is now, in five minutes."

I looked up to see Darnell and Panther ready to go and watching from ten feet away.

Ten minutes after the call, we moved out. There's a factor in the infantry called the "pucker factor" where the butt draws up tight. On a scale of one to ten, I assumed that everyone's was at a level of ten.

The terrain was all it had been billed to be. For the first hour, we were in thick jungle. Rain fell for a while, then stopped, forming a heavy, eerie mist. We began to move uphill. The jungle changed to smaller, twisted scrubby trees. Rocks began to appear in the mix of brush, and the walk became steeper. There were grunts as soldiers stumbled on or slid off the rocks. Dim light came with the first hints of sunrise, and in minutes it grew to the point that we could see. We arrived just as the sun did, at 0600.

We met with the remaining offices of Bravo Company, the unit that had been hit. The commanding officer, a captain named Ziegler, briefed us, his eyes like pool balls. He told us about the ambush, his company's struggle up the rocky hill, and their efforts to retrieve the wounded and carry them as they went. He described the horror of not being able to use his artillery for fear of killing his own soldiers strewn up the hill side, and their final efforts to recover the rest of the wounded.

Charlie-Six laid his hand on Ziegler's shoulder. "What do you need us to do?" Ziegler stared at him. "What if we set up a perimeter and allow your soldiers to rest," Charlie-Six suggested as an afterthought. "What about a landing zone for the choppers?"

"There's not a flat spot anywhere near," came Ziegler's frustrated voice.

"OK, Captain," Charlie-Six said. "Let us take charge from here. You get some rest."

At full sunrise, the medics began to arrive. A very small piece of uneven ground, hardly big enough to allow choppers one at a time to hover over it as they were unloaded, became the busiest spot on the mountain. Field medics arrived with three doctors—captains—all disembarking from the aircrafts as the pilot fought to hold it steady a foot off the ground. Another one arrived with enlisted specialists with cases of supplies and medicines, and it exited the same way. Bama's platoon became stevedores busying themselves with everything from unloading supplies to carrying wounded on stretchers to outgoing aircrafts. Combat medics began to triage the wounded to get them back to established hospitals. Each chopper left with six to eight wounded.

At 0800, the perimeter was hit once more at the bottom of the mountain where the battle the previous day had begun. They were immediately stopped by gunship helicopters swarming over the area like angry hornets, firing into the jungle around the base of the mountain with all that they had and stopping the assault. It did nothing to quell the anxiety or the unbearable level of fear that the enemy still lurked all around us.

A cloudless sky without a hint of a breeze was fiercely hot in the open sunshine, and it stank of drying pools of blood. The area hummed as what seemed to be millions of insects fought with the corpsmen over the bodies. In an hour, the wounded had been evacuated, and the gruesome task of loading the dead became the top priority. When they ran out of stretchers, a large cargo net was brought in and spread on the ground. Bodies were wrapped in ponchos and placed on it, until about half of the dead were carefully arranged there. A cargo master dropped to the ground and worked to pull up four steel rings at the corners and fasten them to a hook on the bottom of the aircraft. During the process, the huge aircraft dipped and bobbed like a Rose Bowl parade float as it fought to remain steady and hover above. The smell of blood, fresh vomit, shit, and tension filled the air. Soldiers began to fill the second net, occasionally screaming and cursing at the overwhelming frustration. In thirty minutes, the last of the bodies were placed on the net, the rings brought together and hung beneath the second Chinook. It lifted and in seconds was gone.

Bama's and Professor's platoons collected rifles and other items in the area halfway down the hill, while constantly watching for snipers in the jungle below as they searched.

At 0145, the remaining uninjured soldiers of B Company fell in with Charlie Company, and we made our way to a camp several hundred meters away. The perimeter of the camp was to be guarded by armored personnel carriers and another company of infantry.

The men of Charlie Company were zombies: tired, frustrated, angry, frightened, and not ashamed occasionally to cry at what they had seen and done. Hot food was brought out, but little was eaten. An engineer company had set up hot showers. There was no levity, no discussions of three-titted women or hot rods. The faces were longer than ever before. There was no talking. And the offering of cold beer did little to change the mood.

I found myself shaking and stuck both hands in my armpits to calm down as I lay on my pack. Stomach acid churned and rose into my mouth to be fought back down.

I recalled a famous painting of a totally drained, emotionless soldier from World War II called *The Thousand Yard Stare*. To a man, this was the look on their faces, which so well captured the condition of their souls.

The next day was spent in quiet time, with an overworked Colonel Chaplain Urrutia busily carrying his word with single individuals and church impromptu services.

The next two days were spent in a task force of six companies, searching the area for the enemy Army that had attacked the company. Viet Cong bodies found scattered through the surrounding jungles were searched by intelligence teams and left where they were.

We found dead campfires, tracks in mud along creeks, cigarette butts, and bits of trash with words in Vietnamese. The only living creatures to be fought now were the ants that climbed over us, mosquitoes, twitter birds that occasionally flitted above us, and our fellow foul-smelling soldiers.

At the end of the next day, God granted us a most welcome trip back to Phuoc Vinh. Sears and Roebuck was the most beautiful sight I had ever seen.

Twenty-Six

SHOTS ON THE ROCKS
MARCH 6, 1966

Two days later at 0800, we were once again underway, moving across an abandoned rubber plantation beneath a blistering, dry, cruel sun. As we walked through tall, thick brown and dead grass, fine dust rose around us, sticking to the sweat on our exposed skin. Professor's platoon had the lead. Charlie-Six and his group, Darnell, Panther, and I were with them. This was open country with few trees, and we stood out to potential snipers like sitting ducks in the event we came in contact with the Viet Cong. By the same token, we were somewhat vulnerable to mortar fire.

Morale sank, and the men began to moan and complain. At around noon, a ridge of large rocks, four to five feet in diameter, began to appear to our front. Bama was behind us to our right, and Allegretti was working an area slightly to our front and left. I paused to find the rocks on the map. I rarely had such clear terrain features as this, and I quickly identified exactly where we were. I turned to Charlie-Six. "I think I should call the artillery battery and ask them to plot these locations beyond the rocks, just in case there's someone's dug in up there. Are you good with that?"

"Yeah," he said, tentatively staring at my map. "Yeah, that's a good idea."

I began. "Destroyer Two-Three, this is Destroyer Niner-Three. Fire mission." I relayed the location and asked that they be marked as potential targets.

Flash's voice came back. "Destroyer Niner-Three, you have three concentrations." He gave me the numbers for each one. These would be pre-recorded data that could be used to hit a target quickly.

"Roger, Two-Three. I will—"

Suddenly a burst of rifle fire came from the rocks. Snipers! We dropped into the concealment of what grass there was. There were screams behind and to my left, followed immediately by one of Professor's men yelling, "Soldiers down!" Our only real hope seemed to be to stay down and out of sight in the tall grass.

Caulk-caulk. Seconds later, two mortars fired from the other side of the wall of rocks in front of us.

The VC had first fired rifles at us while we were walking. As we were unaware of their presence, they had an opportunity to hit some of us. Once the troops were down and not as vulnerable to rifle fire, the VC fired their mortars. Bile rose into my throat, and I swallowed hard as I squeezed the radio handset. Professor's men began to fire toward the rocks even before the mortar rounds hit the ground.

I was immediately on the radio to Destroyer Two-Three, asking him to fire the concentrations—the middle one first. In two minutes, the first two rounds were in the air.

"On the way over," came Flash's voice.

Seconds later came the single word: "Splash." Panther yelled to inform the company.

I took the radio mic. "Destroyer Two-Three, fire for effect. Put eighteen rounds where I need them."

"Roger, wait," came Flash's smooth, calm voice, as if he were at a tea party. I tried to picture the scene that must be going on where he was. I silently stared at the second hand of my watch. It seemed to be slower today, as the company hunkered down.

Flash was back. "On the way, over."

My eyes burned, and I realized that I hadn't blinked for some time.

"Rounds on the way!" I yelled. As I looked around, I realized that my warning had not been needed.

The rounds hit among the rocks over a pattern that covered a major portion of the target, half of them critically close to where the mortar smoke had originally risen. I called for the next sets of rounds to be fired. They hit and all was quiet.

"Good job, Pearce," said Charlie-Six. "Now let's let Allegretti and Bama work it from the two sides.

We caught only glimpses of 3rd Platoon as they darted toward and finally into the rocks on our left. There was a pause, and then a gun fight broke out for several minutes. Then it was totally quiet. A soldier climbed atop one of the rocks in front of us and waved his helmet. All was clear.

The only sound was the ringing in my ears. I heard shouting from behind and to my left, and in two minutes, Professor crashed to the ground beside Charlie-Six. "I have three men dead."

Charlie-Six grimaced. He turned to me. "Fire several more volleys just beyond the rocks, in hopes that I might catch VC gathering there."

Six removed his glasses, threw them into the grass, and pinched the bridge of his nose. I sat silently for several minutes. Finally he muttered one word. "Fuck."

Charlie-Six turned to Swizzledick. "Call in a medevac at—" and I gave him the coordinates.

Charlie-Six continued to sit in the grass.

The radio chirped, and I took the call and then turned to Charlie-Six. "Uh-huh-uh-huh, we'll throw yellow smoke to mark the landing field when you come in."

"We have some intelligence spooks coming in," I said. "Do you want me to tell Allegretti?"

Charlie-Six turned to me. "No, I will," he said as he fumbled for his glasses in the grass and found them. "Get Bama on the horn too." He turned to Swizzledick. "Get Battalion, for me." In a few minutes, he was explaining the situation to his counterpart: "OK. Yes. Sounds good to me."

In minutes he was back on the radio with all three lieutenants. "We have intelligence officers coming in, so tell your men not to touch anything that might be valuable to them in their investigation. I'm almost there. Start forming a ring centered on the area where the mortar was fired earlier. We'll set up there for the night."

The investigators arrived with an interpreter and two specialists. A specialist fifth class began searching three dead VC for information, as two officers immediately blindfolded and isolated each of four VC prisoners. Each, including the dead, was thoroughly searched. Those still alive were bound with cord at their knees, their arms tied behind their backs and a blindfold placed over their eyes. The Butcher tended two VCs for minor wounds.

The collective search of their belongings yielded six rifles—two M16 rifles and the others of an odd assortment. There were rifle shells, eight flashlight batteries, and four hunting knives. The stash included small bags of rice, C-ration coffee packets, and salt; small amounts of a mixture of Vietnamese Piastres and American currency; and pot. One had an American baseball-like card with a picture of Raquel Welch printed on it. Each VC was gagged and isolated among the rocks where one of Allegretti's soldiers stood guard. One by one, they were brought to an even more remote location and interrogated by the spooks through the translator.

After an hour or so, the senior investigators, Captains Jacobs and McCloud, called the company officers together.

"Some of the prisoners are local VC, but some of them are not from this area. Their dialogues are strange to us. They are most likely from North Vietnam. We will get them out of your hair and back to Saigon for detailed analysis. I won't offer to answer questions, as we don't have any definitive answers. Their dead were hit by your artillery and your rifle fire. Sorry I can't tell you more." He looked at each of us. "I—we appreciate what you do. We'll be out of your hair in a few minutes." He paused. "Can you think of anything else we should know?"

Charlie-Six looked at Allegretti. "Do we?" he asked. Allegretti shock his head from right to left. The senior intelligence officer shook hands with each of us, and they were gone, carrying all collected materiel and all prisoners.

"Are we set for the night?" Charlie-Six asked as he looked at each of us. One by one, we nodded yes.

At first light the next morning, we stepped out.

The next three days were uneventful. Days of wading through rivers and swamps as our minds conjured up thoughts of reptiles in the water around us. Days of heat, insects feasting on exposed skin, and unimaginable body odor. Days of wishing for a break, for cold beers instead of the rancid smelling water treated with iodine tablets to make it safe to drink that now filled our canteens. Days of pain in shoulders that supported eighty-pound packs. Days filled with dreams and desires to hear from home. Days spent counting how long it had been since we last kissed girlfriends or wives. We made our way to a large clearing with command tents and two artillery units.

The next morning at dawn, the choppers began to arrive. Even we knew that we would be the last to leave the camp. It boded well that we would be back in camp at Phuoc Vinh by dark. Spirits rose beyond belief as the slips, groups of choppers, began to arrive. As each group left, Charlie Company began to pull the defensive perimeter back around what remained. By 0600, Charlie Company was all that was left. Our ships arrived, and the last batch of Charlie, Bama's platoon, left just before sunset. By dusk, we arrived at The Plantation.

The first day back was dedicated to cleaning equipment and bodies, removing stubborn ticks found during our showers, and attending to minor cuts and scratches. After that, every piece of equipment was brought up to standards. The cooks once more had prepared a meal of roast, French bread, salads, baked potatoes, and blueberry pies.

On the second day, each soldier was told to be ready in thirty minutes for the services. Each man was solemn and soft spoken, as he read letters and magazines and spoke softly to each other.

I watched as Professor and the first sergeant signed the final inventories of the personal effects of the three soldiers killed at the rocks.

I met with Chaplain Colonel Urrutia and Professor, who gave him the names of the soldiers killed at the rocks. He frowned for several seconds and tucked it into a writing pad. Professor shook hands and left to join his platoon, which was preparing for the burial services.

"Shall we go?" Colonel Urrutia asked softly. He asked about me and about Darnell and Panther as we walked. It was quiet with a warm breeze that pulled at the rubber tree branches. We walked roughly a hundred yards into The Plantation to where Darnell and Panther were standing, and then stopped where a small, portable folding lectern stood next to a black leather speaker, its front covered with black mesh and the rest with artificial leather.

We were joined by two specialists who spoke softly to the colonel, showing him how to operate the portable sound system. The colonel tapped the microphone and was rewarded with soft thudding noises. He leaned over and softly said, "Testing." He nodded to the two specialists, and they withdrew to a spot roughly twenty yards away. In front of the podium, ten feet away, three square holes had been dug. They were twenty-four by twenty-four inches wide by eighteen inches deep, and at eighteen inches apart, were perfectly aligned. Each had an M16 rifle in front, stuck bayonet-end first. On top of each rifle was a plain helmet with no cover or lining.

The eeriness of the afternoon with shadows dancing on the ground was heightened by the harsh calls of birds to the south.

I looked up at the distant sound of muffled voices coming from the road in front of the command tent.

It began with muffled commands, then the cadence of marching men and the shuffling sound of boots passing through dead leaves, and grew only slightly louder as they turned twenty feet in front of the podium. "Left face," called a voice softly, and the unit turned to face the podium. Allegretti turned toward the entire company and softly said, "At ease."

Captain Novak came from behind the column, shook hands with Colonel Urrutia, and moved to a spot next to the podium.

Urrutia began, "God has given us this beautiful day to remember and to celebrate the lives of three men, three friends, three soldiers. He gives us the peacefulness of this spot, this garden, in which to remember them. They were good men, good soldiers, and good friends.

"The Bible speaks of war: 'Psalms 144: Blessed *be* the Lord my strength, which teacheth my hands to war, *and* fingers to fight; my goodness, and my fortress; my high tower, and my deliver; my shield, and *he* in whom I trust.'" He paused and looked at the company. "The Bible recognizes what we as soldiers do.

"It also speaks of promise and hope. Psalm 23, perhaps the most comforting in the Bible, has always given us courage and strength to do what is expected of us as Christians, as soldiers. The Lord is my Shepherd; I shall not want."

I suddenly remembered vacation bible school as a child.

He continued as those around him joined in. "Yea, though I walk through the valley of the shadow of death..."

The chaplain stared into a tree above, as if gathering his thoughts.

He turned to where three holes had been dug. "This is a unique ceremony, one I've not seen before, but it is a beautiful way of remembering our friends who have gone to God. This is a special, necessary moment. A moment of closure. In this war, we rarely see those soldiers that perish. They are with us in battle, and then their mortal remains are long gone, back to their homes to be buried there. This is our way of saying goodbye."

Then, without any introduction, he spoke their names, the names of the men killed at the "Rocks": "Corporal Leonard Anderson, Specialist Fourth Class Willard Turner, and Specialist Fourth Class Amos Davidson—all of the 1st Platoon, 1st of the 2nd Infantry."

"Let us pray. Our Father, who art in heaven..." Muffled voices, like water bubbling softly over rocks, were barely heard as they spoke.

He stepped back as three soldiers marched from the back of the formation to a position behind the three rifles and square holes. Each man knelt on one knee behind each rifle, removed the helmet from atop the rifle, and placed it in the hole in front of him. Somewhere behind the group, a bugle sounded taps.

"Enjoy this beautiful day. Enjoy the company of those with you. And enjoy the blessings of the Lord. I will be in the company area all morning if anyone wants to talk to me."

He turned to face Charlie-Six, who moved to the front of the formation and yelled, "Company, attention!" The sound of shuffling boots moving over fallen leaves was followed by "Company, dismissed." They turned and walked silently toward the tent area.

The two remaining soldiers pushed the soil into the holes and packed them with entrenching tools. They brushed leaves over the fresh dirt, retrieved the rifles, and walked back to the tent area.

Twenty-Seven

AN *AMERICAN* FOOTBALL
MARCH 12, 1966

On my eighth birthday, my older brother bought me a cast iron Tonka toy howitzer, six inches long, complete with hard, rubber, cleated tires. As I watched, I remembered that it had most of the characteristics of the real guns now belching flames from their tubes beneath us, hurling explosive rounds to the west of us.

We had received the call at noon the day before that we were to be picked up the next morning and taken to a clearing in Tay Ninh Province. And here we were once more, looking down from the chopper at a village of Army tents and bustling activity racing beneath us. I stared at the world passing below, a panorama of peaceful pastures, small lakes, and the jungle-like broccoli. The choppers that delivered us rocked, tilted, and then finally sat down. Our feet had hardly hit the ground before the aircrafts rose and left.

I joined the other company officers as a captain, who looked like he wasn't old enough to shave, met us and pointed us in the direction of a copse of hardware trees to the west of the clearing. "You'll set up temporarily from roughly that tallest black tree there," he said in a highly officious manner as he pointed with his index, middle, and ring fingers extended and his little finger and thumb wrapped toward his palm, "to where those soldiers are standing." He turned to Charlie-Six and said, "You and I have a meeting with Colonel Barker in—" He glanced at his plastic army green watch. "—fifteen minutes in that middle tent. There," he said, pointing once more with three extended fingers, "where those two captains just walked out. That's Battalion headquarters."

As he left, Bama asked, "What's with the Boy Scout salute?"

Charlie-Six watched him leave, then turned to the four lieutenants. "OK, you heard the man. You know about as much as I do for now." He turned to me. "Go to the battery firing over there, and see if they will be the ones supporting us." He turned to Allegretti. "You are in charge until I get back. Get everyone set up where the captain indicated," he said as he pointed to the assembly area, three fingers extended and locked. We all laughed boisterously as he turned and walked away.

"Professor," Allegretti said, "you take the right third of our new position. Bama, you take the left third, and my platoon will take the center. Make contact with the guys on our right and left, and find out who they are and if they know any more than we do about what is going on."

We broke and moved into our new positions, looking forward to a place where we could drop our damned backpacks.

I couldn't help but grin as Darnell, Panther, and I approached the guns. It was Alpha, 1st of the 5th—my home battery. It was Flash Gordon and Hangover and Captain Turner. As Darnell and the Panther walked toward their friends in the battery, I turned to see Lieutenant "Hangover" watching me, a smile wrapped across the bottom of his face. "My God!" he yelled, "I feel so much safer now that you're here."

"The feeling is mutual," I said as we shook hands.

"I wouldn't be surprised if we finish this shitty little war up by the end of the week with you, Allegretti, and Alabama Wilson—all three, leaning forward in your foxholes."

The conversation ceased as the battery fired once more toward the west, as concussions from the cannons curled clouds of dust that rolled along the ground for fifteen to twenty feet and then upward into the air. The smell of spent cordite drifted over the area. "You've gotta love that smell. That's the smell of peace negotiations," he said as he smiled. "It's good to see you. Let's go see Captain Turner. I'm sure he would appreciate that."

We walked among the guns, now silent, past men wiping the barrels, cleaning aiming devices, and restocking piles of artillery shells. I spoke to them, surprised at how many I remembered. To my right, a section chief was yelling at a soldier about "doing a job right," threatening to "shove a ram rod so far up your ass that you'll sing soprano."

We passed one of the gun sections, and I walked out of my way to pat the howitzer barrel, still warm from the firing. It was Angry Anna. I turned to Hangover. "Seems like a long time since I first saw this."

I looked up to see Flash Gordon come out of the fire direction tent, a breeze tugging at his unkempt mop of orange hair, smiling broadly as he approached. We shook hands, and he nodded at Hangover and said, "Haven't we discussed that we need to be more selective as to whom we allow into the neighborhood?" It was the first time I had seen him since arriving in Vietnam. "What with riff-raff like this being allowed to walk around freely, our women aren't safe, our children aren't safe. My god," he continued, "this man has been living with infantrymen, most likely screwing *water buffaloes!*"

We embraced and shook hands. "Good to see you, Pearce," Flash said in his soft tenor voice as a generous grin came over his face.

"And you," I returned. "I appreciate your help. It's always good to hear your voice on the radio. And it's better to hear your rounds passing overhead when we need them."

"That's what we get paid the big bucks for."

The set of officers was made complete as we were joined by Captain Carlton, smiling and holding up a Melmac glass of ice-cold sweet tea in each hand. "I would have assumed that you wouldn't waste this on a commoner like me," I said as I took the cup.

"Nothing's too good for our men in olive drab, even if it *is* muddy, disgusting, and stinking olive drab." He stared at my filthy fatigue uniform. "My god, man. When was the last time you had a shower and change of clothes?" he said.

"It feels as though it must have been at my christening."

"And to what do we owe this honor?" the captain asked.

"Well, I'm on a mission of mercy. Here's the deal," I said, looking at my watch. "I have to be back for a meeting with Charlie-Six, Captain Novak in a bit." I stared at Captain Turner with pleading eyes. "I noticed that you have a mess tent. What is the chance that my smelly friends and I might bum a hot meal tonight?"

He smiled broadly, held out his hand, and pretended to write on it with an invisible pencil. "And how many will be in your party, sir?"

"There will be five—no, seven, counting Darnell and Panther."

A puzzled look came over his face. "And I assume that you are aware of our dress code?"

"What you see is what you get."

"Of course we can scrounge something up to eat. When will Charlie-Six be through with his briefing?"

"I'm not sure."

"Then let's shoot for 1700?"

"That will work. See you then." He turned to leave. "Oh, and you are required to wash your faces and hands before you return." He smiled, turned, and left.

We all bathed in a small stream, shaved, and changed into clean underwear, most likely killing every form of life in the water. We were back at the battery at sunset. Everyone re-introduced themselves. After all of the "How have you been?" questions were addressed, we made our way through the chow line and then to the shade of the fire direction tent flap. We sat on two rows of 105 ammunition boxes. Charlie-Six turned to Captain Turner. "So, you're the captain closest to the battalion tents. What is your spin on this operation?" It was a meal of fried chicken, corn, mashed potatoes, and cherry cobbler. He chewed as he talked.

"Well," Captain Turner said, "all I hear is that our fearless leader, General Westmoreland, is pushing the concept of search and destroy missions as *the answer* to what we need to be doing. The idea is that we send units out, like ours, to search for Viet Cong. When we find them, we force them to fight. And we destroy them. The new term for that is 'Find, Fix, and Finish.' What a simple concept that is, huh? All you have to do is find the VC, force them to fight, and finish them off."

We all laughed.

Captain Turner took a bite of bread, gestured toward Captain Novak, and continued to talk, chewing between words. "So what's your take on that, Captain Novak?"

Charlie-Six took a drink of iced tea. "We," he pointed at the four lieutenants, including me, "will tell you that it is not going to be easy to do this 'find, fix, and finish' thing. Our experience, with a couple of minor exceptions, tells us that if Charlie doesn't want to be found, he won't. Hiding in a jungle is his specialty, or working the fields in his black shirt and trousers. So if he is found, it is usually because he wants to be found...because he has an ambush set up. The 'fix' bothers me, for the same reason. They set up an ambush, stay there for a short time, and slip away like a breeze. The only way that works is if we can surround them, and that takes a lot of troops. These people can slip through a fish net."

He drew from his Melmac tea mug. "Different Vietnamese armies have been fighting intruders in these jungles since Moses was a lad, and therein lays the rub. We're on their turf, and if they don't want to be found, they probably won't. There are rumors that there are as many as 10,000 Viet Cong between here and the Cambodian border in a space the size of New Hampshire, and we have trouble tying them down. And if we can't do that, the 'fix them' part, the 'finish part' probably won't happen."

"So you think it won't work?" Captain Turner asked.

"First of all, there are men a lot smarter than me directing this show. We know that it will work in some cases. But in my opinion, it's the VC's game, not ours. I think for the most part, if we put enough men in the jungles, there will be cases where we can kick their ass." He paused as the mess sergeant passed quietly behind us delivering ice cubes for our glasses.

"So, back to the philosophy. This is their jungle. Here's the rub, the 'finish' part. The statistics we see in the *Stars and Stripes* newspaper rarely, if ever, show any really lopsided victories. They are normally closer to break-even fights. And, if it becomes a war of attrition, we will have a hard time winning in the long run."

"Yeah," Hanover said, "but the difference is that you have an overwhelming advantage with Captain 'All America' Allegretti on your side. You're safe."

The company officers and I were back at our camp just after dark, sitting on our helmets in our semi-circle. Charlie-Six had just returned from the final briefing of the day. "We have been given an opportunity to make a dent in this war," he began.

"I've been with Colonel Barker, the battalion commander," he said. "We've been selected for a special mission. All hush hush. We are to set up an ambush and hope for a larger unit to hit us. It's our turn to win."

Bama held up a finger, and Charlie-Six turned to him. "Yes—"

"Pardon my interruption, Captain Novak," Bama began in his buttermilk drawl, "But aren't those the words Colonel Travis used to begin his briefing at the Alamo?"

"I can assure you that I wasn't there," Charlie-Six continued.

He paused for a moment as he passed out four crisp, clean maps. Once we folded them, he read the coordinates.

"We will move out at 0430 tomorrow to a position two kilometers from here. The plan is that we will set up an ambush on a trail there and stay for up to two days."

"According to Battalion, B and C Companies will be located close enough to us that they can reach us in fifteen to thirty minutes. They will be located at..." as he rattled off their location. He turned to me. "Pearce, in the morning, we will be supported by Delta Battery." He paused a moment.

"Here is the beauty of this plan. It took around 100 chopper flights, according to Captain 'Glued Fingers,' over the past twenty-four hours to get everyone into this location. In two days, everyone except us will fly out in 100 helicopters. They will have light loads with their passengers sitting on the outside edge of the seats to make it look like all seats are occupied. There were 100 choppers in. There will be 100 choppers out. It will give the impression that everyone who came in has left, and they will get back to normal, walking this trail or going to where we are now, which will be abandoned."

He held up his map. "This trail," he said as he traced a black line on the map with his black forefinger nail, "is where we will set up. Intelligence says that it is well used by the VC for hauling goods in from Cambodia. The hope—by the command group, at least—is that we will be lucky enough to ambush them in that activity." His face was jubilant, like Washington's might have been when his rowboat crunched down in the gravel on the far side of the Delaware.

"Intelligence has strong reasons to believe—their words exactly—that we might be able to ambush as high as a regiment size element, maybe larger." He scanned our faces once more.

"If we do, Alpha and Bravo companies will come in for the fight. We have additional artillery, and the Air Force is in on this."

As I sat there, I thought I felt my rear end suck up a foot of my trouser material. "Be still, my heart," I thought, and from the looks on the other faces, I was not alone.

After a long pause, Bama raised his hand. "So we're gonna be the bait."

Six frowned. "No, no, no. We are going to be a well-deployed infantry company with excess ammunition and mines, with every element of surprise in our favor, positioned to ambush a larger unit and hold it while other units close in on our position to help finish them."

After pausing, Bama said, "So we're going to be the bait!"

Six ignored him. "We will be heavily loaded with Claymore mines, one per man, and will wait, adhering to strict no radio traffic rules, with exceptions for purely tactical support, for two nights. Alpha Company will be located a half a mile away in another area in case we need help. Bravo will be between us and the river. If we get hit, the two of them can be there in thirty minutes." I wanted to point out that if we got hit by a regiment and didn't have help for thirty minutes, they could probably save the taxpayers some money and not come at all. I didn't.

"As usual, there'll be no letters or identifying papers on you. If you have them, you can send them back to the company with the clerk.

"From the time we get there to the time we leave, no one talks unless we have a tactical reason for doing so."

He picked up an empty C-ration box and took a grease pencil from his pocket. He began to draw. "This is the trail you see at the coordinates I gave you. We will set up in a football-shaped formation on either side of the trail."

He paused for several seconds and then said, "An *American*-shaped football."
He took a moment to draw a curved line on either side of the trail, and he
held it up for us to see. "Bama, you will set up on the northeast end of this
football. Allegretti, you will on the southwest end. And Professor, you will be
in reserve on either side of the rest of the football. We will meet back here in
one hour. That will give you time to get your maps folded and study
them." He turned to me. "And Pearce," he said, "you look at the map and
determine where we want the rounds to fall if we need them.

"And the same rules apply. And don't forget...if anyone has perfumed
letters, put them in the mail bag back to camp tonight. They will be there
when you get back."

Bama interrupted. "Sir, the only person here who needs to hear this part
of the briefing is Pearce. He has two perfume users! The rest of us old married
farts haven't received a perfumed letter since college."

As the laughter subsided, Charlie-Six continued. "And there are to be no
cooked C-rations until we are back in camp, and bury the cans to cover the
smell. Are there any questions?" He glanced at each of us. There were none.

"Wherever I can serve my country best," Bama said as he picked up his
helmet and rose. "That's where I want to be."

As the meeting broke up, Professor ambled over to where I stood. "Care
for my opinion?"

"Company with you I always cherish."

Professor lit up a cigarette, reared his head back, and blew out a string of
smoke. "I'm afraid he might be right," he said finally.

"Who's right?"

"Bama is, about 'Find, Fix, and Finish.'" I think there should be one more
'F' word." He turned and walked away.

Everything that needed to be done had been done. C-rations had been stuffed in combat socks and tied to our packs, ammunition clips had been refilled, and we had spent thirty minutes setting up target locations around tomorrow's position. I had finalized every firing point: every stream bed, trail intersection, and hill. We had discussed the operation and our roles together for the last time. These would only be fired in the event we were hit.

Panther, Darnell, and I met beneath a tree with black bark a yard in diameter. I imagined that if I could climb it, I might be among the stars. We talked a while, and Panther left to visit with Dieters. I removed my boots and leaned against the trunk of the tree in the deepening shade as fairy-like shadows danced in the final stages of sunset.

Twenty feet away, I watched Swizzledick talking softly to B.J. Tucker and the Butcher, waving his arms like Leonard Bernstein. He was interrupted periodically by soft laughter.

Darnell and I sat in silence. He was shaving the layers of bark away from a piece of tree branch with a small knife, with no apparent purpose other than just taking his mind off of what tomorrow might hold. He reached into his blouse pocket and pulled out a stack of pictures, on which he had already written "Hold for Darnell," and then finished his beer. He rolled onto his side to face me, watching as I thumbed through the snapshots. "Wow, she's growing up," I said, turning to a picture of his daughter. He grunted. There was no mischief in his eyes, no music in his voice. I looked through the rest and handed them back. He placed them in his pocket as I leaned back against the tree trunk.

It was quiet for several minutes before he spoke. "Have I ever told you about my bridge?" There was a hint of melancholy, of aching in his voice.

"You have mentioned it. But to clarify, you *own* a bridge?" I asked, without opening my eyes.

"No, I don't own it, but it's still my bridge. When I was growing up, I spent so much time there that everyone called it Darcy's Bridge."

"I see," I replied.

"Well, there is this old bridge—"

I interrupted. "You didn't ask me if I *wanted to hear about* it. You just asked me if you had ever told me about it." He threw a twig and hit my side.

"Do you want to hear about it or not?" he asked, disgustedly.

I rolled slightly, stretched and crossed my legs, opened one eye, and replied, "I am your captive audience. Please, tell me about your bridge."

Somewhere to the west, far away, something screeched—a bird or an animal. Darnell stared toward the source of the sound and then resumed the wonderful task of doing nothing.

After several minutes, he sat perfectly still, staring at the curled rolls of white shavings in his lap. Then he turned his eyes to me and spoke. "There's this old bridge, seventy or eighty-years-old, about three miles from where I grew up, not too far from our farm. It's *my bridge*," he said as he smiled broadly. "Pretty much everyone in town calls it my bridge. I spent so much time there, that the people of the area just assumed that that was where I would be...on it or under it or jumping off of it. The Cottonwood River runs beneath it, pushing cool air up onto the bridge. It's a pretty place, a good spot for catching catfish." He shook his head, pursed his lips, and brushed the chips from his lap.

"As kids, we pretended to be Union soldiers, or Brits, or whatever struck us at the time. We'd cut up broom sticks into ten-inch-long pieces, paint them red, bind them together with electrical tape, drill holes in the end of each one, and push pieces of string into the ends for fuses. These were our 'explosives.'" A wide grin appeared on his broad face, and he shook his head slightly. "Then we would spend hours crawling through the infrastructure beneath the surface of the bridge, stuffing them into crevices." He smiled once more with his lopsided smile and folded the knife, stuffing it into his pack.

"We fished from there—big catfish, some carp, some perch."

He lapsed into silence once more, brushing through the pile of wood chips between his boots. "It was three years ago today. That's when I asked Amanda to marry me."

"Congratulations," I said softly, realizing how stupid I must have sounded.

"We were at my bridge once more. Snow was falling that night, just enough to cover the pavement. We'd seen a movie that night, *Love With the Proper Stranger*, a real mushy one. And then we went to the center of the bridge. I shuffled my feet together and drew a large heart, stepped to the center, and dropped to one knee. Her laughter was always like angels singing. I pulled the ring from my Levi watch pocket—it was a ring that had belonged to my grandmother—and held it up to her. In two steps, she was in front of me, kneeling as I was."

"Will you?" was all I asked.

"You know that I will. I love you, Darcy Darnell."

"Well, you romantically inclined old dog," I said with a smile.

"I nearly split my britches when she said that," he said. And then I watched as the smile left. He pulled the knife back out, retrieved the stick, and began shaving it once more, apparently unaware that I had even commented.

After several minutes of silence, he asked, "*Love With a Proper Stranger?*" It took a moment before I realized what he was asking, and then I grinned. "Sorry, that's not the song. Better luck next time. And I don't want a cigarette either."

Twenty-Eight

THE OVERWHELMING SOUND OF EAR-RINGING SILENCE
MARCH 14, 1966

The silence could be felt, like smoke wrapped around us, before dawn the following morning. I stood next to Charlie-Six, the radio rats, and Professor, ten yards inside the ominous dark wall of the jungle with its decomposing odors and the smell of mulch. Panther and the Butcher stood a short distance away in the pre-dawn light.

Charlie-Six looked at Professor. "Is the ambush team ready?" he asked in a hoarse whisper.

"As ready as they'll ever be," Professor replied in the same voice as he pointed to his first squad, ten men twenty feet away. They were in positions that allowed them to see, but not to be seen from the clearing that we had occupied the day before. They were nearly invisible as they lay behind logs and in hastily created fox holes, positions that allowed them to look onto the clearing we had occupied.

Six turned to me. "And Darnell?"

"He is already with Professor's ambush team." I nodded my head toward where he knelt.

Charlie-Six turned to Professor. "Dance" was all he said in the same soft voice.

Professor motioned for his remaining three squads to move out away from the clearing and further into the jungle, pumping his left arm, bent at the elbow, like someone pulling the emergency cord on a bus. From several yards away, I watched as each man passed. Each had a half-inch piece of white tape on the back of his helmet, a patch worn by everyone in the company to make it easier for each man to see the soldier in front of him as they moved toward their destination in the dim light. Each face was covered with black and olive drab camouflage makeup. There were no smiles. There were no jokes, no "your wife is fine" comments.

Once 1st Platoon had passed, Charlie-Six looked at his watch and then motioned for the rest of us to follow, and the command group fell in line behind Professor's last man. I looked back to see Bama's platoon, poised to join the column as they fell in behind us.

The sounds were those of insects chirping softly around us, the shuffling of boots, and the occasional grunts of soldiers stumbling over unseen roots and low branches as we worked our way into the dense foliage.

Fluorescent, citrus-colored, pre-dawn light gradually appeared, as the sun seemed to squeeze through the foliage and replace the near total darkness of the jungle.

At 0600, we stopped as Charlie-Six confirmed his location. Heavy drops of dew fell on giant, predominantly mahogany trees, tapping softly just above us.

In thirty minutes, we reached our destination: a straight trail, prominent enough to indicate that it was well-used, passed through the jungle. Along one side of it, Bama's platoon began to form a curve, which would be an arc along the west side of the trail when finished. Allegretti did the same on the east side. When two squads met, it formed a football—an American football—roughly forty yards from top to bottom. Both lieutenants quickly set up listening posts, and Claymore mines were positioned for protection. Six called Bama twenty minutes after our arrival. "We're here, my listening posts are out, and I have my Claymore mines in place—thirty of them." In another ten minutes, Six called Bama. "Are you set?" he asked softly.

"Set and ready," Bama responded in a soft voice. "Bring 'em."

Each side of the football was in place.

Professor's platoon came next and entered to the center of the football, a second layer to serve as a backup.

In forty-five minutes, everyone was set. In addition to the machine guns, Claymore mines lined the entire perimeter. Listening posts were in place. Darnell and I had coordinated artillery concentration points with a battery to our north on the previous day. We had nothing to do but wait, observing total silence.

Occasionally, someone would rise along the perimeter and disappear into the underbrush, then return to his stitch in the football, fastening his trousers.

At 0700, I squeezed the radio control button twice, causing the rushing noise to stop temporarily. In less than a minute, Darnell did the same thing at the ambush site. These were a predefined set of signals for telling each other that we were "open for business."

And then, the real enemy arrived—silence and total boredom. We listened through the morning as choppers arrived at the main campsite to pick up tents, tables, equipment, supplies, and finally, the personnel. By 1300, the site had been abandoned and everything was gone. The same number of choppers left that had arrived two days earlier, to give the impression that everyone had left.

I opened a small can of crackers, peanut butter, and jelly, all with my trusty Army P-38 can opener. As I ate, I watched a two-and-a-half-inch black scorpion approaching my boot. I spread the peanut butter over both crackers and laid one on my right leg and one on my left. He was as still as a plastic bug. I ate the right leg cracker first in one bite and chewed slowly, actually enjoying the sweet grape flavor, as I watched his every move. He turned away, paused, and turned back. For a second I couldn't see him, and then he reappeared on the side of my boot and moved over my laces to my trousers. I bit into the second cracker. The insect had reached my pant leg and stood staring, its stinger still curled, his wide pinchers opened. He stopped, turning to his right and left. He sat perfectly still as I chewed my breakfast. When he reached just below the knee, I smashed him against the stiff material of my fatigues with my canteen. I scooped out a hole in the loose earth with the cracker can, the size of a snuff can, and placed the hapless creature inside. I bent the lid down, and, using the peanut butter can, I dug a hole and buried it along with the other two cans. I made the tasks of breakfast and burial last for fifteen minutes.

I cleaned my Zippo cigarette lighter, trimmed the wick, and spun the wheel to check the flint. I hadn't started smoking, but I enjoyed carrying it to start the fires for my coffee...coffee that I wouldn't be allowed to drink for the next two days. I opened the four-pack of C-ration Winston cigarettes and pulled one out. I put it between my lips. The tobacco had a soothing smell to it.

I found a green branch that had fallen from a tree. I took out my pocket knife and began carving notches. Panther was ten feet away leaning against a stump. I watched as he wrapped a filthy handkerchief around his finger, wet it on his tongue, and began to rub it vigorously against a spot on his radio.

Charlie-Six had set up his post fifteen feet away, with his radio operators and the medic within ten feet of him. Even Swizzledick was quiet.

The call came just before 1000 hours the next morning. I jumped at the three short pauses in the radio signal and immediately sat up. Darnell was calling. Panther handed me the receiver. I pressed the button twice. At the same time, a call came to Charlie-Six, and I turned to see B.J. Tucker handing him the handset.

"Go," I said softly.

"We have activity," Darnell said on his borrowed radio. It was a terse way of saying that there were VC soldiers on yesterday's campgrounds. "Ten to fifteen by my count," Darnell said. "There may be more in the tree line beyond. They are armed. At least three of them have M16s, and several are in uniforms of some sort. The rest are in black. We need to fire Concentration D10," Darnell said, his voice barely above a whisper. "Then fire the other two."

Six was kneeling next to me as he spoke softly.

"The Tiger Patrol has company. About fifteen people. Viet Cong with weapons. Some are in uniform."

"I got the same message," I said.

"Call it in. This is your specialty," he whispered to me.

As I began the mission, Darnell, Flash, and I were on the same radio frequency and could carry on a three-way conversation. Flash's voice came on. I gave him the information for the fire mission.

Within two minutes, Flash was on his radio once more. "Splash," was all that he said, a code that the rounds would hit at the location I had requested in seconds. Darnell's radio was on the same frequency. "I copy, Niner-Three," he said.

The rounds exploded with immense intensity, like a thunderstorm. And the infantry Tiger team joined in with rifle fire, dropping the scroungers where they stood. Some ran, only to be caught by the firing soldiers and the next two volleys of artillery fire.

Darnell was back on the radio. "Add 200, left 200, fire for effect."

Flash responded with the corrections, and rounds fell once more. I could picture the survivors of the first firings as they moved for the jungle beyond the trash pile. Darnell was following their movements with additional rounds. In fifteen minutes and one more set of rounds, he was finished.

Finally the firing stopped: "Destroyer Two-Three, end of mission."

Charlie-Six was on his radio to the Tiger Patrol. "Uh-huh-uh-huh. Great work. Let's sit tight for an hour and see what happens."

The hour passed in total silence. Six made the call to the ambush team. "Come on in. We are sending someone out to meet you."

Darnell's excited voice came over his radio as a tinny hoarse whisper. "We got every one of them...at least every one of them we could see. So I guess there aren't any more. If there are, they didn't join in the shooting," he said excitedly.

I keyed my mic. "Roger. Good shooting," I acknowledged. "Out." In thirty minutes, the Tiger Team joined the rest of the company in the football. Darnell's adrenaline had maxed out. He described what had happened in a hoarse whisper, drawing a map in the dirt as he described every detail to Panther and me.

"Good job, Darnell. Now that you have it down pat, I may just retire," I said finally. "Get some rest. I'll wake you in an hour."

Since Professor's platoon was split in half on either side of where I sat, Professor sat only yards away from me. Charlie-Six and his radio operators were at the same location. All was quiet...and somber.

If the morning had seemed long, the afternoon was unbearable. All I could think of was that fifteen humans that had been alive this morning were not now. I wondered if they were really soldiers, or simply scroungers going through the trash that we had left behind. Finally I decided: they had all had weapons, so they were soldiers. So case closed. I couldn't talk to anyone about it.

More suspense and boredom.

I tried to name all of the John Wayne movies I had seen. I tried to recall a favorite poem that I had learned in Mrs. Jernigan's eleventh grade literature class. I stumbled over the words until finally they came. *Invictus:*

"Out of the night that covers me,

Black as the pit from pole to pole,

I thank whatever gods may be

For my unconquerable soul."

Then I racked my brain to remember the author...Henrey...Herney. Finally it came: Earnest Henley. Then I racked my brain to determine why such information was important to me!

I struggled to recall the villain's name in every James Bond movie I had seen. I cleaned my lighter again and searched my mind for the names of the Seven Dwarfs, then the members of the 1965 World Series team. Nothing worked.

Hours went by, and although the sun had not been seen all day through the canopy above, it finally set. I was thankful for the darkness as it came, because I imagined everyone looking at me to see how I was handling the amazing success of the morning.

I took the radio watch at midnight.

Panther relieved me at the radio at 0200 hours. I was asleep in minutes.

Except for an occasional call from a bird in the distance, the day began to arrive, noiseless, with gray light beginning to show on the company. I mixed a brown envelope with stenciled letters indicating coffee with tepid water from my canteen and stirred it with my plastic spoon. I took one sip, shuddered, and poured the rest onto the ground and watched it seep into the soil. There was an instant, a minor pang of regret, as I realized that I could have used it for boot polish.

I thought of Angie. I thought of Julie.

Caulk-caulk-caulk-caulk-caulk. The machine gun seemed to shake the entire area, and I felt my heart rate double. *Caulk-caulk-caulk-caulk-caulk.* Soldiers along each side of the northern boundary joined in, firing into the wilderness for several minutes, and then it was quiet. I called Flash, and in minutes his artillery was poised to fire on targets I had coordinated the previous night, well beyond where the ambush had occurred.

Then he looked at me. "Let's go," he whispered, and he was up following the trail, the center lace of the football, to the point from which the firing had occurred. The world was perfectly still.

Two frightened, excited, young machine gunners looked up as we approached. One was Dieters. He looked at me with soulful eyes and tentatively pointed down the trail, as if to say, "Look what I did," and at the same time asking, "Was that alright?"

Fifteen minutes later, Bama and ten men from his platoon had moved to a position on either side of the trail to investigate the shooting. Once there, they had set up outposts. I looked up to see him and his radio operator as they silently appeared as wisps of green grass along the trail.

"They're out there about fifteen yards."

I glanced once more at Dieters, who was watching me, his face stretched like a rubber mask. He immediately looked down at the sites of his machine gun and began rubbing the rear site with his thumbnail once more. I glanced at the other machine gunner. It was Mueller, the Chicago tough guy.

"How many?" Charlie-Six asked Bama.

"So far we have found six along the trail. Two more tried to run away. Made it to some underbrush before we got them. Total of eight," he answered.

"In uniform?"

"Several were in military uniforms—two or three. The rest were in black pajamas."

"Weapons?" Charlie-Six asked.

"Yes, sir, they all had rifles," Bama replied. "They did. They *definitely* did."

"Did they get any shots off?"

"Hell no," Bama said as he turned to Dieters and Mueller. "These two guys saw to that."

"No, sir. They never knew what hit them," Mueller agreed as he scratched at a spot on the machine gun barrel that had probably been there for some time, but now seemed to demand his total attention. His eyes were wide.

"There were eight of them killed that we know of. Some may have gotten away," Bama said. "There was not much on them. Some cigarettes, some photos, a couple of letters, a few pocket knives, and some dried fruit. Each of them had small black bags of C-rations—*U.S. C-rations* with openers—and a handful of bullets for each weapon." He pointed at small stacks of the items as he spoke. "And there is the stack of weapons. One of them was obviously taken from an American at some time." He pointed at an M16. "I have one squad farther up the trail looking for anything else."

Panther and I followed Charlie-Six along the trail to where the eight bodies lay at odd angles on either side, each bleeding out into black puddles of motor oil-like blood. Their faces had already begun to stretch and swell in the heat. One had been hit in the face. I estimated them to be in their late teens to early twenties. Charlie-Six turned to stare into the jungle to the east. "Drag the bodies over behind that tree," he said to two infantrymen, "so they can't be seen by anyone approaching us on this trail. Cover them with leaves. Check their pockets once more for papers, or anything else."

"Are you ready for artillery?" Charlie-Six asked, turning to me first and then Bama.

"Where do you think it would do the most good?" Bama asked.

I held the map in front of Charlie-Six and Bama, and I pointed out six small black x's in a semi-circle, which were well beyond where the bodies lay. I said, "If what you just shot up was the advanced party for a bigger unit, I recommend these six targets. I've already called them in. They're waiting for you to give me the word. Your call."

Six turned to Bama. "Get your men back inside the football. Pearce, execute your plan. You're right. Assuming this was the advanced party, there might be a larger unit out there. Let's mess up their day if they are. It's not costing us anything."

He looked at me and then Bama. "I want you to let me know the second every man is inside the line." He turned to me. "After that, I want balls in the air in two minutes." He turned to Bama and said, "Get your men in."

In ten minutes, everyone was accounted for and inside our lines.

Charlie-Six turned to me and said, "Do it." We returned to the spot where the machine gun was. Mueller and Dieters had been replaced by two other gunners.

The first six rounds hit. Firing continued for ten minutes by three more volleys.

Six held a meeting with the platoon leaders thirty minutes later.

"First of all, good work. Bama, you and your platoon were superb. And Pearce, the same to you and your crew. You all did a great job. And compliment those who were not directly in the same thing."

"Yeah," Allegretti joined in, patting my back. "You did great for a country boy."

"OK, then," Charlie-Six said. "Bama, Country, good work. Make sure your men know what I said."

I made a mental note to congratulate Darnell and Panther.

The second search by Bama's men was more thorough. They found nothing new.

Charlie-Six continued as he haplessly attempted to wipe his smeared glasses. "I want everyone in the company to know that I am proud of them. No one panicked. No one fired unnecessary shots. I want everyone to know that they are damned tough, seasoned soldiers.

"Battalion thinks that we've pretty well lost any element of surprise with the activity a while ago," Charlie-Six said. "We are to stay here tonight." He turned to me. "I want lots of artillery. Pick it out and fire it. I don't need to approve it. We are to leave at 0600 tomorrow morning. We need to redouble your efforts until then. Stack all the trash and burn it in the morning. Pick up all of the brass shells from the ambush. Nothing *remotely* useful to the Viet Cong gets left."

Twenty-Nine

RAISING CANE
MARCH 17, 1966

Gray, somber clouds formed a low ceiling the next morning as Allegretti's platoon led us from the football. We moved northeast, eerily quiet in the gray light with the feel of a scene from a Hitchcock movie. The command group followed after his platoon, then Bama, and then Professor.

Within forty-five minutes, spirits lifted as we crossed a clear stream, knee-deep and fifteen feet wide, flowing over a flat rock bottom, and sparkling with silver flecks of sun on the surface. We were stopped there for thirty minutes, taking turns standing guard while everyone took the opportunity to wash their bodies. A flock of birds rose to the treetops, fussing at having been disturbed, and a gentle breeze welcomed us as we left the jungle into a magnificent dawn beneath a pure azure sky. We skirted a clearing onto an open plain of waist-high grass. It was good to be moving, and the breeze seemed to cleanse our thoughts, replacing the past two days and what had happened there with hope and promise.

In spite of the fact that we still carried the Claymore mines—approximately one per man—and excess ammunition, weight we would have preferred to be without, our spirits rose. The haggard faces lifted with the cool morning air.

In an hour, the terrain began to rise slightly into elephant grass, becoming thicker and beginning to dominate the plain. As we moved, it became taller so that in three more kilometers, it was over ten feet high in every direction. The company's eight machetes were drawn, and Allegretti's men began to hack away at a trail.

Six called a stop, and after fifteen minutes, the three platoon leaders and myself dropped beside him.

"It's like cutting through leather straps," Bama was explaining to Charlie-Six as we stopped. "It's going to be slow."

We paused to study the map, which suggested no other way to get to Battalion than through the pale green vegetation shown on the map. Gnat-like insects had come from nowhere, buzzing frantically at the feasts they had found, and repellent was quickly applied.

"It's as wide as it is long, and there doesn't appear to be any other way to get to our location than to go through it. At the rate we're going, it's going to take us into the night to get through, and God only knows what shape we'll be in." I wasn't sure whether he was asking us for advice or giving us a lesson in map reading. He exhaled deeply. "The shortest route looks to be a thousand meters, or more. Let's keep working it."

"And it's getting hotter by the minute with no sign of relief. What do you think?" Charlie-Six asked, staring at Allegretti.

"Like you said, hack away," Allegretti said. "Seems to be all we can do."

Charlie-Six took a call from Battalion, wanting our status.

"We're slowing down. We are in the heart of this cane break. The men are starting to show signs of heat problems. There is not a breeze here."

"What is your expected time of arrival? Over."

"Hard to say. This is going slowly, over," Charlie-Six returned.

"Can we get choppers in to pick you up? Over." asked the voice.

"It would be chancy. This grass is as dry as gunpowder, and if we set it on fire, it might fry half my company, over."

"OK," said the voice over the radio, "it's your call. Keep us posted on your progress. Out."

Allegretti's platoon stepped up. He watched as the two men of his platoon took turns hacking at the wall with the machetes. There was no banter, no smart comments. The cane wall ahead of us had taken that all away.

Allegretti screamed. "No more," he said as he stood like a crazed animal, his nostrils flaring. "No more. No damned more!" He glanced at me, his eyes rimmed in red and his face covered in dust.

He looked back at one of his soldiers. "Give me your Claymore." The young man jumped up, removed the sling from around his neck, and carried it to Allegretti. Allegretti turned to Charlie-Six. "You might not want to see this. But if you do, I suggest that we concoct some cock-n-bull story about snipers in the cane breaks." Charlie-Six stared at him, tugging at his ear lobe, as Allegretti planted the Claymore mine facing the wall. He fed out the line, yelling as he did: "Fucking jungles, fucking cane, fucking war." He stopped, dropped to one knee, and stuck the mine into the ground facing the wall to his front. "Stand back!" he yelled, as everyone within fifty feet fell back, not needing to be asked twice. He twisted the plunger. The explosion was horrendous in the confine of the cane. He looked at his work, not as clean as removing it with the machetes, but there was now an opening before us in the wall of cane. Dust rose in the silence that followed, and he walked ten yards to the end of the newly created forward edge of the break. He walked back to his point man, pointed at the Claymore on the man's hip, and said, "You do it, Gilmore." The soldier grinned broadly, laid down his rifle, and ran to the new edge.

Allegretti turned to Charlie-Six, his face covered with sweat and dirt and frustration.

"Lieutenant Allegretti," Charlie-Six called out, motioning to a spot away from the lead soldiers. "Come here, please." Allegretti joined him.

"There are no snipers, and we both know it." Allegretti's eye's flashed, and his face filled with anger.

"You know you didn't hear snipers. You know there are no snipers. Don't you." Allegretti removed his T-shirt and began to wipe sweat from his torso. He turned to face Charlie-Six, his face a mask of defiance.

"What you heard, Lieutenant, were enemy mortars. I suggest we use Claymores to destroy them." Allegretti turned to see the broadest grin he had ever seen on the Captain's face. He ran to where his troops sat.

"Don't just sit there!" he yelled, "Didn't you hear those mortars?"

Smiles are contagious. Charlie-Six smiled. "Give it a try," he said finally, smiling broadly. He gestured toward the end of the trail. "I think I heard the sound of more mortars coming from in there."

"Specialist Jackson, Specialist Ramirez, take out those mortars." Both men grinned and stepped up to the edge of the cane. By now everyone's face was covered with towels, dirty T-shirts, or whatever else could be found.

In a minute, another Claymore was set off, followed by another Claymore two minutes later.

Allegretti turned once more to the faces of his platoon. "Sergeant Wilson, you're up. Then you, Turner, and you, Benavidez."

Charlie-Six looked up to see a helicopter approaching above them. "Charlie-Six, this is Danger Thirty-Six. What's happening down there? Over." It was the voice of the battalion S3, the operations officer, passing above and to the east in a chopper.

"Danger Thirty-Six, we've been fighting this cane for two hours now."

"Don't you have machetes?" came S3's voice.

"It must be 120 degrees down here and dusty...and alive with mosquitoes. We tried machetes, but they are virtually worthless against this shit, and my men are fading fast. Would it do any good if I told you that we are receiving mortar fire?"

The chopper hovered above. The voice came back. "Mortar fire, you said?" the Major asked.

"Yes, sir. That's what it sounded like to us."

"Well, then," came the voice, literally from above. "I suggest that you protect yourself with any weapons at your disposal. Carry on." The chopper banked and flew away.

In forty-five more minutes, the cane became smaller. In another fifteen, there was a horizon. Grass covered the slope to a stream, and beyond that were the tents of Battalion. They washed and drank from the flowing water. Charlie Company formed into a combat column and moved into the clearing.

We approached the battalion perimeter in early evening. I could make out Lieutenant Colonel Urrutia, the Chaplain. He had a long scarf around his shoulders and his arms up into the air. He shouted, "Follow me, and I will take to you to a land of milk and honey!"

Ten minutes later, we surrounded a tarp filled with ice and bottled beer. "Two bottles per man!" shouted one of the cooks as they handed out the frigid bottles of "33" beer.

"One hell of a lot better than milk and honey," I thought, as I received my beers from the soldiers passing them out. "Thank you, Lord. Thank you, Lord!"

On the first day back in camp, Charlie-Six held a meeting. There were to be three more days in the field...days that, as it turned out, were wonderfully uneventful, consisting of sorties in the area to check out suspicious sightings by chopper pilots. Our legs, cut and bruised by the cane, healed, as did our spirits.

At 4:30 on the evening of the fourth day, in a brief meeting, Charlie-Six gave the word. "We have one more site to visit tomorrow. That's the bad news. The good news is that we will be back in Phuoc Vinh and The Plantation by 1500 tomorrow. Are there any questions or comments?"

"A comment," I said.

"Shoot," Charlie-Six said.

"Well, I may not be able to join the group tomorrow." All eyes turned to me. "General 'Hammer' has invited me to join him in Saigon for a weekend of drinking, dining, and whoring." Everyone laughed.

"Clarify something for me," Bama said, a wry grin forming. "This whoring...will there be women involved, or is it just you and the General?"

Thirty

TALIA MAREAU LIVES!
MARCH 21, 1966

The night was clear, and the stars shone above for a change. Part of my reconnaissance training at Fort Sill had included many hours studying the stars and constellations and their usefulness in surveying. The irony was that the majority of my training had been in the Northern Hemisphere, and all of the stars above me were Southern. I thought of my life, of why I was here. I thought of dying. I thought of living and then of Julie and Angie. And finally, I relaxed and listened to the constant conversation of the "radio rats," the soldiers now sitting around the dying embers of a small fire.

"Well, I can top that," Darnell said. "There's this bridge not far from my home in Kansas. Me and this friend of mine and his girlfriend were there late one evening just before dark, drinking beer. So he was sittin' on his Harley, talking to me, and she comes right over and straddles him so that her back was toward the handlebars on the bike. And she is naked as a jaybird. Boobs out to here," he said, holding his spread, cupped hands toward him. "Well, she starts to squirm and twist, and they pick at each other, and the first thing I know, they're getting it on. He pushes the throttle, and they roar away humping like crazy."

The subject turned to a discussion of a strong community of wealthy French landowners near the Michelin Plantation, not far from where we were, with beautiful trees, swimming pools, and golf courses. They were discussing the possibility of "living like that" when a radio call came in.

Swizzledick took the radio call. "Charlie-Six," he said.

There were three pauses in the rushing noise of the radio speaker. It was an "unofficial code" from his counterpart at Battalion headquarters, Keaton Fullingham, whom Swizzledick had known since their communications training days.

He turned and stared at the receiver, then pressed the *send* key on his handset. "This is Charlie-Six, over," he said, almost in a whisper.

Both operators knew that they could get into trouble for violating radio communications protocol and the misuse of the radios, but this was their means of gossiping. Such infractions would most likely be considered minor since there was nothing going on, yet both knew that they had to do it. For the soldiers of the command group, this was vitally critical, but totally unauthorized, gossip.

"It's true," whispered the soft voice in response. It was the voice of Keaton Fullingham, Swizzledick's confidant at Battalion that he often communicated with over this network.

"What's true? Over," Swizzledick responded, maintaining some semblance of protocol in case someone was listening in.

"Charlie-Six, are you prepared to take a message? Over," asked Fullingham.

"Wait one minute," Swizzledick said as he quickly snapped his fingers at B.J. Tucker and scribbled in the air with an imaginary pencil. Tucker grabbed a pen from his pocket, tore the top from a C-ration box, and handed it to him. All eyes were on Swizzledick, his mouth hanging open. "Send your message," he said softly.

"The message is: thirty-eight-twenty-six-thirty-eight," Fullingham replied.

Swizzledick scribbled the message on the cardboard lid, his face a mask of confusion, and then his eyes widened as his jaw dropped. Every man in the circle stared intently at the radio operator. They knew that the message was about her!

"Don't kid me, man," he whispered hoarsely, looking around quickly to make sure Charlie-Six was not in the area.

Fullingham continued softly: "There's more. Tango-Alpha-Lima-India-Alpha. Last name Mareau. Sighted yesterday near the Michelin Rubber Plantation at—oops! BIA. Out." BIA was their code for "boss in area," a sign that his commanding officer, a major, was approaching.

Swizzledick covered his eyes with his hand, and immediately a freckle-bunching smile appeared. "You are not going to hockin' believe this!" he said, lowering his hand and turning from one to the other in the dim light. "The message is: thirty-eight-twenty-six-thirty-eight."

There was confusion on each face. "Her name is—" He pulled up the crushed C-ration box he had written on and read his message. "T-A-L-I-A," he continued, "Talia Mareau." And she was spotted yesterday in the Michelin Rubber Plantation!

"And it has been confirmed by Colonel Forrester at Brigade. Keaton Fullingham drives for him, and Fullingham overheard him talking to a major about a *hot* woman who lived at one of these jungle country clubs very close to where we are. He indicated that the colonel described her as being 'stacked like a French dessert' and looking like Aphrodites—whoever that is. He said that she rides around the plantation on a giant horse, a Perch...Percher—"

"Percheron," B.J. said.

Swizzledick glared at him, apparently annoyed at having been interrupted. "What?"

"It has to be a Percheron," B.J insisted.

"OK, damn it. Anyway, and she stays by herself, swimming and sunbathing."

"Bull shit," Panther said. "That's nuts. I don't believe you."

"My source is hard to dispute," Swizzledick said, somewhat indignantly. "Anyway, I also talked to 'Cargo' Thompson, and he said that he had heard something about the same thing."

They all stared, slack-jawed, like goldfish at the side of a bowl. "Talia Mareau lives," Swizzledick said softy.

Finally Panther spoke. "Please don't tell me," he said slowly, "that she has any more than the standard number of tits."

She was a legend among the soldiers...a reportedly beautiful woman who often traveled through the jungles with nothing on but a bikini. "And she has definitely been spotted and identified, somewhere near where we were."

I smiled at the thought that she might just be real.

The rain came at dusk, big splats of water hammering the trees and falling into puddles beginning to form along our trail below. It continued, wetting everything around. Ponchos did little good as the water ran along every seam, finding its way inside. The final insult for me was when it ran beneath my waistline and into my crotch. I gave up, stood up, and made my way to the base of a large tree, where I re-wrapped my poncho and sat down.

Just after noon the next day, we were picked up by choppers. We were back at The Plantation by 1530 hours.

As usual, every piece of equipment had to be cleaned and inspected before we could relax. It was an excellent incentive, and the soldiers threw themselves into their tasks. Extra water tanks had been brought in, and by late afternoon, the chores were done and showers completed. The men walked around in boxer shorts, T-shirts, and rubber thong sandals as rock music played in the background. Dinner from the mess hall consisted of sirloin steaks with gravy, green beans, French bread bought from a bakery near Sears and Roebuck, and cherry cobbler.

I stuffed my allocation of three cold beers in the cargo pockets of my pants and went back to the tent. As I walked, I decided that the definition of luxury varies with how desperate one is. On this late afternoon, with a warm meal, three beers, three letters from two ladies, and a cold shower, I considered myself to be in the midst of it.

As I entered the tent, Allegretti was sitting on his bunk holding a letter. His face was a mask of strained muscles and gritted teeth and tears that still glistened on his cheek. He held a photograph in his hand.

"Is everything okay?" I asked.

He snorted and cleared his throat. "If having a wife that I haven't held for five months, a child whom I haven't seen in that entire time, a child who took her first step, who spoke her first word, all without my being there, and having a rash from my knees to my crotch, then everything is okay."

I pulled a beer from my cargo pocket, searched until I found an opener, and handed it to him. I walked to my bunk and sat everything I had carried in on top of my foot locker. I picked up my letters and my calendar covered with x's and stepped over my bunk to my chair outside.

I picked up the first letter: Wind Song. It was from Julie.

"I'm thinking about painting the entryway, and I can't decide which color to use. Right now I'm down to two possibilities: 'Easter Dawn' or 'Pansy Dream'. Both are pretty colors. I've enclosed paint samples- let me know which one, if either, that you like. Trish, the girl in the apartment next to me is engaged, and it is not to Robert! A major shocker! I talked to her yesterday- she said to say hello. Mrs. Eaton, the school secretary was in a car wreck—she is fine.

"Be careful and stay down or whatever you are supposed to do. And by the way, I was wondering if Vietnamese women are beautiful. Care to comment on that? We are getting a new principal- Larry Parker, you remember, Larry? He said to tell you good luck.

"This letter is the most pitiful collection of dribble I have ever written. With a college degree I should be able to do much better. And here is the only thing *in this entire dribble* that is important, and needs to be said- 'I love you Craig Pearce'. Please take care of yourself- With all my love, Julie."

The next letter was from Angie: Chanel No. 5.

"How's my cowboy? I hope you are fine, and that you stay that way. I have big plans for you when you get back here. I had dinner with Dinky and she told me to tell you 'hello'", "So, 'hello' from Dinky." There was little information in the letter. I appreciated the fact that after a letter a day, day after day, it became impossible to find new things to say. "Tom and Alicia broke up. Randy wrecked his pickup. I am thinking of getting my hair cut so that it wraps around. Write me. Stay safe. Hugs and kisses from me —love Angie." The dot above the letter 'I' in Angie had been circled with dashes to form a small flower.

The third letter was from my mother, and while I was thrilled to hear from home, it paled in comparison to the other two.

The check-off calendar was next. I began carefully putting an "x" in each blank box since the last time I had done so. Beginning with the last "x" I had filled in during the last session, I carefully drew an "x" from corner to corner until I came to March 21—today—and then I counted. I drained at the thought that I had far more unchecked blocks than those I had filled.

With that thought, I wilted. "I could have received a shorter sentence than that for manslaughter in El Paso," I thought, as I carefully folded everything and put it in my locker. As I placed each letter in its own stack in the foot locker, my voice came to me: "You really need to address this situation, jackass!"

As my head touched my pillow, I stared outside the tent into the waning light of The Plantation, the flash of random stars temporarily visible as breezes toyed with the trees and the whisper of the wind. *It was a beautiful place*, I thought, even with all the hate, fighting, and deception that each side in this war could heap on one another.

Life had already become a nasty string of events. I already dreaded the next operation. I already dreaded those things that caused me to become a beast of burden: the pack, the rifle, the helmet, the rashes, and the pain. I shook as I thought of the constant stench from my clothes, the smell that hung like a foul cloud around me each day. I hated the athlete's foot fungus that lived in the boots that I wore and the pain of pulling knee-high, foul-smelling socks over my feet each day.

I pondered the fact that my new definition of true luxuries in my life never seemed to rise above expectations of cold water showers every week to ten days, that gourmet meals in combat came out of little green cans, and that fatigue shirts and trousers weren't really dirty until they had sweat stains under the arms and in the crotch, were covered in dirt and mud, and caused me to itch all over. I thought of the near-orgasmic feelings that came from the thoughts of a new razor blade roughly every three to eight days. Even now, back in camp after a pleasing shower with soap that had brought me as close to being normal as I could expect, could all be lost within the first four hours of the next jungle hike. I shook my head at the thought that I now considered the greatest single feeling in life to be scratching crud from my scalp.

I hated the thoughts of quiet moments like I was now enjoying, being shattered in an instant, filling my body with fear and excruciating pain caused by the unexpected sound of gunfire as every muscle in my body seized and quivered.

I despised the conflicts in my brain that took place when we were fired upon. The "love thy neighbor" shit that had been taught in Miss McKenzie's Baptist Vacation Bible School, and the automatic burning need to kill other humans at the sound of gunfire could not be reconciled. The good book says, "Thou shall not kill." The doctrines of war say, "Thou damned well better kill if *thou wants to live!*"

Tomorrow we would be allowed to stand down from this shitty war for two days. There would be beer for each man, hot meals from the mess tent, naps, and conversations with friends...friends who, like me, had come to hate the same things that I did.

How pitiful it is when a man reaches a point where his thrills are perfumed letters and three cold beers. "Keep 'em coming ladies, please!"

"Professor," drawled Bama softly from his cot. "I think that I am at a point where I can recognize which one of country ladies' letter he is reading, just by the fragrance." Bama chuckled and continued, "So much for the total loss of privacy in the Army."

I said softly, "You poor, jealous, old, married farts. Eat your hearts out."

"We're not the ones who need to worry about getting our hearts eaten out. As soon as either 'roses' or 'lilacs' realizes that they are *both* on your Christmas card list!" Bama returned.

Thirty-One

OPERATION MONROE
MARCH 25, 1966

It was a gray day, one that matched the mood of everyone there. We stood in the mist, our clothes already becoming soaked in spite of our ponchos. The trucks had dropped us off earlier, and the men stood now in small groups waiting for the choppers to pick us up. It was quiet except for short bursts of laughter, which released cigarette smoke into the gray day.

The sound of the choppers clapping against the moist air began to be heard, and in less than five minutes, their rotors, slinging even more water on those of us waiting, began to arrive.

They landed in groups of six or seven at a time for loading. Allegretti's platoon boarded the first six choppers, followed by the command group. The engine revved, and we began to rise as the chopper tilted forward and to the left. The next ships carried Bama's platoon and then Professor's. The sign and its reminder that "San Francisco" was 1500 miles away blew down in the blast from the rotors, sailed past and beneath us, and shattered as it hit the fence post. I looked down and watched as the other two slips lifted.

The moment was cool and hypnotic as we rose through a light fog, scattering it like powder as it banked to avoid an artillery battery firing to the south, and then climbing into the morning sky. Sears and Roebuck passed beneath as a woman entered, followed by three small children like a string of ducks. The same filthy geese waddled in the sewage ditches on either side of the street. I craned to see if I could spot Ebony Eyes, but didn't. We climbed several minutes more and rose into a brilliant, blinding morning sky, framed in hints of gold and red to the east. We passed over the road that led to The Plantation and rice paddies filled with birds feeding on the freshly planted rice sprouts. Then the jungle, like huge green sponges, began to pass beneath as the morning air rushed through the cabin. If there was peace anywhere in Vietnam, it was here in the sky.

"This is being touted as a critical mission, a search and destroy operation," Charlie-Six had told us the evening before. "If you draw a line from Saigon through Tay Ninh to the Cambodian border and cut it in half, that puts you right about here." He read the coordinates. "That is where we will be." He lowered the pencil he had been holding against his temple and placed the point on the map, just northeast of part of the rubber plantation.

"Due west is the Cambodian border. And right in the middle of that curve is part of where the Ho Chi Minh trail empties into Vietnam. That's where, according to the intelligence guys, the Cong have some of the biggest stock piles of supplies in Vietnam. It is easy for them to move it by water directly into the interior of the country."

He looked up to each of us. There were no comments, so he continued.

"This area is also where some of the biggest concentrations of VC units in the country are. No allied troops have been in here for up to ten years. The intelligence guys have proof that the Viet Cong have built hospitals, training areas, assembly plants for making 'homemade' Claymore mines. According to them, there are pictures of bunkers two stories underground with all sorts of supplies and equipment. They even make uniforms there. And we are going to pay them a visit."

"Why doesn't the Air Force take it all out?" Professor asked.

"They have destroyed some of it, but the intelligence people are convinced that there is a lot of important information there. They want you ground pounders to secure it enough for them to come in and investigate. We have been given this information by spies...spies that have seen it. This is apparently a *very* important mission."

"We will start near our old friend, the Rach Chi Bat—the same river which is part of the Cambodian Border—and work that area for a couple of days, doing some reconnaissance and search and destroy missions. Reports are that it is a mix of everything from heavy jungle to abandoned rubber plantations.

"Meanwhile, the Quarter Horse Cavalry and parts of the 2nd Brigade will be setting up in an area to the east. The whistle will be blown, and we will start toward each other, hopefully smashing a lot of critical supplies...and VC.

"And for this, we take our gas masks. Are you ready for that?" he asked, looking at me.

"Yes sir", I replied. "I hope to hell we don't need them, but we're ready."

"We land at a forward position where Battalion is. I'll get details at 1300 at Battalion, and we'll meet at 1400 to go over every final detail, and out in the morning. You can tell the men to be prepared for at least ten days." He locked eyes with each of us.

He stretched his arms, palms up above his head, then leaned back in his folding canvas chair. He reached behind and pulled out a piece of cardboard with writing that read "Company Mess Tent—eat here and get a free grease job. Or don't eat here and add years to your life." It was signed "the Phuoc Vinh Phantom." Six continued in a low voice. "Tell your men that *when* I catch whoever is doing this, I will cut his nuts off and serve them to him on a plate of Sergeant Zeigler's spaghetti." He scanned the circle, then placed the sign behind his chair and turned to face us once more. "We need to stop this. The cooks deserve better. Are there any questions?"

He waited several seconds before speaking again. "OK. I'll be back from the briefing about 1400 hours."

I was ready. I sat in my shorts and T-shirt and wrote letters to my mom and dad, to Julie, to Angie, to my sisters, and to several college friends. I told them about the country, about watching water buffalos tilling soil and working fields, about Sears and Roebuck, and other mundane things in my life. I indicated that "things were safe where we were, and that the probability of actually being in combat was almost zero." I carried them to City Hall and dropped them in the mail bag.

That afternoon, three letters were in my mail.

Mother's letters were very transparent. She knew she needed to write to me to keep my morale up, but she had little to say and nothing to ask. She was intent in not saying anything that she thought would bother me. She described the livestock and a new hay-bailer. She spoke of quilting circles, Eileen Davis and her ulcers, and her knitting. She spoke of emerald deep green alfalfa fields, of baby chickens, ragged looking in their new feathers, and of new calves. She provided a list of neighbors, all of whom had asked her to "tell me hello" when she wrote.

Angie talked of her job and how she hated it. "My boss is a lecher, and is always sneering or saying something out of line. I told him that when you got back you would 'kick his ass.' The 'gang' said hello — Randy and Denise are getting a divorce — it rained some, but not enough. I love you — and I miss you." It was signed simply "Hug, Kisses, and the 'really good stuff' await your return. Angie"

Julie talked of our summer trip and thanked me again for it. She described her favorite scenes: her memories of waterfalls, of seeing large grazing animals near the glacier, and of chilly evenings on the deck. "I miss you terribly. Please be careful - you're carrying my heart around with you. Saint Christopher told me to tell you hello. My love forever- Julie."

The next morning we left into heavy, damp, hot air.

GIs rarely used the phrase "it could be worse," as if doing so all too often fulfilled a prophecy. And that it did. As we approached the strongholds, ambushes became more common, with a VC soldier firing two rounds at us and then dropping into a tunnel and disappearing. We started using tear gas early in the morning, often causing as many problems for us as the VC. The tunnels often ran several miles with multiple entrances and exits. Gas thrown in one opening could travel for long distances, coming up anywhere and hanging in the air. By mid-morning, the air was filled with the pungent odor of tear gas. Even when it was used properly, sweat mixed with the agent could make its way beneath the rubber covering the forehead, causing irritation inside. Our eyes were rimmed in deep red. Our men ran, fell on the ground, and—the worst thing possible—they began to remove their masks. It was so painful, so wicked, that fellow soldiers who still wore masks began to lead them back to safe areas.

For the most part, the VC coming out of the tunnels did so firing at us, and in most such cases they were killed. Some came out only after holding up a stick with a piece of cloth on the end of it and were handled as prisoners of war. That in turn created the need for guards, and ultimately military police had to be summoned to remove the prisoners.

They arrived in two choppers, twelve men and equipment with a new mission for us: provide protection for intelligence teams sent to determine what was there. In another hour, everything was secure.

At noon, two intelligence captains—two that we had worked with before—arrived. We re-introduced ourselves, and Captain McCloud began to explain what they intended to do.

"We expect this to be a treasure trove of information. We could spend a good deal of time here," Captain McCloud explained, "but we realize, Captain Novak," he said, turning to Charlie-Six, "that that is not practical. So, here is our plan. As I understand it, it has been decided that your company will provide security for at least two, hopefully three, days. Is that what you've been told?"

"It is," Charlie-Six replied.

"Good," McCloud continued. "So for the first day, we will identify items that we need to get back to Saigon. Those will be loaded on choppers to be flown back by the end of tomorrow. The following day or two, we will go through the remaining items. And around noon, demolition teams will be brought in to do the rest.

"So, in the meantime, your infantry company will set up and maintain security for the area for two to three days. We will be joined by A Company to help sometime later today." Charlie-Six paused and nodded, indicating that he agreed with the plan.

"You know the Cong are pissed at us for messing up their playhouses, and they may be ready to give us some shit," McCloud said. "We are aware of that, and that is the primary reason for getting this over quickly. You will not be asked to do anything here other than that."

Just after dawn the next morning, Charlie-Six got a call. We assembled.

We had set up a perimeter around the area, which included a landing zone large enough to support a Chinook helicopter if necessary. By 0630, the show began. The huge twin rotor aircraft came with welding equipment, power saws, chain saws, demolitions, twenty perforated burn barrels, a small forklift, and crews trained to operate all of that. It was like a circus rigging up:

ten to fifteen welders, mechanics, and quartermaster specialist all to help in sorting materiel and intelligence information, loading what was to be kept on choppers. The rest was to be destroyed as much as possible.

Shortly after noon on the second day, McCloud was back with the Charlie Company officers. "For your information, everything we find is being placed in one of three stacks. One will be what we considered classified information, and we will handle that. One will be recoverable items, tools, generators, so forth. The final one will be material to be rendered useless by demolition experts. The first stack is ours and will be out of here by choppers by sundown.

"The rest, the stuff to be demolished by the quartermaster engineers, is starting this afternoon. All documents will be burned. In the morning, as I understand, the major tunnels will be blasted away. And finally, when we have all left, the Air Force will come in and do their business."

At mid-afternoon, the Chinook arrived. Two hours later, everything of importance to the spooks had been loaded. All of the equipment brought by the quartermaster people was loaded on a different Chinook. In an hour, both left.

Engineers arrived with more C-4 explosives than we had ever seen and began placing it deep inside tunnels. Just before sundown, they began pushing plungers to trigger it. This was the part that gave the engineers erections. The paper in the burn barrels, which remained, was burned.

We maintained the perimeter and patrolled the area, supported by more than the usual number of helicopter gunships. The piles grew. By noon the next day, the spooks met with us once more. "We will be leaving within two hours. This has been very worthwhile," Captain McCloud began.

"Did you find anything of interest?" Charlie-Six asked.

"Indeed," he answered. "This compound has been in place here for years. They weren't what we normally think of when we speak of tunnels. Some rooms had block walls where we found several small safes. One area was two floors deep, framed with railroad rails and finished with timbers and concrete. One last Chinook is due in to pack up any remaining tools—generators and all of the remaining 'stuff.'"

I established twenty points in the area and assigned artillery concentrations to each. In an hour, we were in our defensive position for an uneventful night.

By noon the next day, we were home. "Home," I whispered. "What a twisted concept."

Thirty-Two

THE RAINCROW
MARCH 28, 1966

The trees were blending into the charcoal evening sky as small birds flitted about, busily catching flying insects to take home to unseen nests filled with hungry mouths. Even the white paint-like aroma of rubber oozing from the trees, which had smelled acidic and rank when I had first arrived, had somehow become soothing.

I was homesick. I carried my folding stool, my rifle, my helmet with a new canvas camouflage cover, and a black magic marker to the edge of The Plantation. For the mood I was in, its orderly, symmetrical rows of trees were somehow pleasant and calming, as a breeze tugged at the small branches and silver spots of light danced on the carpet of leaves.

I spread the chair legs and straddled the canvas seat. I lifted the helmet and placed it in my lap. It consisted of two parts: the steel shell, which had been designed to protect soldiers since World War II, and an inner removable liner, which was made of layers of molded plastics to form an inner shell. I separated the outer steel cover from the inner helmet liner, which fit snugly inside and provided the interior webbing to allow the helmet to fit properly on my head. I unfolded a new camouflage canvas cover, stretching it over the steel pot and pulling it over the outer shell. With the heel of my hand, I smoothed the material until it fit smoothly over the steel exterior and tucked the remaining material inside. I pushed the remaining liner into place and folded the retainer straps over the front and back of the pot. It was now covered in patterns and shades of olive to lime green, deep brown to tan, and gray to black. I placed the holding band around the edge of the pot and inspected my work. I rubbed remaining wrinkles with a stick until it was combat ready. I placed it between my knees, picked up a black magic marker, and began to draw a small figure on the left side, no larger than the bottom of a mess hall coffee cup. Finally it was finished: a solid black sketch of an American raven, Daddy Bud's Raincrow. I brushed it off and placed it on the ground next to my chair.

As crude as it was, it brought back memories of my childhood, of similar early evenings at home with Daddy Bud, my grandfather...as we talked, played checkers, sang gospel hymns, and whittled. My heritage, including this Raincrow, would always be there for me.

The greatest sensation I had had since my arrival back in camp had been a cool two-minute shower. I ached everywhere: where the pack straps had ridden my shoulder all day all week, in the small of my back from carrying the weight of everything I owned for the mission, and in my head where the ringing of explosive memories still resonated. But that began to fade, as I was now clean. As I finished a beer, my thoughts returned to the boy, wrapped in a poncho somewhere in an abandoned village. I wondered if his family, or friends had held a proper funeral, whatever that was. I wondered if he had a grandfather, and once more, my thoughts returned to Daddy Bud.

I heard a soft conversation and looked up to see Darnell and Panther coming my way. They seemed as quiet and moody as I was, especially

Panther. They came bearing gifts: six cold beers—two each—and a sack of sweet C-ration canned peaches. We discussed what we had learned and seen in the last few days. They seemed to be here now just to talk and massage their minds. All three of us seemed content to just sit and feel the relatively cool evening air around us. My second beer and the first can of peaches were opened, and the conversation started.

"So what's with the helmet?" Panther asked, staring at me. "Are you carrying it with you...afraid you are going to get attacked in your shorts and thong sandals?"

"I ripped my old cover getting out of the chopper earlier. I got a new one and felt that I needed my own trademark on it." I held it up.

"A bird?" Darnell asked. He took it from me, studied it, and passed it to Panther.

"It's not just a bird in my family. It's a Raincrow."

"A what?"

"It's a Raincrow."

"So what's his story? Is it some kind of a New Mexico thing? Is it an Indian thing? Apache? Navajo? Whatever?"

I smiled. "Nothing that exotic," I returned. "It's just a family thing."

"So...what's with it?" he repeated. "Aren't we family by now?" he asked. I grinned broadly, my first smile of the day.

"I suppose you are," I began.

"Daddy Bud lived next door to us on the farm, just north of Hobbs, New Mexico. He had become too old to farm, and as a boy, I used to spend a lot of time with him, sitting on his small wooden front porch, eight by eight feet and thirty inches off the ground with three steps leading down the front. All around the porch, fragrant pink four o'clock bushes grew in the summer, creating my 'hideout.' I loved to crawl beneath them and lean against the house, with the sounds of Daddy Bud rocking above me. It was where I became Frank Lovejoy leading his Army squad across Italy, or the men of Easy Company with Broderick Crawford moving through the olive groves of

Tunisia in World War II, or Audie Murphy, or John Wayne on Normandy Beach.

"He always dressed in khaki pants, a white shirt buttoned up to his Adam's apple, a narrow black belt, thin socks, and 'old-man' lace-up shoes. He would sit and stare and whittle with a small pocket knife, carving little square trucks out of white pine scraps of wood. Then he would sit for hours rubbing the knife blade on a whetstone to sharpen it." I smiled broadly as I remembered his offerings. "The carvings were crude enough that anyone of them could serve as a car, a truck, or even a tank. Well, they were good enough for me because he had made them. He would sit for long periods of his mornings in his ancient wooden rocking chair. And while he could not see me at the end of that porch, behind my bushes, he always seemed to know when I was there. 'Boy,' he would ask, 'are you there?' 'Yes sir,' I would reply.

"He would stand up, take the two or three shuffling steps to the end of the porch, place his latest carved creation on its edge, and return to his rocking chair. I would ask him questions, and he would always wait for a couple of minutes before answering, allowing the chair to stop rocking.

"On one such morning, a real crow feather had been placed on the receiving spot at the end of the porch. I picked it up and ran it along my fingers, looking at the hues of blues and greens formed by the light on its ink black surface. I brushed it over my face, feeling the strong veins of the feather."

"Was he some kind of an Indian?" Darnell asked, interrupting.

"No, he was just a quiet, loving old man. I remember asking, 'Daddy Bud, why doesn't a crow have a yellow beak like a chicken?' The squeak of the rocking chair stopped as he thought. 'For the same reason, you don't have a yellow beak, boy. You weren't designed that way.'

"Well, anyway, I can remember listening to discussions between my mom and dad, speculating about the possibility of rain, the fact that the water tables in the lakes beneath the ground were dropping and how desperately the crops needed moisture. I remember them on one morning mentioning a Raincrow.

"Later that day I sat beneath the porch, listening to the soft sound of the rocker moving above. From my position behind the four o'clock, I asked, 'Daddy Bud, what is a Raincrow?' The rocking stopped. 'It's a special crow. One that God gave us. It can tell us when it is going to rain.' The rocking resumed. 'Are all crows Raincrows?'

"I can still remember how the creaking of his rocking chair stopped once more. 'No, only the Raincrow is special,' he said in a burnt out baritone and raspy voice. He kept a soup can at his feet, and he picked it up and spit tobacco juice into it. He daubed a handkerchief at the corners of his mouth, returned the can to the floor at the edge of the rocker, and continued. 'He has a different call, almost a screech.' He rocked for several seconds more and then stopped. 'But when you hear his special call, it is going to rain. He's unique. He will see us through. He will bring the rain.'"

Darnell had picked up the helmet and was studying the drawing by the fading light. "So was it a religious thing?"

"No, I don't think it was. Daddy Bud was special, but not really a prophet.

"I was ten at the time, but I knew what water meant to my family. I knew that in June, as the heat of that arid land began to evaporate what precious moisture there was, those vapors would collect into towering clouds thousands of feet high, like giant ghosts, and float across the plains, pushed by the wind. My dad called these clouds 'practice clouds,' as they rarely produced rain. He and other farmers had irrigation pumps that ran deep into giant lakes beneath the Earth's surface to draw pure, crystal clear, clean, and cold water to ditches to keep the crops alive. It was borrowed water from the Ogallala Aquifer, and everyone knew that without the rains to replenish the water in those lakes below, the country would become a desert."

I took a long drink from my bottle and stared into the growing darkness before continuing. "Anyway, in July those clouds would begin to grow in mid-morning every day. Breezes would rise and push them from Arizona through New Mexico to Texas like huge, beautiful parades.

"My friend, a kid named Bobby, and I would lie in the shade of an elm tree and pick out objects hidden in them, like a face or a car or a Nazi airplane, which we would fire at with imaginary rifles from below. Each day these clouds would grow in size and quantity, teasing the people.

"I remember my Dad throughout those days stopping from whatever he was working on to raise his hat to shade his eyes and stare as they passed, as if searching them to see if 'this would be the one.' We would watch as he gazed at every wisp of a cloud, every streak of white in the sky, until it disappeared.

"And then finally, on a still, scorching day that began with azure skies, fitful breezes would gather strength, rising to enormous heights, skirting the land, and tossing the plants like eager messengers of a storm as bird's race for shelter. Distant clouds would turn blue and black and rise like a gigantic ancient goddess, twisting and roiling to demonstrate her power and reclaim her world. The breezes would turn to blasts of hot wind as laundry was hurriedly brought in from clothes lines. Equipment would be driven from the field and parked by workers beneath overhanging roofs attached to the barns. And as if these farmers weren't paying enough attention to what nature was doing, she would split the sky with streaks of lightning, creating crashes of thunder, which temporarily stole the breath from everyone below. Prayers would be offered: 'Please give us rain, God...but no hail.'

"In late July, light showers would occasionally fall. My father called them promises, and while they were welcome, they weren't what the farmers had been praying for. They would stop in their pickups along dirt roads to confer about the miracle to come and speculate about when.

"Finally, on a day in early August, it would happen. Daddy Bud would tell me on that morning, 'I heard a Raincrow just a while ago.'

"Giant black splats, like a slap, would begin to hit the baked ground, only to be greedily absorbed into the soil. More drops would come until finally the deluge would begin in earnest, sending solid sheets of water. We would gather in barns with their giant doors open, knowing that everyone on every farm around us was standing in open doors or on porches, listening to the roar of millions of drops pounding on galvanized metal roofs above them. Children would dash from beneath overhanging porches, screaming and laughing as the huge drops pelted their bodies, then return to the shelters where they would squeal with every ominous clap of thunder or shaft of lightning.

"Then, in late afternoon it would stop, leaving brilliant sunlight glistening on the plants below. A wonderful, earthy aroma would fill the air as toads emerged from beneath the soil where they have been since the previous summer. They'd make their way to puddles of rain, belching praise in their deep voices for their cleverness in having found these temporary lakes. And as if vying with the sunset, a brilliant fluorescent rainbow would arch from horizon to horizon, as the final drops slipped away from trees and tin roofs.

"Rain gauges would be checked to see how much came. Farmers would get in their pickup trucks and drive, and stopping along farm roads, they would roll down their windows to tell each other what a blessing it was, but how it wasn't enough. They would recall rains of years ago, saying 'We need one like the summer of '58.'

"Rain, taken for granted in other parts of the world, never is in Southern New Mexico," I said, looking at Panther.

"That Raincrow, with his screechy caws, would have foretold of this storm and kept his promise. He was special to farmers. And to a young boy who learned of him from a magic old man, he became a symbol of hope, amazement...and fulfillment."

I opened another beer. "Throughout my life, when I needed optimism and hope," I said, "I would think about that crow. He was like religion to me. He saw me through." I held up the helmet. "And here he is." I raised my bottle. "To hope. To dreams. And to the Raincrow. He'll see me—he'll see us through."

We all three drew deeply on the bottles, content just to take in the last few minutes of dusk.

Finally Darnell spoke. "I know what's bothering you, Lieutenant. You're not sharing the truth."

I turned to him, a quizzical look on my face.

"You need to open up." His grin began forming. "Now be honest. Is your song 'Get an Ugly Girl to Marry You?'" Panther blew a mist of beer from his mouth and choked as he laughed.

We walked back toward the tents, stopping at the trash barrel to deposit the bottles and then they continued to the latrine. "I appreciate you guys," I said as I extended my right hand and shook with each of them.

Thirty-Three

THE THRILL OF A CONVOY
MARCH 29, 1966

Allegretti ducked as he entered the tent, his face twisted into a broad grin, a rare facial expression for him. "Well, gents, we're going for a ride."

Professor and I stared, waiting for him to continue. Professor sat down his Melmac cup of lemonade and said, "Well, don't keep us in suspense, big man. A ride to where?"

"To Ben Hoa, that's where! We leave in two days. The convoy is finally on." Allegretti's eyebrows lifted as he spoke. Ben Hoa was a relatively busy supply point south of Phuoc Vinh.

"And you know this how?" Professor asked.

"I was with Charlie-Six when he got the word just forty-five minutes ago. He said he would brief us when he gets back from Battalion."

I had not said anything as I watched and listened. I recalled a conversation several nights earlier about how occasionally it was necessary to run a convoy between Phuoc Vinh and supply points in and around Ben Hoa to pick up supplies, food, fuel, medicine, and ammunition for everything that fired a round...and most importantly, for beer. Now, it was obviously happening.

B.J. Tucker suddenly appeared behind Allegretti. "Captain Novak is back. He asked me to give these to you and asked you to pass them out before the meeting." He handed Mike four sets of maps. "The meeting will be held in thirty minutes at City Hall." City Hall was the name we used for Charlie-Six's tent.

"A convoy, it is," Allegretti said as he turned and walked out.

I looked at Professor. "So what does this mean to someone who has never been on a real combat convoy?"

Professor retrieved his lemonade from the earthen floor beside him and took a sip before responding. "It's our turn to support the monthly convoy."

"OK, I gathered that. Yes, I *know* what a convoy is. And yes, I even know how to spell it. So what does it mean to me? What's our role? And more importantly, what's my role?"

"Well, as a group we will be expected to ride—not walk—to a stretch on the road, set up points to protect the convoy vehicles as they travel to Ben Hoa empty, and return to Phuoc Vinh full. We'll sit there for two to three days protecting them as they go back and forth. There might be some minor missions while we are there, but they rarely amount to more than a half a day. And what's your role, you asked?" Professor continued. "I'm sure it will continue to be, as in the past, to protect the rest of us." He stood and walked away, mumbling "what to wear, what to wear?"

Forty minutes later, Charlie-Six arrived. Ten minutes later, we were at the City Hall—his tent.

"We are going on a convoy," he began. "On March 31. We leave somewhere just after dawn. The convoy will be handled by the battalion military police leading us, just as last time. We will join in at the entrance to

The Plantation. Bravo and Alpha are both already involved in missions south of here, so they will join in as part of the route defense.

"The route is much the same as last month's convoy. It will be Route 1 to Ben Hoa. Security will be for the same stretch of road from last time. This is the same area we secured during Red Ball V in January, maybe even the same foxholes and bunkers. Make damned sure if you use them again that no one jumps into one of them until we verify that they aren't booby trapped." He looked around the circle, making eye contact with each of us.

"Our primary mission will be to secure the highway for the convoy vehicles and personnel. Once again, as I said, Charlie Company has been assigned a stretch of the road three kilometers during the day and rolling up into our defensive perimeter each night," Charlie-Six said.

"The MPs and the Quarter Horse Cavalry will lead the convoy to provide security. There is at least one, maybe two, infantry brigades along the way, and as I understand, that an Australian unit will also be involved. Then when it is safe to travel, empty fuel, two-and-a-half-ton trucks, and medical wagons will make a dash south to the resupply points at Ben Hoa for supplies...everything from food to medicine to toilet paper and yes, beer. Then they will return to Phuoc Vinh."

He looked once more at each of us. "The initial passwords for the operation will be 'Quantum.' The response will be 'Lilly Pad.' As usual, it will change each midnight we are there. If I find anyone giving out a password for a piece of ass from some whore around our area, I will personally shoot him. Remind them: This is not a game."

Charlie-Six looked down at a small green notebook, and then continued.

"Bama, tomorrow I want you to familiarize Pearce with the armament on the trucks." He turned and looked at me. "This will give you a chance to see how well protected we are. OK?"

"Yes, sir, I would appreciate it," I said.

"He will appreciate it," Bama said, looking at Charlie-Six, "because you have chosen me to brief him, not Professor, whose *briefing* would last longer than the war will."

Professor turned to stare at Bama as he spoke. "Captain Novak. I request permission to form a firing squad after the meeting, please."

"Pearce, you will continue to be supported by Alpha Battery in case we need artillery support." Six flipped the notebook to the next page.

Several administrative items were discussed, until finally Charlie-Six adjourned the meeting. We all knew that there would be another one the next day.

"Oh. And one more thing before you go." He held up a sign, which had been painted on one of the flaps of a C-ration box using black shoe polish. It read "In the future the shit-barrels will be burned each day from 1100 to 1300 to mask the smell of lunch being prepared by the cooks." It was signed "The Phuoc Vinh Phantom."

"When I catch him, I will hang him! This is an embarrassment to the company and not fair to the cooks. Let your men now that I am pissed!"

The next day I met with Bama at one of the trucks. I knew little about what we would be doing and was pleased when Bama showed me around. We walked to where a standard Army two-and-one-half-ton truck, a deuce-and-a-half, was lined up along the road, with soldiers making last-minute inspections, modifications, and maintenance corrections along the line of trucks.

"Son of a bitch!" a soldier screamed, as the lug wrench slipped and he smashed his hand against the ground. "Piece of junk! Shit!" His teammate motioned, and he turned to see us. "Sorry sir—sirs."

"Nothing to be sorry about, Specialist Montez," Bama said. "Are you okay?"

"Yes, sir."

Bama began. "The first objective is to do anything we can reasonably do to get to where we are going. We'll start here. Rule number one: the flak vest is a must. Wear it on convoys. Rule two: If you have two of them, put one under your butt in case we run over a landmine. In short, we need every form of protection we have, or can think of."

We stopped at one of the trucks. "We'll start here." He began as he balled his fist and held up one finger. "The objective is to get us to our assigned section of road. Correction," he said. "To get us to our assigned section of the road...unharmed! To do that, some modifications have been made. As you can see, the canvas covers have all been removed from the cargo areas of the trucks. This makes it easier to watch what's going on along the road, to have better lanes of fire so you can be able to shoot in any direction, and to get out of the trucks quickly if we are hit by an ambush."

We walked around to the side, and he pointed to three three-by-twelve rough cut boards the length of the truck beds. They had been bolted to the outside slatted sides of the vehicle. "Someone came up with this idea in case we get hit with Claymores along the road. These," he said as he slapped one of the boards, "absorb most of the blast. And, we will attach Claymores on the outside of these," he said, knocking on the timbers once more, "facing away from the road to set off our *own Claymores* toward the VC in case of an ambush. That's a hell of a deterrent. If we get hit, we trigger the Claymores away from the road and hopefully into Charlie."

"Clever, you American pigs," I said, "Clever indeed."

"Wasn't our idea. Some brain at the Pentagon came up with it."

"To hear Allegretti tell it, there *are* no brains in the Pentagon," I said with a smile.

"I won't argue with Allegretti on anything."

We moved to the front of the truck where he pointed out a piece of two-inch angle iron that had been attached to the massive bumper. It rose straight up for three feet and then turned at a forty-five degree angle away from the hood. Notches had been cut into the leading edge of the forty-five degree angle slots in the piece of iron. "Charlie loves to string wire along the roads. Early on, that's all they did...just string a piece of wire between two trees just high enough to clear the hood. A truck or jeep comes along with the windshield down, which is how we have to travel, and zing." He made a slashing motion with his forefinger across his neck. "Everyone inside the cab area is gone. We didn't think of that either, but it worked. Then Charlie decided to attach a Claymore mine on one end of the wire on your side of the jeep, tie it to a tree at four feet off the ground, so when we came by, the wire would get caught by the angle iron up front and set off the Claymore, killing everyone in the jeep. That's what I call evolutionary science."

"So what happens when the Claymore goes off?"

"It can kill everyone in the jeep," he said, a smile forming. "And oh, by the way, you'll be riding in a jeep."

"Thanks for pointing that out. So where does the VC get the Claymore mines?"

"One source is our military manufactured Claymores, the M18s. These have been reported stolen from military vehicles when some careless jackass is stupid enough to leave them there. We have had incidents of them being traded to 'sidewalk ladies' for a piece of ass." He looked at me with a smirk and nodded his head.

"The power of *love*," I said.

"And, they also make them. At least their version."

"They make them?" I asked.

"Indeed they do. They steal the parts from wherever they can find them. They start with a cheap wash pan like the one you bought the other day, some C-4 explosives, again from a truck or in trade for something, a strip of commo wire, which is strung all over Phuoc Vinh for everything from clothes lines to fences. And finally, a blasting cap—again, from a lot of places. And, oh yeah, the bolts that hold artillery ammo packing boxes together.

"The C-4 is pliable like children's clay. It gets stuffed into the pan about half full and pressed tightly. The ammo rods are cut up into half-inch pieces and spread over the C-4. Then they make a silt solution of sand and clay and pour it over the ammo rods. Let it dry, turn it over, punch a hole in the back of the pan, insert the blasting cap into the clay, and string seventy feet of commo wire away from the blast area. Then touch a double A battery to it, and 'good night, Irene.'"

He picked up a dry twig and carried it like a swagger stick back to my jeep, which had a wire cutter attached to the front. The windshield had been lowered, and flak jackets lay in each seat. Panther would drive, I would sit in the right front seat, and Darnell would sit in the back with the radio. I didn't sleep well that night.

The next morning was like a circus as the company prepared for the ride. I stood next to Professor as he ate a candy bar and we watched the activity. Huge Army trucks sat idling, all lined up in the order in which they would be inserted into the convoy, along the entrance to The Plantation. Charlie-Six would lead, followed by my jeep and the trucks with the platoons.

At 0600, we were ready. A chant began softly from the men in the trucks and grew louder as it was repeated until all had joined in: "Haulin' food, haulin' gas, haulin' ammo, haulin' ass!"

We followed the dirt strip from The Plantation to the main road and stopped behind a military police jeep. The vehicle had a 50-caliber machine gun mounted on a high swivel to ensure that it would clear the front seat passengers if used. It was manned by a grisly-looking sergeant, who wore a zipped flak vest. Two magnetic signs with "Convoy Escort" were mounted on the front and rear of the vehicle. The MP lieutenant looked at his watch, then up the road toward the sound of armored personnel carriers coming toward us on the road. He quickly walked to his jeep and climbed in. In seconds, he pulled in behind the growling track vehicles. B.J. Tucker did the same, and we were on our way to Ben Hoa.

Charlie-Six looked back at me, raised his right hand, and pumped his fist up and down several times. In our jeep, Panther immediately turned onto the road to follow, maintaining a distance of approximately fifteen yards. We were under way in seconds. In the back, Darnell spoke into the radio: "Destroyer Two-Three, this is Destroyer Niner-Three. Communications check, over."

In a moment, the radio sounded again. "Destroyer Niner-Three, I read you. Lima Charlie, out." Lima Charlie meant "loud and clear."

"Roger, Destroyer Two-Three. Out," Darnell said as he turned his portable radio up as loud as it could play. Nancy Sinatra was in the midst of singing "These boots were made for walking." I was glad for a change that we wouldn't be.

For me, everything—every bird, every bump in the road, every patch of plantations that cast shadows across the road—was a new experience. I turned to Panther, and he smiled.

I was amazed at the amount of civilian traffic on the road, walking, riding bikes, and overstuffed vehicles and busses. Those walking traveled mainly in clusters and ranged from mostly groups of women carrying babies and younger children, to elderly men with their bodies bent by time. They clung to staffs made from tree branches that were taller than they were—weapons to stave off the aging process and squeeze a few more steps out of life.

I turned to Darnell, my left arm over the back of the seat, and motioned for him to turn Nancy down. I asked, "Why are all of these Vietnamese out today?"

"They're having a convoy too, taking advantage of a 'safe road.' If the road is safe for us, it's safe for them. We'll see a lot of civilians today."

Ten minutes further along, as if fulfilling Darnell's prophecy, we passed a blue and orange bus adorned with chrome, bound in the direction of Phuoc

Vinh and packed to capacity. A man held two live chickens out one of the windows of the bus by their legs. Three young boys sat on top amid bags and packages tied there. The driver honked continuously as he dodged our vehicles and the pedestrians. Pedestrians passed both ways along the road, carrying baskets, bags, and other parcels, dressed predominantly in their common cloths of black satin-like pants, shirts, traditional sandals, and woven conical hats. Occasionally they would have various items of military clothing mixed in with their wardrobe, such as fatigue pants, military belts, green socks, and military baseball caps.

We passed a man on a bright, three-wheel, motorized tricycle with a small pickup bed, carrying ice covered in straw to keep it from melting. Typically their waves seemed guarded and insincere...never the enthusiastic waves that Frank Lovejoy got when he liberated Paris. Bicycles passed with unbelievable numbers of packages and suitcases tied to them, often to the point that the owner was pushing instead of riding the bike.

I again turned to Darnell. "Where do they come from?" I asked.

The smile appeared immediately. "Ah, come on, Lieutenant," he said in a tone of disgust, "you should know that. Don't they teach biology in New Mexico?"

"OK, I deserved that," I said, laughing. "What do they want?"

"Anything you'll throw to them: food, C-rations, cigarettes, coins. Most people just throw them the finger." As he spoke, he tossed a handful of hard candy to a group of small children who scurried to pick it up.

We drove over dusty roads, enjoying the shadow of the plantations and the breeze in our faces, Panther working to maintain the interval between B.J. Tucker in the jeep ahead of us. We rounded a curve, and I checked the map to find it and confirm that we were where we should be. We were fifteen kilometers from An Sut, where we would secure our portion of the road.

This entailed stringing the three platoons along the road and digging in for the three-day stay. Strong points with 50-caliber machine guns would be placed so that in case of an attack, those points could be strengthened and held. The good news was that along this road, soldiers on previous such trips had dug foxholes while on similar duty. All that we'd have to do to be protected in adequate foxholes would be to check them for booby traps, clean them out, and move in.

We passed a 105 howitzer battery and a group of engineers who had arrived before us and were already occupying their assigned stretch of the road.

With any luck, it would be easy duty. Soldiers had brought magazines— Playboys to be shared until they became too nasty to be held, Time, Sports Illustrated—radios, and stationary.

We passed over the Song Be Bridge one vehicle at a time and waved to the Army of Vietnam soldiers who had secured it. One held out his hand and called out "cigarette" as we passed slowly by. Darnell held his hand up, his middle finger extended upward. I turned around and stared at him.

"Was that necessary, Sergeant Darnell?" I asked.

"Sometimes you just have to be a hard ass with these people," he said. "It's the only thing they understand."

"Life according to *hard ass* Darnell," I said with a smile. "We *must* teach these locals the lessons of life."

We passed more plantations, rice paddies like shallow lakes with green shoots sticking out of the water, interspersed with stretches of vivid green jungle.

We were stopped briefly while a stalled bus was investigated and cleared from the road. The men on Bama's truck disembarked and flanked each side of the road as a helicopter hovered overhead the entire time.

"Dreadlock Two-Three, this is Destroyer Niner-Three. Commo check, over," came Darnell's voice from the back seat.

In a minute, Dreadlock, the battery we had passed, replied. "Loud and clear, Destroyer Niner-Three." I turned in my seat and hit Darnell on his right knee.

"Good job, Sergeant," I said. "We can't be too careful."

"Can't be too careful, indeed," he replied.

A group of children had encircled Charlie-Six's jeep, and he yelled at them to leave. They ran to our jeep. Darnell reached beneath the seat and retrieved his bag of peppermints, giving each child two pieces. They were hesitant to leave. Darnell gave each one more, and they ran to rejoin their families.

"You know, Mathias," I said, staring at Panther as we began to leave once more. "Sometimes you just have to be a hard ass with these people. It's the only thing they understand." He gunned the jeep, and we were on our way once more.

We arrived at our destination in mid-afternoon, the stretch of road that we would occupy for the next three or four days. An hour later, foxholes had been prepared and manned, and we were ready to defend our part of the route.

After we stopped and organized our position, Charlie-Six called a meeting of the officers. He was assured by each of the lieutenants that all sections of the road under our protection had been readied and listening posts were out in front of the lines. "And how about you, Pearce? Have you coordinated the artillery for the night?"

"Yes, sir. They're set, subject to your approval." I had studied the map and identified points around our area where artillery might be needed: trails and streams that might be used by the Viet Cong to travel and low spots where the VC might set up mortars.

Charlie-Six nodded. "Good. Hang around after the meeting, and you and I will go over them."

He continued. "We will be re-supplied every other day, with hot meals, hopefully.

"As I said in the last meeting, we will be directed to conduct short missions in the area to investigate whatever Battalion asks us to. These have always turned out to be less than half a day. And I got the first one earlier this afternoon." He turned to Professor. "Congratulations, sir, the first one is yours. First thing in the morning, you will investigate a spot along the river east of here. There have been reports of possible supply point activities there." He read the concentration points and waited as we found them on the map. "You will investigate it, and we will report back to headquarters. I am to meet to get more details in—" he turned to his watch. "Thirty minutes. We will continue this meeting when I get back to finalize this mission. In the meantime, Professor, give your non-commissioned officers a heads up that they will be on call first thing in the morning. Are there any questions?" There were none.

Thirty-Four

SEPTIC TANK
MARCH 31, 1966

Mid-afternoon on the day we arrived just north of the village of An Sut, a large, filthy, yellow dog with the markings of a Labrador came from a patch of jungle and apparently decided to join us. He had specifically adopted a soldier that I knew only as "Roller Coaster" Randolph from Professor's platoon. The dog, and Roller Coaster for that matter, smelled like a sewage plant.

Early afternoon, a messenger had wandered into camp and delivered a communication radio part to Professor, who assigned Randolph to deliver it to Swizzledick. Randolph arrived at the command group with the dog in tow shortly thereafter.

Immediately Panther grimaced. "What the hell is that smell?" he shouted. He turned to Randolph. "Is that you or the damned dog?"

"It's him," Randolph said. "I haven't had a chance to wash him. I named him 'Terror.' He's French," he continued, as he handed the part to Swizzledick. "If I can find his papers, I am going to breed him." The group roared with laughter.

"Well, when you do, we would like to watch," Darnell shouted.

"How do you know that he's French?" Panther asked, holding the sleeve of his T-shirt over his nose.

"He is. He was found on a French plantation, and he likes the C-ration 'spaghetti and meatballs.'"

"For god's sake, man, 'spaghetti and meatballs' is Italian, not French," Swizzledick said disgustedly.

"Because of his aroma," B.J. Tucker said, "I make a motion that we call him 'Septic Tank.' Do I have a second?"

"Second," Darnell said, grinning broadly.

"All in favor say 'aye.'" A chorus rose. "All opposed? The 'ayes' have it." B.J. looked at Randolph. "From now on, this dog will officially be known as 'Septic Tank.'"

Randolph turned and walked away, shaking his head, Septic Tank at his side.

Across the road from where Charlie-Six's command group had settled was a large rice field, which discouraged any attack because of the lack of cover. Beyond that at about five kilometers was a sizable river. To the west, jungle had overtaken an abandoned rubber plantation that ran north and south for several kilometers. If we were attacked, that would be the most likely approach, so the primary fortifications faced that way, with Allegretti's platoon. Roughly a third of the remainder faced the road and the rice paddy, which was given to Bama. The rest, a curved line that ran between the other two, was given to Professor. This would be the area where we "curled up" each night.

Early the next morning, Charlie-Six was called by Battalion intelligence to a meeting. He was back in thirty minutes, and a meeting was called.

"OK, we have an ad hoc call for assistance. Professor, you get to take this one, as I told you yesterday. The 'intelligence folks' have reason to believe, from information obtained, that supplies and troops are being brought in at a point on the river with heavy vegetation. Their source is a Vietnamese citizen who informed Battalion that supplies and VC soldiers are being moved in and out at that point. We have not been able to see what, if anything, is going on there by air...vegetation is too thick. So, we have the honor of going in to take a look.

"The bottom line is that activity along the river due east of here is where you will go," he said as he pointed at Professor. "Move out as soon as you can, say, forty-five minutes? Bama, your platoon is on call as backup in case Professor gets hit and needs help. You're on standby for a fifteen minute response until Professor gets back." Charlie-Six turned toward me. "You will accompany Professor. Have Darnell stay with us. Are there any questions?"

I met with Professor as he briefed the mission to his platoon, non-commissioned officers, his sergeants.

"We have a mission. It's east of here, probably an hour and forty-five minutes, depending on the terrain, which is mostly rice paddies with some heavy jungle toward the end of the march. Most of the way should be fairly easy walking. There appears to be a Viet Cong supply point there. We are to check it out."

In twenty minutes, the mission was described. "Are there any questions?"

I had already heard the briefing from Charlie-Six, so I allowed my eyes and thoughts to wander. The platoon sergeant was an E-7, and all of the squad sergeants were E-6s. I watched Randolph. He was kneeling and petting Septic Tank. Randolph threw a stick, and the dog retrieved it and was rewarded with a spoonful of something from a C-ration can. He patted the dog's head and threw the stick once more.

We moved due east, following, but not walking, on the berms that surrounded the lush green rice paddies, as the Viet Cong often booby-trapped them. A cool breeze came from the fields, offsetting the heat of the sun that burned through our fatigue shirts. Packs had been removed and left at the main camp, leaving the main strap that held two canteens and two ammunition pouches, a much lightened load.

There was sudden laughter and shouting behind me, and I turned to see Septic Tank atop the berm that defined the southernmost paddy, walking parallel to Randolph and a soldier that I knew only as Fitz below. The dog jumped down and ran to him and was rewarded with a treat of some sort. Randolph and Fitz had been appointed as point men for the march. We continued for forty-five minutes toward a wall of jungle, which grew in height as we approached it. Septic Tank scurried up the berm and ran along it for about twenty yards, stopped to stare at the dense foliage roughly two hundred meters away, and then returned to Randolph, nuzzling his pockets for yet another treat. The dog repeated the process again.

The Professor called a halt. "Take ten," he said. "Does it strike you as strange that this mongrel seems so comfortable here?"

He called two of his squad leaders, Sergeants Simpson and Akins. "Watch for the dog, somewhere toward that lone mahogany tree at the jungles edge." We all did, as Septic Tank continued to run back and forth. Finally he ran once more, but instead of stopping, he ran into the jungle.

"There," Professor said, "where the dog went in!" He turned to one of the squad leaders. "He knows this place! Simpson, I want you to take one team of your squad and go to a point some fifty meters to the left of where the dog went in, and enter the jungle there, say, in fifteen minutes." He turned to Akins. "When Simpson goes in, you move out in front of us and advance directly to where the dog just went in. Assume it is a hot spot and maneuver accordingly." He turned to me. "Would you prepare for artillery on the same spot to which Sergeant Simpson is moving? Just in case."

Thirty minutes later, both sergeants had accomplished their missions. We joined them and walked into the thick forest. The underbrush had been cut away and cleared in a thirty-yard circle, and the ground had been scraped level by the movement of heavy objects, most likely pallets, we deduced. Professor called the 1st and 3rd Squad leaders and told them to set up defensive position facing the entry point. The place where Septic Tank had gone in was a living area, obviously Viet Cong, with two cots, lanterns, and a fire pit. Two cases of Army C-rations, three Army medical kits, two M16s, and a grenade launcher were first spotted beneath one of the cots, most likely to keep them out of the rain. Ammunition for the weapons was also beneath one of the cots.

The river passed the eastern edge of the compound, deep and swift. Huge trees hovered overhead. On the river side, a docking platform made of heavy timber had been constructed. Woven mats hung randomly in the area where the foliage was thin, and camouflage netting had been installed to ensure that nothing could be seen from the air. Tarpaulins covered several stacks of something, which Professor instructed Akins to have someone check them for booby traps. A length of parachute cord was cut and tied to the corner of one of the tarps, and from forty feet away was pulled to reveal a jackpot of materiel. The process was repeated.

"Charlie-Six, we're here," Professor said. "We have a significant dock on the west side of the river built of big ass timbers. There are all sorts of indicators of movement of heavy cargo from time to time. They've built a huge A-frame of twelve-foot logs tied together with what I would say are one-inch chains. There is a winch, industrial size, in the middle of the main frame. It is obvious by the scrapes in the earth that some crates are going through here. All of the area has camouflage netting, *Uncle Sam's* netting, stretched everywhere. The trees along each side of the river have been tied at the top and brought together to form an overhead screen. The result: the river, as far as we can see either way, is covered by a solid roof of trees and vines. There are no signs of huts or buildings on the map. I'll get back to you in fifteen minutes, once we have time to check it out."

"Sounds good," Charlie-Six mused. "Get back to me as soon as you can."

"Charlie-Six, I'm back," Professor said into the radio. "We have hit a jackpot. In that area, we found a variety of ammunition: rifle and mortar shells, even a dozen or so boxes of 105 artillery rounds. We have twenty-five rifles so far. All look to be usable. Eight are M16s. There are several cases of U.S. Claymores. There is a small electrical generator, several wenches, and a tool chest.

"There are two cots and evidence of cooking recently. The dog is sleeping comfortably under one of the cots. There are recent footprints, C-ration cigarettes, some magazines, even some medical supplies. And the icing on the cake is a collection of twenty Playboy magazines. Over."

"Interesting," Charlie-Six mused. "I'll notify Battalion and then get back to you pronto."

"Pronto indeed," Professor said. "This place gives me the creeps. We have formed a perimeter, but it is spread pretty thin."

Six was back in ten minutes.

"OK, listen up. I have been promised that a chopper will be here in thirty minutes to an hour with spooks on board. They seem very interested in what you've found. Hold what you have until they get there."

They came with cameras and a lieutenant and two specialists. In forty-five minutes, they inventoried, packed, and loaded most of what there was...enough that a second chopper had to be called in to carry everything out.

"They've loaded everything, including the Playboys, obviously to be examined as a source of enemy code!" Professor said, chuckling.

Fifteen minutes later, we were headed back to camp.

On orders, we returned a different way to check out one more area and a large—by Vietnamese standards—building. Spirits were high as we skirted the north edge of a large plain of rice fields separated by berms that crisscrossed at intervals of thirty feet, with water reflecting the sky and clouds above. A small road skirted them to the south and finally ended in an open field. We fanned out and continued to march toward the building. Teams approached it carefully, and in a short time we were there. It turned out to be nothing more than what it had appeared to be: a building, an *empty* building. We reported that and were told to "come on in." Once again Roller Coaster was the point man, accompanied by Septic Tank, his back slightly arched, his head down, and his tail between his legs.

The sun was in its full glory, with a comforting breeze. The men of the platoon formed two columns thirty feet apart as we moved along. There was no movement except for us and the dog as he dashed away, then back to Roller Coaster. The only sound was the muffled voices of the men.

At mid-afternoon, we stopped, our attention drawn to a single Vietnamese standing on a compound wall of bags, packed with dirt stacked to what I guessed to be four feet high. He was highly animated, standing on the sandbag berm, shouting and waving his arms. Professor called me over, and we studied the map. He reached for his radio. "Charlie-Six, this is Charlie-One, over."

B.J. Tucker answered the call. "Wait one, Charlie-One. I'll get Charlie-Six."

"This is Charlie-Six, over."

"Six, we are approaching a compound. And there isn't a compound shown on the map, over."

"What sort of a compound is it? You mean a military-sort of compound? With sandbags, machine gun emplacements. Is it that sort of compound?"

"It's that sort of compound. And there is a Republic of Vietnam soldier standing on the nearest wall, motioning for us to go back. He's pretty excited."

"Is he a threat?"

"Probably not, but he's not a welcoming party either."

"I'll call Battalion and see if they know anything about it. Keep me posted, and I'll get back to you."

We began to shift direction to the north. Within seconds, the sergeant increased his antics, his screaming an octave higher as he continued to scream.

He was now jumping up and down on the wall of sandbags and had ramped up his shouts and gestures.

"What the hell is he saying? Sounds like 'limes-rinds.' He shook his head. The soldier had moved to a higher point on the bunker wall, which held a machine gun. He was waving his arms and shouting, "Limes-limes!"

Birds flew above us, snatching insects from the air as we moved through knee-high grass, everyone watching the compound. Professor was on the radio. "I have no idea what this guy wants us to do. We're approaching it as if it might be a problem, over."

"Limes-limes!" the Vietnamese sergeant continued to yell, as he waved his arms wildly.

Suddenly, Panther grabbed my sleeve. "Not 'limes'!" Panther screamed. "The son-of-bitch is saying 'mines'!" he screamed. "Mines!"

Forty yards away, a bird, like a pheasant, burst into the air from its hiding place, startled by Septic Tank six feet away from it. The dog took two quick steps and lunged for it, arching through the air and coming to earth, landing on his right outstretched foot on an M14 U.S. Army landmine.

Every man in the platoon, instantly alert, dove to the ground when the explosion occurred, sending hundreds of pieces of mud, wild flowers, and the remains of Septic Tank into the air.

Every soldier felt the crushing pain of terror in his stomach, as every eye frantically sought movement throughout the area, along the berms and beyond every stem of grass.

A cacophony of sounds rose as Panther yelled into the radio, calling in a fire mission to our supporting artillery battery. The screaming from the Vietnamese sergeant was frantic. He had been joined by two of his comrades.

Professor yelled into his handset, and shouts came from sergeants in the field beside us, positioning their men.

"Roger, Dreadlock, wait out," Panther said softly. He looked at me. "Dreadlock's ready when you are," he said. I shook my head and continued to search the field.

I was kneeling next to Professor.

Six was on the radio. "Is anyone hurt? What happened? Talk to me!"

Professor yelled into his radio. "There is a fucking minefield out here, unmarked, and Randolph is right in the middle of it. The damned dog set the mine off, the best I can tell. There's no report of any casualties...yet."

"Can you get Randolph out?" Charlie-Six asked.

"I don't a have choice, do I, *SIR?*" Professor yelled into his radio. "The ground is dry and grassy. We may not be able to see where anyone stepped going into where he is now." He yelled at Roller Coaster, who was still thirty to forty yards away, frozen like the statue of liberty. "Randolph, are you all right?" Professor called out.

The young soldier simply nodded his head slowly. "Yes, sir. What's happening?"

"Not sure. Looks like a landmine," Professor said. "Just stay where you are. We'll get you out. Don't move!"

Just short of thirty minutes later, Private Randolph now sat where he had been standing, resting his chin on his fists. "The Army's recommended approach to this situation is to have the soldier, Randolph, leave the minefield by stepping in the same footprints that got him where he is in the first place." Professor said sourly. "Good luck with that. It's low grass, and the tracks can't be seen. End of discussion on that. Solution 'two' calls for the soldier to stick a bayonet into the ground at an angle to find mines, and if there is no mine there, it's safe to step there." He yelled. He called two sergeants over, explained the process to them, and told them to get started. After thirty minutes, there had been very little progress, as the soil was baked like concrete.

Professor was on the phone with Charlie-Six. "We're working our way there, but it is a slow way to go. Do you have any other ideas?"

"How far will they have to go?" Charlie-Six asked.

"Thirty, forty yards," Professor replied. "And the ground is hard and dry." There was a long pause. "Charlie-Six, did you hear me?" Professor asked into the radio receiver.

"Sorry. Yes, yes, I heard you."

"And?" Professor asked testily.

"Hang tight and relax," Six said. "I think we have a solution...an angel! I'll get back in fifteen minutes."

In fifteen minutes, the two soldiers approaching Roller Coaster Randolph in the minefield had little progress in reaching him. "It's gonna take a month at the rate we are moving. I don't think—"

Professor told them to stop and wait until Charlie-Six got back to him. We sat on the ground and waited.

East of us, a LOH chopper, a "flashbulb" droned softly. "Destroyer Niner-Three, this is Red Dog Three-Three, over." I had heard the voice but couldn't place it. I looked up to see a light observation helicopter coming toward us and descending. A rope with a large loop hanging down danced in the chopper's down blast.

"Red Dog?" I yelled into the handset. "T-Bone...T-Bone Thornton, is that you?"

"One and the same," responded the voice over my radio. "I got a call from Charlie-Six, and he said you needed my help. We came up with an idea," the voice continued. By then he was directly over Randolph, who needed no instructions to grab the rope and slip into the loop. Five minutes later, Randolph had been gently lowered into the open arms of his squad members, and the chopper banked away to the north.

"I owe you, man!" I screamed into my radio handset, looking up and grinning as widely as I could.

"Yes, you do. You really do. We 'angels of mercy' need special compensation. I would say one steak, two drinks, and three women," he replied, as the chopper continued to rise. He banked and keyed the radio talk button as he sang: "Happy trails to you, until we meet again."

I looked at Professor. "I wish to hell that I was enjoying this war as much as he is. I would settle for ten percent as much."

Shortly later, a chopper landed carrying Charlie-Six, along with Warrant Officer Holcomb, who was here to observe and clear the minefield. They were also accompanied by a specialist fourth class carrying a large plastic case of equipment and a Vietnamese interpreter who introduced himself simply as Johnny Walker Red. They all gathered around the screamer, the Vietnamese sergeant from the compound. By then the ARVN soldier had calmed considerably.

The WO of the group turned to Johnny Walker Red. "Ask him about the minefield."

Johnny Walker turned to the soldier and issued a string of sing-song syllables. The soldier responded in kind for almost a minute. The soldier's face darkened, and he began screaming.

"What did he say?" Holcomb asked as he turned toward Johnny Walker.

He said, "You are full of shit."

"The officer pulled a large knife from his pocket and opened the biggest blade. "Tell him I will cut his nuts off."

In Vietnamese, Johnny Walker responded as he pointed toward the lieutenant. "He said he will cut your manhood out."

"He won't," the soldier said slowly.

"He will, because he is anxious to get back to the asylum where he lives, where it is cool and there is beer...and nurses." After almost two minutes, Holcomb walked toward him, motioning for Johnny Walker to follow.

The sergeant held out his hands. "OK. There is a minefield," the Vietnamese said calmly.

"Tell him that he must show us where they are...all of them. He has to show us. He can't have this, this close to civilians. He has to tell us."

Johnny Walker replied to the soldier.

The soldier screamed a string of words, spittle flying from his mouth as he extended his index finger toward the officer.

Walker turned calmly, grinned, and looked at the lieutenant. "He said 'no, SIR.'"

The Vietnamese continued to scream, and Johnny Walker continued to translate. "You are not here all the time!" the Vietnamese screamed. "Americans are not here all the time," the soldier spoke, seeming to warm up. "You don't see what we see. You want our help, but don't send yours. We're alone."

The lieutenant turned to Charlie-Six. "Go ahead, we'll take it from here. Thanks."

Within fifteen minutes, we were on our way back to camp for the night. There were two letters: one from my mother and one from Julie.

Panther, Darnell, and I were bedded down within ten feet of each other. I stared at the lacy plantation sky. Somewhere in the jungle to the north was what sounded like a large cat screaming at something.

"Lieutenant?" Darnell asked, "How about 'I Can't Help Myself'?"

It took me a minute before I knew what he was asking. I grinned and responded, "No, thanks, I don't dance. My card is already full."

"'Do Wah Diddy Diddy'?"

"NO?"

"'Little Old Lady From Pasadena'?"

"Go to sleep, Sergeant. That's an order."

Thirty-Five

THE GAMES WE PLAYED
APRIL 2, 1966

For a period of time, our convoy duty consisted of manning strips of the highway along Route 1 as trucks went back and forth delivering materiel. This afternoon would be the last run, and we would return to Phuoc Vinh.

In the meantime, letters were shared, as were magazines and newspapers. Those from sweethearts were usually doused with liberal amounts of cologne, which made the inside of the mail bag rival a French lady's lingerie drawer. My mail today had been a surprise: a small portable tape cassette player/recorder from my brother with two cassettes.

I had read the instructions, placed the tiny speaker buds in my ears, and listened to Dvorak's Fifth-*Symphony to the New World*. I became giddy as I listened. My lips trembled slightly, and I felt tears rise along my eyelids. My high school band had played this my senior year. I sat with my back against a tree, amazed at what I was hearing. There is no place in a combat zone for Dvorak's music, I mused, yet there it was. Even if it was only on my new, small, reel-to-reel, battery-operated tape player with earphones...there it was. I listened to it once and played it for the second time today. It was therapy, in its rich, ordered score, yet it seemed incongruous and definitely out of place, as if music didn't belong here.

"So what music does belong here?" I asked myself. What I was listening to was like fine lace: ordered, smooth, and intricate, with trills from the wind instruments building to a dramatic climax, as a French horn quartet joined in. It was beautiful.

What about Tchaikovsky's *1812 Overture*? Or Franz von Suppé's *Light Cavalry Overture*? These were tributes to war, to man's participation in war. Even Mussorgsky's heavy, dark music didn't fit. None of it fit here. Yet, I found solace as I listened to Dvorak.

A sudden flurry of activity drew me back, and I jerked the ear plug out and located Panther. I turned to see two girls—teens—who had gotten too close to one of the soldiers on the perimeter, each holding two bottles of "33" Beer out to him. The squad sergeant yelled for them to leave, waving his arm in the air. They turned and left.

Then I was back to my music, back to my thoughts. So what did fit? It occurred to me that there were no birds, not even sparrows. I had not seen any today. Surely there were sparrows. I couldn't remember any. Had they all been driven away by the mayhem we had brought to Vietnam?

Did anything belong here?

I looked up to see Darnell walking toward me. I smiled. At least his conversation would be entertaining. I pushed the switch on the recorder and pulled the earphones out.

He pointed at the recorder, and I handed him the buds, and he listened to Dvorak for a minute before he handed it back. "Does it play real music?" he asked, "or just this funeral music?" His crooked smile crossed his face.

He showed me new pictures of his daughter in Amanda's lap, both dressed in frill and lace—church clothes, I assumed.

"Two beautiful women," I concluded, and handed it back.

"Yeah," he managed to get out.

"Nobody really wants to be where we are," I said, "but we all had much rather be here than walking the jungles. You may not like the music you are listening to at any given time, but it's a hell of a lot better than listing to the thunder of artillery."

He shook his head. "I'll let you get back to your therapy," he said as he stood and went to where the radio rats were expounding on the miracles of the world.

I turned the recorder off and leaned back against a tree, enjoying what they were saying. Darnell was presiding over a group of soldiers about ten feet away as the never-ending conversation continued. At the conclusion of the story, which was gross even for Darnell, he was jokingly chastised by B.J. Tucker. "Specialist Darnell," Tucker chided, "you, sir, are a hopeless sinner!"

"I don't believe in sin." Darnell said. "Life is easier that way. Do you believe in sin? What exactly is a sin?"

Tucker rose to the bait. "A sin is something you do that's wrong."

"You mean like putting a wheel on a car backwards or wearing your shoes on the wrong feet?"

"Like stealing," Dieters offered, joining the conversation. He was the religious one of the bunch gathered there.

"You never stole anything, Dieters?" Darnell asked with a broad grin on his face.

"No."

"Not even an apple? Not even a piece of candy? Not even a kiss from a married woman?"

"What about eating pork. Is that a sin? Or having a beer on Sunday? Or eating meat on Friday? Or dancing? It's all in the mind of whoever convinces you what a sin is."

"Sins are spelled out in the Bible if you ever bothered to—"

"Oh, I have bothered," Darnell interrupted. "I've bothered a lot. I've read it and had it read to me and been told by men in seventy-dollar suits what it means. The bible is a book report, just like in junior high. Mark, John...they heard the word and wrote it down. Then someone else translated it into a book report, and then someone else translated it, and so on and so on—"

"Well, I believe that—"

"That's nice," Darnell interrupted. "Everyone has to believe in something."

"And what do you believe in?" Dieters blurted out.

"I believe in ME," Darnell said softly.

"And how about murder," Dieters continued after several seconds. "Is that a sin?"

"It depends on the setting. Kill a man in Chicago, and maybe it's a sin...or maybe not. Maybe he deserved to die. Kill a man here, and it's probably not. Even if you shoot a Viet Cong, it's probably not."

I looked up to see Dieters flushed and confused, his mouth open. Darnell was staring at him. Dieters rose, turned, and walked slowly away. The color drained from Darnell's face the way it had on the day of the ambush. "Aw, Dieters. Man, I'm sorry," he said as he trotted to catch up with him. "Please, man, wait up. I-I didn't mean—"

Compared to what we had been going through, this had been soft duty. According to plans, the trucks were to have left Ben Hoa, heading back to join with us on our trips north. When they passed this morning, groups like ours would fall in at the rear of the convoy and join them and travel back, dropping off at wherever they called home—in our case, The Plantation.

We were to be picked up sometime in late morning.

An hour later, the convoy had not arrived. We were over an hour behind already. I could hear Charlie-Six on the radio. "OK, but get back to me ASAP."

He turned to me and shook his head. "Battalion says that the convoy south of here hasn't left yet. They're an hour late. That could put us out of here two hours late, or more."

"So what happens now?" I asked.

He pursed his lips and shook his head. "It beats me." The radio silenced once more—a message. Charlie-Six grabbed it and listened, grunting occasionally. "Son of a bitch!" he said as he put the radio down.

"What is it?" I asked.

"Two ARVN companies that were supposed to be guarding the road pulled out an hour ago, and three other units joined them...all heading north. We have a five-mile gap between here and Phuoc Vinh with no protection."

After twenty minutes, the radio sounded, and he spoke into the handset. "This is Charlie-Six, over. Uh-huh, uh-huh." With each "uh-huh," his face grew darker. "Roger. Out." He handed the handset to B.J. Tucker. "Call the lieutenants. Get 'em over here."

As we sat on our helmets at his feet, he explained the situation. "Part of the road between us and Phuoc Vinh is no longer secure. Three companies that should be between here and there somehow were told to go ahead and start back to Brigade—Phuoc Vinh." He looked at each of us. "We don't have any convoy security between here and Phuoc Vinh."

The radio buzzed again. Charlie-Six took the message. We're not alone in this *friggin'* mess. There are about four more companies south of us, stranded like we are. They are on the road headed here to spend the night. We are to all set up a perimeter when they get here. It will be late by then. We all head out in the morning. Are there any questions?" There were none.

Thirty minutes later, the companies from south of us began pulling into the clearing and were directed to their new location for the night by the Military Police. There was one more infantry company, two 105 howitzer artillery batteries, and a troop of the Quarter Horse Cavalry. With us, they formed a much larger protective perimeter.

It was a beehive of activity as everyone moved into position. Trucks were placed, and the artillery batteries were laid out. The elements of the Fourth Cavalry were interspersed throughout the large circle.

"We're here for the night," he said as he walked away. "Hang tight. I'll be back as soon as I can."

"Well, they taught me at the University of Alabama that military history repeats itself. I just wonder if anything like today ever happened to Stonewall Jackson." Bama threw the contents of his coffee against the base of a tree. "Well, if you'll excuse me, I will go and inform my platoon, like officers in the past, that I have no friggin' idea what is happening!"

Charlie-Six was back in thirty minutes. He described how the other units had been dispersed.

I thought, "I haven't felt this safe since we left the states. I was asleep in five minutes."

Thirty-Six

THE NIGHT OF TOLKIEN'S ORCS
APRIL 2, 1966

I was instantly awake when Panther shook me, his hand over my mouth until I was awake.

"What-what's wrong?" I asked.

"Captain Novak wants to see you pronto!"

"What time is it?" I asked as I stared at my watch.

"Ten past midnight, sir. And I am afraid that you are *still* in Vietnam. And Captain Novak *still* wants to see you." I pulled on my boots and walked to where he was talking on the radio. He looked up and held one finger in the air.

"Allegretti is getting some reports from Sergeant De La Pena. Some occasional movement. If anyone else was reporting it, I wouldn't be as concerned, but he is a solid soldier."

I turned and stared toward Allegretti's platoon area as if expecting to see something. "Is it anything substantial?" I asked finally.

"Probably not, but let's stay awake until they settle down."

For the most part, given the number of men and the amount of equipment, it was incredibly quiet. The rushing noise of the radio stopped, indicating an incoming call. We both looked at B.J., and then he stood and carried the radio to the Captain. "This is Charlie-Six, over."

"Charlie-Six, there's something out there. This isn't like De La Pena. Any ideas?"

Six stared at me.

"How about I fire a flare?" I asked. "If the Viet Cong is out there, they already know we're here. They probably watched us set up for the night. I can get the 105 battery to light up the sky."

Six scratched his chin and spoke to Allegretti. "Destroyer Niner-Three suggests a flare. What do you think?"

"That's a good idea."

"Let us check and see. We have a hell of a lot of folks to coordinate with. Give us five minutes."

Six contacted the other units while I talked to the artillery battery nearest us. No one was opposed.

In ten minutes, I was calling Destroyer, the 105 howitzer battery that was preparing to fire a mission for me.

"Destroyer Two-Three, this is Destroyer Niner-Three. Fire mission, over." It came as no surprise to him, as he had been one of the calls I had made to set it all up.

"We suspect enemy activity beyond listening posts. Coordinates—" I gave him the information, including where I wanted the shell. "Shell illumination. Request one round, over."

"Destroyer Niner-Three, observe one round."

"Destroyer Two-Three, roger. Wait out." I had hardly finished when the explosive blast shattered the silence, shaking the upper branches of the rubber trees. In seconds, a brilliant light appeared in the sky, lighting up what was now the entire battlefield before us and the rubber plantation beyond our lines.

I felt acid begin to rise in my throat.

The silence evaporated immediately as Allegretti's platoon opened up. He was on the line. "We have VC coming our way. I've called De La Pena's listening post in. They are coming in now".

It occurred to me that the VC may well never have seen a flare like this, and they continued to come toward us. The light above, a phosphorus core attached to a small parachute, swung from side to side, illuminating the VC on the field before us as they came. They were crouched and seemed to sway from side to side as they continued to approach. The image of the Orcs from Tolkien's Trilogy came to mind. "They are approaching the line!" De La Pena shouted into his radio.

"We're clear now," Allegretti said on the radio. Charlie-Six reported it immediately, and in seconds the 50-caliber machine guns from our armored personnel carriers opened up with a continuous string of three round bursts: *caulk-caulk-caulk. Caulk-caulk-caulk.* The infantry companies, Destroyer and Dogface, joined in. And the 105 howitzers began firing direct fire at the approaching Viet Cong soldiers.

The silence of the night was gone. The rest of the orchestra that could see the approaching soldiers joined in on the grisly symphony.

"De La Pena says there must be a hundred of them coming at us."

"1, 2, 3, this is Charlie-Six. We have confirmed enemy activity."

Swizzledick shouted into the radio. "Stay alert."

"Destroyer Two-Three, this is Destroyer Niner-Three. We have a mission for another flare. Stand by." Again, the explosion was followed by the brilliant light of the flare.

"They're here, Charlie-Six, to my front." I fired another flare. In seconds it illuminated the field of Viet Cong soldiers moving our way, closing on our position. They were made menacing and grotesque by the contrasting shadows and the flare, and seemed to continue to dance as the flare rocked back and forth above. They appeared as cockroaches crawling over a cake.

Hell was open for business as everyone around the perimeter came to life. The eight-inch howitzers were firing direct fire to their front, as trees two hundred yards away pinwheeled into the night sky and mud flew into the air. Enemy soldiers seemed to disintegrate in the open field. The armored cavalry covered its front, with the 50-caliber machine guns barking and sending their strings of shells across the field.

Just after midnight, it began to die down. Another flare revealed a field of carnage with bodies strewn everywhere. The wounded screamed and wailed with pain, but no one came to help them. Smoke rose from burning grass and trees that had caught fire across the field. And the moon moved behind a bank of clouds as if too embarrassed to watch. The firing dwindled, then ceased. A blanket of smoke, twenty feet above the entire battlefield, trapped the sounds, the screams, and moans. It trapped the hideous smell of split intestines and bowel movements, shattered bodies, and blood. It formed an amphitheater and the smell of dying, crying men.

"Charlie-Six," B.J. said, speaking into the radio. "Yes, sir. I'll get him," he said as he jumped to his feet and carried the radio to Charlie-Six.

"Six, over." Captain Novak said into the mic. "God...no" was all he said as he nodded his head for several seconds, then let his arm with the handset drop to his side. "De La Pena was killed coming in," he said turning to me. After several seconds, he turned to B.J. "Check in with 1st and 2nd Platoons." He turned into the shadows and simply stood there.

It was tense. Soldiers moved about to improve their positions. Smoke filled with the acrid smell of cordite and mixed with the moist air. It hung above the open field before us like evil spirits. I stepped to a nearby tree and threw up at its base.

At 4:30, it began again, this time from the southwest. It lasted thirty minutes, as additional VC bodies fell to direct fire from everyone on the opposite side of our perimeter. There would be no more surprises. Soldiers disintegrated before the heavy direct fire of the 50-caliber machine guns.

Mercifully, at last, the field in front took on a shadowy gray light, and then pale pink, then light as the sun rose, making blood-covered bodies even redder with cheery shades of pink and orange. It was over.

There were bodies everywhere...simply too many to be carried away. There were less than twenty rounds of 105 howitzer ammunition left in the two batteries and less than an average of twenty rounds of ammunition per man. Their basic load at the beginning of the battle had been two hundred rounds per man.

A VC soldier who had been wounded and bled out was found dead within ten feet of the fire direction center for Dogface, another infantry company with us. He had enough C-4 explosive strapped to his body to kill a third of the men in our compound.

By six o'clock, the 'Crisp and Cleans,' the intelligence teams from Division headquarters, began to arrive, two helicopters with six in each one. They contacted Charlie-Six. He called in the officers from all of the other units. After a discussion, he called a meeting with the lieutenants.

"We move out in an hour. Our job is to work with a team from headquarters to try to identify who these people were that hit us last night. The feeling was that they weren't 'run of the mill' Viet Cong. Dogface will go out with another team. A chopper will land in ten minutes with rations, ammunition, and other supplies. We have little time, so let's get it done."

We broke up, and I turned to see Lieutenant Colonel Urrutia with his soothing, plaintiff smile. He shook my hand and held it. "Bless you, Craig," he said softly. "I thank God for seeing you through the night."

"It is always good to see you, sir."

"I prayed for you last night...when I heard that your unit was in trouble."

"I appreciate that, Father. Pray often for all of us."

At 0700, Charlie Company led out across the field of bodies. Part of the intelligence team that had arrived earlier accompanied Charlie Company. They had spread out among the corpses, searching them for whatever their clothing might conceal: scraps of paper, pocket knives, pencils, small amounts of currency, and crinkled, tattered pictures. Another body had been found less that fifty feet from our front line, with a large amount of C-4 explosives taped to his body and a detonator in his hand, lying in a large puddle of sticky, purple blood. He had bled out before he could plunge the trigger device. Some of the intelligence teams were examining bodies for booby traps and personal items that would identify who they were and from where they came.

Charlie Company was directed to serve as a guardian force to take the intelligence investigators into the jungle so that they could further learn from what happened and what waited there. It was bizarre. It was a world of frightened, moaning men, of body parts strewn over a small clearing like a small child's toy chest. The smell of urine, feces, and warming flesh hung in the air. The eyes of maimed, riddled men stared into eternity.

At 0800, the sun had fully risen, accompanied with intense heat. Flies came in swarms, and the intensity of the stench rose with every degree of temperature. Our trek was a nightmare, inundated with the stench of death and bodies twisted by rigor into grotesque shapes. Their mouths hung open as if they had died while talking to someone. They had been left to die, the smell of their blood and ruptured entrails cooking in the heat. Moans rose, randomly drawing shots from panicked soldiers of Charlie Company. Our soldiers fell away and wretched, then re-joined the column as it moved through these scenes. Finally we walked into the shade of the giant trees and vines, shattered by the battle. Soldiers tied their towels away from their necks and wrapped them across their faces.

The trail itself told a tale of a very primitive form of triage. The worst cases that had been dragged or carried from the battlefield were the first abandoned by the fleeing VC Army. They were left just off the trails where they lay twisted like manikins, their eyes already swollen shut.

The second level was those who had some chance of living, but couldn't be carried by a fleeing army, and as such, were still alive and in what appeared to be in some stage of narcotics, with zombie eyes staring past us as we moved along. Soldiers tried to avoid their stares, turning their heads, only to face other dying Viet Cong at the next turn. The only thing given to us that morning was visions that we would have forever.

The hardened men of Charlie Company vomited, paled, and cried shamelessly.

A preliminary body count had been difficult, initially eighty to ninety dead, with fractions of bodies that could only be guessed at.

My stomach burned, carrying me to the point of screaming, as acid raced up my throat.

It was a relief when we finally entered the serenity of what was left of the rubber plantation on the other side. We followed a gruesome trail of blood-stained tree trunks, bandages torn free by tree branches, and occasional bodies left just off the trail and covered with branches. At mid-morning, we returned inside our lines. It was hot, and it smelled like a rendering plant.

The story pieced together by the intelligence specialists was that the regiment-size force, somewhere around 500 soldiers, had information that told them that the force they were to hit was one infantry company and one artillery battery. This had been the force that had occupied The Plantation for the previous two nights. What they had actually hit was the *convoy army* that had come in at dusk the night before.

When the Republic of Vietnam Forces had left their positions early, leaving the road unguarded, the Cavalry, another infantry company, and another artillery battery joined in the current position, creating a force bordering on brigade size.

The intelligence officers were ecstatic, congratulating themselves on the information gleaned from the bodies, as they continued to search the dead. They identified some of them as officers, two of them from North Vietnam. One carried a map with small red x's on it in areas east of the Cambodian borders. There were a large number of weapons. Far too many of them were M16s, several AK-47s, several new automatic weapons that I was not familiar with, and a menagerie of others.

As we returned to our camp at noon, I passed a Charlie Company private who looked to be thirteen. His eyelids were ringed by a blood-colored line, and he held a small silver cross on a chain between his teeth.

As we were released to return to our area, we passed a dozen or so wounded enemy soldiers, alive, stripped down to their shorts, with their eyes covered, tape over their mouths, and their wrists bound.

By 1000 the next day, we turned down the lane that took us to The Plantation. There was no joy, no bantering, or horseplay. By two that afternoon, engineer trucks came with boilers for hot water and portable showers.

I saw no one writing letters.

The mess hall had pork chops, salad, corn on the cob, and cherry cobbler.

There was also mail: a letter from my mom. Everyone was fine—"Mr. Withers said to tell you that he thinks that you were a fine man and a good soldier." The crops were doing fine, and it was branding time.

I looked up to see Father Urrutia wandering among the soldiers, plying his trade.

There was a newspaper clipping enclosed. Seven days earlier, the Hobbs newspaper, the Sun News, relayed how the Eagles of Hobbs High School men's basketball team had vanquished its foe on the field of honor under their legendary coach Ralph Tasker, *slaughtering* them before a crowd of over 2000 screaming fans. What a simple world.

That evening, we badly needed humor. The indomitable spirit of GIs in combat appeared on the flap of the latrine. The sign read "What is the difference between the three-pound lump found in 'Roller Coaster' Randolph's pants in the minefield and a mess hall meatloaf? And the answer is? The stuff from his pants is tastier." It was signed: "The voice of culinary justice, The Phuoc Vinh Phantom."

The next day, seventy-five men, the remains of Charlie Company—dwindled by ten killed and twice that many wounded—listened to the chaplain. An unusually cool breeze tugged at the leaves above as he began to read the names. There were no helmets in square holes; there were simply not enough. Colonel Urrutia simply read the names: Platoon Sergeant Eduardo Tomas De La Pena, Specialist Fourth Class Leonard Tabor, Specialist Fourth Class Ralph Duncan...the list went on and on.

As he spoke, I scanned the trees that were standing on the gently rolling slope, hundreds of them in silent ranks and files. "Lord," I thought, "if you intend for us to fill this entire field with helmets, I had just as soon not have to watch it all."

Thirty-Seven

THANK YOU, BARRY MCGUIRE
APRIL 5, 2014

We were back in camp at the officer's tent. I sat on the edge of my cot, applying a waterproofing compound to my boots and drinking my blues away from a pint bottle of Cutty Sark. Professor, the only other person there, was reading. Bama and Allegretti had gone to Battalion to see some old friends.

Professor sat quietly reading a copy of some new magazine he had received from home, already eight days old. His blond hair, though combed and parted, sported a rooster tail in back. He breathed deeply, looked up at me, and let out an exasperated sigh.

"So," I asked, "what's the latest score on the war?"

"Well, it's not what we learned in reserve officer training in college," he said melodically. "It all seems to still be in the 'defining stage,' best I can tell. The bad guys seem to be wreaking havoc, and the good guys...just now seem to be figuring out that a new approach is needed." He shifted in his chair toward me, his legs crossed with a thong sandal draping from his suspended right foot. He rolled the magazine and held it up. "The times they are changing." He reached down and picked up a mess hall cup and took a drink. "My sources—Time, Newsweek, and Mad Magazine—are what I go by.

"On the one hand, we have 'Big Bill' Westmoreland saying we can win this war in three easy steps." He pointed his index finger at the Coleman lantern suspended above. "Step one, he says, is to have U.S. and Vietnamese Forces form a ring around certain strategic areas, such as Saigon: Tan Son Nhut Air Base, Vung Tau, the major cities. Step two—" He raised another finger forming a V. "We work with the ARVN soldiers, the Army of the Republic of Vietnam, until they are comfortable with the concept. Once those rings are under control and secure, we begin cutting back on the number of U.S. forces and turn it over to the ARVN, and they assume the responsibility of holding it. Well, that's not totally accurate. We will continue to have some allied troops with them. Anyway, we move out and form even larger rings, or rings at different locations, and repeat the process with new ARVN troops, and they take over. The number of circles grows." He paused as he picked up the cup and drew another sip of scotch. "We continue, with more circles, more happy people, flowers, Disney's bluebirds, and peace and progress."

He held up three fingers. "And step three? Well, there seems to be the problem." He belched loudly. "Step three says that we extend the rings further and further out from those strategic locations, each time turning the newly gained territory over to the ARVN. Great plan, Big Bill, except for a couple of itsy, tiny, little flaws. The Vietnamese put up such a great show of manning those positions that the allies turn them over to them, until...until the VC show up. Then the ARVN realize that it's time for a three-day weekend, and everything is lost. The Vietnamese civilians get their collective asses kicked, a few are killed to make an example of them, and the VC melt back into the jungle...or back to running their stores in downtown Saigon. Having the Vietnamese army stand duty at any point or checkpoint is a vicious cycle, with apparently neither firm ground nor firm resolve." He smiled at me.

"On the other hand, we have the philosophy of this guy, this singer from California." Dave licked his thumb and turned through the pages of his magazine until he came upon a face, which he held up for me to see. "Barry McGuire, who is setting the music world on fire with lyrics that admonish us to—" He studied the page, then said, "Ah, yes. Here it is: 'tell me over and over again, my friend, you don't believe we're on the eve of destruction.' And he has a lot of people learning the lyrics because they want to sing along with him."

"And now, Big Bill scratches his 'four-star' chin and says: 'you know, there may be something to what Barry is saying. And what we have to do to avoid that eve of destruction is to continue to keep troops in the circles to help the ARVN. More allied troops.'"

He drained his cup, reached in his foot locker, pulled out his stash of scotch, and poured in a liberal amount. He paused and stared at me, holding up the bottle.

"No, thanks. I am having trouble spelling 'New Mexico' as it is," I said, realizing that I was slurring my words slightly.

"The ARVN aren't totally to blame. They just don't have the military background we do. They just don't share the view of war, or the necessity, that John Wayne taught most of us Americans in *The Sands of Iwo Jima*."

"So, what's next?" I asked.

"Well—" he paused and bobbed his head to clear a belch that seemed to be caught in his throat. "It is clear to me that we need...we need to start showing *The Sands of Iwo Jima* to every Vietnamese male in the ARVN, maybe three or four times each. Or as we capture these strongholds, instead of turning them over completely to the Army of the Republic of Vietnam, we put our people, who did see and were impressed with John Wayne and *The Sands of Iwo Jima*, in the foxholes to help secure them." He watched as I twisted my mouth and eyebrows.

"Just a moment, my friend," Professor continued. "That is precisely what Big Bill Westmoreland is asking Mr. President Johnson to do: to go from thirty or forty thousand of us over here now, to three or four hundred thousand of us over here in the near future. And Congress is squirming and twisting in their collective seats, and Barry's *Eve of Destruction* is going through the roof."

He stopped and belched. "And, word has it that this the new concept starts *for us, day after tomorrow.* " He held the magazine open to a quarter-page picture of Westmoreland. "I think we are heading into a new philosophy—" He paused. "A new philosophy," he said slowly, "where our primary goal is moving away from 'roasting rice' like we did last week to a philosophy which concentrates on stacking up VC bodies."

Finally I spoke. "So what the hell does all of that translate to?"

"It translates to a new concept, my precious friend. One that says from now on we grind at the VC every time we find them, everywhere we find them until they give up. Then we lock our socks and shorts in our duffel bags, have one more round of Vietnamese beer, pro—" He belched loudly. "—promise to meet back here in ten years...and go back to wives and homes." He paused as a crooked smile arranged itself on his face. "Or, as in at least one case, to our multiple girlfriends and their multiple homes."

He folded his magazine and placed it on his foot locker. He removed his glasses, placed them in his lap, and rubbed his eyes with the heels of his hands. "Anyway, either heavy philosophy makes me need to take a shit or heavy shit makes me need to philosophize."

He placed his glasses on his foot locker, stood, and walked toward the front of the tent. "Back in a minute," he said.

He turned and ran into the tent pole and dropped his cup. He gathered himself and stepped outside, rubbing his forehead as he walked into the darkness.

Thirty-Eight

HELL HATH NO FURY—
APRIL 7, 1966

I held it in my hand. It was a letter from Angie...a single sheet of paper, a handwritten note that floated to the ground. I picked it up and read. "*WHO IN THE HELL IS JULIE? AND WHY WAS YOUR LAST LETTER TO HER SENT TO MY ADDRESS? ADDRESSED TO ME!!! YOU SORRY BASTARD!*

My throat locked up, and I couldn't breathe. I stumbled to a nearby tree and slid down its trunk to the ground. I read it again. Then I stiffened against the tree. "Mother of pearl," I thought, "I got the *last letters to them* mixed up." I stared at the sun. "Then-then, that means that Julie got the one intended for Angie!" I struggled to remember what I had said in my last letter to Angie. I had said nothing romantic, I knew. I hadn't even told her that I loved her. I knew that I hadn't done that in sometime.

There was no letter from Julie. After several days, I wrote her and told her what had happened. A week after the letter fiasco, Julie wrote. "Dear

Craig- I was mad at first! Then confused and then, I thought that it was funny- only you could be so bone-headed. I love you. I trust you. I believe you. So, her name is- *was* Angie. Well, that's behind us now- right?" It was signed "Julie- yours forever- I love you. P.S. Enjoy the art."

There were twenty-five pictures depicting superheroes drawn with crayons on Big Chief Tablet sheets. They were all of Superman. "Enjoy. *YOU* are my Superman- and I love you.

Two days later, in shock, I watched as a linen-like envelope embossed with a long stem rose curled around the bottom corner slip from my fingers to the ground. I picked it up, tore the end from the envelope, and slid the contents out. I took out a lacy piece of fabric-like paper. "Ours will be forever" was written in gold foil script, with two more deeply embossed, intertwined roses on the lower left corner.

"Mr. and Mrs. Daniel Weaver invite you to the wedding of their Daughter, Angelina Fay Weaver, and Captain Wayne Cartwright." I ignored the dates and events. The bottom line read "The reception will follow."

I thought, "Yes, and I'll bet that it would be a damned cold one for me." I picked up pieces from the envelope and walked to the burn spot. I lit the corner of the invitation and held it up, guiding the flame until it was a shadow, then dropped it to the ground and stomped it into the dirt.

"Son of a bitch," I whispered. "You've been seeing him all along."

I breathed a sigh of relief. "I really wish you the best," I said as I stared through the rubber trees at a path of blue sky. "And Lord, thanks for your help."

Thirty-Nine

GOOD NIGHT, SWEET PRINCE
APRIL 15, 1966

Professor was reading an article aloud, Bama was cleaning his cigarette lighter, Allegretti was writing a letter, and I was lying on my bunk staring at the black numerals stenciled on our canvas tent ceiling.

It came. Acid ran up my throat and into my mouth. The sound of a round fired beyond the latrines to the south. Immediately, every eye in the camp, every ear, every standing hair was attuned in the direction of the sound. We all four grabbed our rifles and ran for Charlie-Six's tent, the assembly point in the event of an emergency. Platoon sergeants sprang into action to "implement the arc," the defensive plan that had been rehearsed relentlessly for attacks on the camp. I looked at my watch. It was 2015 hours.

Charlie-Six was on his radio to Battalion when we all arrived at his location. "I'll get back the second I know what happened," he said to the major at Battalion. "And you are sure that you know of no friendly activity in this area? Uh-huh. OK, we'll go with that." He turned to us as he handed the radio handset to Swizzledick. "OK, what do we know?"

Allegretti spoke first. "A single shot came from out beyond the latrines, probably a hundred yards." As he spoke, he turned and looked at the other lieutenants as if asking for confirmation.

"OK, everyone, let's get set up." Each officer knew that it was already being done, and within minutes it would be in place. A single line was being formed as Professor's platoon was fanning out in foxholes along the entrance road. Bama's platoon had done the same in holes beyond the mess tent to the south. And Allegretti's men were in place beyond the latrine and the water trailer. Beyond all of those positions, another thirty meters out, two-man advanced foxholes were being occupied, and Claymore mines set up to their front. Every machine gun in the company was in place. It was done. It was quiet.

"Allegretti, I want you to send a squad out to the south to where the shot came from, no more than two hundred meters, and see what you find," Charlie-Six said. "The rest of you finish getting into position...and set tight." The entire time that he spoke, he tapped a yellow pencil against the back of his hand. "Questions?" he asked. "I want each of you to send a runner in fifteen minutes telling me that everyone is in place. This may be a hell of a long night."

"Pearce, check with Destroyer and verify once more that the concentrations that you have at the end of The Plantation are ready."

"I already have," I replied. "We have the same concentrations as we've had since I first got here. I just got off the radio with Flash. Alpha Battery is set to fire high angle fire. Specialist Darnell is finalizing all of that now. I can have balls in the air in five minutes."

The arc was in place. There were no lights, no cigarettes. There was no music. There was no sound, except for the hissing of the army radios as they awaited calls.

In fifteen minutes, the patrol was back. "We have a man down. Dead," Allegretti said calmly to Charlie-Six. "It is safe to go there. It's all over."

Charlie-Six and I followed him to a point in The Plantation where his platoon sergeant knelt just beyond the flashlight circle. He shined a flashlight on a body. "Sweet Jesus," Charlie-Six mumbled.

The entire left side of Specialist Dieters' head was gone. A red cavity dotted with glistening white teeth remained. Blood continued to ooze from vessels in his neck.

The sergeant turned the light to the tree next to the body. A string of white, sticky sap ran from a nail that had been driven to hold a note. It read "The Bible recognizes what we as soldiers do. Psalms 118:17."

"Get me Battalion," Charlie-Six said disparagingly. In seconds, the radio handset was handed back to him. "Yes, sir," Charlie-Six said softly into the headset. "You can stand down. And I need a military police forensic unit as soon as possible."

Fifteen minutes later, two military police vehicles arrived. Lieutenant Cutter and two sergeants stepped from the jeep beside where Charlie-Six stood. The scene was already surrounded with orange tape, with two soldiers standing guard. Thirty minutes later, Cutter met with Charlie-Six and the lieutenants, his preliminary investigation concluded. "Major Travolta has already asked that you meet with him at your convenience somewhere in the morning," Cutter said.

I walked back toward the captain's tent with First Sergeant Flaherty, and we were met by Lieutenant Colonel Urrutia. Charlie-Six shook his hand and explained what had happened. He thanked the priest for "always being there" and departed.

The colonel turned and walked to me. "That young man thought a lot of you. He thought a lot of your radio operator...Panther, right? And how is he doing?"

"He is with his friends."

"And you?" He simply stared at me for several seconds. "Are you okay?"

"Is anyone in Vietnam who is dressed in army green okay?" I asked, smiling. "Yes, I am okay. And I'm not surprised that you are here. Thank you."

"Will you pray with me?"

I took his hand, and he began. He whispered, "Amen."

"God bless you, Chaplain, and thanks for being here," I said as I turned and walked away.

Two days later, the official report arrived. "Death caused by self-inflicted gunfire." *Two disinterested parties*, as required by regulation, the First Sergeant Flaherty and I began to inventory Dieters' belongings to "ensure that nothing was there that could be deemed embarrassing to the deceased's family or the Department of the Army." Allegretti also provided two privates to help us. When they arrived, Sergeant Flaherty instructed them to find a container of kerosene and bring it back in thirty minutes.

We began.

All pockets of every piece of clothing were searched for any item, which were placed in a large manila envelope marked "Personal Effects." His foot locker was examined for any notes or messages. His mattress was examined and tossed outside the tent.

All military clothing that had his name on it and all military underwear, shoes, and socks were set aside to be burned. Personal belongings were set aside for further review, catalogued, and placed in a second envelope.

As if on cue, the two privates arrived. First Sergeant Flaherty pointed to the stack of clothing, boots, underwear, towels, and a Sears and Roebuck mattress. "Take this out to the burn area, douse it well, and stand there until there is nothing left. Oh, before you do, go by the mess tent and pick up a fire extinguisher." He stared at them as if analyzing their intelligence. "And stand upwind when you light the fire."

Sergeant Flaherty turned to me. He held a stack of letters. "This is a tricky part...what to do with them. In one of the earlier cases, we found letters from one of the soldiers killed, showing that he and his sister-in-law were having an affair. So, since then, we do a pretty thorough job of looking through them." He handed me half the stack of letters. My half was thirty-eight letters. I opened each one, read them all, and handed them back. He did the same, and a rubber band was put around the stack and placed in a box marked "Dieters—Personal."

"Do you write the letter to the family?" I asked.

"Not us. Battalion personnel will take care of that, as well as filling out the forms. They have most likely already notified Department of the Army, who has contacted someone in the area—probably in the middle of the night—who, along with another officer from the base nearest his home, will notify the family in person. That has already happened, I imagine." He looked up at me. "What a shitty job that would be!"

We inventoried everything that remained. The first sergeant read the list of personal belongings, and one of the company clerks recorded everything there: "One two-blade Kabar pocket knife, two bibles, a gold cross and chain, a high school class ring, a pair of thong sandals, a civilian belt, a small picture album, a wallet with three pictures in it, and..." He paused as he counted the cash inside. "Fifteen piastres and ten dollars American cash, and a small card, like linen, with Psalms 119:74 printed on it, and a Duncan yo-yo." First Sergeant pulled out a cigarette and lit it.

I stared at the box with all of his belongings. "Not much of a testimony to a good man," I said.

"That's it, Lieutenant," Sergeant Flaherty said, picking up the box. "I'll have some papers for you to sign later today. Personnel at Battalion will take care of the rest." He stuck out his right hand, and we shook. "And thanks for your help." He turned and left.

When finished, Dieters' entire life in Vietnam was packed into a cardboard box, twelve inches by twelve inches by six inches, sealed by the company clerk and hand delivered, along with the required forms, by the first sergeant to battalion personnel.

I walked farther away from camp into The Plantation and lay down, my head against one of the trees. I watched pure white clouds pass overhead, clouds created by God, which could have come from Arizona into New Mexico into Vietnam, sent there for young Vietnamese boys like me and Bobby to ponder.

Forty

JUST ANOTHER CASUALTY OF WAR
APRIL 18, 1966

Under a cloudless, breezeless, treeless sky, the heat seemed to burn through the sweaty, green, khaki-like cloth, and my steel helmet had turned into an oven.

We had spent the day moving through craters created in a B-52 bombing raid to evaluate the damage to the terrain. We were forced to crawl through, over, and under craters twenty yards across and ten deep, surrounded by huge trees, split and twisted from top to bottom. Matters were made worse by the fact that rains from two nights before had turned the craters into mud pits. As a result, we were caked like pigs.

We had worked an entire day, going no more than three thousand meters. In late afternoon, we came to the end at the edge of an abandoned rice paddy. We stopped for the night near a gift from God: a small, clear stream. On the map, a small village lay to the north. The perimeter was quickly set up along the walls of the berms. Darnell called in the artillery locations. "I couldn't have done it better myself," I said as he finished.

Panther joined us, and the three of us took turns bathing in the stream that ran just outside the wall.

Forty minutes before sundown, muscles had relaxed. I sat on my helmet and ate C-ration canned peaches from a small can. Relaxation was a rare, cherished moment, and I savored it.

Just before sunset, as the camp settled down, a shot rang out not far from where Charlie-Six and I were discussing tomorrow's activities.

"What do you have?" Charlie-Six asked Allegretti, who was closest to where the shot had been heard.

"Just one shot so far," Allegretti said. "And we caught a glimpse of the shooter there, just to the left of that dip in the berm wall." He pointed at a waste-high berm roughly twenty-five yards away. "Got it?" he asked.

"I do," I said.

"Hit that spot, and I will owe you a beer."

I turned to Darnell. "Call it in, Darnell," I said. He smiled and took my map. He studied it, wrote down the coordinates, and held them up for me to see. They were beyond the berm, but that suited me fine. "It looks good to me." In two minutes, Darnell stood beside me as his first two rounds hit, rounds fired to disrupt any group that might be in front of us and beyond the shooter.

He then turned to Allegretti. "Do you want more, sir?"

"No," Allegretti said. He turned to a lanky squad sergeant. "Check it out, Sergeant Paxton."

"Yes, sir" was the reply, and his squad was on the move, slithering over the berm and out of sight.

I turned back to Allegretti and resumed my gaze. Another shot, followed by a yell. "There the mother fucker is...two berms over." Shots were fired along the second berm as the squad slid over the wall and made its way over to the next one farther away and ducked for cover.

The Viet Cong's head rose for several seconds to see where Allegretti's men were, a deadly mistake, as what sounded like a dozen individual shots rang out. As they did, the members of 1st Squad were across the open space where the VC had last appeared. Two groups of two men ran, converging from different angles along the berm, and then slid to the other side.

The world was silent as Allegretti joined me.

Sergeant Paxton raised his head. "All clear!" he yelled.

Allegretti turned to me. "Come on, Pearce. Let's go check it out." We were there in two minutes. Darnell was still talking to the artillery battery. Panther was over the wall with ease. Then, just as fast, he jumped back over the wall towards us, vomiting his soul out.

In fifteen minutes, the corpse had been wrapped in a poncho atop the berm. I sat inside the berm and ate a can of peaches, the only thing that I thought I could hold down.

In forty minutes, everything had been done, and with the exception of listening posts thirty meters around the berm, we were inside our defensive lines once more.

My nerves were shot as acid erupted into my throat, and my body, tense like a piano wire, shook constantly. I had seen the enemy soldier, the one that now lay there wrapped in a poncho and placed on top of the berm wall. Once inside the makeshift compound, we were in for the night. In the fading light, I could make out the small wrapped package: a girl child lying alone atop a berm.

Somewhere in the action, a small handful of yellow wild flowers had been placed on the corpse.

I stared for several minutes, until the sun set. Darkness came like smoke in a starless night, turning the world black. I slid down along the inside of the earthen wall, my face pushing hard against its rugged surface, and cried as quietly as I could, biting my filthy fist. My stomach muscles and intestines cringed into tight balls of stinging pain. Finally the tears subsided, replaced by heaving sobs. I rubbed my eyes against the filthy fatigue blouse and waited as my breathing returned to normal.

I was quiet for several minutes. "God," I whispered finally, "did we really need this day? Did we truly, honestly need this day? Was there no way we could have done without it?"

Forty-One

HOW MANY DEATHS WILL IT TAKE TILL HE KNOWS?
APRIL 22, 1966

As I enjoyed my last canteen cup of bad C-ration coffee, I stared at a series of roughly twenty-by-twenty-yard earthen squares, their walls two feet thick and two feet high, each partially filled with rancid water. Together they formed a large checkerboard pattern of rice paddies. Occasional movements in the water, most likely frogs, I assumed, darted just beneath the surfaces. In the fifteen minutes I had been there, I had watched the sheet of water as it changed infinitesimally from dark brown to rich pastels, of rich pastels of reddish orange and bright yellow as the sun rose. Finally it turned to deep blue, mirroring the sky. Sprigs of rice, recently hand-planted inches apart, protruded through reflections of huge white clouds passing above, as small gray-and-black birds skimmed along the water, snatching insects from the surface. In one square, a heron or crane stood on one leg, unmoving and patiently staring at the water at its feet.

The field stretched to the east, ending at two rows of rubber trees. Beyond that, the rusted tin roofs of the village huts were barely visible, with their gray mud stucco exterior walls. Ribbons of white smoke rose from them in thin lines as breakfasts were cooked, before joining to create horizontal layers of smoke. Beneath the layer of smoke, there was what looked like a small Buddhist temple. The faint sounds of voices carried on the moist air, a rooster crowed, and a water buffalo lowed impatiently. The air reeked of stale manure and human feces that had been worked into the soil to fertilize the crops.

As I stared at it all, I imagined a young Vietnamese boy following his father as they walked along the top of one of the berms, the child listening to stories of how this would all be his one day.

God was at peace for the moment.

I turned to see the company beginning to gather across the trail from where I stood.

At the morning staff meeting earlier, Charlie-Six had laid out the day. We were given the map coordinates that defined our final destination today, and each of us dutifully wrote them down with grease pencils on our plastic map cases.

"We'll approach from the northeast. We'll have some marshes to put up with, but that's nothing new. For the first part of the day, it's rural, with small huts grouped in little clusters and mostly farmland.

"Somewhere around noon, we'll start to move into shallow swamps, the light green areas on the map with dotted lines through them."

"Shit," Bama interrupted as he stared to the area Charlie-Six was describing. "Another day up to our ass in stinking mud and pigeon-size mosquitoes."

"You're right, Bama," Professor said. "There are swamps and bogs all over the place. That's the bad news. The good news is that dinosaurs haven't been reported in any of them."

Swizzledick interrupted with a radio call, which gave us the opportunity to familiarize ourselves with the small villages and terrain. The map showed small, black squares that represented huts and dotted lines that indicated a trail beside them. The final destination was deep green jungle.

"And look at this," Bama continued with his rant. "Right here on the bottom of the map, in the legend, it says that where we are going is 'subject to inundation.' The whole damned country is subject to inundation!"

"OK, here's the scoop," Six continued after returning from his call. "Day after tomorrow, we officially enter the first day of Operation Birmingham." He described the mission as I scanned the map. Two kilometers to the west of where we were was a large river, the Rach Beng Go, which had flowed and twisted for centuries to form what resembled a giant bear's head growling into Cambodia on the map. "This is one of the major crossing points, and the intelligence folks say there has been a lot of Viet Cong traffic back and forth across the river, bringing in the usual supplies: rifles, medical equipment, explosives. From here, we will move to our primary objective today at coordinates—" He paused and gave us a set of numbers. "This is just south of a village called Xom Ray. And then on the next day, we will set up an ambush position there before dawn. In the meantime, two elements of the 2nd of the 18th will be working down the east of the river and its swamps. The intent is that Charlie Cong will be driven into us. Bravo Company will land at first light about thousand meters from here and will move to support us in the event we are hit. Bottom line is that's a lot of troops.

"By my calculations, the first part of today will be through rural areas with the usual village squares, surrounded primarily with rice paddies and small plantations, just like what you see all around us.

"Shortly after noon, by my estimations, we will move into some thick ground foliage. That's where we set up the ambush and camp. Same rules as before: no smoke, no fires, and *no* noise. Once more, we have another opportunity to excel!

"The location around there reportedly has a shit-load of storage areas," Six said, "filled with supplies, VC hospitals in some of the tunnels, training areas...it's pretty critical to the VC. There was even a report about a treadle sewing machine that had been converted to drive a dentist drill." He smiled, then continued. "And we, along with one of the biggest combined infantry efforts we've ever been a part of, are going to mess that up. Questions?" he asked. There were none.

"Allegretti, your platoon will lead off this morning in—" he held up his arm and looked at his green watch. "Thirty minutes." He turned to Professor. "You'll follow him. And Bama, you go last?"

"Alright," Charlie-Six said, "let's do it."

Later I stood with the command group, watching as 3rd Platoon prepared to move out, tightening pack straps, pulling at each other's packs to center them, and having a final cigarette for a while. At ten minutes on the dot, 3rd Platoon began to move. After half of his lead squad passed the command group, Allegretti came by, his face tightly bunched around his nose. He looked at me, smiled, and pumped his closed fist with his thumb extended, leading the already tired-looking young men of his platoon.

"Stay behind us. We'll keep you from getting lost," he said to me as he passed, allowing a broad grin and punching my shoulder. His men followed. Each wore filthy, long-sleeved, lightweight jungle fatigues with their sleeves rolled up above their elbows. On each left arm at the shoulder was the darkened patch of the 1st Infantry Division, the "Big Red One." It was the origin of the taunt that if you are to going to "be one, you might as well be a 'big red one.'"

Each soldier had his M16 rifle resting over the top of one of his two canteens at his waist, an arm holding it in place. Each had C-rations stuffed into a long green sock that hung along their suspenders, a small first-aid pack, and an attached backpack that contained additional ammunition, a razor, toothbrush, two T-shirts, a comb, and three pairs of briefs—all dirty. A rolled plastic poncho was attached to the pack just above the buttock. In total, somewhere around seventy pounds of dead weight.

They bantered back and forth softly as they passed the command group radio operators, such things as "are you getting as many letters from your wife as I am?" or "your sweetheart was great the last night before we left" or "does your girlfriend still wear those black panties with the hearts embroidered on them?" or "I got a letter from your wife. When did she get her nipples pierced?"

Their cloth, camouflaged helmet covers carried individualized messages written with black markers, messages such as "Philly's where my filly is," "Native Oklahoma Indian, and proud to be one" with the division patch where the word "one" should have been, "California Dreaming," and "John Wayne never fired a shot." A number of the messages proclaimed "God is my point man." I smiled as I saw one that I had seen before. It was misspelled and read "God is my 'pint' man." And still, others bore simple crosses with lines radiating in a circle around the center.

The only things in common were that although their faces were freshly shaved, they were still dirty, and they reeked of stale sweat and liquids from the C-ration meals.

I heard Panther behind me checking in: "Destroyer Two-Three, Destroyer Niner-Three, over."

"Loud and clear," Flash responded in his trademark-like voice over the radio.

As the last of Allegretti's platoon passed by, Captain Novak, his radio operators, Sergeant Darnell, Panther, and I stepped into the column and joined the string. We passed Professor's platoon preparing to join in the file. "A great day for a stroll, don't you think, Governor?" he called out in a passable Cockney accent. "Just an ever-so peachy walk in the park."

In thirty minutes, we walked to the north of the first set of huts I had observed earlier. Smoke rose from two fire pits. There was not a soul to be seen.

By noon, I estimated the humidity to be 300 percent with the temperature in the high nineties. My neck already itched where the collar rubbed against it, and my body smelled of odors accumulated over the past six days from sweat and mildew in my armpits, beneath my stiff collars, and inside my helmet. My forehead ached constantly where the headband inside rode. The acrid smell of insect repellent, which failed to ward off pesky clouds of mosquitoes that hovered around us, and sweat hung in the air as ants dropped from the trees above into our open collars, crawling inside and stinging us as they did. Sweat trickled down my neck, irritating the bites left by the ants, past my chest, my armpits, my belt, and into my shorts. Yet, except for occasional clinks of metal from the heavy packs we carried or the slapping sound of a mosquito being killed, we moved silently.

The movement of the column paused briefly as we crossed a shallow, crystal clear stream, causing me to stop in the gently rolling water, allowing it to ooze through the siding of my mesh boots. I looked down as some leggy creature that was several inches long crawled across the toe of my boot. I shook my foot to dislodge it and then ground it into the pebbles of the stream bed.

Shortly after noon, we incurred four injuries: three from snipers and one killed from a Claymore mine. With each one, we had "neutralized" the enemy, waited until medical evac helicopters could haul away the wounded and dead, and then trudged on. I remembered the sound of the rotors of each medevac chopper slapping the moist air as it left with the latest cargo. I remembered pondering how God had determined who would fly out on one of the choppers and who would stay with the ants, spiders, the aches, and the heat. "Just another day at the office," I whispered to Panther.

We stopped for the day, the perimeter was set, listening posts were set up beyond the line, and everyone sank to the ground like molten lava.

Bivouac that night was quiet. The antics of the command group were solemn. Even Swizzledick, the company clown, sat subdued, drawing in the dirt. Darnell rested on his poncho against a tree, facing me, five feet away. Panther was humming a song in his soft, falsetto voice.

"Panther, you okay?" I asked

He nodded and continued softly with his song.

"How many times must a man look up?

Before he can see the sky?

How many ears must one man have?

Before he can hear people cry?"

I smiled and said, "Good song. Peter, Paul, and Mary?"

He grinned.

"No. Bob Dylan?" I asked.

"No," he said as he smiled. "It's the Chambers Brothers."

"Oh yeah," I agreed, nodding my head.

He turned and stared into my eyes. "Is that what we're doing here, Lieutenant Pearce?" Is it really a matter of 'how many deaths it will take till we recognize that too many people have died?' Is this fuckin' war just about hurtin' mankind just to save our own asses? Just to show the world we can? That'd be a shame if we are. A damned shame. It ain't supposed to be about hurtin' little girls...killin' children." He sat quietly for several minutes, and then he removed his boots and rubbed his feet. He took off his dirty blouse and spread it over a tree branch and then lay down wrapped in his smelly poncho blanket.

"Panther makes a good point," Darnell mumbled softly over his shoulder, as he snuffed his cigarette in the dirt and then lay back on his poncho. "There always seems to be some way to make the dark darker," he said softly as he turned away and pulled his poncho over his head.

I toyed with the insert pack of my last C-ration box. It held a small roll of toilet paper, two flat cans—one of jelly, one of peanut butter—a small box that held four cigarettes, and a paper packet of matches. I opened the four-pack of Winston cigarettes and pulled them out. I bent the first and second in half until the tobacco was exposed. The third I sniffed and touched the tobacco to my tongue, and then I unrolled it and tasted it. I placed the fourth between my lips, struck the match, and softly drew the smoke through.

I heard Darnell chuckle ten feet away. "Gotcha!" he said softly.

Forty-Two

It began with peaches. The rounds began to fall.

Shrapnel smashed through trees in the clearing, accompanied by flashes, like lightning. Red hot pieces of steel careened through the air in front of us as each shell exploded to expose the terror inside, so close that I imagined I could hear the steel of each round splitting before the sound of the explosion.

I raised enough to see Darnell sprawled out beside Butcher, where he had landed after pulling free of me, as Panther continued to hold me down.

The first six rounds were followed by the next six. I felt as though I was on the head of a pin with no place to hide, curled like a baby waiting for the devil to smash me. I glanced at those around me, protected behind the short barrier, yet curled up in fetal positions against the onslaught. A tree just beyond the clearing split from top to root, roaring like thunder, as if proclaiming the end of the world. I realized that I was screaming at Darnell, unheard against the noise. I could still feel Panther's grip around my knees. I felt like I was waiting to be smashed by the incoming shells. It seemed as if

God Himself had decided to stop our foolish part of the war by destroying this part of the world.

Then it was silent, except for the noise roaring in my brain. I grabbed the radio, shaking uncontrollably.

"Destroyer Twenty-Three, rounds observed. Wait, out." Destroyer Two-Three responded, but I could barely hear him through the ringing in my ears.

I realized that I had vomited in the sand beneath me and on my blouse, and I quivered almost uncontrollably. It was still...and quiet. Panther asked if I was alright, in a tinny voice like an ancient radio.

Darnell! I yelled at Panther to release my legs, and then I jumped up and ran into the clearing. Nothing heroic. I simply didn't care. I ran to where Darnell lay, as Panther fell beside him. He was breathing heavily. "He's alive!" I screamed at Panther. Get a medic!" An ugly blue piece of flesh was folded back on the side of his face, his upper cheek. He was breathing raspy breaths.

"Are you okay?" I shook his shoulders. My voice echoed in my head. I could barely hear myself. There was no response. I ripped my pack away, dropped my helmet, and knelt beside him. I put my hand on his chest. He was breathing. "He's alive!" I screamed. "Unconscious, but alive." A wave of warmth rushed over me. "You are damned lucky you didn't get killed." I swiveled to face him and put my hand beneath his head to straighten his body, quivering as I did.

The side of Darcy's head behind his left ear was wet and warm and covered with sweat...or mud? I pulled my hand back. It was covered in crimson and small pinkish chunks of what looked like cottage cheese. I fell back, crab-walking away and screaming for the medic, pushing frantically and rubbing my bloody hand on the grass.

"Medic!" I yelled as I returned to his side. I grabbed Darnell's helmet.

I became aware of mottled green and gray shadows, hunched forward at the waist and jogging past me on either side, like specters, as the men of Allegretti's platoon moved to join in the chase of any enemy survivors. I felt a hand on my shoulder and looked to see Allegretti squeezing it as he passed by.

"He's alive, Mike. Darnell is—" I yelled.

"That's good," he responded softly as he continued to move to where his platoon manned their portion of the defensive "doughnut," facing into the shredded jungle.

I turned and stared at the Butcher. My mind swirled through twisted thoughts as I tried to make sense of what was happening.

Panther handed me the handset.

I cleared my head. "Destroyer, add one thousand meters and fire for effect, over." Eighteen more rounds would hit farther away in the direction that Allegretti was moving, yet considerable distance away from his unit, hopefully catching the bastards as they retreated. As I spoke, I watched the rise and fall of Darnell's chest...still breathing.

I was aware of movement at my side and looked up as the medic from B Company pushed me away and began examining Darnell.

I sensed someone next to me and looked up to see Charlie-Six behind me, with Swizzledick and B.J. Tucker. "Let's go," he said softly, looking down at me.

I stared back at Darnell.

"Now," came the same softened voice of Charlie-Six. "I need you, Pearce. Allegretti needs you. Now."

I shook my head vigorously to clear the webs inside.

I stood. Six turned and followed Allegretti's platoon. I fell in behind him. Behind me, I heard Panther on the radio doing his job to ensure that we were still in communication with Flash.

"Destroyer Two-Three, Destroyer Niner-three. How do you read me, over?"

"Loud and clear," Flash replied.

Allegretti was on his radio just beyond the clearing, coordinating the movement of his platoon that was moving even further beyond us. I spotted a number of bodies—ten, fifteen black, pajama-clad bodies lying just a few feet away—and realized that there were parts of others.

Charlie-Six was beside me. "Allegretti is headed here," he said. "What do we need to do? Where should we fire in some rounds? Call in some artillery here to soften it up," he said, drawing on the map. "B Company is to our south," he said as he drew another circle on the map and printed the letter "B" beside it. "They're somewhere in here." He drew a line on the map and looked at me. "Don't shoot anything past this until we get a better idea where the other companies were." I stared at my map. "And be thinking about where we'll need to set up our firing points for the night?"

"He was working me," I thought. He knew as well as I did where we needed to hit with the artillery. But I didn't care. I touched a junction of two small streams. "There," I said. "It's a likely spot for them to re-group." I pointed at a saddle of land between two hills. "And here."

Charlie-Six yelled, "Well, get them in the air! We've got men dying out there. Do your job!" I called them in. Rounds fell in five minutes in the direction of the stream junction. I called for another set of rounds on a dotted line on the map: a trail. It began to quieten. Firing could be heard, but it was farther away. It moved farther still.

As the next hour passed, everything began to quieten around us. To the west, far away from us, firing continued. Bama and Dave had set up positions along the trail and stream junction I had hit earlier, as squad-size teams— angry men—probed even further ahead, searching for someone to kill. Small arms rifle fire could be heard to our right front. Somewhere, big stuff—eight-inch artillery—was firing steadily toward the Cambodian border.

In an hour it was almost quiet.

Charlie-Six called a meeting of the lieutenants. "The firing we hear is from our A Company and from units of the 2nd of the 16th Infantry. There's still some heavy shit going on there. We've been told to curl up where we are for the night, Allegretti...here." He traced a small stream. "With that, each of the platoon leaders knew where their part of the perimeter line would be. You need to know that B Company will curl up to your northwest, probably no more than a couple of kilometers." He turned to me. "Be careful if you fire in that direction. We'll coordinate with them to keep up with their location." He stared at me. "Two more medics are on their way." He paused. "Country, you did a great job a while ago." He reached and pulled my map from me and placed three x's in the area in front of where we were. "Set these up with the artillery in case we need them. Keep it up." I turned to him and stared at his face. He had never called me "Country" before.

It was almost dark by the time we were set up for the night. I was breathing normally, but still shaking slightly. Acid seemed to be pooled in my throat and esophagus, burning as if I had had far too much coffee, yet I had had none. Darnell and the rest of the wounded had been moved to the center of the C Company area, where they were being tended to by a medic from B Company. I walked to where they were.

As the melee subsided, choppers began to arrive, bringing medical technicians. One was now kneeling beside Darnell. "Any change?" I asked, staring from a spot five feet away.. The medic continued to probe and feel his chest area. "He's breathing...that's good...right?"

"He's breathing. Yes, that's good." I tried to study the B Company medic's face in the reflection of a small flashlight, but there wasn't enough light.

"Will they get any medevac choppers in for the wounded?"

"Not as I understand it, sir. They say that there is too much artillery in the area, and full darkness is too risky." He looked up at me, turned, and left. I realized once more that there were others wounded and he had to attend to them. I settled down beside Darnell. Within minutes, Panther was with me, handing me a canteen cup of warm C-ration coffee. In just the light of my small light, I could tell that Darnell's eyes were swollen shut. I grasped his knee and squeezed it as I took the cup and sat it at my side. What remained of the peaches, so treasured just hours before, had turned to bile and acid that gnawed at the walls of my stomach and throat.

I heard Panther behind me, still carrying on the business. "Destroyer Two-Three, this is Destroyer Niner-Three. Commo check, over." I stared into near total darkness at his silhouette, almost lost to the night.

"Thanks," I said, and I patted his leg. "You okay?" He didn't answer.

The light was gone, and with it, all of Darnell's features. I shook, but my breathing had begun to settle. I realized for the first time that he might never return. I put my hand on his chest and shivered in the heat of the summer night. He was still breathing.

Behind me, I heard Charlie-Six talking softly to Bama, Professor, and Allegretti. "We have a total of eight wounded, thirteen killed, two missing. We can't get any more choppers out because of firing in the area. The 2nd of the 18th and our A Company, 1st of the 2nd, are getting hammered and need the fire support. B Company sent over a medic. I want each of you to send up a volunteer to help him do anything they can to help the wounded. It's all we're gonna get."

I settled next to Darnell and whispered his name. The smell of his body, of blood, sweat and perspiration, his bowels, and his wounds—and his ragged breathing—was all he offered in return. I was glad it was dark. I cried quietly as my body simply shut down.

Sometime later, Panther was beside me holding out a canteen cup of water, kneeling on one knee. "Drink this," he said, followed by, "How is he?"

"He's still with us,'" I replied as I put my hand on his knee, squeezing it. "He'll be okay." My ears were still ringing, and my voice sounded like an ancient phonograph record. "His breathing is better now," I said. "Don't you think?" There was no response.

"He was trying to get to Butcher when he got shot," Panther said softly. "Darnell was trying to save Butcher." I looked up to where I knew Panther was, but could not see him.

I heard Charlie-Six on the radio. I turned once more to Panther. "The Viet Cong didn't kill our wounded right away. They were using them as bait. Did you know that, Panther? They actually wanted someone to go into the clearing to help him." There was a grunt from him, but nothing more.

Panther simply exhaled a heavy sigh. I knew he could tell I was crying, but I didn't care. After several minutes, without comment, he moved away several feet to the radio.

Around midnight, the medic was back. He held a small flashlight in Darcy's face. "What do you think? His breathing is better, isn't it?" I asked timidly.

"I hope you are right, Lieutenant. I hope it's a good sign. I have to check on the others."

Then he was gone.

Charlie-Six was several feet away on the radio to headquarters. He recapped the dead and injured list. "The medic says that of the remaining eight wounded, six are not critical. He doesn't think that two will make it."

I jerked toward Charlie-Six as he said it, and then leaned to whisper in Darnell's ear. "That's not you, Darcy," I whispered. "He's not talking about you. Stay with me."

I awoke sometime later, jumping with a start. His breathing was raspy, like a sheet of metal being dragged across concrete. It sounded as though he had just run a mile. I held my hand on his forehead, a stupid gesture I had learned from watching my mother as she tended to us kids when we were sick. Then I drifted back to sleep.

Later on, the ringing in my ears had somewhat subsided. My head throbbed, my stomach was on fire, and my throat burned. Suddenly, I sat up immediately and realized that there were worse things than the raspy breathing sound I had monitored all night. He was now totally silent. I jumped to my knees, waiting, feeling his chest. I called for the medic as loudly as I dared. In minutes he was there. He felt Darcy's body, probing, squeezing. "Sorry, Lieutenant" was all he said as he moved away.

I stared into the darkness where I knew Darcy's face was and grabbed his T-shirt, trying to lift him. I fell beside him, pushing him. Then I sat up slugging him in the chest. "Stop this shit," I whispered hoarsely. There was no reply. "God, please. God, please. No." I waited, and then I slugged him in the chest...once...twice. I prayed. I cried. I asked God why he no longer cared.

Then it was quiet. Hints of sunrise finally came, pushing night from the sky. Darkness began changing imperceptibly to gray shadows, with faint tinted patches and hints of citrus fruit colors: peach, pink, and orange. Shadows began to leave like haunts, allowing light between openings in the trees, as though God were playing with children to make them feel better.

Darnell's lips were curled back, and his face was bluish-gray and swollen and puffy. The wound on the side of his face and head were deep red and purple, his eyes were swollen shut like prunes, and his neck had grown to deformed proportions. His blood, caked on his T-shirt, was now the color of dark molasses.

Finally it was light.

A chopper landed and left, to be replaced by others. In five minutes, the B Company medic, attended by two clean soldiers—medics from the chopper—

dropped beside Darnell. They had shoulder patches on their sleeves that I had never seen before. They unrolled a zippered bag and flattened it beside Darnell, one grasping beneath his armpits from behind and one poised to lift him by his knees.

"On my one," the ranking medic said softly. "Three-two-one." Both grunted and placed him on the spread of plastic. The two of them wrestled him inside and began to zip it closed.

"Stop, please," I said. Each looked up at me. I placed the photo of Amanda and his daughter, which I had taken from inside his helmet, and placed it on his chest. "Thanks for all of those peaches," I said softly, and then I stood and walked away.

Charlie-Six was on the radio again. "We haven't had a chance to do a thorough search for VC bodies, but we will this morning. Best we can tell from accounts, there were good hits on about twenty of them. We've found six."

"Yeah," I thought. And Battalion would report to Brigade that "fifteen kills were confirmed with ten additional estimated." Brigade would report to Division that "between thirty to forty enemy soldiers were killed, and fifty more were wounded." And Division would report "one hundred killed and thousands wounded."

"Zero to ten," I thought. "Ten to thirty, thirty to three hundred." These were the complex frustrations of grown men who simply couldn't admit that Americans had been killed in combat with little to show for it.

A short, gentle shower fell, a gift from God tapping gently on my helmet. I removed it and stared into the falling drops. My throat hurt from acid that had fluxed into my throat and mouth all night. I imagined that that must be what an electrocution would feel like. My eyes burned like coals. My mind didn't seem capable of working. I turned to see Panther behind me, and I embraced him. Then the weather cleared.

I sensed that Charlie-Six was at my side. "You gonna be okay?"

"I'm fine, thank you," I said curtly. He left. I didn't know if I was going to be okay. My brain was not working. It had gone into a surreal copse of clouds where nothing could be seen or heard. I was shaking uncontrollably.

I was snapped back to my senses by the flat, cracking sound of an incoming helicopter, and I walked to the clearing with Panther at my side.

I watched as the wounded were loaded and whisked away into the sky. Minutes later another landed. Four men, wrapped in body bags, were strapped onto stretchers. One of them was Darnell. One by one they were loaded into racks. I watched as a sergeant at the chopper made a notation on a clipboard, then crawled onto the chopper as it rose and disappeared.

I went to a stream and removed my blouse and T-shirt. I pushed my head under the cool water and held it down until I had to breathe. I did it twice more and then wiped water from my head and arms with a smelly towel. I soaped my hair, then rinsed and combed it. I seemed to be totally out of touch with my body as I put on my last, almost clean T-shirt, which was soaked with sweat by the time I finished. I pulled my razor and cream and then my toothbrush from my pack. I shaved, brushed my teeth, and dressed once more in my second set of fatigues. The filthy ones, the ones I had been wearing, I carried to a tree and stuffed them beneath the thick vegetation at its base.

I filled the canteens with water from the stream and dropped two quinine tablets in each one.

I stared at the Raincrow on my helmet: fifth grader's art.

I looked for the hope in my mind, hope that had always come from the Raincrow.

There was none.

I thought of Daddy Bud saying, "he is a very special bird, when times are tough, he will see us through." But where was the Raincrow now?

There was no Raincrow here. There was no hope here. There never really was. If anyone was going to pull me through, it would be me. Daddy Bud had lied to me. Westmoreland had lied to all us. "Screw you both," I thought.

I reached for a palm full of mud and smeared it over the crude drawing, grinding against the camouflaged canvas with the heel of my hand. I watched as the figure of the crow faded with each stroke, leaving only the faintest sign of the drawing on the helmet cover.

"Fuck you, crow," I said. "There is no place for you here either." Darnell was gone, and so was the Raincrow. I was on my own.

I re-washed my hands. It was 0650.

I ignored everyone as I walked back to camp. They moved like zombies. Charlie-Six looked up and watched me coming toward him.

"Good morning, Captain Novak," I said cheerily. "It's going to be a beautiful day!"

"Good morning, Lieutenant." He had a strange look on his freshly scratched face. His eyes were crimson from lack of sleep.

"You look like you had a rough night," I said solemnly.

He stared at me for the better part of a minute and then threw out the remains of his coffee. "Country, I'm gonna send you back to camp. You can join us in a couple of days."

I found myself ignoring his suggestion as I raised my hand. "Don't we have a staff meeting now?" I asked, feigning confusion.

"We can get someone from B Company to help handle the artillery."

"That won't work, sir. I have as much time invested in this outfit as you do." I gritted my teeth. "So," my voice came as a slight snarl through gritted teeth. "Again," I asked flatly, "don't you have a staff meeting to conduct, Captain Novak?"

He was silent for some time. I looked into his eyes. "Can you do your job?" he asked

"That's the second time since I met you that you've asked me that. The first time was the day we met. You still have doubts?"

He pulled the black scarf from around his neck, removed the remains of his glasses, and rubbed the single remaining lens with the sweaty rag. He looked at me once more.

When I spoke, it came as a growl. "I'll tell you what. I'll do *my* fucking job, and *you* do yours. In the meantime, if I fail, you can send me to camp. And I will go. Or you can shoot me for treason...or insubordination, for all I care!"

I heard shuffling behind me, and I turned to see Allegretti, Professor, and Bama standing fanned out there. "In the meantime," I said, "I'll wait to go back to camp when they do." I gestured with my thumb at the three of them standing behind me. Allegretti dropped his steel helmet on the ground to my left and eased himself down on it. His leg brushed my arm as he did and remained there. Seconds later, Bama and Professor did the same, and each pulled out their map cases.

"Is this the meeting we're supposed to attend?" Allegretti asked, looking up at Charlie-Six.

Novak placed the frame and single lens over his nose and knelt several steps away. I glanced at my watch, then pulled my map case from my side pocket, withdrew a grease pencil and my memo pad, and looked up at Charlie-Six.

He knelt and began to lay out the day.

There was no way I was going back to *The Plantation*.

After the meeting, I joined Panther and discussed the meeting without the theatrics. "You okay?" I asked as I finished.

"Yes, sir," he growled in a flat voice. "I'm rearing to go.

Fifteen minutes later, Allegretti's platoon passed by the command group. He stepped over to where I was, squeezed my shoulder, and then rejoined his platoon as they passed by.

I looked as the soldier with "God is my *Pint* Man" scribbled on his helmet passed in front of me.

"Nice art work," I said.

"Why thank you, Lieutenant. I done it myself."

Epilogue

DARCY'S BRIDGE
MARCH 6, 1976

At 9:00 a.m., I parked at the outer edge of the parking lot of the Hired-Help Cafe and made my way inside. Tables were crowded together, a situation made worse by the fact that all of the customers were stout, heavy men. There was a constant drone of conversation, which reminded me of the sound of boiling water, and the air smelled of cigarette smoke, sweat, and fried bacon. Metal signs hung on the wall at eye level around the large single room: Farmall, John Deere, International Harvester, and Allis-Chalmers. A long hat rack made of pegs and drilled into a two-by-six strip of unfinished redwood held several dozen baseball caps, with logos from farm seed products to sports teams to John Wayne. Behind the bar, the décor was an extensive collection of black, wrought iron planter plates. A gaudy Wurlitzer jukebox was playing "Your Cheatin' Heart" barely audible above the conversations. The cashier/receptionist/waitress pointed out what seemed to be the only vacant seat, a chrome stool with a red, vinyl, plastic cushion at the far end of the bar that overlooked the entire room. Behind it was a large, framed picture of a prize bull with ribbons hung outside the frame. I weaved my way among tables to get there, as farmers nodded politely and helped me along the way, their cheeks stretched with food as they talked. The menu was already open when I got there.

"What will you have, sweetheart?" asked a waitress with a pinkish orange muff of hair with a pencil stuck into it. She wiped the countertop with a damp towel, then pulled the pencil and waited patiently. "It's all good," she said. "Just look at these fat farmers if you don't believe me." She wore a lime green blouse and red apron, with a name tag that read "Fayleen." I ordered the *City Slicker Special*: a slab of brisket, two large biscuits, mashed potatoes, and gravy over everything, and a large brown mug of black coffee. I managed to eat half of it. It was wonderful.

From my vantage point, I could see it all. I eavesdropped on a group of four men near me at the table to my right, all dressed in dusty bib-overalls. I had grown up listening to the same conversations they were carrying on: concerns about a lack of rain and concerns about *too much* rain, the price of corn, rumors of blight that was affecting cotton crops, and the price of propane. One of the farmers, who I assumed to be my age, wore a black baseball-style cap with "Vietnam Veteran" in gold embroidered letters above the bill, and a string of military ribbons.

"Nice hat," I said. We spent a couple of minutes discussing when we had been in Vietnam and where. I asked for directions to the bridge and then shook hands with all four of the men.

I realized that I was nervous at the thought of what I was going to do. By 11:00 a.m., the place was almost empty. I had no more excuses. It was time to do this, once and for all.

Thirty minutes later I was there. A cool, eye-watering breeze was coming from the south along the river, gently tossing the smaller branches of the massive trees that lined each side of the river. I parked in the shade of several giant cottonwood trees beside two concrete roadside tables on a grassy knoll west of the bridge. As I got out of the car, I startled a crow that had been feeding from a trash can. It screamed and flew from the barrel to the trees and then to the crest of the bridge. From its new perch, the crow continued to chastise me before finally flying into an adjacent field and landing behind a tractor that was tilling the earth. I turned once more to what I had come to see. This was Darnell's bridge. I was finally here. After all of the excuses and procrastination, I was at his bridge.

I walked to where the bridge met the paved highway and stepped on to it, stopping to admire the architectural art all around me. I walked to the slanted steel upright beams to the north and a stamped cast iron plaque, the proud signature of an ironworks company in Chicago. I stared at it for several minutes.

I walked to the opposite side of the bridge where two more plaques— bronze—were attached. The larger one was weathered to a dark bronze green and attached to the angular upright beside the right lane that ran into town, proclaiming it as a Kansas Historical Society monument. It was dated March 10, 1902. A smaller bronze plaque, nine by twelve, was attached just above and read "In Memory of Darcy James Darnell — a Son of Kansas and a hero — March 23, 1947-April 15, 1966." Just above the lettering was a small, bronze replica of a 1st Infantry Division insignia. I removed my glove and ran my forefinger over the cold, smooth outline of the letters, my feelings a mixture of pride, disappointment, and anger.

I left the bridge and strolled along a slope that led to the river below. The seventy-five-year-old concrete support buttresses looked remarkably well-preserved, streaked with rusty lines caused from water dripping from the metal struts above. Two large pieces of concrete ran down the slope and into the water. On one of them, faded graffiti proclaimed that "Franklin loves Linda," that "Franklin loves Diane," "Franklin loves Rebecca," and finally, one admonishing Franklin to "roast in hell."

I walked and slid to where the concrete sloped into the moving water, ran my hand over its cool, smooth surface, and sat there for some time.

Flowers with small, yellow buds pushed upward through grayish-black straw...remains of their ancestors. I bent and picked up a beer bottle that was partially hidden by the foliage and walked slowly to the trash barrel to deposit it, then turned once more to stare, as his stories began to reel through my brain.

The bridge itself—the metal—had recently been painted, and one lateral brace had obviously been replaced, evidence of diligent maintenance. I walked up the rise, onto the pavement, and to the railing on the north side. I stared at the water below, the sun reflecting in thousands of silver dots that danced there. It had the look of a moderately deep river, green and gently rolling and twisting, seemingly chasing the breeze to reach the bridge. I was drawn from my thoughts once more by the screams of the crow that had returned to a large cottonwood that hung above the bridge. This was apparently his territory.

I crossed onto the bridge. As an architect, I have always been fascinated by truss bridges; and the one on which I stood over, a branch of the Republican River, was a masterpiece of steel I-beams, thousands of mushroom rivets, and massive moss-covered concrete buttresses. I wrapped my arm around one of the support beams and resumed staring at the shimmering deep green and silver currents below, which seemed to chuckle as it passed beneath. The metal surface felt cool and solid against my arm.

I had spent the last three days in meetings discussing every period, every comma, and every penny of a federal government paving contract within Fort Leavenworth that had been awarded to my company. It had been three days of too much bad coffee, too much stale air, too many fast food meals, too many arguments, and too much nit-picking.

Now I was finally here. Now I was on Darcy's Bridge. I leaned over the upstream side of the bridge railing and stared into the cool breeze whispering through the cottonwoods. My eyes watered as every hint of tension was drained from me, like the water passing below.

The silence was interrupted as a truck driver, on the interstate several miles to the north, pushed his rig through its gears, roaring as he gained speed. I realized that in the time I had arrived over thirty minutes before, not a single car had passed over the bridge where I stood. At this instant, at this spot, nothing existed except the crow and me.

This was the place Darnell had talked about, the spot where he had made me promise we would meet after our war. It was where he and his friends had jumped from the bridge, where they had fished and gigged frogs with sharpened sticks. It was where they had played war, fighting Union soldiers. They had stood on the upper level of the bridge in a contest to see who could piss the furthest, and he had fallen and broken his foot. As boys, they raced across it on bicycles, and from it they had fished for carp, using cane poles and twine with safety-pin hooks covered with bread balls.

This was where the starting lineup of the Bison State Football Champs jumped into the river, wearing nothing but purple and green jockstraps.

This was where he had first kissed his future wife.

I watched gently swaying cottonwoods with grayish-brown trunks the size of barrels and tiny, mint green buds on branches above. They were intertwined along the shores with gnarled oak trees to form spectacular, solid walls of varying shades of pale spring green as far as I could see along each bank of the river.

An Erector Set patterned bridge stretched over the two-lane highway where I stood, forming a tunnel-like passage through which traffic could enter onto the bridge at either end. They cast shadows that danced on the pavement. Through that tunnel was my reason for being here today.

Through *that* bridge was Amanda Kay Darnell, and today, after years, I would answer her questions.

Suddenly the combination of the morning feast, the thought of seeing her, and the excitement of being there caused my meal to rise in my throat, and I turned and vomited into the water. I watched, shaking, as a school of shad frantically darted over and began to devour it.

I walked back to the car to warm up and slid in behind the steering wheel. I sat listening to a hog report on the radio as I looked at everything in sight. I left the car with my heavy jacket and walked back to where I had been. A pickup, followed by a tractor, passed over the bridge. Both drivers waved, and I did the same as I turned my jacket collar up.

Then, for the first time in a long time, *his voice* came once more. *"So, what the hell brings you here?"* We had argued with each other for years.

"I thought you'd be here," I said, half expecting to see him as I turned.

"I've been here since my life stopped...ten years ago," Darcy's voice came clear and calm. I looked around once more, still expecting to see him, but knew he wasn't there.

"I want to see her." I said aloud, the beginning of a conversation I had carried on with *him* hundreds of times over the past ten years.

"You've been saying that for years. So what's changed?"

"I'm finally here this time. That's what's changed!"

"And you intend to talk to her?"

"Of course I intend to talk to her," I replied.

"And you'll expect me not to bother you when you do? I've bothered you for the past ten years. Why would I stop now?"

I didn't answer, but I looked down at the river, not sure if I was calmer or more disturbed that he had entered the conversation with me.

"You intend to talk about me?"

"Of-of course," I said, not as self-confident as my last reply.

"And do you plan to start the conversation the same way?"

"As usual, I suppose."

"There has never been an 'as usual,'" came his voice. *"You have never spoken to her in all these years. Oh, you have said that you would, but you never have. So how can there be an 'as usual' approach?"*

I wrapped my arms around one of the upright supports and thought of what I would say to Amanda Darnell. The solid iron felt cold against my cheek. "I will tell her that you were a good soldier...and a better friend."

"And do you think that will soothe her, calm her thoughts? What if she has already calmed those thoughts in her own way, years ago? What if she isn't interested in talking to you? You've started on this venture before and never have completed it."

"I'll ask her if she got the medals, if she knows what they are...what they mean."

"And that's your best first shot? The best approach you've got? The same old hack, the same old grateful nation, which regrets to inform her? Bullshit."

I didn't speak for several minutes. "I know, I know. I have addressed that a thousand times."

"Yes, and with the same results: 'No answers, no comfort."

I stared for a long time, facing into the wind...wind that was growing chillier. I was scratching at the thick paint on the railing with my fingernail as a gust of wind bullied piles of leaves across the bridge and into the water.

"I will tell her that you were a hero."

"Ah, that lame approach that we have discussed a hundred, no, a thousand times, only to finally decide that there is no consolation to be had there either. There is no consolation in the medals. There is no consolation to be had for a growing daughter. None from a small

town minister, none from a handsome soldier that had accompanied my coffin and delivered the hollow form letter ten years ago, announcing my death."

"She needs to know!" I yelled at my reflection on the water.

"Ah, yes, that pathetic, useless chess move that you make every time we talk of this."

"Then help me. Tell me what to say, what to do. Tell me!" I screamed until mucus ran down my upper lip.

The crow above burst from the branch on which he sat and cawed as it flew away down river, leaving me once more alone. I watched a log floating lengthwise downstream, dipping and bobbing in the cold water.

His voice came in my mind. *"As before when we have discussed this line, there is nothing to say. There is nothing to do, except to go home to your family. Besides, there's no assurance that if you go to her, you will ease her mind at all. You may only upset her more as you dredge forgotten memories."*

"The medals...I want her to know what they mean. I want to tell her, to make sure she knows what they represent." I continued to scratch at the paint atop the beam.

"Trinkets, worthless trinkets," said the imaginary voice calmly. *"We have discussed this before. Trinkets probably made in Taiwan to soothe a president, a congress, a grateful nation...and do little, if anything, to soothe a grieving widow with a child who has asked where daddy was a million times. And a nation whose best approach to the situation was to put me in a clean uniform, lay my body in a coffin, and send it to Kansas!"*

I stared into the west as it changed into evening colors in the late afternoon sky, as hues of gold, red, and umber reflected on the water, erupting into hundreds of ripples of lights like Christmas tree bulbs strung across the water. The wind, which whispered ominously past my ears, was out of the west and had turned even colder...my eyes watering as I stood staring into it.

"And if she asks how I died, will you calmly say with the back half of my head gone?"

I pulled back, jolting at the thought.

"And if she says 'it was a stupid war. Fought for what—for political egos?' What if she says that I was stupid for going to this war...and that you were too?

I grimaced at the thought. "It won't be like that. I just know that she wants to know."

"And what makes you think that she doesn't already know all of this? What if she remarried and has a new life? What if I'm no more than a dusty box on my mother's mantel? What if she burned the certificates and threw the medals out there in the river?"

No answer came. No courage to speak once more, grew.

From out of nowhere, a large, white bird flying overhead—a stork— dropped into the river thirty yards away and retrieved something silver that thrashed as the bird rose and flew toward a sandbar beneath cottonwoods fifty feet away, its prey continuing to flap wildly. The bird thrashed its head from side to side and then pointed its beak toward the sky, and in a series of savage jerking motions, swallowed its meal. I said nothing for several minutes.

"It's your move," said the voice softly.

I leaned against the girder one more time and felt the deepest coldness of my life come through my coat sleeves and into my body. I rested my chin on my folded fist, shivering violently. "I will tell her—"

I suddenly recalled the months—years—that my wife, Julie, and I had fought demons in my mind and terrible nightmares and how she had been the cure...how she would calm me and, once done, go into the adjacent bedroom and cry.

I shook my head violently and walked from where I stood to the railing on the far side, then back. "It had to mean more than that," I said, barely above a whisper. I bent my body, slammed my fist against my thighs, and screamed. "There has to be truth, understanding, whatever the hell you want to call it. I can't just dismiss all that happened in those few months as a poorly executed fiasco, as a nightmare." I wiped my nose on my sleeve like a schoolboy. "I can't leave without her knowing..."

The sun, now behind the trees, formed a fragmented collection of orange and red slashes in the western sky. I watched for some time as it seemed to slowly melt into the horizon, leaving the world gray and cold. In minutes I would be alone, on his bridge, in darkness.

"She needs to know. All of it," I said as I stood up straight, summoning my voice.

"Bullshit," his voice said flatly.

"You are a hero. She will want to know what that means."

"More bullshit. I was a fool!"

"She has to know!" I screamed.

"No. You want her to know," said the voice once more. *"She has resolved herself to not caring."*

I paused for several minutes.

Finally his voice came once more. *"What if she says that the country was at war for no other reason than to soothe political egos, that it was a chess game for dried up generals and senior politicians, an opportunity for them to flex their shriveled dicks? What will you tell her then?"* asked his voice mockingly.

I stood silently and stared.

"I'm waiting."

I looked toward the tractor as a bullbat circled above the fence line, looking for something that he probably wouldn't find.

Darnell was a friend. And I couldn't keep this one, simple promise—the simple promise that I had made to him. "I'm sorry, Darnell," I whispered as I began to shake violently.

The next time he spoke, his voice was kinder, more understanding. *"What if her idea of a hero would be of a husband who came home after work every night with warm kisses, with chocolates and ice cream? Or sat on the floor each day and read to his daughter? Or helped her cut out paper dolls? What if her view of the war was frustrating and frivolous, or terrifying? What if the medals have no more value to her—to me—than something that came out of a Wheaties box?"*

I simply stared into the dark gray horizon.

"So answer my question. What would you tell her?" asked the imaginary voice.

"I'm not sure I know."

"OK. If you don't know, do you really think it would be wise to go to her and stumble and fumble with words?"

I straightened quickly, looking around, my stomach boiling and cramped as I walked from where I stood to the other side of the bridge and vomited once more. I wiped my mouth with my glove and looked up as a flock of ducks flew overhead, quacking loudly like Marines in a bar.

Finally, the sky was the color of charcoal. My breath came in sobs. I was alone, on his bridge, in near darkness. Black clouds began to pass just above the treetops. The farmer had left his field. I imagined him climbing down from the tractor, closing the valve on the propane tank, and slapping his gloves against the huge tire to remove the dust before placing them on the empty seat. The highway to the north was eerily quiet, except for the random growl of semi-trucks.

The crow was nowhere to be seen, or heard.

I was silent for a long while. "I would tell her that she is right. That she wins." I folded my arms across my chest and stood there. Chill, moist air with the stench of fish passed over me, like salvation.

I wrapped my arms around the cold upright beam and shivered violently. "I would tell her—" I paused as the wind dried my cheeks. "Darnell," I called loudly as I stood, looking frantically about. "Darnell," I called once again, more loudly, looking frantically at each end of the bridge.

I was answered only by the softly whistling wind. I was empty.

After several minutes, I wiped my nose on my jacket and stared at the black water for several minutes. "If I leave now," I said aloud, "I can get back in time for room service and the second half of the Phoenix Suns-Celtics game. Surely Phoenix is good for at least one more win."

In spite of the cold and goosebumps, I walked slowly back to the car. I removed my coat and threw it into the back and then slipped into the driver's seat. Chill, moist air passed over me once more. I started the engine, shivering as the heater slowly warmed the interior. My breathing was calm once more. I turned the radio station to KOMA in Oklahoma City. The sound came like liquid butter. "Get ready, there's a train a comin', people get ready to climb on board."

I sat up immediately, my eyes beginning to water. It was the tender, tenor voice of Curtis Mayfield of the Chambers Brothers from the rear speaker. Tears began to flow, and a lump grew in my throat, and my chest tightened. In spite of all, I smiled and screamed, "You got it! Darnell, you finally guessed it! *That's my song.*" I screamed as I began to laugh and continued to cry. My shoulders heaved back and forth.

I sang along, crying hot, stinging tears as I did, squeezing the steering wheel with both hands.

"There ain't no room for the hopeless sinner,
Who would hurt all mankind just to save his own.
Have pity on those, whose chances grow thinner,
for there's no hiding place against the Kingdom's
throne."

The heat was wonderful and began to fill my body like a warm liquid.

"So people get ready, there's a train a comin'."

I pulled the transmission lever into reverse and backed away from the picnic table in a curve that pointed my rear bumper toward the bridge.

I sat there staring into the rearview mirror as the red tail lights bathed over Darnell's plaque, the bridge, and the massive ghost-like figures of the trees that seemed to be protecting the world. I sang along with the last verse.

"So people get ready, there's a train a comin',
You don't need any baggage, you just get on board.
All you need is faith to hear the diesels hummin',
don't need no ticket, you just thank the Lord."

I pushed the radio button, and quiet came. I lifted my foot from the brake and gently pressed the accelerator, watching the scene directly behind me the entire time. In minutes, I covered the two straight miles to the stop sign. A sign that proclaimed the road crossing in front of me led away eight miles to the interstate access. I turned off the ignition and the lights and stepped out of the car to look back. Beneath a billion stars, I stared into the blackness.

Cold, stinging air dried my face once again. I walked several steps away and continued to stare into the total darkness in the direction of the bridge.

There were no trees to be seen there, just black shadows where the river had been.

There was no "love" graffiti about Franklin and his girls, no memories of the "Mighty Bisons."

There was no sound of rustling water.

There were no thoughts of a ring from a benevolent grandmother and no memories of Darnell kneeling in the snow to slip it onto Amanda's small finger.

There were no boisterous ducks, quacking and flapping their wings overhead in cold, fishy-smelling air.

There was no burnt orange sun reflecting off the river. No thoughts of Daddy Bud and his Raincrow.

There was no bridge. No bronze plaques.

There were no memories of an Army helmet with the photograph of two beautiful people taped inside.

It was all gone.

"Thanks for all you did for me. Thanks for your friendship," I said softly as I dried my eyes on the sleeve of my jacket and tossed it onto the passenger seat of the car. I slid in behind the steering wheel, started the engine, and drove onto the access road.

Tomorrow night I would be with Julie and Cody.

Tomorrow night...*I would be home.*

The End

CPSIA information can be obtained
at www.ICGtesting.com
Printed in the USA
BVHW031139270520
580420BV00001B/2/J